G000066533

THE HEALER'S CURSE

THE SEQUEL TO THE HEALER'S SECRET

HELEN PRYKE

Copyright © 2020 Helen Pryke
The right of Helen Pryke to be identified as the Author of the Work has been
asserted by her in accordance to the Copyright, Designs and Patents Act 1988.
First published in 2020 by Bloodhound Books
Apart from any use permitted under UK copyright law, this publication may
only be reproduced, stored, or transmitted, in any form, or by any means, with
prior permission in writing of the publisher or, in the case of reprographic
production, in accordance with the terms of licences issued by the Copyright
Licensing Agency.
All characters in this publication are fictitious and any resemblance to real
persons, living or dead, is purely coincidental.
www.bloodhoundbooks.com

Print ISBN 978-1-913419-90-5

ALSO BY HELEN PRYKE

Romance Saga

The Healer's Secret

Suspense

The Lost Girls (Maggie Turner Book #1)

Right Beside You (Maggie Turner Book #2)

Women's Fiction

Walls of Silence

Autumn Sky (a short story)

Children's Books

(under the pen name Julia E. Clements)

Dreamland (also available as audiobook)

Unicorns, Mermaids, and Magical Tales

Adventure in Malasorte Castle

The Last of the Guardians (a short story)

For Marianne, who has believed in me from the beginning.

JENNIFER

1

MARCH

I n the early morning haze that hung above the Grove at the
bottom of the garden, I could almost imagine the ghost-like
forms of healers from the past drifting towards me through the
mists of time. I blinked, and they were gone. All I could see were
the plants and fruit trees of the Grove once more. I pulled my
cardigan tighter around me and returned indoors.

It had taken me a while to get used to life up here in the
mountains, but with the help of my warm-hearted, lively Italian
family, and local handyman Francesco, I was more at home here
than I'd felt anywhere before. I had overcome alcoholism, begun
a new life as a healer with my cousin Agnese, and found love
after so much heartache and loss. There was only one thing left
for me to do, and I was determined to succeed this time.

Later that afternoon I stood back, satisfied, and looked at the
blazing fire inside the wood stove. Orange flames leapt around
the oven, devouring the wood I'd carefully prepared earlier,
determined to get a fire going this time. I glanced at Agnese,
who'd watched over my amateur attempts with interest.

'I think I've done it!'

'Well done, it's only taken you all winter. It's a pity it's spring now and we won't need to use it anymore,' she replied dryly.

My shoulders drooped. 'I never could get the hang of that bloody thing. I'll probably have forgotten by the time we use it again.'

'Don't worry, it's like riding a bike. You never forget.'

'Forget what?' Francesco barged through the back door carrying a large bag of tools in his arms. Bella, our adopted dog, jumped up and weaved excitedly around his legs, almost tripping him up. He dumped the bag on the floor and stood up with a groan.

'All right, Bella. Yes, I missed you too.' He ruffled her fur and gave her a treat from his pocket. 'Signora Cappellini insisted I mend the hinges on her shutters, then she wanted me to fix her leaky taps, and take out some warped wooden beams and replace them. I had to take the whole tool bag as I didn't know what she'd ask me to do next.' He strode over to me and gave me a quick kiss on the cheek. 'Everything okay here?'

I smiled and stood back so he could see the results of my handiwork. He looked at me, a bemused expression on his face.

'Ta-daa,' I cried, gesturing towards the stove.

The penny dropped. 'Oh wow, you did it.' He picked up the long metal hook and lifted out the middle iron ring on top of the stove. The flames flickered hungrily, the blazing fire inside spilling heat into the room.

'We never gave up hope, did we?' Agnese said, her eyes sparkling with suppressed mirth.

'Nope, never,' Francesco agreed. 'We knew you'd get there eventually, it was only a question of perseverance.'

I threw a nearby dishcloth at him. My inability to get the wood stove to work was a standing joke by now, and I'd despaired of ever learning. My attempt today had been make-or-

3

break time; either I succeeded, or I'd never try again. I'd set everything up, even though I was convinced the flames would fizzle out like a damp squib, as usual. Instead, the paper had caught immediately and the small twigs I'd placed underneath had started to burn as well. Hardly daring to breathe, I'd added some larger sticks, one at a time, waiting until each one started burning before adding the next, until the wood was glowing red and crackling in the heat of the flames. Only then did I finally close the door without fear of the fire fading as quickly as it had sprung to life.

'I guess the stars and planets were aligned today,' I said, only half-joking.

'Whatever it was, we're very proud of you.' He gave me a hug and handed me back the dishcloth. 'You're now a fully fledged member of the Innocenti family... healer, apothecary and wood stove lighter extraordinaire!'

I punched his arm, but couldn't help laughing. Francesco and I were on the same wavelength, and often made fun of each other. It was a fundamental part of our relationship that kept our love growing every day.

He officially moved in the day after Malva was born, even though he'd been practically living with us for some months while he carried out repairs on the cottage. I imagined the gossips in town were having a field day – a man living with two women, one divorced, the other a single mother! But we were happy with the arrangement. Francesco was busy all week long; his reputation of being able to fix anything meant he was in demand throughout the area, and he worked long hours. This meant Agnese and I could dedicate our days to our new lives as healers.

During the weekends, Francesco had turned the old, dilapidated garage into a modern laboratory where we could prepare everything in a clean, sterile environment that had been approved by the council. This meant that indoors there were no longer saucepans of boiling water on the kitchen stove, but the cottage still retained a faint perfume of herbs, as if it had permeated the walls over the centuries.

While Agnese had been recovering from Malva's birth, I hadn't been idle over the winter. Even though there was nothing for me to do in the Grove, I'd collected enough plant cuttings to keep me busy, testing new recipes, perfecting the ones I already knew, until there was a wide variety of products to offer our customers. Several local shops sold our body lotions and creams, with regular orders coming in every week, and people came to us for homeopathic cures, just as they used to go to my great-grandmother Luisa.

With spring finally here, we could spend our days working in the Grove, Bella never far away, doing her own thing, or in the laboratory, where she waited outside the door, whining. We tended the plants, picked what we needed for our cures, prepared the various concoctions, then stored them in glass jars and bottles in the pantry. Malva would sleep most of the time in her pram, and we'd take turns entertaining her when she was awake.

The cottage was big enough for us to have our own space when we needed it, or keep each other company when we felt like it. Agnese and Malva had Luisa's old bedroom, as it was the biggest, and Francesco and I had the spare room on the other side of the corridor, which had a view over the garden and the Grove, with the mountains as a backdrop.

My life was finally getting back on track. I no longer craved alcohol; in fact, I never wanted to return to those dark days of oblivion ever again. I had a man I loved and who loved me, who somehow sensed when I was having a down day and encouraged me to talk about the babies I'd lost. I had my Italian family, who drove me crazy with their worrying and fussing, but made me feel so wanted and protected that I could put up with anything. I'd made my peace with Mum, and our relationship was better than it had ever been, even though she was back in England. Or maybe because of that. We spoke often on the phone, revealing parts of ourselves we'd never revealed before.

And I had Agnese and Malva. My cousin and I had connected right from the beginning, and we'd shared experiences that made our connection even deeper. I'd been delighted when she'd accepted to become a healer together with me, it was as if it was meant to be. When Malva had been born, I'd been there right alongside Agnese, holding her hand and encouraging her. I would never forget those hours in the nursery, cradling Malva in my arms, full of love for this tiny creature, realising that my future was about to begin, and excited to find out what it held in store for me.

Everything was perfect, except for the one thing that kept happening to me. I pushed the thought to the back of my mind, refusing to dwell on it.

'You can put the coffee on, using the wood stove that I've *finally* got working,' I said, smiling smugly at Francesco. 'I'm going out to the Grove to pick some leaves for the oil we need. There's a lot of coughs and colds going around, it's better we stock up.'

'After the day I've had, I need a shower,' Francesco grumbled. 'Signora Cappellini is a slave driver.'

'I'll put the coffee on while you have a shower and Jennifer gets the leaves,' Agnese said. 'You two sound like an old married couple already.' She put Malva back in her pram, ignoring her daughter's whimpers. 'I know you want to stay in Mummy's arms, but Aunty Jennifer and Uncle Francesco must have their coffee, otherwise the world will come to an end.' She turned, her mouth twitching.

I poked my tongue out at her. 'Thank you, cousin Agnese,' I

replied sweetly and made a small curtsey. 'I'll make sure I'm quick, so Malva doesn't start crying.' Chuckling, I made my way outside, Bella close at my heels, never one to turn down the chance to go out and explore.

The sun was about to sink below the mountains, and its rays shone directly in my eyes as I walked down to the Grove. The air was full of the sounds of new life, as the wildlife rejoiced in this new-found warmth after the long, cold winter. The gate to the Grove creaked as I swung it open, and I made a mental note to put some oil on it. I stood still and breathed in the unique aroma of the garden, each plant giving off its own scent as insects brushed over them or the wind rustled the leaves. I never tired of being here. Even during the winter I'd often come to stand and take in the calming atmosphere.

I took the secateurs out of my pocket and set to work, cutting the pieces I needed. The sun warmed the top of my head while a cool breeze blew around the rest of my body, chilling me. I moved over to the plant near the wall, my fingertips brushing its soft, silver-green leaves, the sweet scent drifting in the air. A dragonfly appeared, and hovered in front of my face. I stopped to watch, remembering the events of the year before, when it had guided me to the grave in the middle of the garden. The grave that had led me to discover my great-grandmother's secret.

I'd been told the Grove had been full of dragonflies once, but these days only the one remained. *My dragonfly*, I thought hazily as my mind clouded over. I turned to follow it, my limbs stiff and heavy, and ended up standing in front of the grave. Everything around me faded away.

I was standing in the middle of a cabin, the floor swaying under my feet with the swell of the waves, my hand over the slight round- ness of my belly. I pressed harder against my stomach, concentrating my mind on the tiny being inside me, feeling the energy flow from my fingertips through my skin and beyond. Movement fluttered under-

neath my hand, making me gasp. I delved deeper inside with my mind, searching, and was rewarded with a faint ripple of life flowing through my flesh. My heart skipped a beat; if only Ted could have been here to feel his daughter's first kicks. Standing motionless, a blissful smile upon my face, I felt the connection between us become stronger as we reached out to each other. And then there was something else, something dark and menacing, that made me feel as though I was suffocating. I gasped, trying to draw air into my lungs, but the air was too dense. It filled my throat, clogging my airway. A figure appeared before me, its dark eyes hidden in shadows. There was only a glittering pinprick of light that got bigger and brighter as it got closer. Fear engulfed me and I tried to move away, but my feet were stuck to the floor. Terrified, I could only watch as the something approached, sucking all the air from the room.

A knock on the door made me jump, breaking the spell. Suddenly able to move again, I clasped my arms around my belly. No one will hurt my baby, Ted's baby, *I thought, determined. A voice called out...*

'Jennifer!' The voice penetrated the darkness around me, disturbing my thoughts. I tried to ignore it. I wanted to stay where I was, feel the baby kick once more.

'Jennifer.' It was closer this time. A hand touched my shoulder lightly. I shuddered, dreading to see who was standing behind me. 'Jen, open your eyes. It's okay, you're here in the Grove.'

2

Francesco. It was Francesco's voice, not *his*, not the man who haunted my dreams lately, his eyes blacker than his soul. I slowly opened my eyes and blinked at the harsh sunlight. I'd half-expected to see the dark shadows of the ship's cabin, where the only light came from a flickering candle. I turned and threw myself into Francesco's arms, sobbing violently.

'Come on, let's get you inside,' he said, holding me tightly. We left the Grove and made our way up to the cottage, my sobs subsiding into small hiccoughs. I glanced down at my stomach without thinking, dismayed to see it as flat as ever. I surreptitiously moved my hand across it, knowing I would never feel movement there, but hopeful all the same.

Agnese was pouring the coffee into cups as we entered, singing a lullaby to Malva, who was lying in her pram, sucking on her hands. She took one look at my face, put the percolator down, and rushed over to help me to a chair.

'It's happened again, hasn't it?' she said to Francesco, placing a hand on my brow. He nodded. 'She hasn't got a temperature, so it's not heatstroke. This is the third time this week. What's going on?'

'I've no idea,' he replied. 'I keep finding her by the grave, standing there in a trance. And when I call her, it's like she doesn't want to come back from wherever she is.'

'*She* can hear you,' I said, looking up at them both. 'I-I was on a ship, in the middle of the ocean. I could feel the movement of the deck going up and down with the waves, a-and I was pregnant.' I faltered, unable to speak for the moment.

'What?' they exclaimed, the incredulous looks on their faces making me want to laugh. I tried to remain serious as I knew that Agnese would insist I took something to make me sleep if she saw I was getting hysterical. Malva snuffled in her pram, waving her arms about as if she wanted attention too. At only three months old, she'd already wormed her way into our hearts and our lives, and we were all deeply in love with her.

'The baby,' I said pointedly.

Francesco went over and picked her up, breathing in her sweet perfume as he cradled her in his arms. 'You're not off the hook just because you distracted us. Tell us what's going on, otherwise we'll have to speak with Liliana, see if she can get the truth out of you.'

I gulped. Aunt Liliana was a force to be reckoned with, and had her ways of getting any information she wanted out of someone. 'That's cruel.' Francesco raised his eyebrows, his face stern. 'Okay, okay. Can I have a glass of water first, or are you going to torture as well as interrogate me?'

Agnese brought over a glass of water and placed it on the table in front of me. I drank it down in one go, partly to quench my thirst and partly to delay the inevitable explanation. Francesco placed the now-sleeping Malva in her pram, then sat at the table in front of me. Agnese remained standing, her arms crossed.

'We're worried about you,' she said. 'Francesco keeps finding you in trances, and he says you're not sleeping well either. What's going on?'

I glared at him. 'Telling tales now, are we?'

'Come on, Jen, there's something wrong. Tell us. We want to help you.'

I shrugged. 'I don't know. It's the same every time. I go down to the Grove to get some cuttings or fruit, and somehow end up near the grave. And then the next thing I know, you're calling me, and I don't want to come back.'

'Did you touch anything? In the Grove, I mean. Some plant, something toxic, maybe,' Agnese asked, finally sitting down with us.

I considered it for a moment. 'No, I don't think so. I know every single plant, and which ones I need to wear gloves for. But now I think about it...' I stopped.

'Yes?' they both said, the frustration plain in their voices.

'The dragonfly. I remember seeing the dragonfly, and I thought it was odd as it's still a bit cold. I was getting a cutting off the plant near the wall.' They nodded as I hesitated. The unknown plant was an important ingredient in our homeopathic cures, but we still didn't have an official name for it. The original healer, Agnes, referred to it as 'silver leaf' in the recipe book. 'So, I saw the dragonfly and went over to the grave to see if it was the same one from before. I know that's impossible,' I added as I saw Francesco open his mouth. 'I know they don't live very long, but it seems to me this dragonfly has been here a lot longer than we think. Can I go on?'

'Please.' He gestured for me to continue.

'I was standing in front of the grave, looking at the dragonfly, straight into its eyes. It was as if I was getting sucked down into them and I could see images swirling around. I felt like I was fainting, so I grabbed on to the headstone to steady myself, and then I was on the ship. The other times it's happened, I'm usually walking around the deck and there's an old woman who keeps looking at me. It should give me the creeps, but it feels like I know her. This time, I was in a dark cabin, by myself.'

'Pregnant,' Agnese said.

'Yes. I could feel the baby kicking.'

Francesco frowned. 'What sort of ship was it?'

'Oh, I don't know. It was wooden, with sails,' I exclaimed, huffing. 'I'm not a ship expert, am I?'

'Not a modern-day boat, then?'

'No, not really. What are you getting at?' Then it suddenly hit me. 'You think it's flashbacks from the past, like with Luisa?' I'd watched my great-grandmother's story unfold before me only a few months earlier, after drinking some of her specially brewed 'wine'. It had been a harrowing experience that had revealed some shocking secrets about her, which I'd only shared with my mum, Agnese and Francesco.

'Aren't you curious to find out who she is, this pregnant woman?' Agnese asked.

'Well, yes and no,' I replied. 'It's strange, being her and feeling the baby kick and everything, but there's something else there too, something nasty. When you called me, Francesco, I was scared it was him, coming to get me.'

'"Him" who?' Francesco said.

'I've no idea. I remember feeling terrified that he had found me, and he wanted to hurt both me and the baby.'

Malva woke up and started to cry, her wails echoing around the room.

'Dinner time already,' Agnese groaned, going to her daughter. 'That must be the quickest nap ever. I'll go outside, leave you two to talk this over.'

I watched as she took her screaming daughter out into the garden, closing the back door behind her.

'Do you think it's dangerous, when you go into your trance?'

Francesco looked worried, and I couldn't blame him.

'I-I don't think so, it's not like I'm there. I'm only seeing it through this woman's eyes.' I tried to smile reassuringly at him, but it didn't seem to have the desired effect.

'When you saw Luisa's story, it wasn't like that.'

'That's true. It was like watching a film play out before me. Do you think the plant and the dragonfly have anything to do with it?'

He rubbed his chin. 'It would certainly seem so. I don't think it's a coincidence that you see the dragonfly while you're working on the plant. What is it, anyway, this silver leaf? Didn't you try googling it?'

'Yes, many times, but I've never managed to find out what it is. It's not on any site. What do the dragonfly and the plant have to do with this? Why am I seeing this person?'

'I'm not sure. When it happened before, you were reading Luisa's letter, right?'

'Yes, and drinking the juice she'd made. But I didn't touch the plant. I was indoors, with Bella.'

'Did you touch anything else in the house before these trances started? Anything at all that might have a connection to the past.'

I thought. 'Aunt Liliana, Agnese, Giulia and I cleaned the house from top to bottom after I moved in, but I don't remember there being anything like that. There were the usual knick-knacks, Luisa's bits and pieces she'd collected over the years, but no family heirlooms. There was only the wine she'd made, nothing else. And the book, after I inherited it from Uncle Mario.'

'Do you think it could be the book?' Francesco asked, glancing at the cupboard where I usually kept it.

'It's not really likely. We use the printed sheets now, and hardly touch the book anymore. Anyway, nothing's ever happened to Agnese when she touched it. And we haven't drunk any juice since Mum left, so it can't be that.'

'Didn't you say you found a wooden box at Tommaso's house? You mentioned it but never showed it to me.'

'Yes!' I'd forgotten about the box. It had remained at the back of my wardrobe since Mum's visit. 'There's a dragonfly carved on the lid, it's where I found the recipe book.' I hesitated. 'And it had a false bottom. For hiding things.'

'Really? You never told me.'

'Sorry. I've had other things on my mind, I forgot all about it. The day after Mum left, I wrote Luisa's story in a notebook and took out the chest to put it inside for safekeeping. I noticed it looked deeper than it actually was, and found it had a false bottom.'

'And? Did you find something in there? Good grief, Jen, don't keep me on tenterhooks like this!'

I grinned. Francesco was normally so calm and relaxed, it was funny to see him riled for once. 'I eventually managed to open it and found an oiled silk bag. Inside that was...' I paused for dramatic effect, pretending not to see his clenched fists.

Agnese came back indoors, holding the baby over her shoulder and patting her back. Bella was close on her heels, eager to see what she was missing out on.

'So, are we any closer to solving the mystery?' she asked as Malva expelled an enormous burp.

'Jennifer was about to tell me what she found in the wooden box,' Francesco said through gritted teeth.

'Ooh, sounds exciting. What wooden box is that?' She sat down on the sofa, sighing heavily. 'You may be only three months old, young missy, but you weigh a ton already!' Her daughter opened her mouth and dribbled milk down her chin. 'Ew, why does she always do that?' Agnese picked up a nearby bib.

'Learned from her mum,' I said, laughing. She threw a cushion at me.

'All right you two, let's get back to the subject in hand. What... was... in... the... box?'

'*What* box?' Agnese repeated.

Francesco snorted. 'The damn box Jen inherited from her uncle Mario.'

'Ah, *that* box.' Agnese raised an eyebrow. 'So?'

I giggled. 'Okay, I'll put you out of your misery. It was a tapestry.'

'A tapestry?' Francesco looked disappointed.

'About the size of an A3 piece of paper,' I replied. 'It was beautiful, and the colours were so bright it looked like it had just been woven, but I reckon it was pretty old.'

'What was on it?' Agnese asked.

'It was divided into two parts. On one side there was a scene of Gallicano, and the Innocenti coat of arms. On the other was what looked to me like an English village, with a maypole in the middle of a green.'

'Why didn't you show it to us?' Francesco asked.

'Okay, now you're going to think I'm crazy,' I replied.

'Try me.'

'Because when I touched it, it seemed to come to life. I could hear voices, music, children singing, and the figures on the tapestry started moving.' I lowered my head, waiting for them to burst out laughing. Their faces remained as serious as ever.

'Had you drunk any of Luisa's juice?' Francesco said quietly.

'I think we drank some the day before, but I can't remember. Although, now I come to think of it, there were some dried leaves in the silk bag as well, they had the same scent as the silver leaf plant. Why?'

'Luisa added some dried leaves from the silver leaf plant to the juice while we were making it,' Agnese said.

'I think we've found our connection.' He looked at me. 'Is there any juice left?'

'The cupboard's still full, we haven't touched a drop since Mum went home. You're not suggesting I should repeat what happened with Luisa's letter? Drink the juice and touch the tapestry? Oh no.' I buried my face in my hands. Could I really go through all that again? I'd hidden the wooden box away because I couldn't face it before. Was I strong enough now?

He came over to me and put his arm around my shoulders. 'It's either that or keep going into these trances, sweetheart,' he murmured, kissing my hair. 'Someone wants you to know the truth, just like Luisa did.'

I cleared my throat. 'I guess so. Why does it have to be me, though?'

3

We sat under the shade of the horse chestnut tree, watching Giulia and Piero's nine-year-old daughter, Beatrice, playing with Bella. Bea threw Bella's squeaky ball as far as she could, then burst into giggles at the sight of the dog charging through the grass after it. When she found it, she'd pounce on the ball as if it were a rattlesnake and toss it up in the air, catching it in her jaws and chewing furiously. The painful squeaks coming from the toy made Bea double up in fits of laughter, until Bella brought her back the ball and the pantomime began all over again.

'I wish I had some of that energy,' Giulia said, glancing over at the pushchair where their younger child, Antonio, was fast asleep, sucking his thumb.

I looked at the black shadows under her eyes. 'Is he still not sleeping?'

'Worse, he wakes up at three o'clock and starts singing,' she grumbled. 'These two sleep right through it, so I have to get up.'

'I hope Malva doesn't decide to do that,' I said, alarmed. For a newborn, she was a little angel, only waking for feeds during the night. I hardly ever heard her, luckily. I already wasn't sleeping very well, and didn't need to add that to my list of problems.

'Maybe Piero could get up sometimes.' Aunt Liliana cast a disapproving look at her son. 'Give your wife a break every now and then, poor woman. She's got enough to do, what with running around after Bea and caring for the little one. I thought I brought you up better than that.'

Everyone joined in at that point, and I sat back in my chair, watching my Italian family in action. Aunt Liliana was a force to be reckoned with, like a tidal wave bending everyone to her will as she crashed over them. But the others managed to shout her down on occasions, even her stoically silent husband, Dante. I enjoyed listening to the hubbub of chatter, content to observe from the edges. Francesco leaned over and held my hand.

'You look happy,' he said.

'I am.' It was everything I'd ever dreamed of, this sense of being at peace with the world.

'So, when are you going to ask them about the family history?'

'It's probably a waste of time. Agnese doesn't know anything, I've already asked her.'

'Still, maybe they can give you some clues, so you know what to expect.'

I'd tried googling the Innocenti family but hadn't found anything useful. All the information seemed to only go to the 1700s, and I had a feeling I needed to go further back.

'Later,' I said. 'They're enjoying themselves, I don't want to ruin their day.' I was reluctant to bring up the subject, as I remembered Uncle Dante's reaction when I'd asked about my grandmother, Bruna. His sudden anger had shocked me back then, and made me wish I could crawl into a hole. I had no desire to repeat the experience.

'Mamma, Mamma, come and see this!' Bea suddenly yelled.

We all turned to see where she was, expecting her to still be close by.

'She's over at the Grove,' Agnese said, pointing.

'What's she doing down there?' Giulia said, irritated. She sighed and started to get up.

'I'll go,' I said, jumping out of my chair.

'You sure?' she asked, but the look of relief on her face was plain to see.

'Of course. She's probably seen a lizard, or some new plant, and wants to show it off to someone.'

I walked down the garden path to the entrance of the Grove, where Bea was waiting impatiently. Bella sniffed around in the grass, intent on following some insect she'd found.

'What's up, Bea?' I asked.

She gestured towards the Grove. 'Look,' she whispered.

I followed the direction of her finger and gasped. Every bush, plant, and tree was covered with dragonflies, the vibration of their shimmering wings making the leaves tremble. The Grove was a riot of colours; iridescent greens, blues, reds and yellows were dotted among the plants everywhere I looked.

'What's happened here?' I said, stunned.

'Isn't it pretty? Can we go in?'

'No, let's leave them alone, shall we?' I was in awe of the scene before me, somehow aware that we shouldn't disturb them.

Francesco arrived, stopping as he took in the incredible view. 'What on earth?'

'Shh,' Bea admonished him. 'You'll scare them if you make too much noise. Even Bella isn't barking.'

I realised she was right. Bella was still running around, but she was strangely silent. The others joined us, curious to see what all the fuss was about. They stared, astonished at the scene inside the Grove.

'What's made them hatch right now?' Uncle Dante asked, his booming voice unnaturally low.

Bea stood up straight and clasped her hands behind her back. 'We've been studying dragonflies at school. They lay their eggs either on a plant or in the water, then the egg hatches and the larva turns into the dragonfly after a few weeks.'

'Ah, so you do listen at school, then,' Giulia said, ruffling her daughter's hair.

'Mamma!' Bea twisted her head to get away.

'But isn't it a bit early for them to hatch?' Piero asked.

'They don't really have a specific time, it just needs to be the right temperature or something,' Bea explained to her father.

'And it's been quite warm lately, so that's probably why,' Agnese added.

My attention was caught by a dragonfly landing on the headstone in the middle of the Grove, its familiar blue-green body glinting like a jewel in the sunlight. The others' voices faded into the background as I stepped forward and unlatched the gate. I entered the Grove, my gaze focused on the dragonfly, everything else forgotten as I walked towards the grave. It remained on the white marble, its large black eyes staring at me with the wisdom of centuries hidden in their depths.

I reached out my hand, palm up, unsure why I was doing it but unable to stop myself. I wanted to hold the insect, let it transmit its secrets to me and teach me everything it knew. The world around me folded in on itself as I sank into the now-familiar trance, the salty smell of brine in the air.

'Jen, wake up.' Someone took hold of my outstretched hand, rough callouses scratching my palm. Startled, I came back to the real world with a jolt. Francesco stood beside me, still holding my hand.

'You've got to stop doing that,' he said, smiling down at me, but I saw the worry etched on his face.

'I-I don't know what happened,' I stuttered, confused. Looking around, I saw that the dragonfly had disappeared.

'Come on, let's go back to the others,' he suggested. As we turned to go, the dragonflies flew off from the bushes, filling the sky with a colourful, shimmering cloud that swirled and swooped, before breaking up as the insects flew off in different directions. We joined the others outside the gate, as stunned as we were by the spectacle.

'Now I see why it was called the Dragonfly Grove,' Agnese said. 'Do you think they'll come back?'

I glanced at Francesco. 'I think they're here to stay.'

He squeezed my hand reassuringly. 'I don't think it's a coincidence they're here, do you?'

I shook my head. 'I'd say something's going to happen and we're going to be a part of it, whether we want to or not.'

Aunt Liliana looked at me, shocked. 'What do you mean, something's going to happen? Are you in danger? Luisa took her healing seriously, and often spoke of the dragonflies as if she could talk to them, but we thought it was just mumbo-jumbo and humoured her to keep her happy. My mother left home as soon as she could to get away from the madness here! Are you saying it was all real?'

From the expression on her face, I knew she had no qualms about packing up our things and insisting we move into her house in the village that very moment. I had to say something before things got out of hand.

'Oh no, Aunt Liliana, that's not what we meant. Dragonflies aren't dangerous! I think it's our hard work paying off; we've got the Grove back to its former glory, and the dragonflies have returned. Didn't it look pretty before, when they were all over the plants?'

'Yes, well,' Aunt Liliana huffed. 'So why did you go in by

yourself? And why did Francesco panic when he saw you go to the grave?'

Agnese spoke before I could open my mouth. 'Jennifer's fascinated by these insects and keeps saying she wants to capture one so she can keep it in the house.'

'Cool,' Bea interrupted. 'A pet dragonfly!'

'That's what I thought, Bea, but Francesco and Agnese insisted it wouldn't be right to keep one captive. They're so beautiful, they belong outdoors in their natural habitat,' I said, grateful that Agnese had come up with an excuse so quickly.

'I thought she was going to catch it,' Francesco interjected. 'So I rushed in to stop her. Lucky I did, too, otherwise she'd have hurt it. They're very delicate,' he added, winking at Bea.

'Like butterflies?' she asked.

'Just like butterflies.'

'In that case, you have to leave them alone,' Bea said firmly.

I hid a smile, and put on a suitably downcast face. 'You're right, all of you. I'm sorry, I won't try to catch one again.'

The crisis averted, we returned to our chairs underneath the horse chestnut tree. Bea came over to me and put her hand on my shoulder.

'I'll make you a dragonfly out of paper, so you can keep it indoors and look at it whenever you want,' she promised. 'I'll make it exactly the same colour as the one you wanted to catch.'

'Thank you, Bea, that would be wonderful,' I said, touched. But I felt a knot growing in my stomach as I realised that Francesco and Agnese were right. I would have to face whatever secrets the tapestry held, sooner rather than later.

4

We got used to the dragonflies in the Grove, flitting around our heads as we worked. Malva stared at them as she lay on her blanket, playing with her toys, entranced by their flashing colours. Bella ignored them completely, going about her business as if they weren't even there. I'd imagined she would have chased them, or at least tried to snap at them, but I was pleasantly surprised.

Every Saturday, Francesco and I drove down to the market in the main square of Lucca to stock up on supplies, Bella sitting in the back of the van with her head out the window, her ears flapping wildly.

We loved walking around the open-air market amongst the bustling crowds of people, the various stall-owners shouting as loudly as they could, trying to entice us to buy their wares. The sweet perfume of fresh fruit was overlaid with the more pungent aroma of strong Italian cheeses or the musty odour of salami hanging from stall canopies, while all around people haggled for the best price, tutting loudly when they felt they hadn't got the bargain they'd been looking for. The elderly women were the worst, squeezing the fruit and vegetables with a grim expression, audibly doubting the freshness of the products and complaining about the prices. Then they would walk away, smiling a toothy grin, satisfied with their victory as the owner threw an extra something in the bag, grumbling that they drove a hard bargain.

I didn't have the courage to haggle with the stallholders, but I enjoyed watching these performances every week. Today, we needed to buy more bottles, ribbons and labels for our products, so we slowly made our way through the throng of people to the stall on the other side of the square. I kept a tight hold of Bella's lead, worried she'd run off if she managed to get loose. She'd been eyeing the salami, her nose pointing upwards while licking her chops greedily.

Encouraged by the warmer weather, there were more people than usual, and it was hard work to make our way through them. As I rounded a corner, past the last food stall, I saw a tall, blond-haired man walking ahead of us. I stopped, and pulled Bella to my side. *Mark?* Seen from behind, the man looked familiar.

'Jen? We need to go over there.' Francesco nudged my shoulder, pointing at a stall in the far corner.

'What? Oh yes, just a moment.' I craned my neck, searching for the man among the people milling around. I was about to give up when I saw him again. The way he moved, that arrogant swagger to his walk... it couldn't be. He was gone, we'd chased him off that night. I still had nightmares of the night he'd broken in and tried to drag Agnese away after finding out she was pregnant. If Mum hadn't turned up, I dreaded to think what could have happened. She'd told the cheating bastard to leave, and then she'd called the police. He'd be stupid to come back, the *carabinieri* would still be keeping an eye out for him. I'd almost convinced myself that I was wrong, that Mark was miles away, maybe even in another country, when he turned to look at something on a stall. I gasped in shock. It was him all right.

'What's wrong? You look like you've seen a ghost,' Francesco remarked.

'I think I have,' I said. He knew about Mark; he'd been so angry when Agnese and I had told him what had happened, and declared that he'd kill him if he came within punching distance ever again. I didn't dare tell him that he was here, only metres away from us.

I thought we'd seen the last of the bastard, and I couldn't for the life of me imagine what he was doing in Lucca. I prayed he'd stay far away from Gallicano and the cottage, but a feeling of dread crept into my heart. *Oh, Agnese, Malva.* My heart ached for them and I almost cried out, as if it was a physical pain.

I fixed a smile on my face. 'Let's go, then, shall we?' I looked behind me a couple of times as we made our way over to the stall, but Mark had disappeared in the crowd.

Francesco got out of the van and opened the gates. Bella jumped out with him and ran into the garden, barking wildly to let Agnese know we were home. He climbed back in and drove through, then parked near the cottage.

'Jen? Is everything okay?'

I'd hardly spoken during the drive home, and hoped he hadn't noticed. Of course he had. We spent so much time together that we were attuned to each other's feelings and knew instinctively when something was wrong.

'It's fine,' I replied, stepping down onto the drive. 'I'll give you a hand taking everything in.' I opened the back of the van, took out a couple of bags, and went into the cottage without looking at him.

'Hi, Jen, you're back early.' Agnese sat at the kitchen table, eating a plate of pasta. She looked up and made a face. 'It's cold. I've only just sat down. Malva cried all morning and wouldn't settle. I think she had a bit of wind. She did a couple of loud farts, then went straight to sleep. Pity it took her all morning to get rid of it!'

When I didn't laugh, Agnese looked more closely at me. 'Are you all right? You look a bit pale. Come and sit down.'

I sat opposite her and leaned my arms on the table. I opened my mouth to speak, but nothing came out.

'Okay, now you're scaring me. What's wrong, Jen?'

'At the market, in Lucca,' I whispered. I looked at her face, so innocent and trusting, and knew that my next words would change all of that in an instant. 'I saw him. I saw Mark.'

She stared at me, her mouth open. 'No, you're mistaken. It can't have been him,' she said, tugging at her hair. 'He wouldn't be so stupid as to come back.' She looked beseechingly at me, as if willing me to start laughing and say it was a joke.

'I'm sorry. I thought I was mistaken at first, then he turned around and it was him. No doubt about it.'

'D-did you speak to him?' Her voice trembled slightly.

'No. He disappeared before I got a chance to get any closer. And Francesco...' I jumped as the back door banged open. Bella came bounding in, followed by Francesco loaded with bags.

'Christ, these are heavy! How much stuff did we buy this morning?' He dumped them on the kitchen counter and started unpacking. 'I'll put everything away, then you two can tell me what's going on,' he said, smiling at us.

'What makes you think something's going on?' I asked, trying to act innocent.

'The fact you haven't spoken since we left the market.'

I got up. 'I'm tired, that's all. I'll make us some coffee, that should perk me up.'

'Don't bother making one for me. If you're sure there's

nothing wrong, I'm going to sort out that tree in the drive – if I don't cut back its branches, it could be a risk to the house. I'd rather do it now, while it's not too hot out there.' He walked out the back door, whistling for Bella as he went.

Agnese pulled at my sleeve. 'Leave the coffee. Come and tell me what happened.'

She listened closely, her face white, as I told her what I'd seen down at the market.

'You're absolutely certain it was him?' she asked me once again.

'Yes. One hundred per cent. We'll inform the police and make sure we keep everything locked. He'd be an idiot to come back here, and I'm sure he knows that.'

'The police weren't much help last time, they couldn't find him,' Agnese said.

'I thought I'd try something else. I was thinking on the way home about some remedies I came across in the book. More than cures, they seemed to be charms, or for want of a better word, spells.'

'Spells?' I could see the doubt on Agnese's face.

'Spells,' I repeated, and refused to say any more about the matter.

5

The newly painted laboratory was filled with glass jars containing dried herbs from the garden, distilling equipment, and pots and pans hanging from hooks on the shelves. The stainless-steel worktops glittered in the daylight. Francesco had got everything for us at next to no price, calling in favours owed and using his contacts down in the valley. It exuded professionalism and hygiene, and mirrored our dedication to our new lives. Every time we opened the door, the delicate aroma of herbs wafted out, filling my heart with pride.

Agnese and I had worked hard over the months, learning the craft of making natural cures for every sort of ailment, and now people from all over the area came to buy them from us. Healers. The word still made my stomach flutter with delight at the thought that we were carrying on Great-grandmother Luisa's legacy, and I hoped she would have been proud of us.

During the winter months, I'd dedicated my time to painstakingly copying the recipes in the book on to my computer. We now had a binder full of printed recipes which we kept in the kitchen, and I'd put the original book back into the wooden box with the dragonfly carving on the top. It hadn't been easy deciphering some of the earlier entries, but Agnese had a smattering of Latin and Aunt Liliana had been surprisingly helpful in translating the poorly written Italian. My friend Google helped with the rest. The end result was a binder full of clear, easy-to-read recipes, each one stored inside a plastic wallet to prevent it from being ruined by splashes. I'd found some interesting recipes too: love potions, earth spells, charms for visions and astral projection, spells for healing, sleeping, and breaking other spells, and the one I was currently studying — a charm for protecting your loved ones.

The herbs were laid out before me on the work surface, in the right quantities. We'd picked and dried leaves from the plants in the Grove before winter set in, and had a vast selection already prepared. Some of the containers were getting low, though, and I was thankful that at last we could replenish our stocks.

'Who would have thought I'd have become so countrified!' I giggled, amused that just over a year ago I'd been working in a boring nine-to-five job as a secretary, and now I watched the weather every day, worried that the plants would get damaged by the cold or rain and we'd have nothing to make our products with. Even though the plants had survived for years on their own, centuries in some cases, I still felt responsible for them.

I picked up the box of small muslin bags I'd bought in Gallicano. They were originally intended for home-made *bomboniere*, wedding favours, and the owner had looked at me eagerly, expecting an announcement for my own upcoming nuptials. I'd hated to disappoint her; it was obvious that by now everyone in the village knew about Francesco and me, but I didn't want the gossip to get out of hand. I'd mumbled something about a party for little Malva, and managed to escape with my eccentric Englishwoman reputation still intact.

I took out the semi-transparent bags in various colours and

placed them next to the herbs. Each spell required a coloured bag and different herbs to make it work. The pink and purple ones hadn't been a problem, and for the brown ones I'd used hessian-type bags, but the black ones had been a bit more difficult, not being a common colour for weddings. The owner had suddenly had a brainwave and had gone to the storeroom out back for some minutes before returning, triumphantly waving a handful of black bags left over from Halloween.

I read through the recipes again, making sure I hadn't forgotten anything. The black bags were for protection, the brown ones for blessing the house, pink for protecting Malva, and purple for driving away evil. The herbs were all there – agrimony, angelica, basil, feverfew, nettles, and vervain, to name but a few. I'd also added some ivy taken from the tombstone in the Grove, bird feathers, twigs, and other bits and pieces I'd picked up from the garden. According to the book, items such as these were essential to make the charms even more powerful. As they were for keeping Mark away, I thought we'd need all the help we could get. I'd already lit several green candles, which I'd sprinkled with some of the silver leaf plant, and placed them around my working area, their light flickering weakly in the morning sunshine.

I read the instructions carefully, making sure I'd understood everything.

Place the herbs in your bag, concentrating on your intentions as you fill them.

Well, that seemed easy enough. I spooned the dried plant leaves into the bags, focusing my attention on the gates, firmly locked against the outside world, and the cottage, the garden, and the Grove, our safe haven.

Put a piece of paper with the name of the person and your intention written on it inside the bag.

I'd already prepared rectangles of paper with our names on

them, one for each charm, and the words 'keep me safe' written underneath. I folded each rectangle twice and popped it inside a bag.

Close the bag, and visualise a light entering you through your head, passing through your body, down to your feet. Visualise this light flowing through your fingertips into the bag, and focus on your intentions. When you've finished, visualise a protective light surrounding the bag. Give thanks to the energy and forces you believe in and make known your wish.

That last one had been more difficult. I wasn't sure what I believed in, but I had to make sure that the charm would work. In the end, I'd written a few lines that I hoped would appease the 'forces'.

I thank you for helping to keep us safe in our home.

I thank you for the light of these candles to keep away the darkness.

I thank you for the plants in the Grove that grow strong and healthy.

I ask you to protect me, Francesco, Agnese, Malva, and Bella, and help keep us from harm.

I ask you to protect us from Mark and to keep him away from the cottage and our lives.

I thank you for your love, friendship and protection.

I got a lot of it off the internet, but I reasoned that it would be just as effective, provided I said it with sincerity. I finished preparing the bags and pulled the drawstrings tight on each one.

'Here goes,' I said, glad the door was locked and there was no one about to watch me make a fool of myself. I took a deep breath and picked up the first bag. Closing my eyes, I followed each instruction in my mind, visualising the light and then reciting my request to whatever forces were present. I did this for each bag until I'd finished.

I slowly opened my eyes. Everything seemed sharper,

clearer, when I looked around me. I could see tiny grooves in the stainless-steel worktops, a small nick in the blade of the knife I'd used to chop up the herbs, small sparks leaping off the candles as their wicks fizzed in the molten wax. I felt both dreamy and alert, the same sensation I'd had when I'd drunk the wine and seen the dragonfly for the first time.

The aroma coming off the candles filled my nostrils, heightening my senses, making me feel powerful, able to deal with a whole army of Marks if necessary. I breathed out, a long, deep breath that seemed to last forever, and the candles all went out at the same time.

I dropped my head and leaned heavily on the worktop, my arms bearing the weight of my body as the energy left me. I realised that something important had happened, that I was capable of so much more than healing, and the knowledge scared me. What was the legacy our ancestor Agnes had left us all those centuries ago? Why was it reappearing in me and why now, at this time?

I gathered up the little muslin bags and placed them on a tray, ready to distribute later. I would put them under everyone's pillow and under Bella's blanket, and place a few around the edge of the garden and on the gates. I glanced at the candles, debating whether to put them away. Wisps of smoke still rose from the blackened wicks, and a vague scent of herbs lingered in the air. In the end, I placed them in a circle around a small, heart-shaped stone I'd found down by the old chicken coops, and left them there. I checked that I'd left everything in order, then picked up the tray and went back to the cottage.

6

I'd done everything I could to protect us, and only time would tell if it would work. Francesco expressed surprise at the muslin bags, but I told him that it was for our well-being and he accepted it in the end, if only to please me. I placed them under our pillows, under Malva's mattress, in Bella's bedding, inside coat pockets and handbags, and even attached some to the trees bordering the garden and on the metal gates at the driveway entrance. I tried tying one to Bella's collar, but she merely blinked at me and used her hind leg to scratch it off straight away. Agnese raised an eyebrow at the little shrine I'd created in the laboratory with the candles and stone, but I asked her to humour me and she left it alone.

The stress brought out the worst in me. I was agitated most of the time, as if waiting for some impending doom, and my OCD raised its ugly head once again. I worried that I was making it worse than it really was, but the images of that evening kept playing over and over again in my mind: Bella throwing herself at the back door, desperately trying to get in, the look of hatred on Mark's face as he threw me to the floor, Agnese's fear as he dragged her down the hall.

I decided to phone Mum and ask her advice, remembering how she'd helped me before when I was trying to get off the booze. She'd be worried, obviously, thinking that I would give in to my demons. I was worried too, as there were a few times when I would have done anything to sit down with a glass of chilled prosecco. But I knew I wouldn't go there anymore. I'd come through so much and wasn't about to ruin it for a drink and a hangover in the morning. Temptation was a nasty monster, but I was determined to defeat it.

I heard the rattling of plates and cutlery in the background as we talked. 'Have I rung at a bad time? Are you eating?'

'No, no, we've just finished. Kevin's loading the dishwasher.'

'You've already got him trained? Not bad going, Mum.'

'Yes, well, um, he moved in a couple of weeks ago.'

I could imagine her cheeks burning bright red at the other end of the line. 'Ooh, that *was* fast!' I laughed.

'Y-you think so? Should I have waited a bit longer?'

'Oh, Mum, don't be silly. I'm really pleased for you, I'm glad it's working out.' I could hear the doubt in her voice and felt guilty for laughing at her. 'Honestly, if you're happy, then I'm happy.'

'Thanks. You know, I never imagined I'd find something like this again. I spent so many years alone, and then you had your problems...' She coughed. 'I wanted to grab this with both hands and do something for myself.'

'Mum, you don't have to explain yourself to me. As long as he treats you well and you're both in love, then anything you do is fine.'

'When you told me Francesco had moved into the cottage, I thought, Why not? Why shouldn't I have some happiness as well?'

'And are you? Happy, I mean.'

'Yes, I am. I never believed I could be, not after your dad, but I am. I'm glad I did it, Jen.'

'Me too.' There was a pause while I wondered how to bring up my reason for calling.

'So, why did you phone? Was it only for a natter, or is there something else?'

I never could fool her, it was like she had a radar that could detect my problems.

'There's something I wanted to speak to you about. Francesco doesn't know, and Agnese doesn't really want to talk about it. The whole situation is becoming quite stressful.'

'Go on. I'm here for anything, you know that.'

I took a deep breath. There was no easy way to say it, so I blurted it out. 'It's Mark. I saw him at the market in Lucca. I-I think he's come back, Mum, and I don't know what to do.'

'Mark? The maniac? I thought the police were looking for him.'

'It's been a few months, they probably assumed he left the area.'

'Are you sure it was him? Did you see his face?'

'Yes. I'm positive it was him.'

'Why didn't you tell Francesco? I can understand Agnese not wanting to talk about it, after everything she went through.'

'Because I'm scared he'll go after him and do something stupid,' I admitted. 'When I told him what Mark did to us, he said he'd punch his lights out if he ever saw him. I don't want to see Francesco go to jail because of that arsehole. And maybe he'll stay down in the valley. I'd be very surprised if he shows his face in Gallicano again. Everyone knows him.'

'Hmm, I hope you're right. I can see your dilemma, but I think you should tell him, Jen, I really do. Firstly, because you can't carry this stress by yourself...' I tried to interrupt but she wouldn't let me. 'I can hear it in your voice, Jen, there's that little tremble it used to do when you were going through detox. I'll never forget it.' Her voice caught, and she took a moment to compose herself. 'And because Francesco needs to know. What if Mark does turn up? You all need to be ready, so you can defend yourselves. He almost dragged Agnese off last time, God only knows what would have happened if I hadn't turned up. He was going to come back for you too, Jen, I've no doubt about that.'

'You're right, Mum. I've tried to forget that night, but he was crazy. He wanted to hurt us, both of us, and we couldn't stop him. I-I've been having problems since I saw him the other day. I keep wanting to clean everything, like I can scrub away the dirt he's left behind. But I found a charm in the book that's supposed to provide protection for the people you love. I made some herbal bags and performed the spell, then told everyone to keep the bags with them. Francesco thinks I'm mad, and I know Agnese isn't convinced it will work.'

Mum didn't laugh, as I'd expected. 'The book is powerful, and if you found a spell in it, it will probably help.'

'You believe me? You don't think I'm crazy for having tried it?'

'Not at all. After everything you told me last year, and having seen the effect of Luisa's juice for myself, I'll believe anything you tell me.'

'What about this, then?' I wasn't sure it was a good idea, but ploughed on nonetheless. 'After I carried out the spell, I felt a bit funny, like there was so much more I could do. Like the healing side of things is only the beginning; it's as if something's being opened inside me. I don't know, maybe I'm making this all up and it's the after-effects of the herbs, like getting high. But I keep thinking about the dragonflies, how they're connected to us, the cottage, the Grove, how they seem to communicate with us. There's something more to our family, and I want to find out what it is.'

'I've always told you there's magic in the cottage, Jen, and I believe it now more than ever, after what you've just told me. I guess you're going to use Luisa's juice, see if it works like last time?'

'That's what I was thinking. I found an old wooden box at Tommaso's house the day I was looking for the recipe book, and inside it was a tapestry. I think it was made by the first healer; the dates match, and when I touched it I felt myself being pulled back through time. I could hear the voices of children singing as they danced around the maypole, I could see the little figures moving, weaving in and out of each other...' My voice faded as I remembered how scared I'd felt, seeing the scene unfold before me. 'I-I want to see if the juice will show me the past, like the night I saw Grandma Luisa's life story, but I'm afraid to do it, Mum. What if I can't wake up? Before, I didn't know what was going on, but now I've had time to think about what could have gone wrong.'

'You'll have Francesco and Agnese with you this time, they'll make sure you're all right,' Mum said, her voice trembling slightly. 'But first, you have to tell Francesco about Mark, so you can protect each other. Promise me you'll tell him.'

'I promise, Mum.' I knew she was right, even though I was dreading it.

'And promise me you won't try to touch the tapestry unless they're there with you,' she insisted. 'You'll be safe if you do it with them.'

'I promise,' I repeated. 'I knew phoning you would help, Mum.'

'Even if I say things you don't want to hear?'

'Sometimes I need a kick up the backside.'

She chuckled. 'That's what I'm here for. Keep me updated, okay? Both about Mark and the tapestry. I can always come over, if necessary.'

'Maybe I can meet Kevin at long last,' I said, trying to keep my voice light.

She wasn't fooled. 'Anything you need, Jen, *anything*, call me. I'm only a short flight away.'

'Okay. Love you, Mum.'

'I love you too. Say hi to the others for me.'

I ended the call and put my phone down on the table. I knew it wouldn't be easy, but I had to do it.

7

Francesco leapt to his feet, shoving his chair back. 'You're telling me you saw that... that... arsehole, and you didn't say anything?' he shouted.

'Ssh, you'll wake Malva,' I said, trying to calm him down.

He lowered his voice. 'I can't believe you didn't tell me.'

'And what would you have done if I had?'

'I'd have gone over and punched him.'

'Exactly.' I crossed my arms and scowled at him.

'Okay, so it wouldn't have been the best thing to do,' he admitted.

'Especially with all those people about to witness it.'

'But the police are looking for this guy! You should have told me, we could have gone to the *carabinieri*.'

'He disappeared. One minute he was there, the next, nothing. By the time the police would have arrived, he'd have been long gone. I'm sorry. I didn't know what to do, it was such a shock seeing him.'

'He won't come here. Jen's made the charms.' Agnese's voice was quiet, but I could hear the determination in her voice.

'You knew?' Francesco shook his head and snorted.

'I had to tell her. We phoned the police and warned them, and I put the charms everywhere.'

'Oh, so that's what they were for. Not for our well-being, but to *protect* us. Now I understand.'

'Please, Francesco.' My shoulders slumped. So much for Mum's advice.

'I'm sorry, Jen.' He sat next to me and put his hand over mine. 'It's a bit of a shock, that's all. Do you think he'll come here?'

'I honestly don't know. He'd be stupid to come back, but then again...' My voice trailed off as I thought about the last time we'd seen him, here at the cottage. I shuddered, trying not to imagine what would have happened if my mum hadn't arrived at exactly the right moment. Glancing at Agnese's face, I realised she was thinking the same thing.

'Then he'll have to deal with me, and Bella,' Francesco said grimly. Bella leapt up at the sound of her name, wagging her tail. He leaned over and caressed her head. 'Isn't that right, Bella? You'll protect Jen and Agnese, won't you? You won't let that arsehole get away again, you'll chew his arm up good and proper next time!'

I laughed as the tension eased slightly. 'Bella would have gone for him if Agnese hadn't held her back. She managed to rip up his jacket before he threw her outside. If he shows his face here again, we'll let her loose on him.'

Francesco tugged at his shirt sleeves. 'I want you girls to keep your phones on you at all times and call me straight away if anything happens. That creep had better not show his face again, if he has any sense.'

'Don't do anything that's going to get you into trouble,' I pleaded. 'The last thing we need is you arrested while *he's* free to do what he wants.'

'I won't,' he said.

'Promise?'

He smiled. 'Yes, I promise. Now, no more talk about Mr Psycho. What about we get some lunch?'

I sat back in my chair and watched as he took pots and pans out of the cupboard, banging them down on the counter. He'd promised, but I suspected he'd had his fingers crossed under the table. Francesco was a good man, and I knew he'd do whatever was necessary to protect us. I sighed, wondering if I'd done the right thing in telling him about Mark.

Lunch was a subdued affair. None of us had much of an appetite or the desire to talk. Francesco left for an emergency repair job he couldn't cancel, leaving strict instructions on how to contact him if we needed to. Agnese and I sat down on the sofa while Malva played happily on the floor.

'Are you okay?' I asked Agnese. She was twisting some hair between her fingers, turning it as tight as she could before letting it go and starting again.

'Not really.'

I couldn't blame her. I'd been upset since seeing him, but she had been stoically silent since I'd told her that day. Her face crumpled as she started to cry.

'Why? Why does he have to show up now? Just when we're getting our lives back together and putting everything behind us. I've been having nightmares...'

'Me too.' I sighed. 'But they'll pass, promise.'

'I'm terrified he'll try to take Malva away,' she said in a soft voice.

'He can't,' I said firmly. 'She's your daughter, and after what he did, no one will let him near her.'

She brushed a tear from her cheek and put her hands in her lap, clenching her fists.

'Talk to me, Agnese,' I insisted gently. 'It helps, you know it does. Remember when I found the grave and I told you everything about my babies?'

She nodded.

'So, talk to me. Face up to it, get it out of your system.' I waited.

Sniffing, she picked up a packet of tissues from the coffee table and blew her nose. 'I don't have the dream often, only when I'm particularly stressed. I'm in the Grove, with Malva on her blanket, and he turns up...' I noticed she couldn't bring herself to say his name. I reached over and took hold of her hand.

'Go on.'

'He comes sauntering through the gate towards us, and everything goes dark, as if it was night. Malva starts crying, and I look around in panic, but there's no one there. Not you, or Bella, or Francesco; it's just me and Mark. He grins at us, and his mouth gets wider and bigger, until it fills his whole face. He goes over to Malva and bends down to pick her up. I scream and run to save her, but he pushes me away, and I fall to the ground.

'Then suddenly he's on top of me, still grinning, and I realise he wants to bury me. He's pushing me further and further down into the earth, and I'm sinking, the soil's going over my head and getting in my eyes, my ears, my mouth, until I'm completely covered, and then he disappears. That's when I usually wake up.' Her hand grasped tightly on to mine as she talked.

'It's only a dream, Agnese, it won't happen,' I said quietly.

'But she's his daughter. He could demand to see her, go to court, and I'd have to let him, and he could run away with her...' She burst into racking sobs, her whole body shaking.

I wrapped my arms around her. 'He wouldn't be so stupid. The police are still looking for him, he's not going to go to court.

And if he comes here, we'll set Bella on him. Try not to think about what might happen, concentrate on what you have now.'

She sat up, sniffing. 'You're right. I don't know why I ever fell for his bullshit, really. I was taking stock of my life, as you do; twenty-eight years old, still living at home with my parents, doing odd jobs here and there. I didn't have a future, I didn't even know what I wanted to do. I'd worked as a secretary in a local office, done some waitressing in the restaurants around town, I even did a stint at the tourist information point, but I didn't have any qualifications, or any direction in life. I remember thinking I'd end up as an old spinster, still living with my parents while Piero and Lorenzo became high-flying executives and travelled the world. I didn't want to go abroad, but I wanted something, *anything*, to bring some excitement in my life.' She straightened her shoulders and smiled ruefully. 'I sound pretty pathetic, don't I?'

'Not at all. I was going through exactly the same thing – the mundane job, husband left me, no idea what I was going to do with my life. So I drank. It was easier than dealing with things. I must have made Mum's life hell.' I grimaced, thinking back to some of my more spectacular stunts when I was legless.

'I wish I'd turned to drink rather than him,' Agnese replied, then gave an apologetic smile. 'Sorry. I probably shouldn't have said that.'

'Probably not, but I'm not offended. Drink wouldn't have given you Malva, though.'

She glanced over at the sleeping baby in her cot. 'That's what keeps me going, and stops me from totally collapsing. The fact that I've got a beautiful daughter, and you and I are healers, living here at the cottage. A lot of good things have come out of my stupidity, and I remind myself of that every day. Strangely enough, he gave me the future I was looking for, not all the shit he promised me.'

'How did you get together with him? Only if you want to tell me, though.' We'd never spoken about it since the night he'd attacked us, and I was curious.

'I met him at a bar in Lucca about six months before you came over,' she said, hesitant at first, then gaining confidence as she spoke. 'He said he was divorced but he seemed nice, so I agreed to go out with him again. It was all right in the beginning. He took me to some nice restaurants, drove me around in his flashy car, he was always well dressed and looked like the international businessman he said he was. He told me to forget looking for a job, that he'd sort out his business here and then we'd go to England and start a new life there. I was so excited – at long last it was my turn to be someone and do something with my life. It had only been a few months, but he was so convincing. We were on the point of telling everyone...' She stopped and glanced at me.

'And then I turned up,' I finished for her. 'Oh God, I'm so sorry, Agnese.'

'You weren't to know,' she said, patting my knee. 'And neither did I, apparently. When he told us to cool it off because you'd arrived, I had no idea. I was too stupid to put two and two together.'

'Even if you had, he would have denied it. And he would have convinced you it was your fault.'

'That's true. Anyway, that's the sad story of what happened, right up until he cheated on me.'

'He got me drunk,' I said, so quietly I thought she hadn't heard me at first. There was silence for a few moments.

'What?' she whispered.

'I told you about the caves, right?'

'Of course. Bastard.'

'Well, after that, he took me to the bar and bought me a few glasses of wine, even though he knew I was recovering and couldn't touch the stuff. He got me drunk, brought me back here, and...' I shrugged helplessly.

'You never told me.' Her voice was subdued, her eyes glistening with tears. She reached for a tissue.

'I-I couldn't. I was so ashamed of myself. I threw him out of the house, and told him exactly what I thought of him. But it was my fault, I should have known better.' I stopped, unable to go on. The guilt I'd been carrying around for months suddenly overwhelmed me, suffocating me.

'Jennifer, listen to me.' Agnese's voice cut through the fog in my head. 'You're not to blame, do you hear? You weren't to know he was going to come here and attack us. Christ, you didn't even know he was seeing me. He's the one responsible for his actions, *him*. Not you because you got upset with him, not me because I thought I had a future with him. It sounds like he planned every single detail of what he did to us. We're the innocent ones in all this.' She leaned over, holding on to my arm, looking earnestly into my eyes. 'Please, Jennifer. I don't know what I'll do if he comes here, if I'll be able to face him without collapsing in a heap. Please stay strong for me, for both of us.'

I hugged her back, holding her tightly, and we both wept tears of anger, guilt, and frustration as we let the emotions run through our bodies, until we had nothing left to cry.

Francesco wanted to go in person to the *carabinieri*, even though I'd already phoned them. We dropped Agnese and Malva off at Aunt Liliana's house on our way. I told them what had happened, and they said they'd check out Mark's house and alert the police in Lucca. But it was obvious from their faces they weren't convinced they'd catch him.

When we returned to Aunt Liliana's, the whole family was gathered.

'So?' Aunt Liliana wasn't patient at the best of times, and I could see she was agitated. None of them knew the whole story about Mark, in particular that he was Malva's father, but we'd told them how unhinged he was and that was enough to worry them all.

'They're going to keep an eye out for him,' I told her.

'That's it? Nothing else? They should be out patrolling the streets, looking everywhere until they find him!' she shouted. Uncle Dante patted her arm.

'They will,' he reassured her, but I could see the tension etched on his face. Everyone looked upset.

'I'll be there in the evenings and at the weekends,' Francesco said, 'and I don't think he'll try anything during the day, there are too many people coming and going from the cottage.'

Aunt Liliana stamped her foot. 'He was waiting in the kitchen for them the last time, or have you forgotten that?'

He blushed. 'I know, but he took them by surprise. I'll buy chains for the gates, and Bella will protect them.'

'I don't know. The thought of the two of them up there at the cottage by themselves... maybe we should take it in turns to stay there during the day,' Aunt Liliana said.

'Oh, Mamma, don't!' Agnese snapped. She looked pale and tense, but I could see she was ready to fight for her independence. 'We don't know if he's back for good, or if he'll even come to Gallicano. Maybe he'll stay in Lucca, or he's passing through. You can't keep us under surveillance twenty-four hours a day just because he *might* do something.'

'I agree,' Piero said.

'Me too,' Giulia added. 'Agnese and Jennifer aren't stupid, they know how to look after themselves. And we can spread the word around the village, make sure people tell us if they see him. People are still gossiping about him even now, wondering why he upped and left so suddenly. If we tell them the *carabinieri* are looking for him, they'll help.'

'So, that's settled then?' I asked. They nodded. Aunt Liliana didn't look too happy about things, and I knew she'd be straight on the phone to Mum as soon as we left. I was glad I'd already spoken to her.

'And there's the spell, well, charm,' I blurted out suddenly. Everyone turned and stared at me. 'In the book, there are some... charms. I've made some protection ones, hopefully they'll help.' From the blank looks on their faces, I guessed they weren't too impressed. 'Everything else works,' I said in my defence. 'All the potions and creams we've made so far are effective, so why shouldn't these charms help? I mean, it's probably the ingredients rather than the actual spell, but it can't hurt.'

'A spell?' Lorenzo sniggered, and Piero had an enormous grin on his face.

'Yes, a spell,' I insisted. 'I've read through the whole book, and there are spells for love potions, for sleeping, healing, protection, keeping spirits away, visions; you name it, there's a spell or a charm for everything.'

They stopped laughing. 'I guess it can't hurt to try,' Piero said. 'You'd better watch out, they'll be burning the two of you at the stake as witches if you're not careful!'

The tension broke and everyone started talking, their worries seemingly forgotten as they laughed and joked. I glanced over at Agnese and gave her a reassuring smile. My family always amazed me with their ability to take everything in their stride, and I felt safer than I had in a long time.

8

MAY

A fter speaking with Mum and the rest of the family, I felt more positive. My OCD abated, and I could deal more calmly with the day-to-day things. I checked the herbal bags regularly, making sure they were still where I'd left them. As the days passed and Mark didn't show his face, I started to believe that we'd truly seen the last of him.

Spring had arrived, and our time was divided between the Grove and the laboratory. Even rainy days were bearable; we'd stay in the cottage, the wood-burning stove crackling merrily away in the kitchen, chasing away the humidity and the dull greyness outside. Nobody bothered to make the trip up to the cottage in the rain, so we could spend the day being entertained by Malva.

At almost five months old, she was a placid child, full of smiles for everyone. She was content to sit in her pram and watch us work, or she would roll around in a small playpen we'd bought and filled with toys. The best moments for me were when I could have her all to myself for a while, holding her and talking nonsense to her, singing nursery rhymes off-key, then watching as her eyes grew heavy and she fell fast asleep. After so many years of longing, here I was with a baby in my arms that was a part of my life, and I a part of hers. I would watch her grow up, teach her right from wrong, encourage her, hold her hand and kiss her better when she fell over; she wasn't mine, but she was the next best thing, and I loved Agnese for giving me these experiences. I knew that I would protect Malva with my life, if necessary, from Mark or from any other evil out there in the world.

Since the day in the laboratory when I'd made the herbal bags and recited the spell, I'd not gone into any more trances when near the tomb in the Grove. But my dreams had got worse; vivid, violent dreams infested by strange occurrences, and always the same evil presence.

I was running through a dense forest and could hear the pounding of horses' hooves coming from behind me. I half fell, half slid down a steep embankment, and ended up on my hands and knees by a stream. I looked down at my reflection, startled to see another woman looking up at me, wild eyes full of fear, her hands protectively cradling her rounded stomach. A shout came from above and I turned, terrified, to see a man on a horse at the top of the slope, pointing at me. I looked back at the woman under the water, but she was gone and I was staring at my own reflection, my own round stomach. The man jumped off his horse and slid down the slope towards me, kicking up clumps of grass and plants. I screamed, searching frantically for a way to escape, but there was nowhere to run; the river was behind me and the steep slope and the man were in front of me. I could smell his fetid breath and see the glint of craziness in his eyes, and feared the worst...

I woke up yelling in terror, only to find Francesco holding on to me tightly, pinning my arms to my side as I tried to hit out. Neither of us slept any more that night.

The dreams were always of the same pregnant woman who became me at the end. They haunted my waking hours too, as I wondered who she was. I was almost certain she was Agnes... but why? What was the connection between us? I knew that she was the original healer, the first name in the book, but I couldn't understand why she was haunting me. Why now? I had discovered Luisa's past and let her soul rest in peace, forgiving the things she had done by understanding her motives. I had overcome my own demons, too, forgiving myself for my past and creating a new future full of hope and love. So what did Agnes need from me? What had she done that needed forgiveness?

I was lying on a hard surface in a dark room, the only light a small candle on a shelf above me. I was drenched in sweat and moaned loudly as waves of pain radiated throughout my body. My stomach felt as if it were in a vice, as if I were being squeezed by an enormous snake, then the pain died away and I drew deep, shaky breaths. There was a loud, rhythmic creaking noise that seemed familiar but I couldn't quite place it. I screamed again as the pain returned, much stronger this time, and I felt the sheets beneath me suddenly become damp. I clutched my stomach, a guttural animal noise coming from me that I hadn't realised a human being was capable of making. The door opened, flooding the room with lamplight, and an elderly woman rushed in. She leaned over me, stroking my head, her mouth saying words I couldn't hear. I looked down at the sheets and screamed at the sight of all the blood. The creaking noise got louder and I suddenly realised that I was on a boat, in a cabin at the bottom of a ship, in the middle of the sea, and I was having a baby, oh God, I was having a baby and I was going to die in some Godforsaken place, and they'd throw my body overboard, together with the baby...

Waking up with a jolt, I realised I wasn't on a ship. I was in bed, with Francesco, in the cottage, and there was no blood and no baby. I reached out and turned on the bedside lamp, then looked down at the sheets, to be sure. I touched my stomach, but it was as flat as ever. A sudden sense of desolation washed over me, a split second of what could have been, then it was gone.

I could put it off no longer. I knew I had to find out the mystery behind the family's origins, what turn of fate had led to Agnes becoming the first healer, and what other secrets the cottage might hold. The wooden box with the intricate dragonfly carving was still hidden at the back of my wardrobe. I hadn't taken it out since I put the recipe book back inside it, taking care not to touch the oiled silk bag that held the tapestry. This time, though, I wanted to be prepared before going ahead with my vision, or time-travelling, or whatever it was that happened.

After having researched everything thoroughly, I told Francesco and Agnese what I was planning to do.

'I can't keep waking you up every night, screaming my head off,' I explained. It was early in the morning, and we were sitting around the kitchen table, nursing steaming cups of coffee after yet another disturbed night.

Francesco looked like he wasn't about to disagree. 'Malva should be the one giving us sleepless nights, not you.' He smiled, but the dark shadows beneath his eyes betrayed the stress he was going through. I knew he was worried, even more so than with the trances, and he was feeling the strain of not sleeping enough and having to work the next day.

'I'm going to need your help.'

'Tell us what you need us to do,' Agnese said.

'That's the problem, I don't really know,' I admitted. 'Last time, I drank the juice, fell asleep, and watched a film of Luisa's life play before me. I didn't know what was going on, or the dangers involved.'

'Dangers?' Francesco asked.

'I've been googling things. I know, I shouldn't. But now my

biggest fear is not being able to get back after it's over. What if I get trapped somewhere?'

Agnese gasped. 'Do you really think that's a possibility?'

'I hope not. Everything went well last time, but I didn't know then what I know now. So, will you both stay with me, just in case?'

'Do you really need to ask us?' Francesco said, leaning over and kissing me on the cheek. 'Of course we'll be there for you. Right, Agnese?'

'Let's plan when, and I'll leave Malva with Mamma for the day,' she said. 'That way we can be sure we won't be disturbed.'

Tears pricked at my eyes. 'Thank you. It means so much to me...' My voice broke and I started sobbing.

Francesco put his arm around my shoulders and held me close. 'Hey, it's okay. Everything will be fine, and you'll have the most amazing story to tell us when it's all over.'

9

We decided to do it the following Saturday. Agnese took Malva down to Aunt Liliana's house, together with an enormous bag full of everything her daughter could possibly need during her stay. We'd agreed it would be better if Malva stayed overnight, so Agnese had taken enough for the weekend.

While she was gone, Francesco and I began our preparations. I took out a bottle of Luisa's special juice, raspberry this time, and got a glass from the cupboard. Francesco plumped up the cushions on the sofa and put a fleece blanket over the back.

'Why?' I gestured at the blanket.

'You might get cold.'

'Aw, you're so sweet,' I said, hugging him.

'And these are for if you start dribbling,' he added, brandishing a box of tissues.

'Oi!' I slapped his arm, but couldn't help laughing.

'You *are* going to be out of it for a while,' he said.

I could see the worry on his face. 'It'll be okay. I've done this before and come through it unscathed. You'll see.' The worried look didn't go away. 'Ah, there's one last thing,' I exclaimed.

I ran outside and gathered up the candles from the laboratory, then put them on the coffee table in front of the sofa. I placed them in a circle once more and sprinkled some chopped leaves over them. Francesco watched me, fascinated.

'What's that?'

'It's from the plant in the Grove,' I replied. 'I did this when I made the protection charms, and breathing in its scent seemed to give me more courage. I thought it couldn't hurt to use it today as well.'

He picked up a leaf and turned it over in his hand. 'I can't understand why no one knows what plant it is. Have you tried googling it?'

'Of course. There are similar plants but nothing identical. Without being a botanist, there's no way of even guessing which family it belongs to. Maybe one day we'll contact an expert. But I do know it's pretty ancient. It's in every recipe in the book, right from the beginning.'

'So, what do they call it in the recipes? There must be a name, otherwise you wouldn't know what it is.'

'In the older recipes, each plant is referred to in dialect, which made it really difficult for us at the beginning to understand which plant was which. Aunt Liliana was a great help there, thank goodness! Other healers added their names for the plants too, and that was useful sometimes. But thanks to our friend Google, we managed to decipher all of them.'

'Except this one.'

'Except this one, exactly. Agnes called it "silver leaf", which was used in most of the recipes until the 1800s. Then it became "bitter wort" for a while, the flowers do pong a bit towards the end of the season, and then it became "blood root". It was a process of elimination; we identified all the plants with the various names used over the centuries, until only this one was left.'

'Quite the Sherlock Holmes, aren't we?' Francesco seemed impressed.

'It took us ages, but we got there in the end. On the other hand, we couldn't follow the recipes if we didn't know which plants to use.'

'True. So, this silver leaf – what does it do?'

'We've no idea. Each plant usually has specific healing properties, which are suitable for certain ailments. But this plant is listed in every single recipe, usually in miniscule quantities. Whatever it is, it works. Look how people keep coming back for more of our products.'

'Okay. So, sprinkling it over the candles works how?'

'No idea. I guess the heat releases the scent in the air or something. All I know is that it made me feel different, and I'm hoping it will help today.'

'You sure it's not marijuana?' Francesco joked.

I gave him a withering look. 'That was the first thing we checked out, especially after it had that weird effect on me. And no, it's got nothing to do with it.'

As I fussed over the candles, he stood watching me. 'Come here, you,' he said, holding his hands out to me.

'Just a moment,' I muttered, still undecided if they should be in a circle or lined up.

'Jen.' He took hold of my arm and gently pulled me upright until I was standing in front of him. He brushed some stray strands of hair out of my eyes. 'I fell in love with you the first time I saw you. Remember?'

'Of course,' I replied, a little surprised. *Love?* In all these months together, he'd never said the 'L' word. 'I was in the Grove.'

'Agnese brought me to see you, and I couldn't believe it when you stepped through the gate.' He smiled. 'Your hair was coming out of its ponytail, it was all over the place.' I smoothed my hair self-consciously. It was the bane of my life; usually flat and life-less, it had a tendency to go wild and frizzy if the air was damp or I sweated. 'And you had a smudge of dirt right here.' He leaned forward and kissed the tip of my nose. 'I immediately thought, *I've met the woman I want to spend the rest of my life with.*'

'Seriously? Why have you never told me this before?' I laughed. 'I remember talking nonsense, I sounded like an idiot, gabbling on about nothing. I liked you too, though,' I added. I didn't mention that I'd nicknamed him Rugged Cowboy on sight, I didn't want him to get too big-headed.

'So, Jennifer Blakely degli Innocenti, do you think you could put up with me forever?' he asked, a mischievous glint in his eyes.

'Ooh, I don't know about that,' I teased, automatically going into my self-defence mode of making a joke out of any situation. 'Jennifer Conti. That's going to take some getting used to!'

'But you *could* get used to it?' he insisted.

'I could get very used to it.' I kissed him softly on the mouth.

'Good,' he murmured, and kissed me back. 'Although, here in Italy women keep their own surname, they don't take their husband's. It's for tax reasons.' I pursed my lips and he must have guessed I was about to say something sarcastic. He coughed. 'Maybe we'll carry on this conversation after... all of this.' He gestured towards the coffee table and sofa.

'Give me something to come back for, eh?' I said, only half-joking.

'Something like that.' He held me close. 'Don't forget me, okay?'

'How could I?'

Agnese came through the back door, panting slightly. 'Malva's settled at Mamma's now, I've locked the gates and put the chain on. We only need to turn off our phones and then we can get started.' She glanced at the two of us. 'Not disturbing anything, am I?'

'No, nothing,' I said.

'Jennifer's a bit worried, that's all,' Francesco added.

'I guess we'd better get on with it, then, before she chickens out.' Agnese gestured to the sofa, and we sat down. 'Relax, everything will be all right.' She picked up the bottle of juice. 'Raspberry this time. Nice.'

I smiled. 'I thought I'd spoil myself.'

'Why not? So, how do we do this?'

I was glad Agnese and Francesco were there, even though I felt a bit self-conscious going through this with them watching me.

'First, I have to drink some juice,' I said, trying to remember what had happened the last time. 'Bella was here too, she was lying on the rug. There was a thunderstorm somewhere close by, the lights flickered, and I thought the electricity would go off. I was looking through the recipe book when I almost spilt the juice over it and dropped it. Luisa's letter fell out, and I picked it up and started reading it...' I stopped. 'The box!'

'What box?' Francesco asked, confused.

'The one in my wardrobe, with the dragonfly on the lid. I need the tapestry inside, I need to be able to touch it!'

Agnese handed me a glass of juice. The ruby red liquid glinted in the sunlight, casting blood-tinted shadows over my hand and arm.

'Drink this, I'll go and get the box,' she said. 'Sit down on the sofa and try to keep calm, otherwise it might not work and you'll have gone through all this for nothing.' She looked at Francesco. 'Light the candles, see if that helps Jen relax.'

I watched as Francesco took a match and lit the candles, one by one. Their soft fragrance immediately filled the air around us, and I slowly felt calmer. I sipped the juice, trying not to imagine what lay ahead.

'Think of it as a dream,' Francesco said, sitting beside me on the sofa. 'A vivid dream where nothing's real and you can wake up whenever you want.'

I bit my lip. 'I have to do this, don't I?'

'If you want peace of mind, and you want to find out what's behind the trances and dreams, yes.'

'Okay,' I said, determined. I took a few more gulps of the juice, barely tasting the sweetness of the berries. I breathed in the scent from the candles and tried to relax.

'Here you go.' Agnese placed the wooden box on my lap, its sudden weight startling me.

'This is it then. No going back.' I traced my forefinger over the carved dragonfly on the lid, once again marvelling at the incredible detail. I could feel the juice taking effect, my body entering the dreamlike state that preceded everything else. I opened the box, the delicate aroma of wood, oiled silk, and dried herbs wafting over me. My senses heightened, I saw the shimmering cloud of dust motes float upwards as I took out my notebook, still tied with a ribbon, and heard the paper make a delicate scratching sound against my fingers as I placed it on the coffee table next to the candles.

Agnese and Francesco sat in silence, following my preparations. Bella lay on the rug, softly snoring, seemingly oblivious to what was going on, but I could see the tiny hairs in her ears vibrate, capturing every sound, every detail.

My fingers found the false bottom of the chest and gently pressed down, applying pressure to make the mechanism work. There was a loud click and I saw the bottom had raised up at an angle. Taking a deep breath, I used my fingernails to lift the wood, revealing the oiled silk bag hidden below.

'This is it,' I whispered. I risked looking up at Agnese and

Francesco; they were watching me, enthralled. I smiled as I removed the bag. Agnese leaned over, picked up the box off my lap, and placed it on the floor beside us.

I took another sip of juice. This time I could taste every ingredient: the delicate sweetness of the raspberries, a hint of sage and thyme, and the woody flavour of the Grove, together with an undefinable aroma that blended with the fragrance of the candles. My hand shook, and I felt someone gently take away the glass as the room folded in on itself around me, darkness filling every corner until I could only see the silk bag.

I loosened the drawstrings and tipped the bag upside down. The tapestry slid out onto my legs. I could already hear the children singing as they danced around the maypole, childish voices coming from far away. I gently unrolled the tapestry and spread it open across my lap. The coloured threads were even brighter this time, if that was possible, and a golden glow emanated from them. The voices grew louder, and the stitched figures started moving, imperceptibly at first. I stared at the two sides of the tapestry, so different but so familiar. The right side, with its English manor house, village green and maypole, and the Grove on the left side, together with the cottage, the mountains, and the valley.

The right side was buzzing with activity, people swaying in time with the music, children dancing around the maypole, others carrying platters of food among the crowds. I stretched out my hand towards them, still hesitant, the juice coursing through my veins not yet enough to overcome my fear. My gaze shifted to the left side, strangely silent, darker somehow, as if the golden light couldn't touch it, even though the whole tapestry was glowing. I moved my hand and my fingertips glided over the stitched image of the cottage, skimming the surface as they traced its outline.

Suddenly, everything went dark and a loud scream reverberated around my head. A face appeared before me, a malevolent snarl distorting its features, its eyes piercing my soul, hatred pouring out from it, boring into me, trying to find its way to my heart...

'Jen? Jennifer, are you okay?' Francesco's voice came from far away, as if he was at the end of a long tunnel. Agnese was talking as well, but everything was muffled. I panicked, struggling to get out of the blackness surrounding me, but it was dragging me down. It was the black hole once more, sucking all my hopes, my future, leaving me with nothing as I plummeted into its murky depths.

There was a whine, and something soft nudged my hand, lifting it from the tapestry. The darkness receded and I gradually came back to the surface, gasping like someone rescued from drowning. My sight came back to me, the golden glow filling my vision, Bella's soft fur under my hand. Agnese and Francesco were talking in urgent tones. I willed myself to concentrate and listen to them, but the glow was too strong, the glow pulled me towards it, no matter how hard I tried to get away. Bella moved her head, and my hand slowly slid off and back onto the tapestry. On the right side this time. My fingers tingled as they touched the tapestry, the voices shouting as the manor house burst into life...

AGNES

1347–1370

10

NOVEMBER 1347

T he manor house overlooking the village of Forest Brook
burst into life as soon as dawn broke. The servants rose,
grumbling, from the piles of straw at the far end of the great
hall, yawning and rubbing their bleary eyes as they made their
way to their various workplaces. Chaos reigned as people jostled
each other at the entrance door, spilling out into the courtyard
and blowing on their hands, clouds of white vapour filling the
air on the cold morning. Lord Funteyn, Baron of Upper Fording-
bridge, the land he owned in Hampshire, and his daughter, Lady
Elizabeth, were rarely seen before the sun was high in the sky,
long after the servants had finished their morning chores.

Agnes pulled her tunic closer around her, the thick, coarse
wool helping to keep out some of the chill. The weak winter sun
broke through the clouds, its rays glinting off the puddles left by
the previous night's downpour. She clasped the shoes she'd just
finished cleaning tightly in her hands. The dainty cloth slippers
weren't really suitable for wearing to the stables, but Lady Elizabeth did as she wanted with no thought to the servants who
would have to clean up after her, as Agnes had discovered in the
short time she'd been there. Agnes had been up since half past

five that morning, scrubbing at the muck and stains until her hands had gone numb with cold. Now she made her way over to the kitchen, intending to leave the slippers near the enormous fireplace so they would hopefully dry out by the afternoon, when her ladyship would no doubt demand to wear them once again.

Skirting around the muddy puddles, she failed to notice two lads charging across the courtyard at full pelt, pushing and shoving each other as they ran. They crashed into her head-on, making her stumble backwards. She landed on her bottom with an 'oomph', right in the middle of an enormous puddle, her hands – and the shoes – sinking into the muddy ground.

'Oh, look what you've done!' she shouted. The boys stopped and stared at her, pointing, then ran off, giggling loudly.

'Don' mind them, they're young lads having a bit o' fun,' a woman said, staggering along, her arms laden with linen.

'Having fun? Look at the state of me,' Agnes wailed. 'And look at these. I'll have to do them again.' She held up the dripping shoes covered in mud.

The woman shrugged. 'Them things happen,' she remarked and carried on her way. Agnes slapped her hand in the icy water in frustration, tears filling her eyes.

'Here, let me help you,' a voice said. Agnes looked up and saw, through her blurry vision, a young man holding out his hand to her.

'Thank you,' she said flatly as he pulled her upright. Water and mud dripped from her. 'I'll have to wash my tunic as well, now.' She burst into tears.

'Hey, it's all right,' he said, patting her arm awkwardly. 'I mean, it's not the end of the world, is it?'

'I-I got up early this morning so I could clean her ladyship's shoes, a-and now I have to do it all over again a-and my hands hurt because it's s-so cold...' She was embarrassed by her tears, but couldn't hold them back.

'Let's get you in the kitchen and warmed up, then things won't seem so bad,' he said. 'My name's Ted, by the way.'

'Th-thanks, Ted,' she mumbled. 'I'm Agnes.'

Agnes was sitting on the steps outside the kitchen door a couple of hours later giving a final scrub to the shoes, dressed in an old tunic while her wet one drip-dried indoors, when she heard a mewling sound coming from above her head. After searching for a while, she saw a small black and white kitten on the nearby roof, crying frantically for its mother. At the same time, Lady Elizabeth leaned out of a nearby window, saying, 'Hold on, Poppy, I'm coming to get you!' The girl had already hooked a leg over the windowsill before Agnes understood what was happening. She had a sudden vision of Lady Elizabeth sliding down the roof before landing on the soft, muddy ground beside her.

'Wait, Lady Elizabeth!' she shouted. 'Don't go on the roof, I'll get your kitten.' She ran indoors and got a stool and then, with some difficulty, hoisted herself up onto the roof. The tiles were still slippery from the recent rains, so she moved slowly towards the kitten, not daring to look down.

'You're nearly there,' Elizabeth called. 'Oh, you've got her!'

Agnes held the purring animal in her arms, its body vibrating against her chest. *Now I've just got to get back down*, she thought grimly. She half-crawled, half-walked back across the roof towards the stool, holding tightly on to the kitten. As she reached the edge of the roof, she heaved a sigh of relief. One more step...

The world spun around her as her foot slipped on a dislodged tile, and she tried to protect the kitten as her body fell through the air. She landed with a hard bump on the ground and lay gasping for breath. The kitten scratched her with its sharp claws as it frantically tried to run away, still crying in panic but otherwise unhurt. Agnes let the ungrateful creature go. There was the sound of footsteps running towards her, a girl's voice crying out, then everything went dark.

She awoke in the great hall on her straw pallet a little while later, her head throbbing and her bones aching. She felt someone sponging her face with a piece of linen soaked in cold water, and then heard Lady Elizabeth speaking to her.

'Oh, thank goodness you're awake. I was so terribly worried when I saw you fall like that. But Poppy's safe, you'll be glad to hear.'

Agnes couldn't really have cared less about Poppy but smiled at the young girl leaning over her. Then she groaned as the room swam about her and she turned to vomit over the side of the pallet.

'You, boy, fetch some water and clean up this mess.' Elizabeth's voice seemed to come from far away. 'Quickly, now.' There was a scampering of feet, then Agnes sank back into the darkness once more.

'I have decided that as a reward for saving Poppy, you are to become my maid,' Elizabeth said in an imperious tone.

Agnes blinked as she came to. Bright light streamed across her face. Confused, she found herself lying on a thick rug, a soft cushion beneath her head.

'You're in my room. I thought it best to get you away from all the confusion downstairs.' The young girl knelt by her side. 'Don't try to sit up yet. The last time you did that, you were sick.'

Agnes grimaced. 'I'm so sorry, Lady Elizabeth. I still feel a bit woozy. I'm in the solar wing?' She had heard that there had been great excitement among the servants when Lord Funteyn hired builders to add the extra wing to the manor house a few years earlier. No other manor house in the area had an upstairs floor, and they loved boasting on market days about the modifications their master had ordered. Indeed, the two-storey wing, with its large windows, was impressive, and gave the stately home a distinctive air.

'I sh-shouldn't be in here!' Agnes suddenly exclaimed, sitting up with a start. The solar wing was strictly off limits for most of the servants; a lowly scullery maid would be whipped just for stepping foot inside the door downstairs.

'Don't be silly.' Elizabeth pushed her back down. 'I've spoken with Father, and he says you can take old Emma's place as my maid. The daft thing could never get my hair right, it's always out of place by mid-afternoon. The wonderful news is, you're to start right away!'

'B-but I don't know anything about being a lady's maid,' Agnes stammered.

'You'll learn,' Elizabeth replied breezily. 'Besides, it will be fun having someone my own age, rather than boring old Emma. We'll have so much to talk about!'

Agnes felt guilty as she watched Emma shuffle her way down the narrow staircase, clutching her few belongings to her chest and muttering to herself.

'What will she do?' She feared the old woman would be sent away. She would never be able to live with herself if that happened.

'Mrs Smythe has been moaning about needing someone else to help with the laundry. Emma's the perfect choice,' Elizabeth replied.

Agnes knew Mrs Smythe well; the robust woman with a heart of gold always made time to speak to her while up to her elbows in soapsuds. She couldn't imagine frail, old Emma being much help at all, and opened her mouth to speak.

'It's either that or she leaves the manor, Agnes,' Elizabeth interrupted, a warning tone in her voice.

'Yes, Lady Elizabeth,' Agnes said, curtseying the best she knew how. At least Emma would still have a roof over her head and food in her belly. Without a husband or a family to care for her, it was the best she could hope for.

11

As the winter months passed, Agnes settled into her new life as Lady Elizabeth's maid. She no longer slept down in the great hall with the other servants; she had her own little room up under the roof. Although she didn't miss sleeping on a thin straw pallet surrounded by people who snored, grunted and farted all night long, listening to small animals scrabbling about above her head took some getting used to.

She quickly learned how to dress Lady Elizabeth's hair, first combing it through, then using her hands to deftly part it in the middle and create two long plaits. These she wound round and round until she had made a bun on each side of the girl's head, which she firmly fixed with long jewelled pins. She could imagine the trouble Emma must have had with her arthritic hands, trying to get the pins in the right place, at the right angle. No wonder Lady Elizabeth's hairstyle fell apart after a few hours!

Agnes rose at dawn, as usual, and crept quietly down the stairs to take Lady Elizabeth's washing to the laundry. She was pleased to see that Emma and Mrs Smythe became firm friends from the start, chatting non-stop about their various aches and pains and complaining about the other servants shirking their duties. Agnes often stopped to speak with them, glad there were no hard feelings between her and Emma.

'Tell the truth, I'm that glad to not have to climb those stairs anymore,' Emma told her one morning. 'Up and down, fetch this, get that... young Lady Elizabeth drove me fair mad with her demands. Yer younger, yer legs'll cope with it.'

Encouraged, Mrs Smythe threw in her opinion as well. 'I don't know how ye do it. If I had to do them, with my knees, I'd do meself a mischief! But yer young, and ye don't have my problems. I don't know, the baron spending all that money on those sorts o' things. In my days, the family lived with the servants, and to hell with all that running around after them!'

Agnes tried to keep a straight face. Since Lord Funteyn had added the upstairs part of the manor, Mrs Smythe had moaned about it every day, according to the other servants. Agnes thought it was a great innovation. She loved climbing up the stairs to Lady Elizabeth's room, far from the noise and chaos of the servants downstairs. There was a drawing room to receive visitors and Lord Funteyn had an office where he shut himself away from the world to conduct his business affairs.

Agnes left them there, still grumbling about life's problems, giggling at their conversation, and went across to the kitchen in the hope of getting some bread and a glass of milk. Godwin, the cook, was besotted with her and would often pass her little tidbits to taste while he was cooking. She knew he was a good man, but didn't want to become a replacement for his wife. And besides, there was Ted, the young man who had helped her out of the puddle that fateful day in November.

She'd bumped into him a few times since then, and he always stopped to have a quick chat with her. She learned that he was the son of a villein and worked in the fields, tending the crops. She'd quickly fallen in love with his cheeky smile and witty banter, and his brilliant blue eyes sent a warm feeling through her body every time she saw him. And it appeared he felt the same way about her, judging from the ribbing remarks his friends made as they walked past the pair of them, making Ted flush bright red.

One morning, as she carried the tray of breakfast things into Elizabeth's room, she was surprised to find her sitting up in bed, reading. She usually had the devil's job to wake her up and make her eat.

'Shall I come back later, Lady Elizabeth?'

'Oh no, I'll eat now.' She put the book to one side. 'I should have read this chapter yesterday for today's lesson, but I forgot.' Agnes narrowed her eyes. 'All right, I didn't forget. But you must admit, it was more fun to go down to the stables and see the horses than read this boring old thing.'

'What is it about?' Agnes asked, curious. She'd seen books on the desk in Lord Funteyn's study when the door was open as she went past, and knew that a tutor came every day to teach Lady Elizabeth. Agnes had even picked up one of her ladyship's books once, marvelling at the strange marks on the parchment and wondering what they meant.

Elizabeth grimaced as she sat down at the table near the window and started to eat. She spoke between mouthfuls, dabbing at her lips with a napkin. 'It's poetry... in English! Father wants me to learn English as well as French now, he says it will be useful in the future. Useful to who? I don't plan to read another word once I'm married. I'll be a lady of leisure, free to do whatever I want.'

'But it must be wonderful to pick up a book and be able to read it,' Agnes said eagerly.

Elizabeth glanced at her. 'Agnes, would you like to learn to read? And write as well, of course.'

'Really? I could learn?'

'Certainly. I will teach you myself, and you may remain here during my lessons with Mr Clarke. You can pretend to be busy with some sewing. We'll keep it our secret, between the two of us.' She clapped her hands, delighted at her idea.

'That would be wonderful!' Agnes exclaimed.

'And then you can read to me during the day and help me learn those silly poems Mr Clarke insists I memorise.' Elizabeth jumped up and hugged her. Agnes couldn't help smiling at her devious tricks. She didn't mind; she would finally learn to read and write, something she had wanted to do ever since she had seen the priest reading from the leather-bound Bible in church.

'Will you teach me both? I mean, English and French?' she asked shyly, scared that she was overstepping the boundary. No matter how much they appeared to be friends, Agnes was fully aware of the fact that she was still a servant and could easily be whipped for offending her mistress.

'I insist you learn both. I'm so glad we have something to do now when it is too cold or too wet to go outside.' She pushed the tray away from her. 'I've finished here. Take it downstairs, then come back so you can help me get ready. If you're quick, we may have time for your first lesson.'

Agnes almost ran down the stairs, taking care not to trip and spill the contents of the tray. She couldn't believe how much her life had changed, all thanks to one silly kitten!

12

Agnes stood outside the manor house, stretching and yawning, shivering a little in the cool morning air. Mrs Smythe strode across the courtyard, loaded with dirty laundry, on her way to the enormous tubs where she'd soon be up to her elbows in soapy water. She spotted Agnes and changed direction.

'So, Agnes, are ye ready for bringing in the May tomorrow, then?'

'Oh, yes. Lady Elizabeth and I are going to the woods today to find flowers for our garlands.'

Mrs Smythe shifted her feet, balancing the laundry in her arms. 'Lady Elizabeth will be making one for her betrothed, Lord Remfrey, the Earl of Stanford. Who will ye be making one for?'

Agnes blushed and lowered her eyes. 'Oh, I don't know.'

'Ye don't know? Well, I'll tell ye who it is if ye don't be knowing yerself.' Mrs Smythe tried to wink at her but only succeeded in scrunching up one side of her face. 'We all been seeing young Ted making eyes at ye, and the two of ye going off for walks every spare second yer got! We're waiting for ye both to announce yer engagement, we're looking forward to another celebration. First Lady Elizabeth, then the two of ye. What a year!'

Agnes laughed and shook her head. 'I don't know about that, Mrs Smythe. We enjoy each other's company, but that's all it is.'

The older woman clucked her tongue. 'Well, tomorrow's the first of May. If young Ted's got any sense in his nonce, he'll do the right thing by ye!'

Agnes's stomach did a flip, while she tried to keep her face neutral. She was looking forward to the upcoming festivities, and hoped Ted would finally kiss her. The last time they'd gone for a walk, he'd held her hand the whole time and had kept smiling at her. She'd been so sure that he would kiss her, but then they'd been interrupted by some of the villagers on their way home after chopping wood in the forest. She'd tried not to be too disappointed, but he'd noticed anyway. As they'd said their goodbyes at the manor house, he'd leaned over and whispered, 'Love you, Agnes', before leaving for his cottage at the edge of the outlying fields.

Mrs Smythe's voice interrupted her thoughts. 'Her ladyship will have ye running around after her all the day long, getting ready for the merriments.'

Agnes started. She'd been miles away. 'I know. I've already taken her washing over to the tubs, so that's out of the way. She told me yesterday she wants me to wake her up extra early today,' she said with a sigh. She loved Elizabeth, but she could be very demanding, especially at times like these.

Mrs Smythe nudged her. 'She'll be wanting to talk about the morrow, and garlands, and whatnot. Maybe she'll name ye Queen of the May. And Ted will be king.'

'Get away with you.' She swiped the older woman's arm. 'It's a shame Lady Funteyn won't get to see her daughter married.'

The lord's wife had passed away two winters before from

influenza. Elizabeth rarely spoke of her mother, telling Agnes it was too painful to remember her. Agnes, too, had lost her mother when she had died giving birth to her brother, therefore she understood Elizabeth's reluctance to talk about Lady Funteyn. Agnes's father had turned to drink and women after losing his wife, so Agnes had left the little cottage where she had grown up and found work as a scullery maid at the manor house. The death of her mother, and the little brother who had been stillborn, still weighed heavily on her heart.

Mrs Smythe nodded, a sober look on her face. ''Twas a terrible time, young Agnes. Ye weren't here then. I remember we cried for days, 'twas such a shock. She was much loved, and 'twas a sad day when she died.' She hoisted the bundle of laundry up higher, and sniffed. 'Well, this washing ain't going to do itself. Ye'd better get going too, there's lots to do the day.'

'I'll go and see if her ladyship's awake so I can start dressing her hair. I'll pop over later, Mrs Smythe, with some freshly made bread for you.'

'Thanks, Agnes, yer a good girl.' Mrs Smythe bustled away to the tubs, still sniffing loudly.

Agnes collected the breakfast tray, then walked over to the solar wing and made her way quietly up the stairs. She knocked on the door of Lady Elizabeth's room before entering, wondering if she would still be asleep. However, she found the young girl sitting up in bed, waiting impatiently for her.

'What a beautiful day! We shall have fun making our garlands.' Elizabeth jumped off the bed and ran over to the window. 'Have they cut the maypole yet?' she asked, her eyes glistening with excitement.

'I think they will cut it today and bring it up to the house tomorrow morning. Ted told me,' Agnes blushed slightly when she said his name, but Elizabeth didn't seem to notice, 'that they want to find the tallest tree in the woods. Even taller than last year's!'

Elizabeth clapped her hands. 'I can't wait to see it. Father has bought the ribbons already, they arrived last week. Tomorrow we'll give them to the villagers, so they can decorate the pole.'

'Which tunic would you like to wear today?' Agnes opened the ornately carved wooden coffer, and ran her hands over the delicate dresses inside.

'Oh, I think the green one today. It won't matter if it gets stained or torn, I've had it for ages anyway. You get it ready while I eat.'

Agnes took the light woollen tunic out, marvelling at the finely made fabric. Her own tunic was made of coarse wool that made her itch all day long, especially on hotter days. Elizabeth wore linen undergarments that were cool and fresh against her skin, a luxury Agnes wasn't permitted to have.

After Agnes had helped Elizabeth get dressed, the two girls left the house and went down the path that led to the woods. The sun shone brightly in the sky and soon they took off their cloaks. As no one was around, they pulled up their long sleeves and bared their arms to the warmth of the sun's rays, grinning at each other in their shared rebellion. Showing even a small area of bare skin was a beatable offence, as they both knew, especially in a respectable household such as Lord Funteyn's.

They reached a clearing and sat down on a fallen tree trunk, studying the flowers around them. As well as sturdy oak trees, there were several birches, their silver bark glinting in the morning sun. Agnes noted that they were quite young, their branches still thin and flexible. She took out a knife she'd brought with her and soon had a pile of pliable sticks lying at her feet.

'These are for the base of the garlands,' she said to Elizabeth. 'What flowers shall we put on them?'

'Oh, definitely woodbine, I love the perfume of it! And what about some hawthorn for the base, there's some over there in flower. It's such a pretty bloom.'

'It's perfect. And look, the clearing is dotted with buttercups and daisies. Shall we add some of those as well?'

'You cut the hawthorn, I shall pick the flowers,' Elizabeth declared.

They spent a couple of pleasant hours preparing their garlands. Agnes bent the birch twigs into circular shapes and added branches of hawthorn. Then Lady Elizabeth added the buttercups, woodbine, and daisies to the two garlands. Agnes went searching around the clearing and came back, triumphantly holding a handful of bluebells she had found under some bushes.

'These are for your garland, Lady Elizabeth.'

'They're beautiful, thank you, Agnes.' Elizabeth deftly inserted them into the twisted branches of the garland, their blue contrasting nicely with the other flowers. 'What about you, don't you want to add some?'

'Oh no, we can't have two identical garlands!' Agnes exclaimed. 'Yours must be unique for Lord Remfrey. I will keep mine as it is.'

'Then I shall find you something else to finish yours.'

They walked back through the woods, chattering excitedly about the upcoming festivities. Elizabeth suddenly darted among the trees on the right of the path and returned a little while later with a triumphant look on her face.

'Here, some flowers for you.' She handed Agnes a bunch of pink and blue flowers.

'Oh, they're forget-me-nots!'

'They're perfect for your garland,' Elizabeth said, winking at her. 'Ted will never forget you now.'

· · ·

The manor house was uncommonly busy the next morning. People had come up from the village, relatives and friends of the manor servants, and were milling about the drive, chatting together as they waited impatiently. May Day was a cause for celebration, for getting drunk and eating well, and they were all determined to enjoy it.

A loud confusion of shouting, singing and trumpeting came from the woods. Startled, everyone turned and ran down the drive, to be greeted by the young men carrying the trunk of the tallest tree they had found. Its upper branches were still intact, and the leaves fluttering merrily in the morning breeze seemed to keep time with the men's songs. Four of the strongest men carried the trunk, while the others held aloft branches they had chopped off.

Ted was in front, carrying the bottom of the heavy trunk on his shoulder. His tunic was torn and grubby, and he had twigs and leaves in his blond hair. His face lit up with an enormous grin when he saw Agnes, and he waved at her, nearly making the trunk fall. Agnes giggled as the others cursed and shouted at him to be more careful, and waved back.

'Ye got yer garland ready for him, then?' Mrs Smythe said, standing beside her. Agnes jumped. She hadn't noticed her there.

'My garland's ready,' she replied haughtily, 'but I don't know who I'm giving it to yet. Maybe it's for you, a gift for a friend.' She turned it in her hands, admiring the beautiful flowers decorating it, their colours still as fresh as the day before.

'Well, I won't be accepting it!' Mrs Smythe gave her a shove, almost knocking her over. 'There's garlands for friends, and garlands for lovers, and I've seen yers... it definitely ain't for a friend!'

Agnes blushed deeply and turned back to the spectacle of the men raising the tree trunk on the grass in front of the manor.

There was a lot of swearing and huffing and puffing, but finally the trunk stood tall and proud in front of them all. Everyone cheered loudly, clapping their hands in delight.

'It's the tallest maypole in the land, taller even than King Edward's!' shouted Roger Shaw, the village farrier, making everyone cheer even louder.

The front door of the manor opened, and Lord Funteyn and Lady Elizabeth stepped outside, dressed in their finest clothes. Agnes had spent more than an hour that morning doing Elizabeth's hair, hampered by the girl's fussing and fidgeting.

'What is this infernal racket about?' Lord Funteyn thundered. The crowd fell silent, and a small child burst into tears.

'It's May Day, my lord,' Roger said, stepping forward with his cap in his hands. 'We've brought the maypole, for the festivities later.'

'Is it necessary to make all that noise? It's enough to wake the dead!'

'My apologies, my lord. We were a bit over-excited, that's all.' Roger's face twitched, as though he wanted to laugh but wasn't sure if Lord Funteyn was truly angry.

'Yes, of course. Today is a feast day, is that right?' Roger nodded. 'Well, in that case, I think my daughter has a gift for you all.'

Lady Elizabeth stepped forward, showing a bundle of brightly coloured ribbons in her hands. 'All the way from London. Ours will be the best decorated maypole in the south of England!'

The villagers surged forward and soon every child and woman was holding a ribbon, waiting for the men to tie it to the tree trunk. Lord Funteyn and Lady Elizabeth stood in the middle of the crowd, the one time of the year when the villagers could stand beside them as their equals.

'Did ye wash yer face with the morning dew?' Mrs Smythe asked Agnes as they waited in line with their ribbons.

'Yes, of course. I was up at four, getting myself ready before going to Lady Elizabeth for the big occasion. Did you?'

'Oh, get on with ye,' Mrs Smythe said. 'My complexion is beyond saving. It's a tradition that works when yer young, not at my age! And, my dear, ye do look radiant this morning. Are ye going to stand forward as Queen of the May later?'

'I-I don't think so,' Agnes said, flustered. 'There are plenty of other girls who deserve it more.'

'I'll vote for you!' shouted a lad standing a few feet away from them. 'I might put meself forward as king!'

'Yeah, right,' said his friend. 'An' Ted will knock your teeth out!' The lad punched him and a friendly brawl broke out.

'See, they're already fighting over ye,' Mrs Smythe said with a satisfied air. She folded her arms under her ample bosom, looking like a hen fussing over her chick. 'Now take these ribbons and get yer Ted to tie them to the pole!'

'He's not *my* Ted,' Agnes mumbled, but nonetheless her heart skipped as she went over to him.

'You look gorgeous, Agnes!' he exclaimed as he took the ribbons from her. When he bent over and kissed her on the cheek, she thought her heart would pound its way out of her chest, it was beating so hard. 'Hey, lads, what about Agnes as our Queen of the May this year?'

There was a cheer of appreciation and a few comments that made Agnes blush bright red. She shook her head, about to refuse, when she heard Lady Elizabeth's voice.

'*I* will decide who will be Queen of the May!' She solemnly walked towards Agnes. 'And it will be *you*!' Agnes thought it wasn't possible to blush even more than she already was, but it seemed so. 'And you shall give the King of the May your garland! Now choose!'

The young men lined up before Agnes, bowing with their caps in their hands and laughing as she looked them over. Several of them winked at her, and one made a lewd gesture. She pretended not to notice and continued looking at them, taking her time to come to a decision. Ted stood at the far end, smiling, but with an uncertain expression on his face, as though he were suddenly unsure of her choice.

Agnes drew a deep breath. 'I have decided,' she said clearly. The men started pushing each other in commiseration. She held the garland before her and walked down the line of men until she stood in front of Ted. As she looked into his bright blue eyes, her whole being was drawn down into the deep inkwells of his pupils. She placed the garland in his hands and kissed him on the tip of his nose.

'I choose you,' she whispered, then gasped as he kissed her on the lips, a full, crushing, passionate kiss that took her breath away. When he finally let her go, she became aware of everyone around them cheering and applauding.

'Ladies and gentlemen, I give you our King and Queen of the May!' Elizabeth cried, joining in with the cheers.

The men swept Ted up onto their shoulders and carried him to where two thrones had been placed on the grass. Agnes followed sedately behind with the other women. She and Ted sat on their thrones, which were two plain wooden chairs decorated with lavender, sage and rosemary from the kitchen garden. Lord Funteyn and Lady Elizabeth approached with two identical wreaths made from branches of hazel and yew intertwined with woodbine, and placed them gently on their heads.

'Now, put those ribbons on the maypole and get these festivities started!' Lord Funteyn ordered.

13

The rest of the day passed in a blur. The villagers attached their ribbons to the maypole and danced wildly around it, first two circles of young girls and maidens weaving in and out of each other, then the young lads joined in, the girls passing under their arms, entwining the ribbons, until the tree trunk was a mass of blues, reds, yellows and greens. Ted and Agnes joined in the fun, laughing and dancing until their feet ached and their faces were red and sweaty.

When they could dance no more, the kitchen servants brought out platters piled high with every type of food and laid them on the grass. Soon everyone was sitting down, eating and talking animatedly.

Agnes closed her eyes and sighed in contentment as Ted fed her sweetmeats and apple sauce. 'No more,' she groaned. 'I've eaten far too much!'

He pushed her gently back until she was lying down, then kissed her on the lips. 'You taste sweet.'

'Don't, there are too many people.' She tried to resist his kisses but found it impossible.

'Let's go into the woods.'

'They'll see us go.'

'We're not the only ones,' he said, laughing. She sat up, resting on her elbows, and looked around. Sure enough, couples were walking nonchalantly through the picnickers and making their way to the edge of the woods. Agnes saw a couple kissing passionately under the branches of an oak tree, and gasped as she realised who it was.

'Mrs Smythe!' she exclaimed.

'And old Tom from the stable,' Ted said, amused. 'Well, who'd have ever thought it!' He gathered Agnes in his arms and held her close. 'So, my queen, will you come into the woods with me?'

Agnes felt herself melting under his intense gaze. 'Yes, of course I will,' she whispered, smiling shyly at him.

They walked slowly among the other villagers, stopping to talk to some, until they arrived at the oaks at the edge of the woods. Ted took her hand and led her through the trees, away from the sounds of frantic coupling going on in nearby bushes, further and further into the woods.

They eventually arrived at a small stream that burst noisily out of a gap in two rocks into a small clearing surrounded by birch trees, winding its way among the trees and bracken until it disappeared into the dark shadows of the woods beyond. Ted scooped some water into his cupped hands and Agnes drank thirstily.

He took her face in his hands and wiped the beads of water from her lips. 'I've dreamt of bringing you here, Agnes,' he said, kissing her nose. 'I used to come here with my father, before he passed. He used to bring me fishing in the stream, and told me this was our private place, only for the two of us. I've never brought anyone here up to now. Since he died, I come here to sit and think. About him, about me mum and brothers and sisters and how we'd fare without him. But lately, I only think about you when I'm here.' He bent and kissed her lips, and she could taste the brackish water on his mouth. He breathed in the honeysuckle scent of her hair. 'It's become my haven, this place. And now you're here, with me.'

Agnes looked around, entranced. The small clearing was covered in a carpet of flowers, the stream running through the middle. She could hear frogs croaking, and bees droned among the multicoloured plants, drinking their nectar. Beams of sunlight filtered through the trees, casting a dappled light over everything. Her gaze was drawn to hundreds of dragonflies flitting about, skimming above the water's surface or darting among the flowers. Their jewel-like bodies glinted in the rays of the sun, their transparent wings beating so fast they were almost invisible.

'It's perfect.' She sighed. 'It feels magical somehow, as if it were a place where water-nymphs and fairies come to play in the moonlight. Perhaps they're watching us now, casting a spell over us to make us fall in love.'

'I don't need a spell, Agnes, I've loved you since I first saw you. I want you, now, here, in this place, watched over by fairies and pixies,' he raised an eyebrow, 'and I want to marry you as soon as we can, if you'll have me.'

Agnes kissed him passionately, gazing deep into his eyes. 'I am yours. Forever.' A dragonfly flew near them, hovering above their heads. 'I love it here. It's our own secret place. We should give it a name... or do you have one already?' she added quickly, afraid he would resent her intrusion in the memories he had of his father.

'No. It was just the copse to us. I'm sure you can come up with something better.' Ted leaned over and picked a leaf from a nearby plant. He crushed it between his fingers, and she could smell its sweet fragrant scent fill the air between them. He gently rubbed it against her neck, trailing his hand down towards her breasts and her wildly beating heart. She suddenly became more aware of everything around them; she could feel the vibrations of the dragonflies' wings, sending ripples of air over her body, making her shiver as it touched her sensitive skin. The drone of the hard-working bees filled her ears, sending shockwaves down through her body to her core, making her melt as Ted's hands skimmed over her curves, finding their way to exactly where she wanted them.

He made love to her, gently at first so as not to hurt her, then more passionately as she thrust herself against him, filled with desire and the enchantment of the place. The birch trees loomed above; she could feel the life-giving sap coursing through them, through her veins, and she became one with the trees as she lost herself in Ted's embrace. He shuddered as he could hold back no longer, and cried out her name.

They lay in each other's arms all afternoon, making love, until at last the shadows became darker and the birds fell silent. Agnes watched the dragonflies flittering among the trees, the last rays from the sun glancing off their jewelled bodies. In the half-light, they truly looked like fairies.

'I have a name,' she whispered, afraid of breaking the spell.

'Tell me,' he whispered back.

'The Dragonfly Grove.'

He kissed her forehead. 'See, I told you you'd come up with something better.'

She traced her fingertips over his chest and down along his side, enjoying seeing the hairs stand up as her nails passed over his skin. 'How did you get this?' she asked, curious about the red, jagged scar curving around to his back.

He blushed. 'It's nothin'.'

'*Ted.*' She turned on her side, resting her weight on her elbow, and frowned at him.

'All right. If you must know, it was Tim, the farrier's son.'

'Tim?' She knew the Shaw family, everyone in the village knew them. The father, Roger, was a good man, but the villagers steered clear of the sons, especially Tim. Only fourteen years old, he was a hulking mass of muscle and sinew, having worked alongside his father since he could walk. He frightened her; the few times she'd crossed his path, he'd planted himself in front of her, blocking her way, his harelip causing a permanent sneer on his face. He never spoke, merely made lewd expressions until she turned and went back the way she'd come.

'Yes. It was a while back. He made some comment about you that made my blood boil, and I went for him. I didn't see the knife until it was too late.' He looked sheepish.

'The *knife*? He stabbed you?'

'Luckily it was only a scratch, the bugger hardly touched me.' Ted grinned at her. 'You should have seen him, though; he was even uglier than usual after I'd finished with him!'

'That isn't just a scratch! You should be more careful. You men are only happy when you're fighting.' Agnes paused. 'What did he say about me?'

'I can't repeat it in polite company,' Ted said, winking. 'But I defended your honour, m'lady.'

Agnes slapped his chest and giggled, but soon put all thoughts of Tim and his knife out of her mind as Ted lay on top of her once more.

Agnes and Ted made their way back to the manor and joined in the festivities still going on, until the church tower down in the village struck midnight and everyone started to go home. They left amid drunken salutations and promises to do it all again the next day, smiling at sleeping children being carried over their mothers' shoulders while the fathers weaved their way home, tripping over invisible stones and crashing into each other.

'Tomorrow we'll talk about our marriage, Agnes,' Ted said as they kissed each other farewell. 'I can't wait to make you my wife.'

'And I can't wait to become your wife,' Agnes replied, her eyes shining. She reluctantly withdrew from Ted's arms, and went into the manor house with the biggest smile on her face.

14

Everyone rose late the next morning, groaning and rubbing their heads as they stepped outside, vowing never to drink so much ale again. Agnes had the rare chance to rest a while on her pallet, as no chores needed to be done that day. A posy of flowers Ted had picked in the grove lay beside her, and she thought about seeing him later. She absentmindedly rubbed a silver leaf between her thumb and forefinger, and gasped as a familiar, tingling sensation ran over her skin. She closed her eyes and let her feelings transport her back to the night before. Memories flashed through her mind of forbidden pleasures, of Ted crushing the leaf and running his fingers over her body, his touch awakening a new awareness in her. She lay there a while longer with her eyes still closed, relishing the last few moments of quiet before the day began, then reluctantly got up.

Agnes was surprised to find Lady Elizabeth awake and full of energy when she took the girl's breakfast to her room. She set the tray on the small table, then opened the coffer to take out her ladyship's clothes for the day.

'So, don't keep me waiting,' Elizabeth said, an expectant look on her face. 'Did he ask you?'

Agnes clasped her hands to her chest, wanting to hold on to her secret for a little longer, then relented. She nodded.

'Oh, Agnes, I am so pleased for you!' Elizabeth said. She rushed over and hugged her tightly. 'When I saw the two of you together on the thrones, our May king and queen, I was so sure you were perfect together. And now he wants to marry you!' She ran back to the bed and jumped up and down on it in excitement, laughing wildly. Agnes stood, waiting patiently with Elizabeth's dress in her arms, but couldn't help smiling at the girl's exuberance. She felt like jumping on the bed herself.

'You see, the wreath worked. If I hadn't put in those forget-me-nots, he might not have proposed.' Elizabeth clambered off the bed and sat on its edge, deep in thought. 'I've got an idea. What if we should get married at the same time? Oh, I know we can't do the wedding together,' she added, seeing Agnes open her mouth to speak, 'what with you being my maid, but you could get married the day after me. You and Ted the day after Hugh and myself! We can leave the church all decorated for you, and you can have what's left of our feast. It would be so romantic.'

'I don't know,' Agnes began. 'You must speak with Lord Funteyn, and the earl–'

'Oh, I can convince my father.' Lady Elizabeth laughed. 'He'll do anything I say. As for Hugh, he only gazes at me in adoration and agrees with me. Oh, please say you want to, Agnes!'

'I'll speak with Ted,' Agnes said, her heart sinking. Lady Elizabeth was due to get married in August; she knew Ted wouldn't want to wait so long. On the other hand, the village church would be beautifully decorated with hundreds of flowers and ribbons, and even the leftovers of Lady Elizabeth's wedding feast would be much more sumptuous than anything she and Ted could ever put on.

. . .

The two girls went down to the stables. Elizabeth's dapple-grey pony, Willow, whinnied when it saw them and greedily ate the apple Agnes held out to it. Elizabeth glanced around and, seeing no sign of old Tom, gave Willow two lumps of sugar. The pony snuffled in appreciation, licking her fingertips to make sure there was no more.

'Shhh, Willow, don't let Tom know,' Elizabeth said with a giggle. 'He reckons sugar will make your teeth fall out, so it's our little secret.' She turned to Agnes. 'Will Ted be taking you to the dance tonight?'

Agnes blushed. 'Yes, he said he will come for me at dusk, up at the house. Will the earl be attending?'

'No. He sent me a letter saying that unfortunately his sister is having a crisis and he has to go to her.' Elizabeth's tone implied that she didn't approve of the elderly spinster's hysterics. 'She lives in Christchurch, he can't be back in time for the dance. But I will enjoy myself anyway. I will dance with all the single men of the village until my feet are so sore I can no longer stand!'

Agnes laughed, imagining her mistress having a wonderful time at the village dance. Elizabeth suddenly hugged her.

'Agnes, I'm glad you are my maid, we have such good fun together,' she said, her face serious for once. 'Please say you'll always be my maid, even after you are married. I'll get Father to allow Ted to leave, then you can both come with me to Hugh's house and live nearby. I'm sure there will be a small cottage that would be perfect for you both, and we would see each other every day. We can take our children for walks together, and yours will always have a place of work guaranteed, perhaps looking after mine. I don't want to lose you, Agnes. I regard you as the best friend I have ever had.'

Agnes hugged her back. 'And you are mine, Lady Elizabeth,'

she said, meaning it. But the thought of leaving Forest Brook and going to live in another town frightened her. She'd never been further than the woods outside the village.

The two girls, both entering their fifteenth year, had become friends, although Agnes was always aware of her place in the household. *And I wouldn't want it any other way*, she thought, glancing at Lady Elizabeth. At least she wasn't obliged to marry some old man, just because he was rich and his lands could be joined with her family's. *She* was free to marry Ted, the man she loved, and their children would also be free to marry who they wanted. And there were worse jobs than looking after members of the Funteyn family, as she well knew.

'Come, Lady Elizabeth, let us take a walk with Willow down to the village,' she said, rubbing the mare's forehead. A stable boy ran over and saddled the pony and they set off, Elizabeth riding and Agnes walking beside her. The sun was hot, but there was a cool breeze that ruffled their hair and kept the flies away from Willow. The girls were quiet; neither felt the excitement of the previous day and the late night had taken the edge off their energy.

They passed the manor house, large and imposing with its various annexes, which stood at the top of a small rise that looked over the village further down. Fields of crops and grassy meadows stretched into the distance, in stark contrast to the dark woods at the side of the house. A babbling brook snaked through the countryside, its water glittering silver in the sunlight before disappearing into the woods.

The beribboned maypole stood proudly in front of the manor house, the coloured fabric shining brightly. The loose ends fluttered in the breeze, making Willow shy away. Agnes held on to the bridle more tightly, shushing the animal until it calmed down enough to carry on. They made their way down the drive and onto the dirt track that led towards the village.

As they neared its outskirts, cottages started to appear, placed haphazardly along the side of the road. These were small, one-room huts with timber frames, white-washed walls and a thatched or mud roof. Some were in various states of disrepair, others better kept. Each one, however, had a small patch of land at the back, where the inhabitants kept chickens, geese and ducks, and grew vegetables. Agnes had grown up in the village, in a cottage just like these, and she couldn't help feeling nostalgic as they passed by. In the village centre, the freemen had larger cottages, and even had pigs, goats or cows. Lord Funteyn's bailiff was an honest man who treated the villagers fairly, as long as they gathered a good harvest and cared for the livestock properly. The villagers were, on the whole, happy with their lot.

'Agnes, what do you think being married is like?' Elizabeth suddenly asked. 'I mean, I remember what my mother and father were like when everyone was around them, but how do you think they behaved in private? Do you think mother was more assertive, or did she tiptoe around him as she did during the day? I-I never saw that side of them, if they showed their love for each other. Or even if they loved each other. Mother once told me they never met before marrying; she was promised to Father on the day she was born.' She sighed, and Agnes wondered if she was thinking of her future husband, who was thirty years her senior and owned the neighbouring farmland. 'Do you think love is necessary, Agnes? Or is it enough to like and respect a man, to be able to talk to him and laugh at his jokes, even if they're not that funny?'

'I don't know, Lady Elizabeth,' Agnes replied. 'It is different for you, you have certain responsibilities towards your father. I think that liking a man is a good place to start, then you can build on that as you get to know him during the years.'

Elizabeth looked thoughtful. 'Do you love Ted?'

'Yes, I do, with all my heart,' Agnes replied truthfully. 'But I don't think everyone finds such love. Indeed, I believe that the opposite is true. You only have to walk through the village to see husbands and wives shouting at each other, or worse. I have seen men who are blind drunk beat their wives until they are black and blue, and women so worn out by childbirth and daily life that they no longer care what happens to them and their family. And who's to say that Ted and I won't end up like that? A few years down the line, with a brood of children under our feet...'

Elizabeth laughed. 'How did you get so wise, Agnes?'

'By observing people. And by being realistic.'

'I take comfort from your words. I do like and respect dear Hugh. Perhaps love will come after, and perhaps it will be a greater love for that. Let us return home now, I have no wish to go any further.'

The festivities that afternoon were more subdued than the day before but by sundown the wine and food had restored everyone's energy. Two minstrels turned up, one with a recorder, the other with a lute, and they played until the early hours of the morning.

Agnes's feet ached, but she'd never had so much fun or felt so alive. Twirling around in Ted's arms, their feet dancing in time with the lively music, she wished the night would last forever. Earlier that day, she'd spoken with Ted about the wedding, telling him that Lady Elizabeth insisted on their getting married the day after her own wedding. He hadn't been too enthusiastic, insisting he wanted to get married as soon as possible, but had finally relented after Agnes explained how strongly Lady Elizabeth regarded their friendship. She would have preferred to marry Ted the next day, but comforted herself with the fact that it was only a couple of months more to wait.

'Mmm, two months seems like an eternity!' Ted echoed her thoughts. They moved to one side, away from the dancing. 'Can't her ladyship get married sooner?'

'You'll have to wait,' Agnes said primly. 'Aren't I worth waiting for?' She pulled away and pouted at him.

'Oh, you're worth it, I just don't know if I can,' Ted exclaimed, drawing her back into his arms. 'God, Agnes, every time I look at you, I want to ravish you!'

'Really, Ted, you should be ashamed!' His cheeks flushed red, making Agnes giggle. 'We don't have to wait to be married, you know, you can ravish me whenever you want.' She fluttered her eyelashes coquettishly at him, then gasped as he grasped her hand and ran with her towards the woods.

All was silent in the grove. Agnes imagined the trees and insects as silent sentinels, watching over them while the two lovers lay entwined on the grass among the flowers. She didn't understand why, but she felt safe under their protection.

'You are wicked, Agnes,' Ted murmured. 'I think you've bewitched me and that's why I can't resist you.' He kissed her forehead, slightly damp from the efforts of their lovemaking.

'You've discovered my secret.' She gazed up at him dreamily. 'Now I'll have to turn you into a frog and keep you tucked up in my apron.'

'As long as you kiss me at night and let me become a man again, to keep you warm in bed,' he replied, laughing.

'Every night?' she asked, arching her eyebrows.

'Well, I'll be sleeping in your apron all day long,' he said, nibbling her ear. 'I'll have lots of energy to burn off by nightfall!'

'Do you think you will love me forever?' She propped herself up on her elbows.

'Forever and a day,' he replied promptly. 'Why?'

'It's something Lady Elizabeth and I were talking about earlier. Would you marry without love, Ted?'

He thought about it for a moment. 'If I was approaching old age, and needed someone to have my dinner ready for when I come home in the evening, then maybe I would.'

Agnes slapped his shoulder. 'Be serious!'

'I am,' he replied. 'I can't think of anything worse than being old and alone, with no one to care for me.' He smoothed back her hair with his rough hands. 'But right now, the only person I want is you, Agnes, and I can't imagine ever marrying anyone else. If I can't have you, I'd rather be alone.'

'Me too,' she replied, kissing him passionately. 'Forever.'

15

JUNE–JULY 1348

The May festivities soon passed, and life returned to its normal rhythm. The wheat grew quickly, encouraged by the sunny days, its long green stalks swaying in the gentle breeze.

'Be too much sun, this year,' mumbled old Joe through his toothless gums. 'It hasn' rained all season, 'twill ruin the crops, mark my words.'

Ted looked out over the verdant field, so vibrant and healthy under the summer sun. 'Should we harvest early this year, Joe?' He valued the old man's opinion; he'd learnt everything he knew from him and was sure there was plenty more he would learn.

'Mebbe. I'll keep an eye on the weather. If a storm comes, it'll destroy everything. Could be better to get it in early and lose a part of it rather than lose it all to the rain. 'Is Lordship will want to make a profit this year, what with the wedding an' all.' He glanced slyly at Ted. 'An' you'll be hobnobbing with the earls and lords, you won't want to be seen with us labourers no more.'

'Give over, Joe,' Ted retorted. 'I'd much rather get married at the inn with you as best man and have a good old drink and singsong after! But Agnes feels it's her duty to please Lady Elizabeth, and who am I to argue?'

'That's right, you're only the husband, better you learn your place from the beginning,' old Joe said sourly. 'We'll raise a glass for you at the tavern, while you're sipping wine from crystal chalices.' He laughed raucously and clapped Ted on the back. 'Good on you, lad, get on in life an' make the best you can. No one else goin' to do it for you.'

'Thanks,' Ted said wryly. 'You want some of this ale or not?' He handed a stone bottle to Joe, who drank thirstily.

'Tha's good stuff,' he said eventually, wiping his mouth on his sleeve and passing the bottle back to Ted. 'Make it yourself?'

'No, I "acquired" a few bottles from the May Day festivities. This is the last one,' Ted replied, smiling.

Joe burped. 'Pity, it went down a treat.'

July arrived, and with it a suffocating heat over the land that brought a portentous silence to the countryside. Soon the villagers were muttering about ruined crops and shortages, and rumours began to spread about cows producing sour milk and sows eating their own litters within moments of giving birth. They carted water to the fields all day long, but the rivers were desperately low. Lord Funteyn visited the fields with his bailiff and talked about whether to harvest early or not. The cattle lay in the mud at the banks of the ever-dwindling river, trying to cool down before the earth became dry and hard. A new well was dug at the other side of the village, in the hope that there would be enough water for everyone until the rains began.

Everyone was convinced that the storms would come, eventually. Every now and then, the distant rumble of thunder could be heard but the longed-for rain never came. The oppressive heat was wearing everyone down and fights often broke out at the village inn during the evenings.

Agnes thought that Lady Elizabeth was the only person unaware of the heat and the problems it was causing. Her skin was still as white and delicate as ever, and her enthusiasm for life never waned.

'Of course, she doesn't have to go to work in the fields, or even go outside in the garden,' she complained to Ted one evening, while lying on the narrow pallet in his cottage. 'Her biggest worry is that her dress won't be ready in time for the wedding.' She walked over to the window and pushed open the shutter to let some air in. She could see the manor house across the fields, dark and silent now the day's work was finished.

'Come, Agnes, don't get bitter,' Ted admonished her. 'She *has* given you one of her dresses, after all.'

'I know, I know,' Agnes replied. 'And it is beautiful. It's just that she has me running around everywhere, while she sits on her window seat, fanning herself and sipping freshly made juice. And complains that Lord Remfrey is spending too much time in Christchurch with his sister. She says she won't remember what he looks like by the time of the wedding!'

'That's probably not a bad thing.' Ted winked at her, grinning widely. Lord Remfrey, the Earl of Stanford, had thinning, grey hair, rotting teeth, and a paunch that even his oversized tunic couldn't hide. 'At least we don't have that problem. I'll never forget what you look like, both clothed and unclothed!'

Agnes hit him. 'That's enough of that,' she said primly. 'I've a good mind not to let you near me until the big day, see how you like it.'

Ted put his hand over his heart and staggered backwards, as if mortally wounded. 'No, please, sweet Agnes, don't do that to me. I'll never resist until August!'

'Oh you,' she exclaimed, laughing. 'I don't think I could resist either!'

'My betrothed has sent me a letter,' Elizabeth said to Agnes. She picked it up and read it out loud.

'"*My dearest, beloved Elizabeth, I regret to inform you that I must stay perforce at my sister's house for a little while longer. There is rumour of an influenza in the coastal cities that is much debilitating, and my sister has sent a servant for news of a widowed cousin of hers, who lives in Weymouth. She desires that this cousin comes to stay with her until the crisis has passed, and has asked me to remain here until she arrives, as she does not wish to be alone at this time. Her heart is weak and cannot withstand too much stress, and the doctor has recommended that she is humoured in her every request.*" Hmm, I hope this cousin arrives soon. However, it goes on. "*I reassure you, my dearest, that I will make every endeavour to be at your side as soon as possible. My heart does break to be so far away from you. I am counting the days to when our two families will be united as one. Your most obedient servant, Hugh.*"'

She narrowed her eyes, her cheeks reddening. '"I will make every endeavour!"' she quoted angrily. 'And if his heart is so broken, why is he not here with me? His sister's weak heart, my foot!'

Agnes was shocked at the outburst. 'But surely he is to be commended, looking after his sister in her hour of need,' she said, trying to console the young girl.

'I suppose so.' Elizabeth sniffed. 'But I shall write to him and demand that he returns by the end of the month. I would like to spend some time with my fiancé before the wedding, he owes me that, at least.'

'Why don't you suggest he brings his sister and her cousin to his house here, so that you can get to know them?'

'What a wonderful idea. I shall write to him immediately.'

After much discussion, writing, crossing out and blotting of ink, the letter was finally ready. Agnes took it downstairs, relieved to be free of Elizabeth for a while.

'Here, Lady Elizabeth requires this letter to be sent as soon as possible,' she told William, Lord Funteyn's chamberlain.

'I will get one of the stable boys to take it today,' he replied.

'Tell him to wait for an answer, then return immediately,' Agnes said. 'Lady Elizabeth is impatient to know when Lord Remfrey will be by her side.'

The chamberlain nodded knowingly. 'Aye, I'll send Jack, he's less likely to stop off in a tavern and lose a couple of nights drinking too much ale!'

16

Agnes was walking through the kitchen garden gathering some lavender to take up to Elizabeth's room when she heard a great commotion out in the driveway. She dropped the flowers and ran to see what was happening.

A horse stood in the middle of a group of servants, streaming with sweat, its sides heaving as it blew strongly through its nose, spraying people with thick white foam. But everyone's attention was on the young lad standing beside it, holding his sides as he tried to draw air into his lungs and talk at the same time.

William strode forward and grasped the boy's shoulders. 'Take a moment, lad, then tell us what's so important you had to ride the lord's poor horse nearly to death,' he ordered. 'An' you lot stand back and give 'im some space,' he said to the others, glowering at them. Everyone chatted amongst themselves while Jack got his breath.

When his face had returned to a normal colour, William let go of his shoulders. 'All right, so what's the news?'

Jack took an envelope out of his shirt. 'The Earl of Stanford's reply to Lady Elizabeth's letter,' he said, struggling to talk. 'H-he is on his way back, sh-should arrive by tonight. H-he's coming hhere.' He took another deep breath, then blurted out, 'The e-earl's sister is dead. Most of her servants are dead too. The influenza has taken them all, the townspeople have cl-closed their houses, no one goes out.'

'What?' William exclaimed. 'What do you mean, they're all dead?'

'What I said,' Jack replied miserably. 'The earl told me everyone's fleeing the town; those who have transport, at least. The others have shut themselves in their houses, waiting for it to pass. He left just after me, but his carriage will take longer to get here.' Agnes stared at him open-mouthed, hardly believing her ears. Jack glanced at her. 'You must tell Lady Elizabeth and Lord Funteyn, Agnes.'

'Yes, of course. I will go immediately, so they are ready for when he arrives. And thank you, Jack,' she added. 'I will tell Lady Elizabeth of your good service to her.'

She turned and ran back towards the house, her head full of confused thoughts. *How could the influenza kill an entire household? Affect an entire town?* She was so distracted that she didn't look where she was going and ran straight into Ted.

'What's the rush, Agnes?' he asked, grabbing her and laughing. 'Is someone on fire?'

She quickly explained everything Jack had said, and Ted's face grew serious. 'Go and speak to Lord Funteyn. I'll find Jack and see if he can tell me anything else. We need to know if we're in any danger here.'

Agnes hadn't thought of that. 'Do you think we will get sick too?'

'No. It'll probably get as far as Christchurch or maybe some of the villages nearby, but I shouldn't think it will come here. But better to be safe than sorry.'

. . .

Lord Funteyn was in his study. He listened gravely as Agnes recounted Jack's story, shaking his head when he heard of Lord Remfrey's loss.

'Thank you for telling me, Agnes. I will make ready for Remfrey's arrival, and ensure he has everything he needs. You must go and tell Elizabeth, she will want to comfort him and be by his side in his hour of need.'

Elizabeth burst into tears when she heard the news. 'Oh, Agnes, I was so horrible, and so selfish wanting him here when his sister was so desperately ill,' she wailed. 'And now God will punish me too, I'm sure of it!'

'Don't be silly, you didn't know how bad it was,' Agnes said, hugging her. 'And God won't punish you for wanting your fiancé to be with you before the wedding.'

Elizabeth made the sign of the cross, then dried her face and blew her nose. 'Yes, you're right, of course you are. When will he arrive, do you know?'

'No, Jack didn't say. Probably later today or sometime tomorrow.' Agnes made soothing shushing noises, holding Elizabeth in her arms as she sobbed.

Later that afternoon, Agnes slipped out of the house while Elizabeth was sleeping. Desperate for some time away from the grief-stricken atmosphere indoors, she wandered through the gardens. A familiar figure approached her, and together they walked quietly among the weeping willows that lined the river behind the manor house, holding hands.

'I spoke with Jack, but he didn't really have much more to tell me,' Ted said sombrely. 'He said that Lord Remfrey read Lady Elizabeth's letter, then told him that his sister had died and her cousin was ill in bed. And that most of the town's residents had decided to leave as soon as possible.'

'Jack didn't see any servants, didn't speak with anyone else?'

'No, he said that the earl opened the door himself. Can you imagine? Jack didn't hear anyone in the house, none of the usual noises.'

'Can it really be that bad, Ted? I mean, a whole town decimated by the influenza?'

'I've never heard of it before. I mean, yes, there's always someone who gets sick and dies, maybe even a whole family, but I've never heard of a whole town. And why is everyone running away?'

'We must pray that it doesn't come here,' Agnes said, wrapping her arms around her waist.

'Christchurch is a long way away,' Ted reassured her. 'It can't come this far.'

Agnes shivered and crossed herself. 'I hope you're right.' She placed her hand protectively over her stomach. Now was not the right time to let Ted know he was to be a father. She wanted to wait until the wedding. It would be her gift to him.

17

The Earl of Stanford arrived late that evening. His carriage thundered up the drive and stopped in front of the house in a spray of gravel. The horses stood, snorting and blowing through their noses, their bodies dripping with sweat, as he clambered out. The carriage leaned alarmingly to one side as he descended the steps.

Lord Funteyn strode over to greet him, and clasped the earl's hand in his. 'My condolences.'

'Thank you, Funteyn. It was all so sudden.' He took a deep breath, then smiled at his friend. 'But I am here now, and I look forward to seeing Elizabeth again. I have missed her terribly while I was away.'

'Come, one of the servants will take you to your room so you can freshen up. Godwin has prepared a dinner worthy of a king, and Elizabeth has decorated the dining room in your honour.'

Lord Remfrey patted his round stomach, his waistcoat straining to contain it. 'Ah, Godwin's cooking is not to be missed. I only wish that I had hired him before you!'

. . .

Dinner that evening was a lively affair. Elizabeth sat to her father's left, with the earl in front of her to her father's right. Remfrey, in an effort to overcome his grief at his sister's death, regaled them with stories of his youth, making them laugh. He dabbed often at his forehead and seemed slightly out of breath at times, but brushed off Elizabeth's preoccupations.

'It's nothing, my dear, I assure you I am perfectly all right,' he said. 'It has been a long journey and I am tired, but this delicious food is the perfect tonic. I shall sleep well tonight!'

'I trust you will stay with us a while, Remfrey?' Lord Funteyn asked.

'I must go to my estate in a couple of days, I have some effects of my sister's that I would like to put into storage. I shall return soon, however,' he added, seeing Elizabeth pout, 'and I shall not leave again until after the wedding.'

Elizabeth relaxed. 'And then we shall go to your estate as husband and wife,' she declared.

'Where we shall live happily ever after.' Lord Remfrey sneezed suddenly and wiped at his nose with his shirtsleeve.

'I hope that cold clears up before the wedding,' Lord Funteyn remarked.

'Oh, I'm sure it's only a summer sniffle. I'll be fine.'

Agnes and Elizabeth sat side by side on the divan, dutifully embroidering some linen for Elizabeth's trousseau while listening to the two men talking at the other end of the room. Lord Remfrey stood by the fireplace, his hands crossed behind his back, making his stomach protrude even more than usual. Lord Funteyn walked back and forth, uttering the odd comment, but mostly listening to what his friend had to say.

'You wouldn't have believed it if you'd seen it with your own eyes,' Lord Remfrey declared, his brows furrowing as he remembered. 'Every house in the town closed up, the streets empty, even the market was cancelled. The only place people went to was church, where the priest talked about an apocalypse and how we were paying for our sins. Someone near me remarked that it would be interesting to see if the priest himself would succumb or not, for that would tell us everything we need to know about God's men!'

'Ha, indeed!' Lord Funteyn exclaimed. 'But your dear sister? What happened?'

'Poor Florence. She didn't want to make a fuss and said nothing for some time, but then she complained of a headache one evening. I thought she was rather pale, so I called for the physician, who came immediately. He said it was influenza, prescribed some fortifying herbal teas, and said he would call back the next afternoon. In the meantime, her cousin Georgina arrived and she sat with her all through the night.

'The next day, Florence was worse, so I sent for the physician again in the morning. He said he'd never seen an influenza like it. It was affecting everyone, regardless of age or sex, and everyone who caught it never recovered. Poor Florence died that evening, in dreadful agony, and several servants were ill too.' He started to say something else, then glanced at the two girls and cleared his throat. 'Anyway, then the town crier passed through the streets, shouting that the dead must be left in front of the door on the streets so that their bodies could be collected and buried in consecrated ground outside the town.

'Georgina and I couldn't bear to leave Florence out on the street like a pauper, so we took her to the burial site ourselves. It was...' He clasped his hands together, visibly moved by the memories. 'It was horrendous,' he finished. 'There were bodies everywhere, arriving on carts and being thrown into the enormous pits that had been dug. I saw the priest trying to bless each corpse, but the townsmen were tossing them in faster than he could reach them. I have never seen anything like it, and I hope never to see it again.'

Lord Funteyn shook his head. 'Did you manage to get Florence blessed?'

'Oh, yes. The priest saw us standing there watching and came over. He performed the last rites on her body, at least I have that to comfort me. And the two of us took her over to the pit and put her as carefully as we could inside, wrapped in the blanket off her bed. We gave her as decent a burial as possible.'

By this point, Agnes and Elizabeth had given up any pretence of sewing and were listening open-mouthed to Remfrey's tale. Agnes caught Lord Funteyn's eye and lowered her gaze, ashamed to have been seen. She remained with her head bent, watching the two men through the curtain of hair in front of her face.

'If everyone who is still healthy has left the town, they'll have contained the sickness by now, don't you think?' he said to his friend, cocking an eyebrow at the two girls.

Lord Remfrey nodded eagerly. 'Oh yes, indubitably. By now the sickness must have died out, and only the people of Christchurch will have been affected. We are safe here, thank goodness.'

Elizabeth rose and went over to the two men. 'I am glad you managed to get away from there.' She placed her hand on Remfrey's arm. 'I will go to the chapel and pray for all those poor souls, and ask God to keep us safe from the blight that has hit Christchurch.'

'Perfect, my dear,' Lord Remfrey beamed. 'And now, no more talk of dreadful things. Tonight is my last evening here, and I am determined that we shall enjoy it.' He sneezed violently three times. 'Damn this cold, I can't seem to get rid of the blasted thing!' he exclaimed, searching his pockets for his handkerchief.

18

The sound of the cockerel crowing startled Agnes from a deep sleep. She sat up and rubbed her eyes, remnants of a strange dream still flitting around inside her head. Fuzzy images of black clouds glowering menacingly over the blackened countryside filled her mind, the burnt-out shells of leafless trees stark against the setting sun. A fierce wind howled across the wasteland, flattening houses and carrying cattle along with it. Brittle skeletons turned to dust, and a deep sense of foreboding grew stronger and stronger, until...

'Enough!' she shouted, finally fully awake, and sat up. Some wayward curls fell in her face, making her sneeze, and she tucked her hair behind her ears so that it wouldn't get in her way. She washed in the bowl of water on the table in the corner of the small room, then took off the linen tunic she wore to bed (another of Lady Elizabeth's cast-offs, but she wasn't complaining; this summer was one of the hottest yet) and replaced it with her usual brown woollen one.

Agnes quietly walked down to the courtyard, enjoying the feel of the cool morning breeze on her face. She knew it wouldn't last long. As soon as the sun appeared over the tops of the trees, the day would become hot and sticky. She stood quietly to one side, making the most of her free time before Lady Elizabeth awoke and began her relentless stream of demands. Since Lord Remfrey's departure a few days earlier, she had become unbearable, moping about as she awaited his return.

One by one the house servants got up and began their daily chores, greeting her as they passed.

'William says her ladyship's up.' Hilda, the latest scullery maid to arrive at the house, appeared at the kitchen door. 'Says she's in a fine temper this morning, keeps complaining her head's hurting enough to split her skull in two.'

Agnes sighed. 'I'll take her up some willow bark tea. I told her not to drink so much wine last night.' She went into the kitchen and set about making the tea, filled with a sense of foreboding. After everything the Earl of Stanford had told them, any symptom seemed sinister to her now. She placed the steaming cup on a tray and carried it carefully up the stairs.

'Good morning, Lady Elizabeth, how are you today?' Agnes set the tray on the small table and threw open the shutters. 'It's a beautiful, sunny day. Shall we go and sit in the garden after lunch?'

Elizabeth groaned and turned over, hiding her face from the sunlight. 'It hurts! Close the shutters, Agnes,' she whimpered.

'Lady Elizabeth?' Concerned, Agnes leaned over the girl and touched her forehead. It seemed cool, but her skin was clammy and there were beads of sweat on her face.

'My head hurts, Agnes, and the sun hurts my eyes,' Elizabeth fretted. 'And it itches, under here.' She lifted her right arm. Agnes placed her hand on the girl's armpit and felt her skin, puzzled.

'It seems swollen, Lady Elizabeth. Let me have a look.' With some difficulty, she removed Elizabeth's nightgown and gently lifted her arm. She was shocked to see an enormous boil in the girl's armpit that seemed to be leaking pus. The skin around the boil was dotted with black spots.

Agnes ran out of the room, calling for William. He arrived at once, scowling angrily at her. 'What's all this noise for? His lordship's still asleep. Stop shouting!'

Agnes stood firm and put her hands on her hips. 'Lady Elizabeth is seriously ill. Call the physician right away.'

The physician came out of Elizabeth's room, grim-faced. 'I've never seen anything like it,' he said to Lord Funteyn, who was pacing anxiously in the corridor. 'But I've heard that something is going around in Dorset, people are dropping like flies there.' He noticed Lord Funteyn's worried expression and coughed. 'We're made of stronger stuff here, I don't imagine there's any risk. She should get better in a couple of days, if I lance the boil and rebalance the humours. What puzzles me is how she got it. You haven't been to your house in Bournemouth, have you?'

'We've been here all summer,' Lord Funteyn replied. 'But Hugh Remfrey stayed with us, and told us about the influenza in Christchurch. His sister died of it, a most unpleasant affair. Come to think of it, he had a bit of a cold too.'

'I think I'd better pay a visit to Lord Remfrey later on,' the physician said gravely. 'But for now, may I treat your daughter, my lord?'

'If you think it's for the best, then by all means.'

'I will need your assistance, my dear,' the physician said, looking at Agnes.

'Of course.' She followed him into Elizabeth's room, feeling more than a little apprehensive.

Elizabeth screamed as the physician cut into the boil and Agnes had to repress the urge to vomit as foul-smelling pus poured out of the wound. She collected it as best she could in the small bowl the physician had given her, then pressed clean linen strips against the wound. The black spots had spread over Elizabeth's chest, neck and stomach, and Agnes noticed another boil forming under her left armpit. She pointed it out to the physician, who nodded and set to lancing that one as well. Agnes was grateful when Elizabeth fainted.

'Keep the cuts clean and give her broth and bread to eat,' he said. 'I will pass again tomorrow morning to see how she is doing, but I expect to see her sitting up and asking to go outside. Once the boil has been lanced, the poison leaves the body and allows a rebalancing of the humours. The young lady will soon feel better.'

'Thank you. I will take good care of her,' Agnes said.

But Elizabeth didn't get better. Her boils grew again, this time into hard lumps that were so painful she couldn't put her arms close to her sides. Her body shook with fever, so Agnes soaked strips of linen in cold water, then placed them on Elizabeth's forehead and chest, and squeezed some drops on to her dry lips. She tried to give her some broth, but Elizabeth promptly heaved it back up again, crying out in pain as spasms racked her body. Agnes watched, hopeless, as Elizabeth deteriorated before her eyes, the black spots covering her body completely by the time evening arrived.

Just before midnight, Elizabeth regained consciousness briefly. 'I feel a bit better, Agnes. Can I have something to eat?' she whispered, her cracked lips bleeding onto her teeth.

'Of course,' Agnes replied. She touched the girl's forehead; it was fresh, and the clamminess was gone. *Can it be over?* she wondered.

Elizabeth took hold of her hand. 'It doesn't hurt anymore,' she said, smiling. 'Tomorrow I will take some fresh air, then I will get better in time for our weddings. And you will be a count-ess's maid. Won't that be grand?'

Agnes gently squeezed her hand. 'I can't wait. You will be the most beautiful bride ever.'

Lady Elizabeth was dead by the morning.

19

The entire household was in shock. The servants went about their business in silence, white-faced, the women with red eyes and noses. The physician returned at around midday, his usually cheerful face pinched and tight-lipped. He went straight to Lord Funteyn in the drawing room and the two men remained there for some time.

Agnes had no idea what to do with herself. After assisting with the cleaning and dressing of Elizabeth's body in preparation for the funeral, she retired to her room in the attic. She lay down on her bed and wept, tiny sobs that became full-blown screams of anguish releasing the pent-up stress of the long night. At last, exhausted, she fell into a light sleep, but kept awaking with visions of a huge fire rushing through the countryside towards her, destroying everything in its path.

'Agnes, wake up.' A voice broke through the smoke, and Agnes opened her eyes with a start. She saw Hilda standing over her, looking worried. 'You were crying out in your sleep. William sent me to see what all the noise was about,' she explained. 'You looked so tormented, I had to wake you.'

'I-I'm all right,' Agnes stuttered, feeling bewildered. 'I'll have a glass of water, then I'll go to Lady Eliz–' She stopped as the grief hit her once more and tears sprang from her eyes. 'What happened?' she whispered. 'She was well two days ago. How could this happen?'

Hilda stroked her hair, trying to smooth the unruly curls. 'William was in the drawing room with Lord Funteyn and the physician. He said they talked for ages, they're really worried. He said he'd received a message that the Earl of Stanford is sick too, with black spots on his body and them enormous boils under his pits and in his legs.'

'Like Elizabeth,' Agnes said with a groan.

'And most of the earl's household is sick with runny noses, fevers, the lot. Those servants who can walk have already left the house and gone back to their families, the others are looking after each other as best they can. The physician says he ain't never seen anything like it, and is going to London later today to speak with some of his colleagues. He says there's something going around on the coast, and wants to find out if it's the same.' Hilda sniffed and wiped her nose on her sleeve. 'Do you think we're going to get sick too, Agnes? William is scared. He says he was waiting on the earl the other evening when he was here at dinner. He's got a cold now, he's sneezing like anything. You should hear him!' She started to laugh, then suddenly sneezed.

Agnes tried to stifle the alarm she felt, there was no point in frightening the girl. 'I'm sure we'll be all right.' But deep inside, she was worried. She sensed that this was no ordinary influenza, far from it. She had to find Ted, he would know what to do.

'Ted's out in the field,' old Joe told her. 'But 'e looks somethin' dreadful, said 'e didn't sleep at all las' night. You tell 'im to get 'imself 'ome and into bed!'

Agnes walked across the field to where Ted was standing

with Lord Funteyn's bailiff, Robin, pointing at the dried-up crops.

'We've got to harvest now,' she heard him saying. 'Otherwise there won't be enough to last the winter, let alone sell.'

Robin nodded in agreement. 'I'll organise the men, get them started as soon as possible.' He turned as Agnes approached. 'Ah, it seems we have a visitor!'

Ted looked around and smiled tiredly when he saw Agnes. *Joe was right, he does look awful,* she thought.

'Hello, sweetheart. Have you come to check up on me?'

'I'll be off then,' Robin said. 'Good day, Agnes.'

'Good day,' she replied automatically, hardly aware of him as he strode away across the field. 'Ted, are you all right? You look terrible.'

'Thanks. I didn't sleep too well.' He wiped his brow with the back of his hand.

'You're sweating. Have you got a fever?' She touched his forehead. It felt like it was on fire. 'You're burning up, Ted. Right, straight to bed with you!'

Ted protested half-heartedly but let her lead him back across the field to his cottage. He stumbled over to his straw pallet in the corner, lay down with a groan, and closed his eyes.

Agnes got a bowl of cold water and washed his face gently with a cloth. 'Would you like something to eat?'

'No, I just want to sleep. My whole body hurts.'

Agnes's heart froze. She lifted his shirt and saw the familiar black spots on his chest.

'Oh God, no,' she whispered.

By evening, most of the household was coughing and sneezing. Lord Funteyn took to his chambers without dining. 'His head is thumping like nobody's business,' was how William put it.

Godwin was nowhere to be found, so everyone helped themselves to cold cuts of meat and cheeses from the pantry, washed down with fresh milk. Agnes sat down for a moment on a stool in a corner, too exhausted to eat anything after having been with Ted all day. He had finally fallen into a deep sleep, his breathing regular and even, so she had taken the opportunity to go and get some broth for him. Once she sat down, though, tiredness washed over her, and she wanted nothing more than to rest a little before going back. Only the urgent need to get back to Ted stopped her from closing her eyes. With an effort, she forced herself to stand up, and started ladling broth into a bowl. As she was cutting some bread, Hilda entered the kitchen and ran over to her.

'What's wrong?' Agnes asked, dreading the answer.

'It's Mrs Smythe,' Hilda cried. 'She's got a fever and them lumps in her pits. I thought you might be able to help, she says they 'urt so much.'

Agnes look down at the bowl of broth in her hands. 'This is for Ted.'

'She's in a bad way, Agnes, and you're the only one what knows what to do.'

'All right, I'll come and see. But you'll have to sit with her, I've got to get back to Ted,' Agnes snapped.

She followed Hilda across the courtyard to the enormous washing tubs. Mrs Smythe lay on the floor nearby, her huge body shaking as the fever consumed her. Agnes went over and immediately saw the black spots on her neck.

'Get me some fresh water,' she said to Hilda. The girl hung back, obviously afraid to come any closer. 'Now!' Agnes said firmly. 'And bring some linen cloths too,' she added as Hilda ran to the kitchen.

Agnes lifted Mrs Smythe's tunic and saw the huge, angry, red boils under her arms and others in her groin. She remembered the physician lancing Elizabeth's boils and the screams the girl had made, as if he was cutting out her heart. She instinctively knew that lancing them was the wrong thing to do. If anything, it made things worse.

Hilda returned with a bowl of water and a stack of cloths. She threw them on the floor next to Agnes, then hastily retreated to a safe distance. Agnes glared at her. 'You have to sit with her and keep sponging her, it helps the fever.'

'But I can't!'

'You must. I have to go back to Ted, he's sick too and needs me,' Agnes shouted in a panic.

'I can't, I just can't,' Hilda whimpered. 'I'm scared I'll get sick too.'

Mrs Smythe moaned and tried to turn over.

'Look, Hilda, you have to stay with her,' Agnes pleaded. 'If anything happens to Ted... I want to be with him. You understand that, don't you?'

'I-I'm sorry, Agnes. This sickness, it scares me.' Hilda glanced at the woman on the floor.

'Oh, go! But please go and check on Ted, and let me know how he is,' Agnes shouted, desperate. She turned her attention to the woman before her, sponging her body with cool, fresh water, letting a few drops hit her lips every now and then. She felt so helpless as she watched the woman dying before her very eyes.

Hilda returned after an hour or so. 'A-agnes,' she stammered, out of breath after running through the entire house. 'I-I've checked everyone who's still here. They're all sick, they've either got a fever or these lumps, or their skin has turned bla–'

Agnes interrupted her. 'What about Ted?'

'He's still sleeping. I just came from his cottage. He seems quiet, not in pain like the others.' Her shoulders slumped. 'Oh Agnes, are we next?'

'I don't know, Hilda, I really don't know,' Agnes replied, disheartened.

'I want to leave. I'll go back to my family in the village, stay with them. Do you want to come with me?'

'What if we take the sickness with us?' Agnes asked her. 'Your family could get sick too.'

'But I'm all right, I don't have the sickness, do I? I'm not like her.' She pointed to Mrs Smythe on the floor, barely breathing. 'Let's leave, go somewhere safe.'

Agnes shook her head. 'I'm going to stay and help the others. I think sponging their bodies helps them a bit, the pain seems less. I want to do everything I can for them before I leave.'

'Well, I'm going,' Hilda retorted. 'When you're ready to leave, you can come to me. Bring Ted too. It's the small cottage down in the village next door to the inn, the one with the white walls.'

'Thank you,' Agnes replied. 'I'll join you there when I can.'

Hilda turned to leave. 'May God bless you and have mercy on all of us.' She made the sign of the cross, and then she was gone.

20

Ted was awake when she crouched down next to his pallet. His dry, parched lips cracked as he smiled at her. He tried to lift his hand to stroke her face but lacked the energy. She took hold of his hand and kissed it, trying hard not to cry. She managed to make him drink a few spoonfuls of broth, holding his head as he swallowed.

'Thank you, my darling Agnes,' he whispered. 'Now I'll get better and hold you once again in my arms.'

'I love you, Ted. I have always loved you, and I always will.'

'You and me forever, eh? Till death us do part.'

'Just make sure you're around for a while, please, Ted,' she begged him.

'You can't get rid of me that easy. See, I'm feeling stronger already.' Then he became serious. 'Marry me, Agnes,' he said, reaching out to her.

'There's no priest here. How can I?'

'I know. It's only me and you, with God as our witness.' He coughed, then struggled to sit up. 'I, Ted Grenefeld, do take thee, Agnes Holt, as my lawful wedded wife,' he said weakly.

Agnes sat on the bed next to him. 'And I, Agnes Holt, do take thee, Ted Grenefeld, as my lawful wedded husband,' she repeated, kissing him gently on the mouth.

'I-I have a gift for you, Agnes, my beloved wife. Under those blankets over there.' He lifted his arm to point, but a hacking cough stopped him.

'Here, lie down. I'll get it.' She was full of despair at the sight of how weak Ted was, but tried not to let it show. She went over to the blankets and lifted them up.

'I did it myself.'

She gazed in wonder at the wooden chest she'd uncovered. Ted had carved an intricate design of a dragonfly onto the lid, every detail lovingly etched into the dark wood.

'You must have spent hours doing this.' She brushed her fingertips over the dragonfly, overwhelmed by his gift.

'I poured all my love for you into it, Agnes.'

'It's beautiful. I don't know what to say.'

'I found a tree fallen in the Grove one day, and I used the wood to make the chest. It's full of the magic we found there together.' He groaned. 'My head is spinning. I still feel so weak, dearest Agnes.'

'Don't you dare die on me now that we're married.' She put the chest aside and ran back to him. 'You *have* to get better, so our child will get to know their father.'

He raised his eyebrows in surprise. 'F-father?'

'Yes,' she replied softly. 'Now you understand why you have to get better.'

He lay silent for a while, so still that she was afraid he would never move again. She looked around his sparse room, taking in the details she'd seen so many times before but never really appreciated. Her gaze fell on a dried wreath in the far corner of the room. Her garland, the one she'd made that long-ago day with Lady Elizabeth, when they had been carefree young girls with no inkling of what was to come. Had it really been only three months earlier? It seemed forever.

'The plant.'

'What?' He'd spoken so quietly she wasn't sure if she'd heard him correctly.

'The plant. You remember, the one in the Grove, the one with the silver leaves. Pa always said it cured everything. Maybe...'

She bent over and kissed him on his forehead. 'I'll do anything to make you better. Anything.'

Agnes collected leaves from the strange plant in the Grove and tried different remedies on Ted. She steeped them in water and used them as poultices to wrap around the lumps under his arms. It appeared to alleviate his pain and reduce their swelling, but they didn't go away. She boiled the leaves, making sweet teas from them that she gave Ted to drink. His fever cooled, and his aches lessened. He could even stand up to use the chamber pot she left for him.

Comforted by the fact that Ted appeared to be getting better, she made more of the poultices and teas for the others and spent the next two days going from one patient to another, each suffering his or her own torments of hell. She applied the poultices and helped them drink their tea. Some showed a little improvement, others were too far gone to even realise she was there. The never-ending cycle of tending to her patients wore her down; her exhausted mind screamed against the injustice of this horrific disease that slowly but surely overcame their agonised bodies, and she dreaded finding the next one who had succumbed.

She did the best she could but one by one they all died slow, agonising deaths. Mrs Smythe was one of the last to go, writhing in pain as the sickness devastated her body. Agnes wept bitterly, full of hate for the unknown illness that didn't discriminate among its victims.

As she did every morning, she completed her rounds of the manor house in the solar wing. Lord Funteyn had insisted she treat the worst of the sick before going to him, declaring her fragrant teas and youthful spirit the only tonic he needed. The previous afternoon, however, he had lain listlessly on his bed and hardly acknowledged her presence as she placed the teacup on the table next to him. She hadn't wanted to leave him, but her duties to the other sick called her away. She wondered if he knew that his chamberlain had died a few hours earlier.

She slowly walked up the stairs in the solar wing, trying to ignore the stench of death that permeated the air. With a sense of foreboding, she went into Lord Funteyn's chambers, once forbidden territory to all but William, now a mausoleum to one of the richest men in Hampshire. Like the others, he was covered in black spots and weeping pustules. His bed was soaked with sweat and urine, and his once-handsome face was twisted in a ferocious snarl, as though he'd tried to fight death to the end. Agnes left his room, crying bitter tears of anger and frustration.

She walked as fast as her exhausted body could take her back to the cottage, eager to see her husband and put the images of death out of her mind. She pictured him eating some of the bread and honey she'd left him, and dared to feel hopeful for the future. But as soon as she opened the door, she realised something was wrong. There was a foul smell in the air, and Ted was whimpering in pain.

'Ted!' she shouted, running over to him. He was drenched in sweat, his body burning with a fierce heat once more.

'Agnes,' he mumbled. 'It hurts, Agnes.' He was rolled up in a foetal position, clutching his stomach, waves of agony passing over his face. Agnes held him close, cradling him in her arms, until he suddenly went rigid. Only her desperate sobs broke the silence that hung heavy in the cottage.

21

Agnes closed the door behind her and went to the stables, wandering blindly in her grief. Instead of the usual bustling movement and the air filled with shouts, there was an unnerving stillness. Only stricken ghosts remained, lamenting their sudden passing; whether in her imagination or as ethereal beings, she didn't know, or care. Horses whinnied as she passed their stalls, some kicking the door angrily when she didn't stop to feed them. She carried on, heedless of their suffering, looking for a place where she could release some of her anger and grief.

A sudden noise came from up ahead, towards the end of the stables where they stored the hay for the winter. She lifted her head, startled.

'Hello,' she called out. 'Is someone there?'

'H-hello,' came a faint voice at the back of the building. 'Can you help me?'

Agnes ran towards the voice, scrambling over bales of hay stacked near the far wall. Lying in the shadows was a young boy no older than twelve. He was shaking with fever, but she couldn't see any signs of black spots.

'How long have you been here?' she asked, feeling under his

armpits. His skin was hot to the touch, but he didn't have any boils.

'Since last night, miss... miss...' He started shaking uncontrollably, sweat breaking out on his forehead.

'I'm Agnes. Don't worry, I'll look after you.'

He looked at her in relief. 'I'm Bob. Bob Fletcher. Have I got what they all had?'

'I don't know. You have a fever, but perhaps...' She stopped, unable to go on. A wave of grief for Ted washed over her and she had to sit down for a moment before she fainted.

'Am I going to die? The others did, I saw them. Horrible it was, they screamed like they was being gutted. Those that stayed. Some ran off. Bastards. Leaving the horses like that, closed up in here with no food or water.' He cleared his throat and spat up some phlegm, leaning over to retch as it turned into a deep, racking cough.

'Try not to think about it,' Agnes said. 'Lie back and rest. I'm going to the kitchen to make you a tea that should help.'

'You're leaving me?' he exclaimed, struggling to sit up.

'No. I have something that could help with the fever, I need to go and fetch it from the house. I'll be back as soon as I can.'

'All right,' he mumbled, sinking back onto the straw. His eyes closed, although his body twitched as the fever ran through him.

Agnes hurried back with the tea and a bowl of fresh water to bathe the boy, terrified of what she might find. She was relieved to see his chest rising and falling as he slept fitfully, calling out every now and then. She woke him up and made him drink some tea, then bathed his body to cool him down as he sank back into his feverish nightmares.

She passed the night with him, giving him sips of tea when he briefly came to, and cooling his body as he slept. As dawn broke, she could do no more and fell into an uneasy sleep, dreaming of Ted, the Dragonfly Grove, her improvised wedding,

Ted doubled up in agony as he died... She awoke with a jolt, tears pouring down her face, and wondered if she'd ever be able to sleep properly again.

Bob stretched and yawned soon after, rubbed his eyes, and declared he was hungry enough to eat a horse. 'Maybe not a horse,' he corrected himself. 'They're such beautiful creatures, don't you think, Agnes?'

'Yes, I always loved coming down to the stables with Lady Elizabeth.' A lump formed in her throat. 'Willow is my favourite, she has such a sweet temperament.'

'Aye, Willow is one of the best,' Bob agreed. Then he thought for a moment. 'Has anyone fed or watered them today? I don't hear old Tom whistling while he's mucking out the stalls. Isn't he around?'

Agnes shook her head. 'Nobody's around, Bob. It's only me and you.'

'What! Nobody?'

'They're either dead or gone.' She hated telling him like this, but she didn't have the energy to break it to him gently.

He thought for a moment. 'I didn't die. You made me better?'

'I don't know if it was anything I did. I gave you a tea which helps with the pain, but it didn't cure any of the others. Maybe you didn't have whatever this is.' Agnes couldn't help wondering why God had spared the two of them, while so many other good people had died.

'What are we going to do? Run the manor by ourselves?'

'No, that would be impossible. Us two, looking after all this? We could never bury the bodies by ourselves. It's summer, they're going to decompose quickly.'

'We're leaving?' Bob whispered, a shocked look on his face. Agnes knew exactly how he felt. The idea of leaving the manor was heartbreaking, but she couldn't see that they had any other choice. The sickness had killed most of the servants; the few that had survived had already run away. They had to go to the village, see if someone would take them in and help them until they found a new lord to serve. *If anyone's left in the village,* a little voice in her head insisted, but she tried to ignore it. Going beyond the village was too terrifying to even think about.

'We'll gather our things and some food, and leave as soon as we can,' she decided.

'What about the horses? We can't leave them to starve in the stables, we have to turn them loose,' Bob pleaded with her. 'They'll die otherwise.'

'All right. I'll go and get you something to eat and drink, then when you feel a bit stronger you can help me release them all. Well, maybe not all of them. What if we keep Willow and another one for us to ride?' She glanced at his pale face. 'I don't think you're going to be able to walk much.'

'Where are we going to go?'

'To the village. We'll go to Hilda's house, she told me I could stay with her if I wanted.'

'And the sickness? Will it follow us? Maybe if we make the horses gallop as fast as they can, we can outrun it,' Bob said hopefully.

'I haven't got it yet and I've been tending the sick for days. I don't really know why, I suppose I've been lucky. And you seem to have recovered already.'

'Maybe you've got some magic against the sickness,' Bob said, looking at her in awe.

Agnes laughed bitterly. 'I wish that was so. I would have saved those poor people up at the manor. And my poor Ted.' She sniffed, willing herself not to cry. 'No, there's no such thing as magic, only luck. Let's hope we haven't used it all up now.'

Bob tended to the horses, giving them water and hay, while Agnes went to the manor house. The kitchen was silent without servants rushing to and fro, grabbing the ingredients Godwin shouted out he needed, passing him pots and utensils, tending the great fire that made the kitchen unbearably hot, even in winter. Agnes took some bread and cheese, and heated up a congealed stew for the two of them. Even after she'd ladled it into bowls it still didn't look very appealing, but she decided it was better than nothing. They needed to build their strength back up.

They ate without speaking at the kitchen table, each with their eyes fixed on the bowl before them, afraid to look around in case they saw the ghosts of their friends. As soon as he finished, Bob fled outside. Agnes took a cloth sack from the pantry and filled it with all the food she could find that hadn't yet gone bad. The bread would last for days, and they could soak it in water when it got too hard to chew.

She joined Bob out in the vegetable garden. He was sitting on the stump of a tree, staring into the distance. She stood next to him, her hand on his shoulder, and felt his body shake as he gave way to his tears. She tried to comfort him the best she could, even though she felt empty inside.

A little while later, Bob sat up straight, sniffing as he wiped his nose on the back of his hand. 'Let's leave as soon as we can, it don't feel right staying here.'

'I agree.'

'First, the horses. We need to see to them before they get too het up.'

They went back to the stables. Agnes gave some carrots to Willow and Star while Bob saw to the others. He stroked each horse's nose and whispered his goodbyes, caressing them tenderly before opening the stable doors and shooing them outside. Most of them stood around, bewildered, pushing and biting each other, until Bob started ringing the heavy iron bell that was once used by the family to call the grooms. The horses startled at the metallic clang and charged through the vegetable garden to the countryside beyond in one large group, leaving a cloud of dust behind them.

Agnes turned to see Bob with tears running down his face as he watched the horses gallop away.

'I only worked here for a while, but I loved them creatures,' he wailed. 'They was the best horses ever, I'll never forget them.' Agnes hugged him, then gently led him back to the stable yard.

'We still have Willow and Star,' she told him. 'They need us and we need them.'

He nodded and wiped his tears on his jacket sleeve, leaving dirty streaks down his face. 'Let's go and get them ready so we can leave here.'

'All right,' Agnes said. 'But first I need your help.'

They stood beside a freshly dug grave. They had carried Ted's body out of his cottage, and now they gently lowered it into the ground. Agnes placed a rose from the garden on Ted's chest.

'I will never forget you,' she whispered. Bob waited respectfully as she said her goodbyes, then shovelled earth into the grave.

'Don't you want to say anything?' he asked.

Agnes shook her head. 'I've said everything I had to say.' Her throat tightened. 'I need to fetch something.'

She ran into the cottage and picked up the wooden chest Ted had so lovingly carved for her. Tears filled her eyes as she looked around the room for the last time. Her gaze settled on the dried garland in the corner, fated to remain there until the brittle flowers crumbled into tiny specks of dust, blowing around the room on currents of draughts. She wondered what would become of the manor and the small cottages dotted around its lands. Would anyone come back and continue to farm the land or would it remain abandoned forever, with only ghosts to lament its demise? Shivering more with fear than with cold, she turned and walked outside.

'Can we take this with us?'

Bob looked at the box in her hands, pursing his lips. 'I s'pose we can put some things inside it, then balance it over one of the ponies with something on the other side. Do you have to take it?'

'Yes.' Agnes wasn't going to leave it behind if she could help it.

Bob sighed. 'Right you are. Let's go and saddle the horses, then.'

22

The two horses stood patiently in the yard while Bob tightened their girths and adjusted the stirrups.

'Have you ever ridden a horse, Agnes?'

'A couple of times. As long as we don't go too fast, I should be all right.'

'Ah, good. Here, take the reins. We'll mount out front of the house.'

They led the horses through the gardens to the drive. Both animals jumped at shadows or passing insects, disturbed by the unnerving quiet. There were no servants shouting to each other, nobody rushing down to the well to get water for Mrs Smythe, no Lady Elizabeth calling out for Agnes. The only sound was the ominous hum of flies everywhere, and the stench of rotting corpses filled the air. It was hot and humid, and Agnes felt sick at the thought of the bodies in the house swelling in the heat.

'Come, let's get away from here,' she said, trembling.

'It's a cursed place now,' Bob replied, crossing himself.

They stopped in front of the manor and mounted the horses. Then, turning their backs on the house, they set off for the village. Neither looked back.

Even though it breaks my heart to leave Ted behind, it's a relief to be away from all that horribleness, Agnes thought as they trotted along the well-worn track. Whatever the sickness was, they were leaving it behind them. Perhaps people from the village would come and help bury the dead up at the manor. She felt guilty at leaving them like that, but she and Bob didn't have the strength to bury them all. Everyone deserved a decent burial.

'We need to stop off at the woods a moment,' she said suddenly.

'Why?'

'I-I need to go to the Grove.'

'The Grove?'

'The Dragonfly Grove. It's mine and Ted's special place, we loved it there. I can't leave without seeing it one last time.'

Bob held the horses while she ran through the woods, pushing branches out of her way and getting scratched by brambles. Breathless, she burst into the clearing she'd come to love with all her heart. She knelt by the babbling stream and washed her body with the cool, fresh water, cleansing her skin from the stench of death. Exhausted, she sat against a fallen tree trunk and watched the dragonflies around her, flitting about their business without a care in the world. She half-closed her eyes, wishing she could turn into one of them and fly away, far away from the manor and her memories corrupted by the sickness.

The heat and the steady whirring of the insects' wings made her feel sleepy and she began to doze. As if in a dream, her body left the ground and floated in the air above the flowers and grass. Looking down, she saw hundreds of dragonflies around her, guiding her with their wings as she drifted through the clearing. They gently lowered her body next to a patch of the unknown plants Ted had shown her that first day, when he'd rubbed the leaves over her neck and she'd felt those strange sensations.

She sat up, rubbing her eyes, and stared in wonder. Whether she'd dreamt it or not, she was sitting next to the plants, with myriads of dragonflies buzzing around her. Their brightly coloured bodies lit up the scene; it was as if hundreds of fairies had suddenly appeared. She gasped, and put her hand to her mouth. A dragonfly flew over and settled on her fingers, its wings vibrating so fast they shimmered in the dappled sunlight.

'Come,' she heard a voice inside her head say. She looked around for the person who had spoken, but no one was there. The dragonfly hovered before her, darting from left to right, its dark eyes never leaving hers.

'Come,' the voice said again.

She stared at the insect. It bobbed up and down, then flew away and back again. Agnes stood up, brushing leaves from her tunic.

'Come!' The voice was more urgent, and the dragonfly's movements became more frantic. She followed it around the patch of plants to an ancient hazel tree at the edge of the clearing. There were more of the plants at its base, their roots interwoven with the roots of the tree, and small shoots wrapped around the trunk as though caressing a lover. There was magic in the air; Agnes could feel it thrumming around her, making the hairs on her arms stand up.

The dragonfly settled on top of the biggest plant, its open wings trembling as it rested. Agnes crouched down and gently stroked the plant in wonder. Its green leaves were velvety to the touch, with flashes of silver as they moved beneath her hands. The white flowers each had five delicate petals and a golden centre. Somehow, she knew she was meant to take the plant with her. She searched for a stone or a stick that she could use to dig it up, and soon got to work. Careful not to damage its roots, she gently pulled the plant away from the tree, wincing as its tender shoots came off the bark with a ripping sound. She stood, cradling the plant in her hands. The dragonfly had been joined by others and they hovered before her, a multicoloured cloud of shimmering wings.

She tore a strip off the end of her tunic, soaked it in the stream, and wrapped it around the roots and earth, praying it would be enough to keep the plant alive. Then she stumbled back through the Grove, clutching the plant to her chest, unaware of the tiny, almost invisible, eggs attached to its stem. She glanced back once and bid a silent farewell to the insects still hovering in the air.

With Bob's help, she placed the plant in the wooden chest, nestled among their other belongings, reminding herself to open the lid during the day and give it some light. She would nurture it, as she nurtured the child growing in her belly; she sensed that both would become an important part of her future.

'Look, the church tower!' Bob said, pointing. 'Not long now. Do you think Hilda's family will let us stay with them?'

'I don't see why not. We'll do some work for them, to pay for our keep.'

Bob chatted excitedly as they neared the village, distracting Agnes from her thoughts. She was glad the boy had survived the sickness, she couldn't imagine how it would feel to be alone at this moment. They followed the road, laughing as Bob told her about the time he'd leapt onto Lord Funteyn's prize stallion's back, only to be dumped unceremoniously into a pile of dung by the irritated animal.

They were laughing so hard they didn't hear the cart charging towards them, and only just managed to get out of its way in time. The two horses pulling the cart were frothing at the mouth and covered in sweat, the driver lashing them with his whip. The cart took the corner at a reckless speed and wobbled dangerously on two wheels before righting itself. Agnes and Bob looked on in horror as the driver whipped the horses again, then there was an awful crash and splintering of wood as the cart went down into the ditch at the side of the road.

Bob jumped down from his horse and ran to the overturned wagon. Agnes followed more slowly, holding Willow's and Star's reins. It was an awful sight. One of the horses had broken its neck immediately and lay at the bottom of the ditch, lifeless. The other had been speared by one of the cart's shafts and was screaming horribly, its great body shuddering with violent spasms of pain. The driver got up from the wreckage, holding his arm at an awkward angle and shaking his head.

'You bloody stupid idiot!' Bob shouted at him. 'What the hell were you doing, whipping the horses like that? Look what you've done!'

The man stared at him like a simpleton, his eyes glazed over with fear. 'I-I had to leave the village.'

'What?' Bob glared at him. 'What on earth possessed you to drive like that?'

The man glanced wildly about, his eyes darting from his broken cart to the empty road behind him. 'The village...' he repeated.

'What about the village?' Bob took a step towards the man, his fist raised. 'Speak, or I'll punch you, so help me God!'

'The village... they're dead, or dying... whatever, it's all the same! We've been deserted by God, by Jesus, by all that's good. The pestilence has come, it's the end of the world!'

Agnes burst into tears. 'Oh God, no, not the village. Everyone?'

The man nodded. 'And not only our village. The physician, he came back yesterday. He says there's no cure, there's nothing we can do except run from the sickness.'

'The physician?' Agnes said. 'He's back?'

'Yes, but he's sick too. Says it came on a boat and is spreading throughout the whole country. Everyone's dying.'

'Wh-what is it? The sickness, what is it?' Agnes asked.

'No one knows. I buried my wife and daughter yesterday and decided to leave while I still can.' He started pulling some belongings out of the back of the wagon. 'I'll carry on by foot. I'm not waiting around here for the sickness to get me too.' He sneezed twice as he worked and wiped some sweat off his forehead.

'What about the horse?' Bob said. 'It's in pain.'

'Forget it. It'll be dead by nightfall,' the man answered. He lugged a heavy bag over his shoulder. 'I'm off. Do you want to join me?'

Neither Agnes nor Bob wanted to keep the man's company and declined his offer. He shrugged and set off by himself.

Bob looked at Agnes. 'Do you think he seemed sick?'

'Yes.'

'Do you think we should tell him?'

'No. He'll probably be dead by nightfall.'

Bob gave a snort. 'Anyone who leaves a horse in such pain deserves everything he gets.'

'Shall we help this poor creature?' Agnes said sadly.

Bob took a knife out of one of their sacks and jumped down into the ditch. Agnes turned her head, unable to watch.

They soon reached the village. The houses were all shut up, and only a few lights could be seen through the windows. They made their way to the inn and found Hilda's house immediately. As she knocked on the door, Agnes wondered if anyone was home. No light filtered through the wooden shutters, and no smoke came out of the roof. A young girl no older than five opened the door, wiping her runny nose on her sleeve.

'What d'you want?' She hung back, her eyes full of suspicion.

Agnes crouched down in front of the child. 'We're looking for Hilda. Is she here?'

The girl burst into tears. 'She was 'ere. She 'ad a terrible cold, real bad it was, then she was coughing blood like there was no tomorrow. Mam said she was sick, but then Mam got it too. And now Hilda and Mam are sleeping, and so's Pa and Henry and Odo and little Fred.'

'Oh, God,' Agnes whimpered. She couldn't believe Hilda was dead as well. 'Will it never stop?'

'I feel sick,' the girl said and fainted on the doorstep.

Bob and Agnes carried her into the house and lay her on a pallet bed near the hearth. The fire had long gone out, and there was an unpleasant smell in the room. Agnes ignored the still forms under stained sheets in the far corner, and concentrated on the little girl. Her body was hot and fevered, and she twitched incessantly as she whispered her brothers' names over and over again. Agnes soaked a cloth in water and tried to cool her down, all the while murmuring soothing words. They watched over her for some time, until her body stilled and she whispered no more.

'We didn't even know her name.' Agnes sobbed as they covered the child's body with a grubby blanket. Bob put an arm around her shoulder.

'I think we should get away from here,' he said quietly. 'Far away from the village. We can forage for food and survive until this sickness passes, then we can find others and start living again.'

'Where will we go?'

'We'll follow the road, then cut through the forest. Stay away from the larger towns, keep to ourselves. Maybe we'll find an abandoned cottage where we can stay for the winter.'

'But I've never been further than Forest Brook before.' Agnes chewed her nail.

'Neither have I,' Bob replied grimly. 'But do you really want to stay here, among all this death?'

Agnes shivered. She dreaded to think what secrets the other houses hid. 'No, you're right. We can't stay here.'

'Let's go. The sooner the better, while there's still light.' He untied the horses and handed Agnes Willow's reins. 'We've got a long journey ahead of us.'

23

In the first days of their travels, they came across the same situation in the towns and villages they stopped at – people fleeing from their homes before the pestilence could catch up with them, others dying or already dead and unburied. They travelled towards London, reasoning that if the sickness had started on the south coast, maybe the further away they went the safer it would be. They kept off the roads as much as possible, heading into the woods as night fell to search for somewhere to sleep. Wrapped in their blankets with the horses tied up nearby, they slept fitfully, waking at the slightest noise. They were unused to silence. Their lives had been filled with the cacophony of country life from dawn until they collapsed on their pallets at night. The incessant chatter of the servants that had once annoyed them was now sorely missed.

Wild berries were abundant in the woods, which they used to supplement their diet of bread and cheese. The horses were well fed, and the soft woodland ground was kind to their feet. Bob combed through their manes and tails every evening, making sure he got rid of the burs and grasses that could cause them problems. If she hadn't been so scared about leaving everything she knew behind, Agnes thought she might have been able to enjoy herself. As it was, the sense of foreboding she'd had since the sickness had struck grew steadily worse.

They eventually came across the village of Little Mere, where the locals hadn't yet heard of the pestilence or had any experience of it. They found a family that was willing to give them lodgings in return for some of the rabbits and pheasants Bob had caught in his traps.

'It will only be for a little while,' Agnes explained. 'Bob and I will go to the manor tomorrow and see if there is work to be had.'

'Oh, don't you worry about that,' said Constance, the wife. 'Tell the truth, I'm that glad to have an extra pair of hands here. You can't imagine what it's like running around after this lot.' She waved her hand at the group of children playing on the dirt floor. There were six of them, ranging from the age of one to eight, with another one in a nearby crib. They were playing quietly for the moment, but Agnes guessed it was only a matter of time before a fight broke out and chaos ensued.

'My husband's out in the fields, helping with the crops, and I'm 'ere alone. If you keep an eye on the littl'uns, I can get on with the wool spinning without havin' to worry what they're up to. Every extra bag's a penny more, and we could use that right now. An' if you help with meals and tending the fowl out back, it would give my poor bones a rest. I'm that tired, I can barely eat some evenings.'

'Of course I'll help out,' Agnes said. 'I can spin too, I've done it before. What are their names?'

'That littl'un is Tilly, then there's Albert, Elaine, Denise, and Gareth, and them's Martin and Merek, the twins. You'll have your work cut out for you with those two, they're worse than Satan himself!' She ruffled their hair affectionately.

'I'm sure we'll be all right,' Agnes said, although she'd seen the mischievous glint in Merek's eyes and was already having some doubts about her ability to keep them in line.

'What about me?' Bob asked. 'I can work in the fields, I'm stronger than I look.'

'You speak with my husband, Simon, this evening when he gets back, I'm sure they need help too,' Constance said. 'Your horses can stay in the back yard. There's space enough for them, as long as you feed them.'

Simon was more than happy for Bob to help out in the fields, and agreed they could both stay for as long as they wanted.

'I'm glad you've turned up. I was wondering how Constance was going to cope, she's been that tired since she had Tilly.' He looked affectionately at his wife. 'Some days she barely has the energy to eat! Don't bother going up to the house,' he added. 'They have plenty of servants, there's nothing there for you two.'

Agnes saw the desperation in his face and understood his fears for his wife's health. If she died, he would have to struggle with raising his seven children while trying to feed and clothe them. Agnes's own father had faced the same fate, and had turned to drink rather than provide for his family, which was why she had ended up as a scullery maid at the manor. She shuddered. Life was harsh for everyone, and no matter how much the other villagers wanted to help those in difficulty, some families ended up slowly starving to death, unable to carry on.

'You're right,' she said. 'We'll stay here and help you both, there's plenty of work for us to do anyway.' She glanced at the children, two of whom were pushing stones up their younger sister's nostrils. 'As I can well see!' She slapped the boys on the backs of their hands and retrieved the stones before they got stuck.

'Thank you,' Constance said, and they all fell silent as Simon said grace before beginning the evening meal.

· · ·

On Sunday, they went to church together in the morning, then for a walk through the village afterwards. It was a beautiful sunny day, and Agnes started to relax and feel that things were going right for once. They were slowly getting to know the other villagers, who had been wary at first of the strangers in their midst, but were now beginning to thaw towards them. Bob's youthful exuberance and cheeky manner endeared him to people, whether they liked it or not.

Simon and Constance stopped and chatted with some families, while Agnes and Bob tried to keep an eye on the children. Agnes was about to shout at Albert, who was running around pulling at the girls' long plaits and making them squeal in pain, when there was a great commotion at the other end of the village square.

They stopped and turned, curious. There was a group of ten men dressed in long white robes and white caps with red crosses on them coming along the street, with children from the village dancing around them and taunting them. The adults watched from a distance, distrust on their faces, as the group neared the village pond.

'Hail, people of Little Mere. We come from afar and we bring you the word of God!' shouted an enormous man with a foreign accent. He took off his cap and tucked it into his robes, his bald head gleaming with sweat. 'My followers and I bring news of a deadly plague that is destroying this country! Men, women and children are dying in their thousands, there is no one left to bury them, and the bodies are festering in the summer heat. But God has shown us how to combat this pestilence. By scourging our bodies in His name, we can scourge this sickness from our land.'

He raised his right hand, and Agnes saw that he was holding a whip that split into three at the end. The group of men removed their robes; underneath they wore white cloths over their legs, but their torsos were bare. They lined up in single file and marched around the pond, the leader chanting something in a strange language and the others responding. Agnes was shocked to see that their backs were covered in wounds, some new and others silver scars that criss-crossed their skin. As she was wondering how they got them, the men flicked their whips over their shoulders, backs and chests. She could see that each tail of the whip had a nail pierced through it, and these nails were making fresh wounds on the men's bodies.

'Oh, sweet Lord,' she heard Constance say breathlessly beside her. 'What on earth are they doing?'

Silence fell among the inhabitants of the village while they watched, horrified, as the men flogged themselves. Rivulets of blood ran down their backs, new wounds merging with old until their backs were a raw and bloody mess. And all the while, they continued to chant in their native language. Three times they went around the pond; each time they returned to their starting point, five of them lay face down on the ground while the rest walked over them, whipping them as they passed. At long last they stopped, picked up their robes, and stood proudly before the villagers.

'People of Little Mere, this is the only way to defend yourselves from the Great Plague. We have come to you to save you. Join us on our journey through the countryside and help save others. Only through suffering will you find your way to salvation!'

A few villagers cheered, but most remained silent.

'What is this pestilence of which he speaks?' a woman behind Agnes asked, bewildered. 'Have you heard anything?'

A man cleared his throat. 'We have no sickness here,' he said loudly, so that the foreign men could hear him. 'What are you talking about, and who are you? Where are you from?'

The bald man frowned. 'You haven't heard of the pestilence?

All of the villages between here and the coast are sick, many have died the most horrendous deaths.'

Muttering broke out among the crowd.

'We are the Flagellants,' the man continued. 'We have travelled from afar, helping redeem those whom God has forsaken. By scourging our bodies twice a day, we save your souls from Satan.'

'Who says our souls need saving?' shouted a woman, cackling loudly. Agnes recognised her. Constance had pointed her out one day, saying in hushed tones that she was a 'woman with loose morals'.

'Aye, yours is beyond saving, Gertie!' a man called, and people burst out laughing. Gertie made a rude gesture and poked her tongue out at him.

'And yours is right alongside mine, John Cooper,' she answered back. The man turned crimson and tried to lose himself in the crowd.

'Join us, good people of Little Mere!' the bald man shouted, desperately trying to win back the crowd's attention. 'Your village is as yet untouched by the sickness. Save yourselves by becoming one of us.'

The villagers stood mutely together, distrusting of these people with their strange accents and even stranger customs.

'We will return before sundown to perform our ritual once more,' the bald man continued, sensing he was losing their interest. 'You are welcome to watch us.'

The group of strangers picked up their belongings and headed for the inn. Agnes noticed that a few of them were sweating heavily and had a feverish look in their eyes. She prayed that it was only due to their intense religious activities and not because of the sickness.

Constance touched her elbow. 'Come, let us go and make lunch while Simon and Bob take the children to the fields.'

They made their way home, past villagers gossiping animatedly about the newcomers. Agnes closed the cottage door and the two women went over to the hearth.

'You knew about the sickness, didn't you?' Constance asked quietly, stoking up the fire.

Agnes debated what to tell her, a dozen thoughts running through her mind. In the end, she nodded wearily.

'I saw your face when those... those madmen spoke about it,' Constance said. 'Everyone else looked shocked, but you seemed sad, as though you'd already seen it.'

'Oh, Constance, you have no idea,' Agnes blurted. 'Me and Bob, we had been travelling for days before we arrived here, ever since everyone up at the manor died. Lady Elizabeth got it first. I was her maid and we were preparing for her wedding, to an earl, no less. I was to be married, too.' She laughed, a harsh, croaking sound that startled her. 'Then she got a fever. I tried to keep her cool but it got worse, and she got these terrible boils and her skin turned black. And then she died. So did Ted, my fiancé.'

Constance put her hand over her mouth. 'My poor girl,' she said, hugging Agnes tightly to her. 'And you say everyone there died of this?'

Agnes sniffed, tears running down her cheeks. 'I'm not sure how long I stayed there, trying to make them better. I ran from one to the other to look after them, but they all died in the end. I found Bob in the stable. He had a fever but got better. We couldn't bear to stay there, so we took the two horses and left. We hoped to find somewhere else to live, but every village we passed through had the sickness. This was the first place we found where the pestilence hadn't struck.'

'What do you think of the foreigners?' Constance asked. 'Can they save us?'

Agnes brushed away the tears and shook her head. 'Only God can save us. And I'm not sure they aren't sick, one or two of them looked feverish. I don't know how, exactly, but it seems this sickness jumps from one person to another. Like when a family gets a cold in the winter,' she mused.

'Then we must drive them out of town!' Constance exclaimed.

'How? The villagers didn't welcome them with open arms, but their antics are entertaining. They will watch them just to ridicule them.'

'We will not go to see them this evening, and we will stay away from them until they leave,' Constance stated firmly. 'You put the water on to boil, I will go and tell Simon and the others to come home right away.'

The children grumbled when their mother told them they were not to go near the Flagellants but one stern look from Simon shut them up.

'Simon was talking to one of them after you and Constance left,' Bob whispered to Agnes.

'Then pray the sickness doesn't take this family too,' Agnes whispered back.

24

The Flagellants performed their ritual every morning and evening. After a couple of days, Agnes noticed that the two who had seemed feverish were missing from the group. When she asked the innkeeper, he told her they had colds and he was keeping them supplied with warm poultices. She immediately went back to Constance and told her to keep the children indoors, away from the other villagers.

'I will make onion and garlic poultices to keep the sickness at bay,' Constance said.

Soon the house reeked of boiled onions and garlic, but nobody dared to complain.

'At least we are sure no one will get sick,' Bob said. 'Nothing would want to come into this house now!'

The next morning, as Agnes was walking to the bakery, she saw two men carrying a heavy shrouded object out of the inn. Her heart sank as she realised that the nightmare was about to begin once more. She walked over, her feet dragging, as though they were mired in thick mud.

'What's happened?' she asked, crossing her fingers and hoping it wasn't as she thought.

'One o' them Flagellants 'as died,' the innkeeper said from just inside the door. 'He was black all over, an' 'ad 'orrible lumps under 'is arms. My men are taking 'im to the vicar, 'e can decide what to do with 'im.'

'You must tell the Flagellants to leave immediately,' Agnes said. 'They have the sickness, this pestilence they are meant to be saving us from.'

The innkeeper's face turned pale. 'An' what do you know about it?' he said harshly. 'Them others said 'e drank too much last night and died from chokin' on 'is own vomit, that's why 'e's all black.'

Agnes stamped her foot. 'No, he has the pestilence. I've seen it already, in other villages. The Flagellants have brought it here with them.'

The innkeeper peered at her, frowning. 'You've seen it? An' 'ow come you ain't dead from it, then? Them Flagellants said everyone who gets it dies.'

'I didn't get it,' Agnes said impatiently. 'I helped care for those who had it, but I never got it. I don't know why.' She thought of Bob, who had apparently recovered from the disease, but didn't say anything.

The man made the sign of the cross. 'Take 'im away,' he barked at the two men who were still standing there, holding the corpse. 'An' you, come in an' take a look at t'others.'

Agnes followed him into the inn, wrinkling her nose at the smell of stale beer, congealed food and urine. He led her up the stairs to the rooms he rented out. She didn't have to ask where the sick man was; the stench of vomit, and worse, wafted out of the nearest door, leading her straight to him.

She saw a man lying on the pallet bed, racked with fever, his body twisted with pain. The bald-headed man was with him, bathing his body with cold water. Sweat poured down his face and he mumbled unintelligible words.

The Flagellant turned and saw them standing there. 'For the love of God, man, call a physician. He's getting worse,' he shouted at the innkeeper.

'There ain't no physician, 'e's two days' ride from 'ere,' the innkeeper replied. 'I sent a boy, but I don't know when 'e'll get back. But *she* knows 'ow to cure 'em.' He pushed Agnes into the room.

'No, I don't,' she began, but the Flagellant leapt up and grabbed hold of her arm.

'See what you can do,' he begged.

Agnes approached the pallet. The man appeared to be sleeping, but his eyelids twitched and his limbs jerked. She could see the swellings under his arms, grotesquely swollen.

'Get me a poultice,' she ordered the innkeeper. 'With onions, garlic, or vinegar, it doesn't matter. We'll put it on these and see if we can get rid of them.' He nodded and left the room.

'Some physicians lance them,' the Flagellant said.

'I know, I've seen it done.' Agnes shuddered as she remembered poor Elizabeth. 'It didn't help. In fact, it seemed to make things worse. I'd leave them alone, it may be better to try to draw out the poison with a poultice.'

'Can you save him?'

Agnes shrugged. 'All I can do is help him, his body will have to do the rest.'

'And God,' the Flagellant said fervently.

She turned to him, anger surging through her. 'Your God has nothing to do with this! You and your people have brought the pestilence to this village. They might have escaped the sickness but now they will probably get it too. And I will have to watch everyone die, again.' She burst into tears, her rage threatening to overwhelm her.

'If God has seen fit to bring the pestilence on this village, then He has His reasons,' the Flagellant insisted. 'There are sinners everywhere. God is cleansing the world of evil and will leave only the good at the end, to start all over again. It is like the Great Flood, scourging the land of sinners. And we are the Ark, a select few who will repopulate the Earth with good, decent people, worshipping the one true God and forbidding Satan to enter our hearts.'

'If that is so, then you too are sinners who will be scourged by the pestilence,' Agnes said, staring him in the eyes. 'One of your men is dead, another is dying, and you do not seem too well yourself.'

The man wiped the beads of sweat from his brow and stared at the moisture on his hand. 'No,' he groaned. 'No! I will go and do penitence at once. My Lord will forgive me my sins and save me. Only He knows what is truly in my heart.'

He left the room and Agnes breathed a sigh of relief. She turned her attention to the sick man next to her but realised that it was hopeless. Blood poured from his mouth and nose, and he lay absolutely still. If not for the slight rise and fall of his chest, she would have thought him already dead.

'Here, the poultice,' the innkeeper said, puffing after his climb up the stairs. He thrust the bowl and cloths into her hands and then backed out of the room. 'Is he dead?'

'Not yet,' Agnes replied. 'But I don't think it will take long. You must get them to leave. They are all sick, and they risk making everyone in the village sick too.'

'I'll tell 'em to go,' he said.

She heard him shouting in the next room, but closed her ears to the sound and concentrated on the patient before her. The lumps were enormous and rock hard, but she placed the poultice on them anyway, hoping to relieve some of the pain.

'You! You are the daughter of Satan!' yelled a voice from the corridor. She turned to see the bald-headed Flagellant glowering at her. Blood streamed down his chest from fresh whip marks. 'You will rot in hell for what you have done to us, to this village.' He lunged forward, grabbed her by the throat, and squeezed, spittle flying from his mouth and hitting her in the face. His blood-streaked eyes glared insanely, the image remaining in her mind as she slowly lost consciousness. Then she was on her knees, gasping for breath, as the innkeeper dragged the man off her.

'Leave. Now!' he shouted at the Flagellant, who stood defiantly before him. The man flexed his hand into a fist a few times, then turned and stormed out of the room.

'You all right?' the innkeeper asked hesitantly. He held out his hand and Agnes used it to stand up.

'Y-yes,' she croaked, her throat burning.

'What about 'im? Shall I get 'em to take this 'un as well?'

'No, he hasn't got long left. Let him die here, not outside like an animal.'

'You call me when 'e's gone,' the innkeeper said. 'I'll get me men to take 'im to the vicar.'

The man died just before noon. A final sigh left his body, and then his chest rose no more. Agnes sat on the floor, relieved that it was over, for this man at least. Tears fell down her cheeks as she thought of Constance, Simon and the children. She said a silent prayer for them and all the villagers.

25

The younger men of the village dug huge pits outside the village boundary. Others were posted at both ends of the village to turn away travellers and strangers. The smell of smoke filled the air as the women burned the clothes of the dead, and the white ash seemed to get everywhere. Several days had passed since the Flagellants left, and one by one the villagers had become ill. Agnes tended those who would let her, but found that many distrusted her. They gathered in groups on the streets, talking frantically among themselves, only to stop and stare at her as she passed. The innkeeper had defended her to the end, but he had been one of the first to succumb to the sickness. His wife and children had soon followed, and now all of them were at the bottom of the pit.

Bob and Agnes were the only ones who left the house. Constance, Simon and the children quickly became bored cooped up inside, but Agnes was adamant.

'Bob and I cannot become ill, you can,' she insisted.

'But the crops–' Simon paced up and down, ignoring the children squabbling in a corner.

'Will have to take care of themselves.'

'We will have no food for the winter,' he said angrily.

'But you will be alive,' she answered sharply. 'We will find food when the time comes. For now, you must do as I say.'

The family moaned and grumbled but obeyed Agnes, and no one got sick. The children played outside in the small back yard, together with the chickens and horses. The adults watched silently from the door as carts passed by, laden with dead bodies, taking them to the newly dug pits. The sound of wailing filled the air as husbands, wives, children and parents were taken by the pestilence.

The mutterings from the villagers grew harsher, and Agnes became worried. She didn't want to tell Constance and Simon to leave the village and risk taking the sickness elsewhere, but she feared what the villagers could do to them.

'They are talking about us,' she said one evening to Constance and Simon, when the children were at long last in bed. Bob sat in the corner, whittling a stick. 'They are asking why you don't get sick, why your family is still unharmed when everyone else has lost at least one person. I hear them whispering and making signs when I walk past them. They think I'm in league with the devil.'

Constance laughed. 'That's the most ridiculous thing I've ever heard.'

'I'm worried,' Agnes insisted. 'They are frightened, they are wondering when it will be their turn. We don't know what they will do.'

'Agnes is right,' Simon said. 'The Flagellants told us that this is God's doing, that we are sinners who must be scourged from the Earth so that good can reign once more. The villagers will use any excuse to destroy those they believe to be demons.'

'Then we shall leave,' Bob said. 'Tomorrow night. We have the horses and Simon's cart, we can leave as soon as it's dark.'

'I agree,' Simon said.

'But what if we take the sickness with us?' Constance asked. 'We could make other villages sick, like the Flagellants did here.'

'We shall stay away from other villages and people,' Agnes said. 'We shall live in the forest until the sickness goes away.'

'Oh, how romantic!' Constance squealed.

'Winter is approaching, it will be anything but romantic,' Simon replied, ever the practical one. 'We shall have to make a hut, something small that will protect us from the cold. I agree with Bob, we will leave tomorrow night.'

They woke up to shouting out in the street and somebody banging loudly on the door. Simon pulled on his tunic and told Constance, Agnes and Bob to stay indoors. Gareth started to cry. Constance hugged him close to her breast, shushing him and talking soothingly until he calmed down. Agnes and Bob watched silently from behind the window, taking care not to be seen.

Simon opened the door. 'What do you want?' He had to shout to be heard above the throng of people outside the cottage.

A large man stood at the front of the crowd, his face bright red from excitement. Agnes recognised him as the innkeeper's brother, Wade Thatcher, who had recently taken over his establishment.

'We want the witch,' he yelled, and the crowd cheered behind him.

'What witch?'

'The witch in your house, the one who brought the pestilence to our village,' a woman cried out.

'She is no witch,' Simon retorted. 'The Flagellants brought the sickness. She is trying to help us.'

'Yes, we've noticed your family isn't sick!' shouted another.

'Your children are saved from her curse, while ours are dying in our arms!'

'Your brother defended Agnes,' Simon cried, pointing at Wade. 'Before he died, he told everyone it was the Flagellants' fault.'

'More fool him,' Wade shouted back. 'Look what good it did him, now he's buried in the pit!'

Angry shouts rose up from the crowd, and some shook their fists at Simon.

'What do you want to do?' Simon asked. 'Kill Agnes and see if the pestilence goes away? You know that isn't going to happen. We have to fight this sickness together, not lay the blame on people who have nothing to do with this.'

'We want the witch,' Wade insisted. 'We will burn her and save those who can be saved, while there is still time. You must give her to us, or we'll burn down your house with all of you inside!'

'Witch, witch, witch,' chanted the crowd, their voices growing louder. 'Witch, witch, witch!'

Agnes watched from inside the cottage, horrified, as the crowd surged forward. The children were sobbing. Bob put his hand in hers. She took a step towards the door, but stopped when she felt someone tugging at her skirt.

'Don't go, Agnes,' Denise said, her face streaked with tears. 'They want to hurt you.'

'She's right,' Bob said. 'Wait and see if Simon can persuade them to go away.'

Outside the crowd was getting more vociferous. Simon was trying to make himself heard over their shouting, but the noise was too great. Constance stepped through the cottage door and stood at his side, her hands on her hips.

'Enough!' she yelled. The sight of her incensed face was enough to make the crowd fall silent.

'You should be ashamed of yourselves. My children are inside, crying their hearts out, scared witless that you are going to harm them and the people they love. You, Meg Baxter, and you, Everard Carter, do you really believe that a single girl can bring so much death to our village?'

The two villagers lowered their heads, trying to hide among the crowd of people around them.

'And you, Wade Thatcher. Your brother died after the Flagellants fell sick while staying at the inn, they're the ones who killed him and his family. You know this is true, so why are you tormenting this poor girl who is only trying to help us all? She tended your brother until his last breath, making his final hours as comfortable as is possible with this terrible pestilence. And now you want to burn her? How can you bear to have her death on your conscience? How can you call yourselves Christians? Hasn't there been enough bereavement?'

Wade cleared his throat. 'I didn't want to scare your children, Constance. We want to get rid of this 'ere sickness, and we thought the girl was cursin' us.'

'This mornin' the milk was curdled,' a young woman said. 'I 'ad to throw it away, it was gone right off.'

'An' the sheep are dead,' said another man. 'I wen' out to the field to feed 'em, and every single one of 'em was stiff as a board. I never seen anythin' like it.'

'So we thought, mebbe it was the work of a witch,' Wade said to Constance. 'There ain't nothin' natural to this sickness, it takes people off in a matter of hours. We all seen it.' The other villagers nodded in agreement.

Agnes had heard enough. She stepped out from behind Constance and Simon. 'It isn't witchcraft,' she said, speaking clearly so they could hear her. 'I don't know what it is, or why it's happening, but we must work together–'

'An' you'll save us all, jus' like you saved Simon's family?' a young lad shouted. 'My mam's sick with it, my brother an' sister are dead. My dad's out at the pit all day long, throwing the bodies in, an' says it won't be long before it's 'is turn. So, what you goin' to do about it, then, eh? Remove the curse from our village? If God wouldn't save 'em Flagellants, why's 'e goin' to save us? An' what can *you* do?'

Simon turned to Agnes. 'Tell them about the poultices, any cures you can think of,' he whispered urgently. 'Anything to get them to go, then we can make our preparations for leaving.'

Agnes thought for a moment. 'All right, here's what you have to do. Make hot poultices out of onion, garlic, herbs, anything with a strong smell, and put them on the swellings in the arms and groin. Keep the sick person cool, wash them with fresh water as much as possible. Wash everything with a solution of vinegar and water; this means everything in the house, the bedding, clothes, everything. When tending to the sick, place a cloth over your mouth and a bag of lavender around your neck to ward off the vapours of the pestilence. We must wait for it to run its course.'

'What about 'em swellings?' an elderly woman asked. 'A poultice will draw out the poison good an' proper, but if you lance 'em they'll heal quicker.'

'No!' Agnes shouted. 'I have seen what happens if you lance them. The person died soon after. The swellings grew even bigger and she was screaming with pain.' Agnes still couldn't bear the memory of Elizabeth's death. 'You must only put the poultice on them, then leave them alone.'

Simon moved in front of Agnes. 'Go home, do as Agnes says, care for your loved ones and take care of yourselves.'

One by one, the villagers left and returned to their homes. Finally, only Wade Thatcher remained.

'They'll come back,' he said quietly to Simon. 'They'll watch their families die, an' then they'll be back for the girl.' He glanced over at Agnes and made the sign of the cross on his chest. 'You've convinced me. I don't think you're a witch an' I don't think you've cursed this village. But many do. I advise you to leave, as soon as you can. An' don't ever come back, memories run long round here.'

26

There was confusion in the small cottage. Children were running everywhere, picking up things that were ready for packing and throwing them on the floor, or fighting over favourite items they had already been told were too big to take with them. Albert ran through the house, laughing maniacally, followed by a sobbing Elaine begging him to give back her doll. Bob caught him in the end and managed to convince him to give Elaine the rag doll after promising him the wooden pony he had been whittling out of a piece of oak.

Constance sighed, running her hands through her hair as the boys flung yet more clothes onto the floor. 'It's impossible.'

'Bob, take the children in the yard and get them to start loading the cart,' Simon barked. Bob gathered all the children together and hurried them outside. The house fell silent.

'Thank goodness,' Constance moaned. 'My head is pounding.'

Agnes glanced at her and reached over to touch her forehead.

'Don't you look at me like that, Agnes, it's only a headache,'

Constance said firmly. 'I'm always getting 'em, it's the noise of the children that brings 'em on.'

'You're a bit hot,' Agnes said, her voice quavering.

'Don't be silly! It's all this rushin' around, I'll be better after a good night's sleep.'

'All the same, you sit down an' me an' Agnes will finish here,' Simon said. After a lot of cajoling, Constance sat at the kitchen table while Simon and Agnes finished bundling up their clothes and belongings. Simon carried everything through to the yard, where Bob and the children were busy loading the cart. They spoke in hushed voices; even the children realised the urgency of the moment.

'Me an' Bob will get the horses harnessed and hitched,' he said, returning to the women. 'Then we'll put the children in the cart an' get on our way.'

'You can sit in the cart, too, Constance if you're still not well,' Agnes said.

'I'm feelin' much better now, I'll walk with you. I only needed a rest, that's all. I didn't get much sleep last night, little Tilly kept wakin' up for nursing, and then tonight that rabble woke us up. I'm exhausted.'

Agnes touched her forehead again. 'You're cooler now,' she said, relieved.

'See!'

They stood at the back door of the cottage, ready at long last. The children and belongings were loaded on the cart and the horses were pawing the ground, impatient to get started. Bob held their heads, talking to them and calming them down.

'I hope we come back some day.' Constance sighed, and looked around.

'I'm sure you will,' Agnes replied. 'Soon the sickness will be gone, then you can return home and everything will go back to how it was.'

'Do you really think so, Agnes?' Simon asked.

Agnes thought of her village, where Lord Funteyn, Lord Remfrey, and all the powerful people were dead, and wondered what would happen. Would the servants now become nobles? And who would work in the fields, harvest the crops, make the bread so desperately needed by the survivors? How could things go back to how they were? Of course their lives would change, so dramatically that it would be like living in an entirely different world.

She said none of this to the others. 'Life goes on, Simon, it always does.'

With Bob and the horses leading the way, they left the cottage and walked through the village. Everywhere was silent. The villagers had returned to their homes and gone back to sleep, needing their rest before facing the day ahead. The sound of the horses' hooves was dulled by the dust on the road, becoming muffled clomps that mingled with the creaking of the wheels on the cart. Nobody spoke. Even the children kept quiet, terrified that someone would wake up and look outside, then raise a hue and cry at the sight of them leaving the village.

They travelled through the night, going further and further into the forest that lay all around Little Mere. Simon used the stars and the moon to guide them, making sure they didn't go in circles. None of the children slept, they were too excited about the journey and kept wriggling restlessly in the back of the cart. Just as the new day was dawning, they arrived in a small clearing surrounded by trees.

'We'll stop here and get some rest,' Simon said. He and Bob unhitched the horses from the cart and removed their harnesses, hobbling them so that they couldn't wander off too far. Constance spread some blankets on the soft, dewy grass and they sank down gratefully onto them. Soon they were fast asleep, exhausted from the night's events.

Agnes woke to the sound of birds chirping in the branches of the nearby oaks. She looked at the others, still sleeping, and smiled. Finally, they were away from the village, far away from other people, sickness, and death. She lay back and watched the clouds blow across the sky, counting her blessings.

A little while later the children woke up and soon started rushing around, gathering wood for the fire, while Agnes and Constance made a soup from the vegetables they'd salvaged from the back yard. Bob disappeared into the woods to set some traps and Simon went searching for somewhere to start building their home for the winter.

Constance hummed as she stirred the vegetables. 'We did the right thing, leavin' the village, didn't we?'

'Yes, we did. Look how happy the children are,' Agnes replied. 'How are you feeling today?'

'A bit better. I think I've been bitten by midges, though, I'm covered in bites.' Constance showed Agnes her arms and legs, which were dotted with red bumps. Agnes touched her forehead.

'You're still hot,' she said, worried. 'And I don't have any bites. May I take a look?'

Constance nodded. The two women went a little way into the woods and Agnes lifted Constance's tunic. The woman's body was entirely covered in red bumps, and Agnes noticed some black patches on her chest. Her legs threatened to give way beneath her.

'Lift up your arms, Constance,' she said. Constance did so, her arms trembling. Agnes touched under her armpits but couldn't feel the tell-tale swellings.

She breathed a sigh of relief. 'No lumps.'

'The swellin's?' Constance asked.

'Yes, everyone I've seen had those lumps before they died,' Agnes said. 'And you don't have them.'

'Thank goodness. You see, it was only midges.' Constance burst out laughing, then bent over double as a hacking cough racked her body.

'Constance?' Agnes cried, putting her arm around the woman's shoulders. Constance gasped for breath as she continued to cough, falling to her knees on the soft earth. Agnes pulled her hair away from her face and was alarmed to see blood streaming from Constance's mouth as she vomited onto the ground.

'Albert, Merek, fetch your father and Bob,' Agnes shouted. The boys came over, took one look at their mother prostrate on the grass and ran off, calling frantically for their father.

Precious minutes passed while Constance continued coughing and vomiting blood. Agnes felt helpless; there was nothing she could do to alleviate her pain. Bob came racing over, the children trailing behind him. He took one look at Constance and yelled at the children to stay back.

'W-what can I do, Agnes?' he asked.

'I don't know. Bring me some water so I can clean her, and find Simon. Quickly, I don't know how to help her!'

She heard Bob giving orders to the children, and turned back to Constance. Her breathing was a bit easier now and she had stopped vomiting. Her face was pale and streaked with sweat and blood, her hair plastered to her head.

'Agnes...' she said, then started coughing again.

'Shush, don't speak,' Agnes said, stroking her back. 'Don't waste your energy.'

Constance shook her head and tried to speak again. 'Th-the ch-children. N-not near me.'

'Don't worry, I'll keep them away.'

'It h-hurts,' she whispered. 'H-hurts to b-breathe.'

'Constance!' Simon rushed over. He stopped abruptly at the sight of his wife. 'What's happened to her?'

'I don't know,' Agnes said miserably. 'I think it's the sickness, but I've never seen anything like it.'

'Can't you do something?' he shouted.

'I don't know what to do,' Agnes wailed. 'When she coughs she can't breathe, and there's so much blood–'

Constance suddenly sat up, her body rigid, her eyes staring ahead of her at something neither Agnes nor Simon could see. Then she coughed, over and over again, her face turning bright red as she struggled to breathe. Simon threw himself beside her and pulled her close to his chest, straining to hold her as her body spasmed in pain. After one final fit of coughing she collapsed, lifeless, in his arms, her body suddenly limp. Simon gave a howl of anguish, while Agnes wept bitter tears.

'Mu-mummy?' came Denise's wavering voice as she ran over to them. Bob grabbed her and held her back.

'I want my mummy!' she screamed, kicking him with all her might.

Agnes went over and hugged her tight. 'Mummy's dead, sweetheart. I'm so sorry.'

Denise burst into tears, as did the other children. Agnes and Bob took them back to the clearing where they sat down together on the grass, weeping and wailing. Bob took a spade out of the cart and went back to Simon.

They stood next to the freshly dug grave, Agnes and the children sobbing loudly while Simon quoted a passage from the Bible. Bob laid some flowers the children had picked on top of the mound of earth and made the sign of the cross.

Later, after a subdued meal, Agnes asked Simon what he was going to do.

He glanced across at the children sleeping next to the cart. 'Do you think they will get sick?' he asked softly.

'I don't know,' Agnes replied, her heart heavy with grief.

'An' you can't cure them, or even help them like you could the other sickness?'

'No. I-I don't know how to. I have no idea where to begin.' She felt so helpless in front of this new malady.

'I can't start a new life here without Constance. How can I care for the children, an' provide for them? Constance, she did everythin' for them, I don't know how to do it.' He paused and took a deep breath. 'We'll return to the village and stay in the cottage until the sickness passes, then start over.' He looked at Agnes and Bob. 'You should come, too.'

Bob shook his head. 'Agnes is in danger if we go back to the village. They're scared and they're looking for someone to blame. I don't think we should go there.'

Agnes had another reason for not going to the village. She had seen Simon's calculating expression, the way his eyes looked her over, and she knew he would try to use her as a replacement for Constance. And much as she loved the children, she knew that she couldn't take their mother's place, neither in their hearts nor in Simon's bed. Besides, her pregnancy would soon start showing. Her stomach already bulged slightly but she managed to keep it hidden under her tunic. She wanted to get far away from everyone before it became noticeable.

'By God's bones, you will *not* leave me alone with the children,' Simon shouted, leaping to his feet. Agnes's head snapped up in shock at his outburst. 'You'll come with me. As my wife, you'll be safe from the villagers.'

Agnes edged away from him, frightened by the wild look in his eyes. 'I will not go anywhere with you.'

'We'll see about that.' Simon lunged forward and grabbed her arm, dragging her to her feet.

Bob's fist hit his face before Simon had time to understand what was going on. He staggered backwards and let go of Agnes. Bob stood, his chest heaving, his fist already pulled back to punch him again.

'You'll not touch Agnes!' he yelled at the man cowering before him.

Simon's shoulders sagged, and he collapsed on the grass, his shoulders heaving as he sobbed. He raised his head as one of the children whimpered in their sleep, then buried his face in his hands again.

'I'm sorry,' he said, his words muffled. 'I... she's... oh my God, she's dead...'

Agnes made to go over to him, but Bob held out his hand to stop her. He looked down at the sobbing man, his arms crossed.

'I know it's hard. We've all lost people we love, but you can't replace Constance with Agnes. Give yourself time to grieve, then you can decide what to do next.'

Simon looked up at him, wiping his nose on his sleeve. 'You're right. My apologies, Agnes. I didn't mean to hurt you.'

Agnes gave him a weak smile. 'We won't return to Little Mere, but we'll wait here with you for a few days to see if you or the children get sick. Maybe Bob and I can get this pestilence, too,' she added as an afterthought. 'At least we can help look after each other. But don't touch me again.'

'All right,' Simon said, sniffing quietly, his gaze fixed on her face.

Agnes shuddered, trying not to think about what could have happened if Bob hadn't been there. She lay down and wrapped her cloak around her, hoping that she would soon be lost in the oblivion of sleep.

27

In the end they stayed a week in the clearing. The children planted flowers around their mother's grave and vowed they would visit her as often as they could. Bob and Agnes prepared for their departure, gathering fruit and gutting the animals Bob caught in his traps. Nobody else got sick and Agnes saw that the children were becoming restless.

'You have to take them home,' she told Simon. 'Go to the village and make a new life for yourself and the children.'

'What about the horses? They belong to you, but I can't get the cart back without them. And the children will never be able to walk that far.'

'You can keep Star. He's a good horse, a hard worker, he'll help you in the fields,' Bob said. 'You'll need him, you'll be short of hands with all the sick and dead.'

'Are you sure?'

Bob glanced at Agnes, who nodded. 'We'll be fine with Willow, she can carry both of us if need be.'

Simon clasped their hands in his, squeezing them tightly. 'Thank you.' He stood up and called the children. 'Gather your things. We're leavin'.'

They shouted and danced with delight, then Elaine stopped and looked at Bob and Agnes. 'Does this mean we have to say goodbye?'

'Just for now, Elaine,' Agnes replied. 'When all this is over, maybe we'll come back and visit you.'

'Promise you'll come back, Agnes,' Elaine demanded.

'If I can,' Agnes said, tears pricking at her eyes.

They all hugged each other, then Bob and Simon hoisted the children onto the cart. Star was already hitched up and waiting patiently.

'Are you sure you don't want to come with us?' Simon asked, turning to Agnes.

'I'm sure. You take care of the children, they need you.'

Simon nodded. 'I will.' He jumped up onto the driver's seat and shook the reins.

Agnes watched as they headed off through the woods. A tear rolled down her cheek.

'They'll be all right, Agnes,' Bob said. 'Simon knows to stay away from the others, he'll keep his children safe.'

'If there's anyone left,' Agnes whispered.

'We'll try to go back, after this is over.' Bob squeezed her hand. 'You'll see, they'll be as boisterous as ever!'

'I hope you're right. Now, shall we get on our way too?'

They picked up their few belongings, loaded them onto Willow, and headed off through the woods. They decided to walk as much as possible, so as not to tire the horse too much. There was an unnatural silence all around them, as though even the animals had been affected by the pestilence.

'Where are we heading?' Bob asked after a while.

'I have no idea,' Agnes admitted. 'I thought perhaps we could carry on towards London.'

'Go to the city? I thought you wanted to keep away from people?'

'I don't know what to do. They were suspicious of us in the village, maybe we'll be able to pass unnoticed in the city. We'll need shelter soon, and food. When winter comes there'll be no wildlife for you to snare, or fruit and berries we can pick. And I'll need–' She stopped, reluctant to speak about her baby.

Bob glanced at her, but didn't ask her what she needed. He coughed. 'All right, but I don't like travelling in this silence. Why don't I tell you how I came to be working in the stables?'

'Yes, I'd like to hear that,' Agnes said, as keen as Bob to break the dreadful quiet.

'My three older brothers had already left home. They started working when they were ten or so, and my mam had me and five others to feed. My dad wanted to send me up to the manor, but Mam said to wait, as I was a bit skinny, like. She was worried I couldn't handle the hard work. Then my dad took me up to the stables one day, because old Fabian... you remember him, he was grouchy at times?'

Agnes nodded.

'He needed someone to help. One of the mares was foaling and another had been hurt in an accident, and Lord Funteyn, well, he wanted horses ready for some hunt or other...' Bob's face twisted as he talked, as if he was trying to stop himself from crying for those people he'd never see again. 'So my dad left me there, told Fabian to make use of me as he saw fit. Old Fabian says, "You ever been near a horse, son?" "No," I replies, "but I know which end a foal comes out of!" "That's good enough for me!" he cries, and takes me to the foaling mare. He left me in the stable with her, told me to run and get him if I needed anything.

'He comes back a few hours later, while I'm rubbing down this beautiful black colt, spitting image of its mum, cleaning the mucous out of its nose. I let the mare do what she had to do, and nature did the rest. He pats me on the head, says "Good job, son, bloody good job," and leaves me to finish things. My dad comes back to fetch me at dusk, and Fabian says to him, "Bring the boy back tomorrow. I'll speak with Lord Funteyn, get the lad a job here in the stables. He's got the touch with horses, a born natural." Turns out the mare wouldn't let anyone near her except Fabian. She'd already bitten one stable lad's arm and kicked another in the shin. All I did was talk to her and stroke her, but it seems she took a shine to me.

'And I found out that I *was* good with horses. I could calm them down, talk to them while I groomed them, I understood what was spooking them, why they wouldn't pull the carriage that day or why they threw their rider. Usually that was because they'd beaten them and the horse had had enough,' he added with a wink. 'I thought I was dreaming and I'd wake up back home in bed with my brothers. Old Fabian told me he'd teach me everything he knew.'

'How long had you been up at the manor?' Agnes asked.

'Near on a year.'

'A year?' she exclaimed. 'But I never saw you in the kitchen or the main hall.'

'Me and Fabian ate in the stables,' Bob said proudly. 'Fabian said he'd had enough of people to last him a lifetime, he preferred his horses to humans any day. So we got Godwin to prepare us a tray and leave it by the kitchen door, and I'd run down to get it. Then we'd sit on a bale of hay and Fabian would tell me stories of when he was young while we ate.'

'I'm sure you miss him a lot,' Agnes said softly.

'When I got ill, I thought I was going to die. Then Fabian came and told me I'd get better, because the horses needed me and he wasn't going to make it. All I remember after that is waking up and seeing you.'

'I'm sorry I told you to let the horses go, it must have broken your heart,' Agnes said.

'It did, but better they were left to go free than die locked in a stable. We did the right thing.'

'The colt?' Agnes suddenly remembered. 'What happened to it?'

'My Blackie?' Bob grinned. 'He's running wild with the rest of them now, but I hope to see him again one day. Star was his sire, so I know he'll be a bloody good horse. I suppose, if we found the herd, I could claim him as mine, if no one else gets him first.' He looked hopefully at her.

'Of course,' Agnes said. She didn't have the heart to tell the young boy it wasn't likely they'd find the colt. Better to let him have a dream to cling to.

'And what about you?' Bob asked.

'Me? Oh, I've been up at the house for almost a year too, first as a scullery maid, then recently as Lady Elizabeth's maid.'

'I know about that. We heard how you took old Hilda's place because you saved her ladyship's kitten. Hilda was that pleased she no longer had to run around after the young miss. Said she fair wore her out.' He glanced over at her. 'What are you going to do about the baby?'

'W-what?' Agnes said, putting her hand protectively over her stomach. 'How did you know?'

'Agnes, I've been around enough brooding mares to know when a female is expecting.' He laughed. 'But it won't be easy. You'll start showing soon and we'll need to find somewhere safe to stay before the winter.'

'That's why I want to go to London. I'll soon be too big to travel, and I-I'll need someone to help as well, when the time comes.' Her future loomed in front of her, and she swallowed the panic that was rising in her throat. 'I miss Ted so much. I wish he was here with me.'

Bob pulled her into his arms. 'I'm here, Agnes. I know I'm not as good as Ted, but I'll do my best.'

She held tightly on to him, her body shuddering as she cried, her fear and desperation overwhelming her.

'I can't do it, Bob, I can't,' she sobbed as he smoothed her hair with his hands. The two sat on a grassy bank, Willow grazing nearby, as Agnes gave voice to her grief.

28

The cathedral spire came into view over the tops of the trees as they neared the city, glittering in the midday sun. The road was well travelled and much wider than the dirt tracks they'd been following up to then. Other people joined them, heading towards the city gates where they disappeared on their own business. Agnes began to feel more optimistic as she saw the amount of people hurrying around, taking no notice of her and Bob. They walked either side of Willow, giving the mare a rest after their long journey.

A stream ran alongside the road, its waters dull and still. Agnes saw it was thick with sludge, and understood what it was when the smell hit her. After living in the woods, in the clean, fresh air, the smells wafting out of the stream were an assault to her senses. She grimaced and put a piece of cloth over her nose and mouth, urging Bob to do the same. She noticed a figure in the distance, dangling from a wooden gallows at the roadside, swinging gently to and fro. She grimaced in disgust, and tried to ignore it.

'We've arrived,' Bob said, his voice filled with awe at the sight of the great walls before them. The imposing towers on either side of the gatehouse stood guard over the torrent of visitors to the city. Agnes and Bob passed beneath the archway, their eyes wide with amazement as they found themselves part of an enormous crowd of people milling about. Shopkeepers stood in their doorways, shouting their wares, and a myriad of smells filled the air, freshly baked bread vying with the pungent odour of week-old carcasses hanging on hooks and fish in barrels. Agnes's mouth started watering; their meagre rations had finished days before and they had been surviving on whatever fruit and berries they could find, and the occasional rabbit Bob managed to catch in his snare. The sight of the food around them was almost too much to bear.

Bob rummaged around in the bags hanging over Willow's withers, then pulled out a package in triumph.

'Here they are.' He unrolled the cloth to reveal a pile of animal pelts: rabbit, hare, and even the hide of a fawn he'd brought down with a well-aimed stone thrown at its head. 'We can trade these, get some money for food and lodgings.'

An hour later, after some intense haggling and threats, Bob had traded the skins for a small purse of coins. Agnes looked at him in admiration. She'd never have thought the scrawny child would have been capable of trading with seasoned merchants and come away with a decent price for his wares.

'Tonight we shall eat until our bellies are full and sleep in a bed,' she promised him.

'And Willow shall sleep in a stable, with oats and hay for once,' Bob replied. 'There's an inn down that street that looks respectable, let's try there.'

The landlord was a robust man, with a stout neck joined on to an equally stout body. Thick, curly hair sprouted out from the top of his tunic, and his squashed nose implied he'd been involved in numerous brawls over the years.

'Yes?' he growled, squinting at them.

'W-we need a room for the night, a meal, and a place for our horse,' Agnes stammered. 'We have the money,' she added as he frowned.

'You're a bit young to be travelling, ain't you?' he said, less harshly this time.

'We're here for the market tomorrow,' Bob said boldly, indicating Willow and the bags on her back. 'We only need the room for the one night.'

The man relaxed and leaned back against the door frame with his arms folded. 'Why didn't you say so? The stable's round the back there.' He jerked his thumb towards a narrow alleyway. 'Get the 'orse settled, then come inside and I'll show you the room. Wife's got a stew over the fire, be ready by evening. But first...' He held out his hand.

Bob took out the purse and counted the coins into the landlord's meaty hand, eyes widening as the man told him the cost.

'Good thing we're only staying the one night, the man's a thief,' he muttered to Agnes as they led Willow down to the stables. 'We'll have to find somewhere else tomorrow, or our money will be gone in no time!'

Ready to find fault with everything, even Bob had to admit that the stables were in good condition, well built without any draughts coming through the wooden planks.

'The oats aren't bad either,' he said, taking a handful out of the barrel and sniffing them. 'They're not musty and there's no sign of mould. Let's hope our stew is as good.' He removed the bags and wooden chest from the mare's back, and gave her a pat.

Agnes's stomach rumbled loudly at the mention of food. 'Enjoy your meal,' she said, stroking the mare's neck. 'We'll be back in the morning.' She turned to Bob. 'Now, let's get ourselves settled, I'm starving.'

They opened the heavy entrance door to the inn and walked into a room dominated by an enormous fireplace on the left. Sunlight strained to get through the small windows, grimy with smoke, grease, and what looked like patches of dung that had been lobbed at them. They wrinkled their noses at the stench of sweat and urine that mingled with the sweeter aroma of lavender, which was scattered among the rushes covering the floor. The heat from the fire added to the heavy, stifling atmosphere, the smoke irritating their eyes and making them cough. The room was already full of travellers sitting at the trestle table along the right wall, laughing and talking as they banged their tankards on the table, demanding more ale.

The landlord saw them standing in the doorway and bustled over. 'Here, come on in and close the door behind you. It gets chilly towards late afternoon, and the draughts get into your bones.' He ushered them in and closed the door with a bang.

The air became even denser and the smells more concentrated, making Agnes gag. She glanced around, trying to find a quiet spot where she and Bob could sit unnoticed, away from the rowdier guests.

'You put your things in this corner and grab two stools,' the landlord said. 'I'll bring you over a couple of ales, that'll perk you up in no time. The stew will be ready shortly, the wife says it's never been so tasty. Mind you, next door's cat was fat enough!'

He laughed at their shocked faces. 'Only joking. There's a side of beef in there that came from the best butcher in the district, and the vegetables came from our yard. There's no cat in it. Not this time, anyway. Just so long as the little bugger don't claw me again.' He rubbed at his arm, and Agnes noticed the long red welts down his forearm. She smiled to herself; obviously she wasn't the only one who found the landlord irritating.

They sat on a pair of three-legged stools at the far end of the trestle table, waiting for their drinks, and gradually became accustomed to the smells and noises of the inn. Several dogs lay sprawled out on the rushes in front of the fire, twitching their ears occasionally at the raucous shouts coming from the customers, but otherwise staying still, soaking up the heat from the flames.

'An' I says to him, I says, "Don't you be jesting now! A whole village, everyone gone or dead? That's not possible."' A group of men nearby was deep in discussion. Agnes shifted her stool and listened more closely.

'An' what did he say?'

'He said he weren't jesting. They'd built a pit and thrown the dead in there, then set fire to them, there were that many. He said he could smell a dreadful stench from miles away, it got worse as he got closer.'

'So why'd he go then?'

'Said he was curious, wanted to see what 'ad happened. Said he'd never seen anythin' like it. The silence put the willies up 'im, that's for sure. All them empty 'ouses, said he felt like there were ghosts looking out at 'im as he went through. Nobody was there, not a soul.'

'An' where was this?'

'Woodcot, 'bout twenny mile from 'ere.'

Bob and Agnes stared at each other, aghast.

'It's coming here, Agnes,' Bob whispered, his face pale in the dim light.

'No, no. I-I can't face it again.' She stared at Bob, her eyes wide with fear. 'Oh, good Lord, please don't make me go through it again.'

''Ere's your stew.' The landlord arrived, carrying a tray with two large steaming bowls and two tankards of ale, which he placed before them. 'You get that in your bellies, it'll do wonders for you.'

They ate, ravenous, dipping large chunks of dry bread into the stew, which was surprisingly tasty. The noise level in the tavern rose as the food was brought out and everyone talked animatedly around mouthfuls of bread and large gulps of ale.

Agnes concentrated on her meal, not wanting to hear any more of their neighbours' conversation. The odd sentence drifted over, but most of their words were lost in the general chaos. The smoke from the fire filled the room, mingling with the smells of boiled meat, sweaty travellers, and urine, which she hoped was from the dogs. The heat made her drowsy. Bob was talking to her in quiet tones, and she felt her eyelids drooping. It had been a long day, and she couldn't wait to go to bed and sleep until the morning.

'Then there's the outlaws.' A voice slightly louder than the rest reached her ears, dragging her back to consciousness.

'Aye, the scourge of the land. Worse than any pestilence,' said another. He hawked a gob of spit on the ground, narrowly missing one of the dogs. 'Bastards. They should be hung, the lot of 'em.'

'An' who's going to do it? The sheriffs are run off their feet with people dying left, right and centre, the constables are worse than useless, an' the rest of them ain't worth the ground they stand on! I heard they're getting more reckless, they'll be coming into the city next if we ain't careful. Robbing anyone they find on the roads, causing mayhem, murdering anyone they come across who's sick. It ain't safe anymore, I tell you.'

Their voices became lost in the general hubbub. Agnes put her spoon down, her appetite gone, and looked across at Bob, who was polishing off the last of his stew with some bread. He gestured with his hand, his mouth full.

'Give me a moment, Agnes, then we'll go,' he said when he'd finished, and pulled her plate towards him. 'I'm tired of all this chatter as well.'

Later, Agnes lay in bed, listening to Bob's light breathing beside her. The straw from the mattress dug into her back, making it impossible to find a comfortable position. The rough linen sheets were clean, at least; she'd checked them before blowing out the candle for signs of bed lice or other unwelcome guests. The other bed in the room was occupied by a large man who was snoring loudly.

'Agnes?' The boy's voice was merely a whisper in her ear.

'Yes.'

'You're awake. I thought you might be sleeping.' He sounded relieved.

'I'm trying, but my head is full of so many thoughts, it's impossible.'

'We have to leave, Agnes,' he said urgently.

'I know. We can't stay here, we'll have to find somewhere else to stay.'

'No. We have to *leave*, go far away from all of this... this sickness, this madness that's around us.'

'Leave London, you mean? What about the baby? Where will we go?'

'The pestilence is everywhere. Every place we go to, it's either already there or arrives shortly after. Now there are outlaws roaming the countryside, nowhere's safe anymore. And when it comes to London, they'll accuse you of being a witch again, and maybe this time there won't be anyone to save you.'

Agnes drew in a sharp breath, the memories of the villagers in Little Mere still fresh in her mind.

'Old Fabian used to talk about horses that came from other

lands. Said Lord Funteyn was thinking of buying some Arabian and Italian stock the next time there was the fair at Winchester. He wanted to breed faster, sturdier horses for hunting and riding.'

Agnes felt the bed shake as he let out a sob and kept quiet, wondering what he was trying to say.

'See, I only know horses. They're my life, I can't imagine doing anything else. Autumn is on its way, and after that, winter. My snares will be worthless, and we'll starve if we haven't found somewhere by then.'

'What should we do?' Agnes asked, dreading the answer.

'Go to Winchester. The fair is at the end of August, if I remember rightly. We can speak with the horse traders, maybe they'll know if there's any manor that can take us. I'll try to find a place in a stable and you can ask for work as a... a scullery maid or washerwoman.' He put his hand on her arm. 'It's the best I can think of right now. Perhaps the pestilence won't have arrived there yet, or the physicians will find a way to cure it. For now, I don't think we have much choice.'

Agnes lay in the dark, staring sightlessly at the ceiling above her. Her head whirled with thoughts as the enormity of what they faced hit her. She'd never been out of the village before; now she was in London, contemplating embarking on yet another journey.

It was a long time before she fell asleep that night.

29

The next morning, they gathered their bags and made their way down the rickety wooden stairs. Their snoring neighbour was still sound asleep, his breath whistling through his nose as he slumbered.

'You'll be off already then?' the landlord asked as they entered the hall where they'd eaten the night before. There were a couple of guests sat at the table, but the dogs had disappeared. The front door was wide open, letting fresh air into the place, and a young girl was sweeping the damp, stained rushes on the floor into a pile. The smell of urine made Agnes's eyes water.

'Yes,' she answered. 'We have to get to Winchester. Do you know which gate we should leave by?'

'Winchester, hmm?' He rubbed his chin, his stubble making a scratching sound. 'You'll have to go to the bridge. You need to go to St. Magnus the Martyr's church, ask anyone for directions. Once you're in Southwark, you can ask the way to Winchester from there. But you be careful.' He peered down at them. 'I 'eard them talking about outlaws and the like outside the walls, robbing people and worse. You'd be better off stayin' in the city. You can find lodgings anywhere, just ask.'

Bob shook his head. 'Thank you, but we need to get to Winchester.' He turned to Agnes. 'Shall we go?'

'Here.' The landlord reached behind the counter and pulled out a loaf of bread, brushing it off. 'It'll keep you going until you get to the city walls. You'll find your horse has been fed and watered this morning, my son John doesn't mind 'elping out every now and then.'

They thanked the landlord and went to collect Willow. The horse whinnied when she saw them, and stamped her feet, eager to be off.

'Yes, we're pleased to see you too,' Bob said with a laugh. 'Let's get back on the road, shall we?'

The city walls were behind them and the sun was high in the sky when they decided to stop and eat. Sitting beneath the shade of some trees, with Willow tethered to a nearby bush, they chewed on their bread, each lost in their own thoughts. The journey ahead of them would be long and arduous, Agnes knew, without any guarantee of finding work or shelter when they got there. She started to drift off, having slept little the night before. Bob's head rested on her shoulder, getting heavier as he fell asleep too.

The sound of horses' hooves thundering through the woods invaded Agnes's dreams. She sat up, groggy and bewildered, then suddenly remembered the stories of outlaws they'd overheard the previous day. Terrified, she shook Bob awake. Too late to find somewhere to hide, they remained where they were and waited. Bob gripped Agnes's hand and held on tightly. Willow whickered, her head up and ears alert. Agnes untied her from the bush, hoping they could flee if necessary.

The first horse came around the bend in the path, neighing loudly as its rider pulled hard on the reins. He held up his hand

and the others behind him came to a skidding halt, clumps of earth flying in the air as the horses' hooves dug into the ground.

'What do we have here?' he shouted, looking down at Bob and Agnes. 'Two little dicky birds all alone in the countryside.' He sneered at them. 'Where are your parents? Cat got your tongues, eh? Did your parents die, like the rest?'

Agnes nodded, hoping he would continue on his way.

'Where are you going? London? The pestilence will arrive there too, you mark my words. There's nowhere you can go, it's come from the coast and is making its way northwards. In the villages around here,' he swept his arm in a wide arc, 'everyone's sick or dying. We've seen it. Me and my men, we're picking up anyone we find like us, those who have escaped the pestilence, and heading for Salisford Castle. We're going to start our new lives as lords of the manor, get us some servants and live a life of luxury, like those rich bastards before the sickness. You shall join us, become part of our new estate. We who were once the workers will become the fighters, and we shall overthrow the aristocracy, who have become lazy and fat in these times of plenty.'

The man rested his hands on his horse's withers, waiting for their answer. Agnes glanced at Bob. His face was white, and he was clenching his fists.

She shook her head. 'We thank you, but my brother and I wish to remain alone.' She pulled Bob to his feet and handed him Willow's reins.

'That's not your choice to make, I'm afraid. If we are to succeed in overthrowing the aristocratic bastards, we're going to need everyone who's not sick.' He moved closer, the stench of his unwashed body wafting over her. 'The lad will be trained to fight, then accompany us on our raids.'

'Raids?' Agnes said.

'The other villages around here are rich pickings. As I said, everyone's either dead, dying, or scared witless, and we'll need food and animals for the winter. And workers to help prepare the land for next year's crops. Aye, young lady,' he said, seeing her sceptical expression, 'I'm not as ignorant as you think. We'll need skilled farmhands, labourers, people to help us carry on as before.'

'You do know that if you raid other villages, you risk getting sick yourselves?' Agnes said. He looked startled.

'Many people don't feel sick at first, sometimes there are no symptoms until the swellings under their armpits, and then it's too late,' she continued. 'And I have seen another form of the pestilence that affects people much faster, and they die in an even more terrible way. What makes you think that you can't get that?'

'What are you?' the man asked, backing his horse away from her. 'How do you know all this? Are you cursing me?'

Agnes shrugged. 'I have nursed many sick people,' she replied quietly. 'I have seen much death. I have spoken to people like you, who believed that the sickness would not touch them, and watched them die before my very eyes. I speak only from experience.'

The man's eyes widened. 'You are a witch,' he hissed. 'An evil being spawned by the devil himself. Maybe it was you who brought the plague to our shores.' He crossed himself several times, his men copying him.

Seeing his fear, Agnes grew bolder. 'Don't be stupid. I am just like you, one of the lucky ones who cannot get sick.'

'No, no you're not, you're nothing like me!' he shouted. 'I have never been near the sick, I left my village as soon as I understood what was happening.'

'You ran like a coward!' Agnes gasped, shocked.

'A coward?' he sneered. 'You, who has spread this sickness among our people, striking down old and young alike, dare to call *me* a coward?' He turned to his men. 'I've heard enough. Grab the lad. *She* will be a sacrifice to ensure our good health.'

Chaos broke out, a million images blurred together in a flurry of sweating horses and shouting men. A woman screamed; Agnes realised it was her, she couldn't stop screaming as the horses charged around them, the air filled with noise and confusion. Somehow she was on Willow's back, and Bob was behind her, grim determination on his face as he slapped the horse's flanks.

Hands grabbed at the reins but Willow was already galloping away, back towards the city walls. Agnes held on tightly, her fingers buried in the horse's mane, willing herself not to fall. Bob's arms were gripped around her waist, squeezing her so tightly it was difficult to breathe, but she took no notice. They had to reach safety before the men caught up with them. She chanced a backwards glance, her heart dropping as she saw the group galloping after them. She leaned forward, her cheek against Willow's damp neck, whispering a prayer.

'Agnes, look! Ahead of us!' Bob pinched her arm, and she raised her head wearily.

A few miles down the road, in the midst of an enormous cloud of dust, she could see shapes moving slowly, people, carts, oxen; it was a large group travelling towards the city. She urged Willow on, shouting, slapping her hands against the horse's flanks. Bob joined in, yelling in her ear as Willow's legs pounded across the ground, closing in on the travellers. Agnes saw them turn, startled by the commotion, then stop and point at them as Willow raced for her life. Behind her came angry cries from the outlaws, desperation in their voices as they pulled their horses up and galloped away in the opposite direction.

Finally they reached the travellers, and Willow came to a standstill, flanks heaving as she drew in huge gasps of breath.

Friendly hands pulled Agnes down, concerned voices talking all around her.

A large bearded face came close to hers, and she drew back in alarm. 'It's all right, lass, no one's going to hurt yer. Let's get yer on the cart, eh?'

He picked her up as if she weighed nothing and carried her over to the cart, where two oxen were waiting patiently. He lay her down in the back on a pile of straw and covered her with a cloth sack.

'Yer get some rest now. Those outlaws won't dare come back, yer safe here. Get some sleep till we gets to the city.'

She felt the cart shudder beneath her as it set off, the steady plodding of the oxen soon lulling her into the deepest sleep she'd had in a long time.

30

Agnes slept all through the day, and the night too. She awoke to the sound of seagulls wailing overhead. Opening her eyes, she saw them circling above her in the pale-blue sky. The sun had risen, and a cool breeze blew gently over her. Fully awake, she sat up, wondering where she was.

Boats of all types were moored at the wharf where the cart was standing. Fish carcasses littered the ground and scrawny cats were busy chomping on them, while the seagulls flew angrily overhead. A young lad stood by the oxen, chewing on a crust of bread as he watched the turmoil going on around them.

The area was a hive of activity. Men carried barrels of fish off the boats and set them down on the wharf, keeping a close eye on the cats, dogs, and children that swarmed everywhere, ready to pounce as soon as their backs were turned. The air was filled with the pungent smell of fish; it overwhelmed all the usual odours of the city.

Agnes crawled to the side of the cart, stunned by everything going on around her. Willow tossed her head, evidently unhappy at being tied to the back of the cart.

'Where's Bob?' she shouted to the lad by the oxen, but he shrugged and continued gnawing on his bread.

She jumped down and scanned the crowd around her, desperately searching for Bob's familiar form among the hordes of people. The fishmongers stood guard over their barrels, having emptied their boats, and shouted their wares to passers-by, adding to the confusion. Coins were exchanged for packets of fish which the red-faced housewives placed in their baskets, bustling their way back through the crowd.

Agnes went over to the young lad, unsure of what to do. 'Bob, my friend who was with me yesterday. Do you know where he is?'

'Nah.'

Obviously it was going to be hard work to get an answer. 'Your friends, the people who saved us yesterday, where are they?' Agnes felt the frustration building up inside her, and tried not to let it show.

'O'er there.' He pointed to a tavern on the far side of the dock, where a large group of men were already gathered, talking noisily.

Agnes thought she recognised the large man who had put her in the back of the cart, swinging a tankard of ale around as he laughed at something the others had said. 'I'll wait here, then. They'll be coming back, yes?'

'Uh-huh,' the lad replied.

Agnes suppressed the urge to scream and turned to observe the fishmongers at work once more. Fascinated, she watched intently as the crowd swelled and surged around each barrel, the fishmongers yelling their banter while people voiced their doubts as to the freshness of the catch. She was so engrossed in what was going on that she didn't realise how much time had passed until she felt a tug on her sleeve.

'You're awake, Agnes.'

'Bob!' She pulled the boy to her and hugged him tightly, ignoring his embarrassed grimace. 'I looked for you but it was impossible with this confusion. Where have you been?'

'With Col.' He gestured to the large bearded man, who was striding towards them. 'He introduced me to some friends of his, they're going to help us.'

'What?'

'Agnes! Did you have a good sleep?' The bearded man – Col, Agnes reminded herself – stopped in front of her, hands on his hips. She noticed his strange accent and wondered which county he came from.

'Er, yes, thank you,' Agnes replied. 'I must have been exhausted.'

Col laughed, a loud, booming sound that carried over the noise of the crowd. Several people turned to look, some raising their hands in salutation.

'Young Bob here has been telling me about your troubles. I can help, but first, let's go over there.' He led them towards a quiet area away from the milling throng of people. 'That's better. I couldn't hear myself think!' He smiled down at Agnes. 'Now, as I understand it, you've both been through the mill. Everyone you know died of the pestilence, you were accused of being a witch, and now you want to leave the city because the sickness is going to arrive at any moment, you're with child, and you're afraid they will accuse you of being a witch again, or worse.'

'I told him everything, Agnes, I didn't know what else to do,' Bob said apologetically.

'That's all right, Bob.' She squeezed his shoulder, and tears sprang to her eyes. Even after her long sleep, she still felt exhausted and had no idea what to do next. She waited to hear Col's suggestion, resigned to her fate.

'I speak with many merchants, all the time. I work for them, taking their goods to markets in and around the city, and in return they tell me news from abroad. This pestilence, it has ravaged the continent, from Italy to Spain, Portugal and France, and now it has arrived here. It was a matter of time, no one can stop it or cure it. Where it passes, it leaves a trail of death behind it, but it doesn't return. Those who survive are starting again, with whatever's left. But still people are fleeing their homes, their countries even, to escape this madness. From what I've heard, it will be a terrible thing.' He paused and sighed.

'I cannot imagine what you have seen, but I can understand your wanting to flee. Bob says he is good with horses. I know a merchant – I've bought and sold many horses for him at the markets. I'm to meet him later, to discuss business.'

'You think you can persuade him to give Bob work?' Agnes asked, hope rising in her again.

'He is a good man, he will help you. He will take you both far away from all this, away from the pestilence and the horror.'

'That's exactly what we need. Isn't it, Bob?' She looked at Bob, but he avoided her eyes and shuffled his feet.

'Agnes,' Col said gently, taking hold of her hand. 'This merchant, he comes from Genoa.'

'Genoa?' she said, confused. 'Which county is that in? I've never heard of it before.'

'Italy,' Bob mumbled, his face bright red. 'It's in Italy, Agnes.'

31

Agnes would have preferred to watch England's shores recede into the distance from the deck, the sun on her face and the wind in her hair. Instead, the captain had insisted that his passengers remain below deck in their berths until they got out to the open sea. As a favour to Col, the merchant had given them their own cabin – a tiny, narrow room, to be sure, but better than sleeping next to the hold, where the livestock was kept. There were chickens in cages, a sow with a litter of piglets, and a cow, as well as the horses the merchant had purchased while in England, and a pungent odour emanated from the area. Willow was tied up among them, handed over as payment for their voyage. Agnes knew that once they reached Genoa – *Italy!* – she'd never see the horse again.

She'd listened, incredulous, as Bob and Col had explained their plans to her. She supposed it made sense – the pestilence had hit the continent the year before, and by now had almost run its course. There was still news of occasional occurrences, but life was starting to return to normal there. The merchant would help them settle once they arrived in Italy.

Italy! It seemed so far away, a land so distant that it might as well exist in one of the fairy tales her mother used to tell her when she was little. A lump came to her throat as she thought about how much her life had changed in the last few months. Was it only May when she and Ted had been crowned king and queen? Now it was the end of August, and she was travelling, by ship, to a foreign country.

She lay on her cot, feeling it sway gently with the rhythm of the ship, listening to the wooden boards of the hull creaking, and cried quiet tears as they headed out to sea.

It took Agnes a few days to get used to her new life on board the ship. Worst of all was learning to use the latrines at the bow head – balancing herself over the hole in a wooden board, with the water rushing past far below, made her feel dizzy as she gripped on to the wooden bars at either side. With the added factor of a queue of people waiting for her to finish, she avoided the latrines as much as possible. Although the chamber pot in their cabin had its own drawbacks, especially when the seas became rough.

Bob's youthful energy and enthusiasm endeared him to everyone. From the first day, he made himself useful, helping the sailors around the ship. He soon learned to climb the rigging and run nimbly across the deck as they sent him on various tasks. Agnes envied his natural cheerfulness and his ability to adapt to his surroundings, no matter what. She avoided the other passengers, preferring to sit quietly somewhere and gaze out to sea, thinking about what the future held for them.

After a while, however, she needed to stretch her legs. She took to walking around the deck every day to pass some time, carrying her precious wooden chest that she never let out of her sight, conscious of the others watching her. An old woman, sat in the shade cast by the upper deck, didn't bother to hide her curiosity, fixing her with black eyes each time she walked past. Today, as usual, Agnes ignored her and carried on with her exercise, determined not to let the woman intimidate her.

'Hey, Agnes!' Bob dashed towards her and caught hold of her tunic. He nudged her. 'See that man over there by the mast, talking to the captain?' He pointed to their right.

Agnes saw a man with dark hair and tanned skin talking animatedly, gesturing with his hands as he spoke. 'What about him?'

'He's an Italian count,' Bob whispered. 'The *Conte di Gallicano*, to be precise.' He affected an Italian accent, bowing stiffly.

Agnes stifled a laugh. 'Is that how Italians speak?'

Bob shrugged. 'It's how I imagine they speak! His father is a marquis. By all accounts, the Innocenti family is very influential.'

'And how do *you* know this?' Agnes raised her eyebrows.

Bob had the grace to look ashamed. 'Oh, you know, I listen while I'm working. These sailors love a gossip, they're worse than the market wives. I also heard,' he leaned in closer, 'that he's been asking about us.'

'About us? Why?'

'Well, more about you, really. He's noticed that we've got our own cabin, and he's been asking which noble family you come from.'

'Bob!' Agnes looked at him sternly, her arms crossed.

'I may have mentioned that Lord Funteyn was your father and I'm your servant accompanying you on this voyage.' He winked.

'Bob. You can't.' Agnes groaned. *What on earth would the count be thinking?* 'Look at my tunic, it's dirty and worn. He won't possibly believe I'm a noblewoman. How could you?'

Bob pursed his lips. 'If you haven't noticed, everyone's clothes are dirty and worn. We've been on board more than a week now, even the count's looking a bit shabby around the edges. Agnes, this is your chance. Our chance. You're young, pretty, and you have a baby who needs a father. We're going to a foreign country with no knowledge of what awaits us. If there's a possibility of making an acquaintance here on board who can help us once we arrive, I think you should take it.'

Agnes didn't know whether to shake him or hug him. 'Oh, you! Leave me be. I won't lie to anyone, not even a count.' But she glanced over to where the man was still in deep conversation with the captain, and reflected on Bob's words as he scampered away.

'Lass, come and sit with me a while. The days are long without anyone to talk to.'

Agnes jumped, startled out of her reverie by the old woman's voice. The cool breeze ruffled her hair, sticky after a night spent below deck in stifling heat, and she ran her hand through it, embarrassed.

'I, erm...'

'I have some ale I'll share with you.' She held aloft a wooden tankard, sloshing some of the liquid over the side, and smiled, showing her toothless gums.

'All right, for a little while,' Agnes said. She sat in the shade near the woman, leaning back against the supports of the upper deck, and set the chest down next to her with a deep sigh.

The woman gestured at the box, her expression curious. 'What's in it?'

'My things.' Agnes wriggled her shoulders, trying to get comfortable.

'What things? Something important? You carry it all day with you. Don't you get tired?'

So many questions, Agnes thought. But something about the woman reassured her. Her worn, wrinkled face looked as though it had centuries of wisdom etched into it, her black eyes glinting as she waited for Agnes to answer.

'M-my... Ted made it for me, I don't want to lose it,' she blurted.

'Ted?'

'W-we were betrothed, but h-he died. From the pestilence.' Agnes felt tears pricking at her eyes, and shook her head. She had to be strong.

The old woman reached out and took her hand. 'Many have died. I lost my family as well. My daughter, her husband, their children – my grandchildren – all taken before their time.'

'I'm sorry.'

'We all have our crosses to bear, lass. I am nearing the end of my life, while yours is just beginning, and that of your child.'

Agnes sat up with a jolt. 'How...?'

'I have been caring for women all my life, I know when one is with child. Don't worry, your secret is safe.'

'I'm scared.' The words were out before Agnes could stop them. She put her hand over her mouth, horrified.

'That's only to be expected. Where are you headed?'

'Genoa. And you?'

'I am also going to Genoa. I will take my cures there, where they may be better received than in England.'

'Cures?'

'I am a healer. What many often call a witch, in their ignorance or fear. I use plants to cure many illnesses or heal wounds, and much more besides.'

'Can you cure the pestilence?' Agnes held her breath, desperate to hear the answer.

'No, lass. Do you think my family would have died if I could? But I can help with other things – I have helped many others over the years. I've saved babies from the grave, children whose mothers and fathers then stoned me when they drove me away from the village, thinking that would save them from the sickness.' She gave an angry sigh. 'People understand naught, lass, especially when the fear takes them over.'

'I-I had to leave too, because people blamed me for the pestilence,' Agnes said sadly. A tear rolled down her cheek. 'I only wanted to help them – the plant couldn't save them, but it gave them relief from the pain towards the end. I didn't get sick, though, and that scared them. They couldn't understand why I was well when everyone around us was dying.'

'I knew it.' The old woman took Agnes's hands in hers, gripping them tightly. 'As soon as I saw you, I knew.'

'Knew what?'

'Later. Tell me about the plant, lass.'

32

Agnes discovered that the old woman, Matilda, was full of wisdom. Although she had never seen the plant from the Dragonfly Grove before, she instinctively knew how to use it. She gave Agnes a small terracotta pot to put it in, and she set it in the shade of the upper deck each afternoon. The plant began to thrive once more. She taught Agnes how to care for it, and a short prayer to recite whenever she had to take a part of it for her cures.

'A plant needs love and care, lass. If it knows you won't hurt it, it will willingly let you take what you want without suffering. It will become second nature to you, and plants will flourish under your care.'

She explained the different preparation methods to Agnes – infusions, tinctures, poultices – and taught her about the different plants and their uses. Many Agnes knew already, such as sage and rosemary, but others were unknown to her. Matilda promised to show them to her when they arrived in Italy.

Agnes was a quick learner, and soon memorised the names of the plants, how to use them, and the ailments they cured. When she retired to the cabin every evening, she would go over what she had learned that day with Bob, her enthusiasm too much to contain. In return, Bob regaled her with stories from his antics that day and gossip he'd picked up from the sailors. Every now and then he'd mention the Italian count, but she told him to stop sticking his nose where it wasn't wanted.

After a week or so, Agnes could recite the names of each plant, their healing powers, and how to use them. Matilda nodded, satisfied.

'Once we get back on land, I'll be able to teach you more, but now you know enough to be getting on with.'

'Thank you.'

'You may not be thanking me when people accuse you of being a witch, lass.' She sat back, her dark eyes glinting in the shadows. 'There's little difference between being a healer and being a witch when times are bad.'

'But in Italy things are better, aren't they? They say the pestilence has passed, that people aren't getting sick anymore.'

'Sometimes it only takes a run of bad luck to bring out the worst in people,' Matilda said. 'A drought, the rains, ruined crops... I have been accused many times.'

'Yet you are still here.'

'Yet I am still here. When it comes down to it, people can't do without their protective charms, love potions, spell-breakers, curse removers, and talismans against evil, it would seem.'

Agnes's eyes lit up. 'Please, teach me those as well.'

'Are you sure, lass?' Even though they had become good friends, Matilda never called her by her name, it was always 'lass'. 'Names are powerful things, you need to be careful when using them,' she'd said when Agnes had asked her why. 'I never utter a name unless it is absolutely necessary.' Agnes secretly didn't agree with her, but took care not to say the old woman's name in her presence.

'Yes, teach me the love potion,' she blurted without thinking. Blushing, she avoided Matilda's stare, her fingers fidgeting with the hem of her tunic.

'Ah, lass, methinks you would like a certain person not far from us to fall in love with you. Is that not so?'

'Of course not!' Agnes huffed, offended by the idea.

'Alas, I don't have the ingredients here. Everything I had was left behind, on England's shores. However, I do not think you need a love potion as far as *he* is concerned. But I will teach you the ways, if you wish.'

'Oh, please.'

'Be warned, lass. Once a healer, always a healer. I will show you things that others would call magic, things that you will learn are all around us, within reach, if you know where to look. But you must believe.'

Agnes thought back to the Grove, the way the dragonflies had seemed like fairies to her, the magic of the place seeping into her skin and her bones, right to her core. And she knew that she would believe.

'Lady Funteyn, I believe we haven't had the pleasure.' Agnes jumped as the count appeared before her, interrupting her morning walk.

'Oh, I...' She suddenly found that she couldn't find the words to say a simple greeting. She swallowed, and tried again. 'Good morning, Count... er...'

'*Il Conte di Gallicano*,' he said with a bow. 'But you may call me Riccardo.'

His voice was low and warm, his Italian accent making his speech almost musical to her ears. Although they were both speaking in French, her voice sounded guttural in comparison to his lilting tones. She tried to remember her lessons from Lady Elizabeth. Her young mistress had loved to pretend they were both ladies of the court, about to be presented to the king, and had taught Agnes how to behave.

'Count,' Agnes murmured, curtseying the best she could. She felt awkward under his gaze, and blushed.

'And I may call you...?' His question hung in the air between them.

'Agnes,' she replied, blushing even more. She felt foolish before this man, and wished that Bob was passing so she could give him a piece of her mind.

'Lady Agnes, it is a pleasure to meet you at long last,' he said, taking hold of her hand and pressing his lips against it.

A warmth spread from her hand, up her arm and into her body, filling her veins and travelling to her head, where it exploded in a million tiny lights. She staggered, overwhelmed by her feelings.

'Is everything all right?' He looked at her, concerned.

'Yes, I-I'm sorry.' She looked into his eyes, their deep, earthy glow of sparkling amber reaching into her soul, and for the first time since Ted's death, she felt hope course through her body. Confused, she slipped her hand out of his and took a few deep breaths.

'I've never met a count before,' she said, then could have kicked herself. She was supposed to be the daughter of a lord! She took a deep breath and willed herself to keep calm. 'I am honoured to make your acquaintance.'

He raised an eyebrow, then smiled at her. 'As am I. The captain tells me you are headed for Genoa. Do you have family in Italy?'

'Oh, no. We had to leave England, m-my family are all dead. The pestilence.'

His face became sombre. 'These are bad times, in the whole of Europe,' he said gravely. 'My family, we live in the mountains, and the pestilence didn't hurt us too badly. But down in the valley, and in other parts of Italy, it was a... how do you say, *un disastro*.'

'Where do you come from in Italy?' Agnes was desperate to keep the conversation going, if only to listen to his accent.

'In Tuscany. Gallicano, to be exact.' He laughed at her puzzled face. 'It is beautiful, right in the middle of the mountains. Our villa is prosperous, everyone is content with their lives.'

'It sounds wonderful. Where do you recommend we go, when we arrive in Genoa?'

'You don't know anyone there?'

'No. As I said, we are fleeing the pestilence in England. Genoa was the best place to go, but we have no plans once we get there.'

'I'm sure I can help you. We still have at least three weeks aboard the ship, perhaps we can use the time to become better acquainted, Lady Agnes?'

Her mouth suddenly went dry and she had to swallow several times before being able to speak. 'That would be lovely, Count.'

33

Matilda glanced at Agnes. 'You're looking radiant, lass. I'm guessing it's not the baby, not this time. I'll wager it has something to do with that Italian count.'

Agnes was in turmoil. Every day, Riccardo accompanied her on her walk around the deck, telling her about Gallicano, his family, and the manor where they lived. He would occasionally touch her arm while talking, and the same feeling of warmth she had felt the first time would pass once again through Agnes's body. She spoke little, partly because she was afraid of letting slip something that would reveal her lie, and partly because she was in turmoil over her feelings for him. It was as if she were betraying Ted and everything they'd had together.

'I *am* happy, but I have my doubts.'

When she'd tried to speak to Bob about it, he'd reminded her that she needed someone to protect her and her unborn child. 'If Ted was watching, he'd tell you not to be so stupid and do what's best. The count likes you and you like him, so what's the problem?' She hadn't asked him again.

'Why's that?' Matilda asked.

'It's Ted. I feel like I'm being unfaithful to him.'

'Ted died,' the old woman said gently.

'I know. It's just that...'

'Yes?'

'When the count touches me, even the merest brushing of his arm against mine, I get this sensation of warmth going through my body. It's as if something from inside him passes to me. It's not a bad thing, it's good,' she added hastily, 'but I'm confused. I love Ted, how can I love Riccardo?'

'Interesting.'

'Interesting?' *Is the old woman going mad?* Agnes thought.

'You are more gifted than I imagined, lass. Being able to sense the soul of another... very few are able to do that. My mother, she had the gift, and I have it too, but not as strongly. You remind me of her.'

'Sense the soul of another?'

'You should be grateful it's warmth you feel. It means he's a good man, and he will treat you well. My mother told me of–' Matilda stopped, wringing her hands together.

'Please, go on.' Agnes was fascinated.

'There was a man. She refused to speak to him, and would cross the road should their paths meet. She said she could sense the blackness coming off him, like a dark cloud of evil.' She shuddered. 'He was the local priest. We never went to church again while he was alive.'

'The priest?'

'Yes, lass. You'd be surprised who the devil gets his claws into. You should consider yourself lucky, it's a special gift you have there.'

'But what should I do? Should I follow my instinct? Even though it feels like I'm betraying Ted?'

'That depends on what you want. Or what you need.' She

glanced at Agnes's stomach. 'Very soon it will start to show, you know that. What will you do then? Trust in God to lead you to someone who will help you? Or do you take this opportunity that providence has put before you? You don't have many choices. I'm sorry.'

'That's what Bob tells me,' Agnes replied. 'But to lie like this, about the baby, and the fact that I'm a servant, not a lord's daughter. I don't like it. I'm always worried I'll say the wrong thing, or that he'll find out somehow. And, as you say, soon it will be obvious. The baby, I mean. I-I don't want him to hate me or think I'm a bad person.'

Matilda took hold of her hand. 'You mustn't think these things. I have the gift, though it is not strong, and I sense no badness in you. You are doing what any woman in your position would do... protecting yourself and your child. There is no wrong in that. The count is in love with you and wants you for his wife. He has decided this for himself, without magic charms or love potions. Feel no guilt for this – you are using no trickery or deception. And you love him too. You will be happy together.'

'He hasn't spoken about what will happen once we arrive in Italy,' Agnes said miserably. 'Maybe he won't even ask me to marry him.'

'Oh, he will, lass. Don't worry about that, he will.'

'Perhaps I should tell him the truth.' She glanced hopefully at Matilda, wishing she would decide for her.

'Only you can know the answer to that. If he is a good man, as you think, he may accept the truth. On the other hand...' She shrugged. 'If we were on land, I could make a charm that would help you. But here, it's in the hands of fate.'

A sudden wave of nausea washed over Agnes. 'I don't feel well. I think I'll go back to the cabin to lie down.'

'I'll see if cook has any chamomile tea, that should help. You're looking pasty, lass, go get some rest.'

But once she arrived at the cabin, Agnes was too agitated to lie down on her narrow cot. She paced around and around the tiny room, the candle throwing eerie shadows on the wooden boards as she passed, the flame stirred up by the air from her movement. She came to a standstill in the middle of the cabin, her hand over the slight roundness of her belly. She pressed harder against her stomach, concentrating on the tiny being inside her, feeling the energy flow from her fingertips, through her skin and beyond. Movement fluttered underneath her hand, and she gasped. She delved deeper inside with her mind, searching, and was rewarded with a faint ripple of life flowing through her flesh. Her heart skipped a beat. *If only Ted could be here to feel this*, she thought, *he would have been over the moon*. An image of Ted's face, smiling at her, came into her mind, and she tried to send it down through her fingers, so that her daughter would know her father's features.

Standing motionless, a blissful smile upon her face, she felt the connection between them become stronger as they reached out to each other... and then there was something else there, something dark and menacing, that made her feel as though she were suffocating. She gasped, trying to draw air into her lungs, but the air was too dense, it filled her throat, clogging her airway. A figure appeared before her, its dark eyes hidden in shadows; there was only a glittering pinprick of light that became bigger and brighter as it got closer. Fear engulfed her, and she tried to move away, but her feet were stuck to the floor. Terrified, she could only watch as the *something* approached, sucking all the air from the room.

A knock on the door made her jump, breaking the spell. Suddenly able to move once more, she clasped her arms around her belly. *No one will hurt my baby, Ted's baby*. A voice called out.

'Agnes? Agnes, I know you're in there. Are you all right? The old woman said you were feeling sick.'

Riccardo. Her heart thudded painfully in her chest as she took deep breaths, trying to bring herself back to the present. The dark presence receded, and she felt the fear lift from her mind.

He knocked again. 'Agnes.' She could hear the worry in his voice.

She staggered over to the door, still clutching her stomach, and fumbled with the catch. Riccardo burst into the room and caught her in his arms.

'Agnes! Is everything all right? What's the matter?' He brushed her damp hair away from her face, and she realised she was sweating. He led her over to the cot and sat her down. She burst into tears, and he held her until her sobs subsided.

'What's wrong?'

'I-I thought I saw...' He would think she was crazy if she told him what she had seen. What if it had been a figment of her imagination, something her mind had concocted because of the guilt she felt? She couldn't carry on lying to him; if he hated her, then so be it. At least her conscience would be clear.

'I need to tell you the truth,' she blurted. He sat beside her, his arm still around her shoulders, as he waited for her to continue.

'Wh-when I left England, I w-was... am... with child,' she said, tears rolling down her cheeks. His body tensed, but he remained silent. 'I-I was betrothed. Ted... we were betrothed, but he died. From the pestilence.'

'I see.' Riccardo stood, his brow furrowed.

Her heart sank. 'I understand if you're angry. You have every right to be.'

'Did Ted know?'

'I told him. W-we exchanged vows, before he died.'

'You were married?'

Agnes thought back to when she and Ted had exchanged

vows, just the two of them in his cottage with God as their witness. 'Yes.'

'He must have been a good man,' Riccardo said quietly.

'He was,' Agnes replied.

Riccardo paced around the room in silence, his hands crossed behind his back, deep in thought. Agnes sat on the cot, waiting for his response. When it came, it surprised her.

'How many months are you?'

'What? About three, I think.' The days passed so quickly, she had difficulty remembering how much time had passed.

'And we've been one and a half months on the ship, or near-about.' Still pacing, he glanced over at her. 'It could work.'

'What could work?'

He strode over and knelt beside her, taking her hand in his. 'Agnes, I love you. I've loved you ever since I first saw you, walking around the deck on your own. So aloof, so full of pain. Now I understand why.' He looked up at her earnestly. 'We can tell my family you are carrying my child, they would never know. We can get married, you would be safe with me.'

'M-married?' Her head spun with the suddenness of it all.

'You and the child, you will carry the Innocenti name. You will never be alone again. Please, marry me.'

'Yes, of course I will,' she said, hardly stopping to think.

He kissed her then, with such passion it took her breath away, and held her close as though he would never let her go again.

A little voice niggled inside her head, insisting she tell him the rest, but she shoved it firmly out of her mind. He loved her, and he wanted to raise Ted's daughter as his own. That would suffice for now.

When Riccardo left her room a little while later, she lay back on her bed, exhausted. With all the thoughts whirling around her head, it took her some time to drift into an uneasy sleep. She dreamt of giving birth on the ship, Matilda beside her, cackling as bright red blood soaked the sheets, terrified that she would die and they would throw both her and the baby overboard...

She turned restlessly on the cot, sweat soaking the worn cotton sheet beneath her as they headed into the dark night.

34

Agnes stood at the prow of the ship, watching the coastline gradually grow larger as they neared the port. After more than six weeks at sea, she couldn't wait to stand on terra firma once more, without the constant creaking of the sails, ropes and wooden boards all around her. Bob scampered from one part of the deck to another, helping the sailors prepare for their arrival. She'd missed his constant presence the last few weeks; too busy during the day to talk to her, he usually fell asleep almost as soon as he lay down on his cot at night. She raised her hand as he ran past, and he shouted a greeting to her over his shoulder.

'*Buongiorno*, Lady Agnes,' a voice said from behind her.

'Count.' She turned and smiled at him. In front of the crew and other passengers, they maintained their usual formality. But when he visited her cabin in the afternoons... she blushed and tried to concentrate on what he was saying.

'That, my dear Lady Agnes, is my country. *L'Italia*. She is beautiful, no?' His accent was more marked, as if in anticipation of returning home.

'It certainly is.' Tall mountains rose in the distance, framing the port and the city, which lay sprawled over the countryside.

As they got closer, she could see rows of houses, reaching down to the water itself in some places. The port was a swarming mass of people, reminding her of the morning she'd awoken on the wharf in London.

'Gallicano is beyond the mountains, slightly more than a day's travel by carriage. If you think these mountains are beautiful, wait until you see those of Tuscany.'

'I can't wait,' Agnes said, her heart thumping wildly.

He moved closer, placing his hand next to hers on the rail. 'Our villa is in the heart of the mountains. My great-grandfather discovered the area while travelling and decided to settle there. I hope you will come to love it as much as I do and call it home in time.'

'Your family will be surprised to see me arrive with you,' she said, biting her lip. 'What if they don't like me?'

'Agnes, you are a wonderful person. I'm sure they will love you. I wish you could have known Papà.' A wistful look came over his face. 'But at least you will meet Mamma, and my brothers and sisters. There are many of us, we will give you back the family you have lost. Italian hospitality is renowned for being the best in the world, you know.'

'It will all be so different. A new culture, a new language, a new beginning. It scares me sometimes.' Riccardo had started teaching her Italian, and she was picking it up quickly. His long discourses on Italian politics, however, left her feeling confused; the intrigues and machinations of his country appeared to be even more complicated than those she'd left behind.

'And your servants, they will be with you,' he reassured her. When she had asked him if Bob and Matilda could accompany her, he'd assumed they were servants from her father's household. 'I'm sure Bob would be happy to work in the stables with my father's horses. We have some of the most spectacular specimens in the whole of Tuscany.'

'You are too kind to us,' Agnes said, moving her hand so that it covered his.

'Anything for you, Lady Agnes,' he whispered in her ear.

The coach set off from the wharf, leaving behind the commotion and confusion surrounding the ship and its cargo. Agnes leaned her head back against the velvet cushions, relieved they were finally off the boat. Her body still swayed with the motion of the rocking ship; Riccardo had told her it would take a while to pass after so long at sea. He'd also mentioned how lucky they'd been with the weather. The couple of squalls they'd encountered during the voyage had been nothing compared to some tempests he'd experienced. She shuddered, thankful that nothing of the kind had hit them. The squalls had been bad enough, making her cower under her blankets, thinking that every crashing boom against the ship would be the wave that breached the hull.

Matilda sat next to her, snoring gently, her head rolling with the rocking of the carriage, while Bob and Riccardo sat on the other side. Bob looked out of the window, his body fidgeting in anticipation, unable to keep still. His eyes were still red from saying goodbye to Willow, but he seemed to have accepted losing the last tie to his life at the manor. Agnes was grateful that Riccardo had asked him to work in the stables, it would help alleviate the boy's pain a little.

Agnes glanced down at the wooden chest beside her, her fingers lightly tracing over the carved dragonfly on the lid. Thanks to Matilda's care, the plant had survived the long journey; indeed, it was thriving. This was her last tie to Ted, and she would do everything she could to protect it.

The rest of the luggage was on the floor in a corner, their worn travel bags looking forlorn next to Riccardo's newer ones.

He'd told her that he preferred travelling alone, without servants fawning over him day and night, and always took as few bags as possible. 'My brother, Filippo, will be the next Marquis of Gallicano. I am content to come and go as I please, without having to prove myself to anyone or follow any stupid rules,' he'd explained. 'I'm afraid you will be marrying the black sheep of the family, dear Agnes.' She didn't mind at all; indeed, she was relieved that she and Riccardo would be able to stay in the background. Let Filippo do all the lordly things, while they could live their lives in blissful peace!

The journey took less than she'd imagined, the roads being in a better condition than those of England. They stopped once for a brief meal, before starting out again and travelling until nightfall. Riccardo had made the journey many times, and knew the best inns to stay at overnight. Bob found the inside of the carriage stifling and often sat outside with the coachman, talking non-stop. Matilda complained that the carriage rattled her bones, but spent most of her time asleep in a corner, wrapped in a grey, worn cloak.

Riccardo pointed out the various places they travelled through, and told her about his family. Agnes felt both excited and nervous at the thought of the new future that awaited her.

'We're almost there,' Riccardo said. Agnes jolted awake. They had hooked heavy cloth curtains across the window to avoid the glare of the sun in their eyes, and it was so hot in the carriage that she'd dozed off for a while.

She pulled back the curtain and eagerly looked out. The road led steeply upward through a forest, the rocky tips of the mountains visible above the treetops, a brilliant blue sky dotted with pure white clouds in the background. She could hear the horses puffing and snorting as they strained to pull the carriage uphill.

'It's beautiful,' she said, awed by the view before her. She nudged Matilda. 'Wake up, sleepy head, and look out of the window.'

Matilda grumbled, but did as she was told. Her gasp made Agnes laugh in delight.

Riccardo leaned forward and pointed out of the window. 'This is Gallicano; my home is further up the mountain. Up there you can see the church where we go to Mass every Sunday.' He waved to some people who had stopped to watch the carriage pass by. Laughing, they waved back, the men taking their caps off and bowing.

'They seem friendly,' Agnes remarked.

'We are not afraid to get our hands dirty, and the villagers appreciate that,' Riccardo replied. 'At harvest time, for example, everyone gets involved.' He glanced over at Matilda. 'Well, there are some exceptions.'

35

The carriage rounded a corner and slowed to a halt. Agnes twisted her hands together, clammy in her lap, and looked at Riccardo.

'We've arrived,' he announced. The door opened, and the coachman stood back, waiting.

Riccardo swung himself down, then turned and held out his hand to Agnes. She grasped it firmly and stepped out of the carriage. The bright sunshine blinded her after the dim interior, and it took her eyes a moment to adjust. She heard Matilda complaining as she got out as well.

'Look, Agnes! Isn't it incredible?' Bob tugged at her arm, pointing in front of him. Agnes raised her head and saw Riccardo's home. She'd always thought Lord Funteyn's manor was fit for a king, but the house before her, at the top of a slight rise, took her breath away.

Made from stone and marble, the villa had a tower with crenelated battlements at either end. The main part of the villa had narrow windows on the upper floor only, and a robust wooden door that looked as though it would withstand the onslaught of the mightiest army. Turning around, Agnes saw that they had passed through a stone archway, and a thick stone wall disappeared into the woods surrounding the grounds.

'As I told you, the villa has been in my family for a few generations,' Riccardo explained, taking hold of her elbow. 'There was much unrest in this area for many years, hence the fortifications. Now that times are more peaceful, my brother is in talks with stonemasons to rebuild the villa and make it more comfortable.'

As he spoke, the enormous wooden door opened and several people stepped out.

'Riccardo, you're back,' a little girl shouted, and ran over to them.

'My youngest sister, Savia,' he whispered to Agnes. '*Ciao, bellissima!*' He swung her up in the air as she launched herself at him. She giggled excitedly, then stopped as she noticed Agnes.

'Who's this?' Savia asked.

'This is Agnes,' Riccardo replied. 'Why don't you stay here and say hello while I go and speak with Mamma? Bob, can you get the bags out of the carriage?'

Agnes watched as he strode over to the others still standing by the entrance, then looked down at the girl, feeling helpless.

'*Ciao*,' Savia said, twiddling her hair around her finger. 'What are you doing here with Riccardo?'

As Agnes searched for an explanation, her eyes were drawn to Riccardo and his family. There was a lot of gesticulating going on, and she could hear raised voices, although she couldn't make out the words.

'They seem angry,' Savia remarked. 'Are you sure you're Riccardo's friend?'

Agnes nodded, distracted, still unable to say anything. Bob and Matilda stood beside her, their faces tense. After a few more angry words and waving of arms, Riccardo came back over to them.

'Domenico here will take you to the stables, Bob, and show

you around.' Riccardo pointed at the tall, wiry lad who stood by the horses' heads. Bob picked up his travel bag and followed the other boy. Agnes and Matilda stepped aside as the horses and carriage made its way along the drive.

'He'll be fine, don't worry,' Riccardo said. 'He can work in the stables, I'm sure he'll feel right at home there. And you,' he glanced over at Matilda, 'can go to the servants' door. Ask for Gisella and tell her you're to have Fiammetta's cottage. She'll take you there and get you settled in. Savia, show her to the door.'

'But I... oh, Riccardo!' the girl exclaimed, stamping her foot.

'No buts, do as you're told,' he said sternly, his lips twitching.

'Come,' she said, grabbing Matilda's arm. The old woman clutched her belongings to her chest and meekly followed the girl.

'That leaves you.' Riccardo took Agnes's hand and squeezed it. 'Don't worry, you'll see your servants again.'

'Your family didn't seem too happy,' Agnes said, reluctant to go over to them.

'That's just how they are. They hate change, and they have a strong distrust of foreigners.'

'Now you tell me!' Agnes let go of his hand.

'Don't worry. At least you only have my mother to deal with. Filippo is out on the estate, sorting some problem or other.' He smiled at her, but it was more of a grimace. 'Whatever happens, I'll be by your side. And leave that,' he added as he saw her go to pick up the wooden chest. 'One of the servants will take your things to your room. I'll make sure they're careful.'

The introductions were tense, and Agnes was glad when the contessa told Riccardo to show her to a guest room. The Italian woman pursed her lips, arms folded across her chest, and didn't say a word as they left. Agnes followed Riccardo through the wooden door into the dark hallway.

'It will get better, I promise you,' he said through gritted teeth. 'They need to get used to you being here.'

As they made their way through the house, servants passed them, casting curious glances at the newcomer. Agnes marvelled at the rich tapestries hanging on the walls, burning torches projecting flickering shadows across them, making the figures appear to move.

'The servants' quarters are along there,' Riccardo told her, pointing further down the corridor. 'Back there is the main hall and the kitchen, the courtyard, stables... but I'll show you everything later. For now, we go up here.'

Agnes followed him up the stairs to a bright corridor. Here, there were large windows that allowed more light in. Riccardo led her right to the end, to a door set at an angle.

'I hope you'll be comfortable here,' he said, opening the door. Agnes entered the room, and gazed around in wonder. Never in her wildest dreams had she thought she would ever stay in a room like this. The bed was larger than the entire attic room she'd had when she was maid to Lady Elizabeth, and she was sure the mattress was soft and downy, from its appearance.

An enormous wooden coffer stood along one wall, decorated with richly carved patterns. Three silver candlesticks stood in a line on top of it, ready for the evening. A dark-blue bedspread made from the finest silk was laid across the bed, and a blue tapestry rug covered the cold stone floor. Red silk cushions graced a settle in one corner, and plush tapestries hung from the walls.

She moved to the window, and gasped. She had a view over the garden, with its colourful flower beds, marble statues, and well-tended lawns dotted with trees and shrubs. Lord Funteyn, ever practical, had dedicated his land to crops and livestock; the only flowers had been the dandelions, buttercups and ribwort that had grown in abundance everywhere.

'I'll let you have a rest, then I'll come back when it's time for the evening meal,' Riccardo said, smiling at her reaction. 'You still have to meet my brother Filippo.'

Agnes turned to him. 'I hope he's more welcoming than the others.'

Riccardo pulled her against him and wrapped his arms around her. 'They'll come to love you, Agnes, like I have,' he murmured, and tilted her face towards his. He bent and kissed her on the lips, and she melted in his embrace.

Dressed in a beautifully embroidered green silk dress and delicate slippers borrowed from Olimpia, another of Riccardo's sisters, Agnes entered the main hall. A surprisingly familiar scene appeared before her eyes – the family sat up at a long wooden table at the far end of the hall, with the servants spread throughout the room, some at small tables, others lounging on piles of straw. Dogs meandered among them, fighting over dropped morsels, receiving kicks and slapped noses when they ventured too close to unguarded plates. The fire was unlit, the cool interior pleasant after the baking heat outside. Torches flickered in their sconces, permanently lit along the windowless walls.

A servant approached with a bowl of water and stood before Agnes, waiting patiently. Startled, she panicked for a moment, then she remembered seeing Lady Elizabeth and her father washing their hands before sitting down to dinner, and realised what she was meant to do. Another servant held out a linen cloth for her dripping hands. She took it, blushing furiously, believing that she should be the one serving them. *Will this feeling ever go away?* she wondered. How long would she be able to keep up the pretence?

Riccardo took her hand and led her to the top table, where

his family were waiting for them. She sat quickly, avoiding their curious stares.

'Lady Agnes, I believe we haven't had the pleasure,' a deep voice boomed from the other side of the table.

She raised her eyes and met the gaze of a dark, brooding man, some years older than Riccardo, a thick black beard covering most of his face. He stood and lifted his cup.

'A toast to Lady Agnes,' he cried, seemingly unaware of the stony expressions on the others' faces. '*Benvenuta alla famiglia Innocenti!*'

'He means, "welcome",' Riccardo translated with a whisper.

'Th-thank you, Count,' Agnes said, her voice shaking. His dark eyes, black as coal, seemed to pierce her skull, boring into her mind to seek out her deepest thoughts. He smiled at her, but the smile never left his lips, his expression cold and calculating. She sensed evil pouring from him in huge waves that crashed against her, and was stunned by the strength of it.

He strode around the table and clapped Riccardo on the shoulder, making him fall forwards.

'So, *fratellino*, you go to England and bring back a bride. A beautiful one, too.' He winked at his brother and gripped his arm. 'I always knew you had the luck of the devil.' He turned to Agnes. 'I'm Filippo, I'm sure Riccardo has mentioned me. I spend my days running here, there and everywhere, making sure everything is as it should be, while my dear brother goes gallivanting across Europe, seducing beautiful women.'

Agnes blushed, unsure of what to say. She could feel the tension coming from Riccardo, his body rigid as his brother spoke. The rest of the family sat in silence, watching.

'*Signorina*, it is a pleasure to meet you,' he finished, taking hold of Agnes's hand and raising it to his lips.

Horror ran through her, to her very core, as soon as his lips touched her skin, the hairs on her arms standing on end. She had to use all her force to not tear her hand from his. *What is happening?* She trembled with fear, her body screaming at her to run, to get away from this man, this devil incarnate. He stood, bent over her hand, waiting patiently for her to answer, and she realised that he didn't know she had sensed the evil emanating from him.

'Count,' she said demurely, resisting the urge to snatch her hand away and wipe it on her tunic. 'I thank you for your welcome, and I hope to become friends with you and the rest of your family.'

'And now, brother, I must ask you to return to your place and let us eat in peace,' Riccardo said, standing up. 'We have travelled long today, and I, for one, am famished.' He beckoned to the servants to bring over the trays of food they were holding, and sat back down. 'You will have more than enough time to talk to Agnes, she isn't going anywhere.'

Filippo frowned, then burst out laughing. 'Too true, brother! Well, Agnes, I look forward to getting to know you better.' Still chuckling, he returned to his seat and attacked the food before him with gusto, glancing at Riccardo every now and then.

Agnes shuddered, suddenly unsure of what the future held for her.

The meal was interspersed with strained conversation after that. Riccardo's family were trying hard, Agnes realised, but they found it difficult to know what to say to her. She was grateful when the servants finally cleared the table, and she and Riccardo could escape outside.

'I'm sorry,' he said as they walked along the drive. The setting sun cast long shadows through the branches of the trees and the air was turning chilly. 'My brother can be difficult at times.'

'It's all right,' Agnes replied, even though her stomach was churning with fear. 'My servants. Do you know when I can see them? I'd like to make sure they are well.'

'I will take you to them tomorrow,' Riccardo promised. 'I think you should rest, Agnes, you're very pale.'

His concern touched her. 'Yes, I think I will retire now, if you don't mind.'

'Of course not.'

'Do they know I am with child?'

'Yes. I told them when we arrived, so they would understand why we have to get married so soon.'

'Ah. No wonder they find it difficult to speak to me.' She sighed. 'It's not as if I could keep it hidden for much longer, anyway.'

He put his arms around her shoulders. 'We will be married as soon as it can be arranged, Agnes, and then they must accept you.'

Agnes wasn't so sure, but said nothing. She leaned into him, relishing the comfort he gave her merely from his presence. She felt a twinge of guilt once more for Ted and pushed it away. The most important thing now was to protect her child.

36

NOVEMBER 1348

The first few months in Italy passed quickly. Agnes soon settled into the villa, and learned which members of his family to avoid. She loved spending time with Savia; the young girl's curiosity and vivacity reminded her of Lady Elizabeth, while Riccardo's oldest sister, Olimpia, was a quiet-spoken woman who was always pleasant to her.

Agnes missed Bob and Matilda, and often felt homesick for Forest Brook and everyone she'd known at the manor. She had gone to Matilda's cottage the day after her first meeting with Filippo, to see how the old woman was settling in and to ask when they could begin her lessons once more. She was eager to learn more about the art of healing, and she enjoyed listening to her reminiscing about the past. While they were talking, she had suddenly burst into tears, unable to hold her emotions back anymore. Matilda took her in her arms and made soothing noises, stroking her hair, until her sobs had subsided.

'I-it's Riccardo's brother, Filippo. I met him for the first time yesterday.'

'Tell me, lass.' Matilda's voice was calm and soft, giving Agnes the strength to speak.

'There's something about him, something... something bad. When he touched my hand, I felt it. There was a darkness in him, an evil that scared me. I can't explain what it is, but it made me want to run away.' She sat back, breathing heavily.

Matilda pursed her lips. 'I told you on the ship you had the gift, but it's stronger than I imagined. That you can sense evil like this; it's not everyone can do it, you know. My mother, God rest her soul, had the gift, but you have a power even greater than hers. I must teach you...' Her voice trailed away as she became lost in thought. She shook her head. 'What am I saying? First, we must protect you and the child, before it is too late.'

'Protect?'

'I need to prepare the charm.' She hurried to her feet, pulling her shawl around her shoulders. 'Come back tomorrow morning, everything will be ready then.'

Since that day, Matilda had fussed over her constantly, but Agnes saw the look of fear in her eyes that the old woman tried to keep hidden.

They walked through the forest, their breath foggy clouds in the air. Agnes was glad of the fur-lined gloves she wore; it was bitterly cold, and the grey sky above them was heavy with the threat of snow. Riccardo stopped beneath an enormous chestnut tree and covered Agnes's eyes with his hands.

'Where are we going?' she giggled, trying not to trip over her feet. Her belly was much bigger, and always getting in the way.

'It's a surprise! It's not much further, just be patient.'

He took her through the woods, guiding her through the trees so she wouldn't get hurt. They made slow progress, but eventually he stopped.

'Now, I'm going to uncover your eyes. No peeking!' he added

as she tried to pry his fingers apart. He took away his hands and stepped back.

Before them was a pretty stone-walled cottage with a slate roof, set in a small clearing in the forest. The watery noon sun forced its rays through thick, grey clouds, lighting up the cottage as if to show it off in its full glory.

'Do you like it?' Riccardo asked, his voice hesitant.

'It's beautiful,' Agnes said, staring in awe.

'It's ours.'

'Ours? Really?' Agnes shrieked in delight and threw her arms around his neck. 'They said yes?'

Riccardo nodded. 'It took a lot of persuasion, but eventually they saw things from my point of view.' They stood hugging each other as Agnes gazed on her new home.

After their wedding in September, Agnes had hoped Riccardo's family would have become more accepting of her. She should have known it wouldn't have been that easy. The contessa had glared at her all the way through the ceremony, and hadn't smiled once during the wedding banquet. While Savia and Olimpia had enthused over her red velvet dress and the daisies entwined in her hair, no one else had even spoken to her. Except for Filippo. After the ceremony, he had bent to kiss her cheek and whispered in her ear, 'I imagine we won't be finding any blood on the bedsheets in the morning, I see my brother has already tasted your wares', then winked at her before striding away to talk with some other guests. Agnes had remained rooted to the spot, humiliated, her face flushed with shame, and her wedding day ruined.

Things had got worse with Riccardo's family after that. His mother, in particular, snapped at her for no reason, and found fault in everything she did. Agnes had been reduced to tears many times when her Italian mother-in-law's sharp tongue lashed out at her. The last time Riccardo had found her lying on their bed, sobbing her heart out, he told her that he had had enough of his mother's interfering and they would move out of the villa. It seemed he had kept his promise.

'I came across the cottage a few weeks ago, while out on my horse. It needed some repairs doing, otherwise I would have brought you sooner. It's far enough from the villa to be on our own, but near enough to send for help when we need it.' He stroked her belly. 'So, do you think you can be happy here, Agnes?'

'Oh yes, it's perfect,' she exclaimed. 'We can use that part of the garden for growing our vegetables, and over there we can keep some chickens. Oh, and there would be perfect for all the herbs and plants I've been learning about. We'll need a pantry too, to store them in. Somewhere dark and cool, where they won't go bad.' She closed her eyes and dreamed of the time when they could call the cottage their home.

He smiled and tugged her arm. 'Come, Agnes, I'll show you around.'

They went inside together, hand in hand, excited about their new future.

They moved into the cottage a week later, and Agnes hardly had time to sit down for the first couple of days, she was so busy sorting everything out. They only had a few servants, enough to help with the daily chores. Agnes felt uncomfortable giving orders to people like herself, and it made her feel even more guilty about deceiving Riccardo. Bob dropped in most days to see her, excitedly telling her the latest events up at the stables. She'd gone to see the horses with him a few times, and even she could tell they were highly bred animals.

She envied Riccardo his freedom to go out on horseback whenever he wanted, and vowed that she would join him as soon as she could. He had promised her a bay mare, sired by the stallion he rode, and she couldn't wait to explore the surrounding area together. She didn't venture very far these days. The baby weighed her down and she tired quickly, but she occasionally went into the woods for a walk.

There was never silence in the cottage. Even though everything was in order, there was always a servant bustling about, or the cook banging pans in the kitchen, or people shouting to each other. Agnes sighed and leaned back in the intricately carved armchair made especially for her, and touched the pouch on the cord around her neck. Its presence reassured her and helped her feel safe. Matilda had shown her how to make the charms and taught her the spell to recite. Agnes had placed pouches around the cottage, and she always made sure she had one on her person. Whether it was a coincidence or magic, Filippo hadn't bothered her since. He glowered at her from afar, naked hunger in his eyes, but never dared approach her. She noticed, however, that he had become more aggressive towards Riccardo lately, and it saddened her to think she was the cause of their falling-out.

As she was clearing away her sewing, a movement outside caught her eye. She looked up as Matilda came into view, her cloak wrapped tightly around her to protect her from the winter wind. She pulled on her own cloak and went out to greet her.

'To what do we owe the pleasure?'

'Can't an old woman come to see how her mistress is faring?' Matilda said grumpily, but she had a twinkle in her eye.

'Can I offer you something warm to drink?' Agnes asked, used to her ways.

'That I wouldn't refuse. Then you can show me that garden you've been blathering on about!'

They stood, side by side, looking over the patch of ground

Agnes had decided to use for the plants. Matilda's wrinkled face lit up as she gazed about her, picturing the area in her mind.

'We can't plant anything now, but we can decide what you need and get everything ready for the spring. This is perfect. That wall there will protect the plants from the cold and wind in winter, and you could put a hedge around the other free sides to keep animals and people out. You don't want them trampling over everything.'

'Yes. I'll speak with Riccardo, and make sure everything's ready as soon as it's warm enough. I can't wait, Matilda. Think what we can do with a garden this big. You'll have to tell me which plants I need, how to look after them–'

'Calm down, lass, we've got a few months yet,' the old woman said, her mouth crinkling at the corners as she smiled at Agnes's enthusiasm.

Agnes looked down at her ever-expanding belly and grimaced. 'This little one is due in February, I'd like to have everything planned by then. Who knows afterwards...?' She paused. Her dreams lately had been filled with nightmarish visions of her giving birth and drowning in blood, screaming as a red river slowly covered her head, filling her mouth and gushing down into her lungs. She shuddered.

'It will be all right, you'll see. Every woman worries about childbirth, but I'll be there with you. I won't let anything happen.' Matilda patted her arm, trying to reassure her, but Agnes saw a flicker of fear cross the old woman's face before she remained impassive once more. She hadn't spoken about her dreams to anyone, but she knew that Matilda could sense things as well.

'We'll decide how big we want the garden, then Riccardo can get everything organised,' she said brightly, casting aside her doubts.

'That's the spirit,' Matilda replied.

They spent a pleasant morning walking around the garden, deep in conversation. Matilda pointed out the best place for each plant, and Agnes listened carefully, trying to picture how it would look afterwards. She wished it was already spring, so they could start planting.

After Matilda left, Agnes needed to get away from the cottage, the servants, and all the confusion that moving in had brought. Walking around the garden with the old woman had made her realise how much she craved some peace and quiet, and she couldn't face going back indoors. The winter sun warmed her enough to keep the chill of the wind away. Without saying anything to anyone, she headed into the forest with a light heart.

37

She found some late berries on a bush and picked them, creating a pocket with the hem of her cloak so that she could take them back to the cottage. She carried on, going deeper into the forest, half-wishing she would see fairies light up the gloom under the trees. She had no idea how long she'd been walking, but thought she had better turn back before the sun disappeared behind the mountains. A noise in the undergrowth startled her, and she stopped, her eyes searching.

Another twig snapped, and this time she heard a huffing sound of heavy breathing. A horse! It was a horse snuffling as it made its way through the trees. Perhaps it was Riccardo, come to find her. She headed towards it, a smile already on her face.

'Good day, Agnes.' She came to a sudden halt, dread filling her. Filippo's dark face looked haughtily down at her from the horse's back.

'Wh-what are you doing here?' She couldn't keep the tremor from her voice.

'This happens to be my land, so I think I can go wherever I want,' he replied with a sneer.

'My apologies.' Agnes lowered her head and desperately wished he would go away.

'I think the question is, what are *you* doing here, alone?' His horse stamped its hoof, straining against the reins.

She hesitated. 'I-I wanted to go for a walk.'

'It's a bit far, especially for someone in your delicate condition.' He raised his eyebrows, and she instantly felt soiled, as though he could see the secrets she hid.

'Let me see. You met my brother at the end of June while travelling to Italy, so that means the child will be born about April time, is that right?' He didn't give her a chance to reply. 'It will be interesting to see if it comes early, as so often seems to happen in these cases.'

'What are you insinuating?' Agnes's mouth was dry with fear.

'I'm insinuating nothing, Agnes, merely making an observation. I'm certain my dear brother has already made sure of the dates. Heaven forbid he should bring up another man's child!'

Agnes lifted her head and looked into his dark eyes. There was no warmth in his gaze, no soul behind those black irises, only a cold arrogance that made the hairs on her arms rise.

'Your silence hides a thousand truths, dear Agnes. But I can keep your secrets. For a price.'

Agnes saw his flushed cheeks, the glint in his eyes, the quickening of his breath, and understood what the price would be. *Run!* her mind screamed, and somehow she found the strength to scramble away from him. The berries fell to the ground as she ran, heedless of branches thudding against her body and brambles catching at her cloak, through the dense forest, the pounding of the horse's hooves coming from behind her. She half fell, half slid down a steep slope, ending up on her hands and knees by a stream. She looked down at her reflection in the water, startled to see her wild expression, full of fear. Her hand moved to cradle her rounded stomach.

A shout came from above and she turned, terrified, to see Filippo on his horse at the top of the bank, pointing. He jumped off his horse and slid down the slope towards her, kicking up clumps of grass and plants.

She searched frantically for a way to escape, but there was nowhere to run; the river was behind her and the steep slope and Filippo were in front of her. She felt at her neck for the charm, but the pouch was no longer there. She stood, shaking, waiting for the inevitable.

'*Lady* Agnes, I find this behaviour most intolerable. We were merely having a conversation, there was no reason for you to run from me.' He leaned towards her until his face was a nose-span from hers. She could smell his fetid breath and see the hint of craziness in his eyes. She remained silent, fearful of angering him even more.

'My brother has always had the best in life,' Filippo said, spittle collecting at the corner of his mouth. 'No responsibilities, travelling around Europe looking for fine specimens of horses to bring back to my father, good food, good wine, and women. Oh yes, Agnes, he has had many women,' he sneered.

Agnes remained impassive, hoping he wouldn't notice the drops of sweat forming on her brow.

'And then he finds you. Gentle, lovely, beautiful Agnes. What man wouldn't want you?' He moved closer until they were almost touching. She could see a swirling cloud around him, drifting away and coming back, changing from transparent grey to a deep black the angrier he became.

'What are you, Agnes?' He reached out and took a lock of her hair between his fingers. 'What spell have you cast over me, to make me want you this way?'

She stepped back, pulling her hair from his hand, her foot

splashing in the water behind her. 'I have cast no spell, Count.'
Fear gripped her, and she was truly afraid of what he might do.

'I believe you are a witch,' he said. 'How else did you escape
the pestilence when everyone else died?'

'No!' she shouted. 'I am *not* a witch. You have no idea what it
was like! I tried to help everyone, my friends, the servants, L–'
She stopped herself before she said 'Lady Elizabeth'. 'I had to
watch them die before my eyes, unable to do anything for them.
Do you think I would have let them die if I were a witch? They
were people I loved. Don't you think I would have saved them if
I could?' She paused for breath, then lifted her chin defiantly.
'Rather, you should tell me, Count – how did your entire family
survive the pestilence, when so many others died?'

'*Witch*,' he sneered, spitting on her. 'I'll tell you, shall I?
You'll be impressed. After all, it was one of your kind who
helped us.'

'What did you do?' Agnes whispered, dreading the answer.

'The wise woman, Fiammetta, who lived in the hovel where
your servant now lives, told me what to do. It was simple. I had
to sacrifice one of my family to save the rest of us.'

Agnes's hand flew to her mouth as she staggered back,
unable to believe her ears. 'S-sacrifice?'

He sighed. 'Just one person. That was all it took to let the rest
of my family live. How could I refuse?'

'Who?' Agnes could barely get the words out, her mouth was
so dry.

'I considered Riccardo. He's a constant irritation in my life
that I desire to be rid of, but we needed him and there was no
one to take his place. It had to be someone who meant nothing
to us, but yet was of our blood. So it had to be Rossella.'

'Rossella?'

'Riccardo hasn't told you about her? That's no surprise, no
one mentions her anymore. She is – was – our sister. Two years

old, silky black hair that Mamma liked to plait, so talkative and inquisitive. It was a shame, but it had to be her.'

'They all agreed?' Agnes thought her heart would break. What kind of family had she married into?

'Oh no, they didn't know anything about it. It's our little secret, Agnes. One of those dark secrets that will tie us together, till death us do part.'

'But how...?'

'It was easy. I couldn't kill them myself, so I convinced the crone to take Rossella down to the valley and never come back. Many were perishing of the pestilence there, I knew neither of them would survive. She refused, of course, but when I threatened to have her burned at the stake for witchcraft...' He shrugged. 'As you can imagine, she preferred to take her chances with the pestilence.'

'You killed them both.'

'It was their destiny. A month after they left, people stopped getting sick and the pestilence moved on. No one else in my family died. So you see, it was for the greater good.'

'You're evil.' The words left her lips before she could stop them.

'And you, *Lady* Agnes, are a witch. I have my doubts that you are even a lady.'

Agnes shook her head, but he carried on speaking.

'You and I are destined to be together, Agnes, to bring my family even greater power than it already has. I know things, but I need another to assist me.'

'Never,' Agnes spat, holding her head high. 'I will only do good, I will never help a murderer such as yourself. And if you come near me or touch me,' she warned as he made to grab hold of her, 'I will put a curse on you, the likes of which has never been seen. Your crops will die, your family will suffer terrible poverty, and you will never have children to carry on the family name. Yes, I see into your soul, Filippo, and I know what you hold most dear. I will take all of that away from you if you so much as come near me again.' Stunned, she fell silent. *Where on earth did that come from*? she wondered. Then she heard a voice in her head, as if far off in the distance. *We're coming for you, lass, hold on a little longer.*

'I could kill you now,' he said quietly. The black cloud around his body no longer swirled, but had become a heavy, solid mass that hugged him like a cloak.

'But you won't.' Agnes stood her ground, warm strength flooding her as the voice in her mind grew louder.

He stepped back. 'You're right. I won't. But I may kill Riccardo. And then, as head of the family, you will do as I say.' He turned to go back up the slope, then stopped. 'I warn you, Agnes – if you say one word of this to anyone, I will make sure that everyone you love suffers. Do you want that on your conscience?' He climbed back up to his horse and mounted. 'Our little secret, Agnes,' he called down to her, then kicked his horse's flanks and disappeared into the forest.

Agnes sank to the ground, unable to stand any longer. She knew she couldn't tell Riccardo the truth about his sister, or what his brother had done. She would spare him that pain, at least. All the terror and anguish from the previous months suddenly washed over her, leaving an aching desolation inside her. She had to talk to him about the pestilence, about the things she had seen, how impotent she had felt as the people around her died in agony, otherwise she knew that she would go mad.

She heard voices coming closer and knew her friends had almost arrived. Agnes made up her mind. Soon she would tell Riccardo everything about her past.

38

APRIL 1349

The world was dark and still, the birds and insects asleep, resting in the final moments before dawn, when they would fill the air once more with their chaotic sounds and incessant movement. Agnes slipped quietly out of the cottage, taking care not to wake the rest of the household.

She made her way down through the garden, the dew on the grass soaking her thin slippers, sending cold chills up her feet. She pulled her cape tighter, and opened the gate to the fenced-off piece of ground that was her own private space. Stepping inside, she breathed in the rich aroma of freshly dug earth. She'd planted the last herbs the day before, and now her garden was complete.

When Agnes had proudly shown it to her husband, she'd enjoyed seeing the look of amazement on his face as he'd gazed upon the work she'd done. From the beginning, he'd insisted she get the gardeners to do everything, telling her it wasn't work for a noble woman. She'd let them plant the hedge and the large fruit trees, but she hadn't trusted anyone else with her precious herbs.

'What on earth?' he'd cried out as an insect flew near them, its wings vibrating with a low hum.

'It's only a dragonfly,' she'd replied, laughing. 'It's full of them here. Look.'

He'd stared in wonder as he saw the insects on every plant and bush, their brightly coloured bodies shining like jewels in the sun.

'I'm going to call this place the Dragonfly Grove. What do you think?' Agnes had chewed her nail as she waited for his answer, needing his benediction.

'I think it's perfect,' he'd replied, putting an arm around her.

She'd looked down at the baby in her arms, held in a sling across her body so that she was free to move. 'Now she's sleeping,' she said softly. 'Not like last night.'

'She's got a right pair of lungs, hasn't she?' Riccardo had grumbled, rubbing a hand across his face. 'Thank goodness we don't live up at the main house, my parents would have thrown us out.'

Agnes smiled at the memory, glad her daughter had passed a quieter night and they'd all managed to get some sleep. She moved quickly through the garden, having no need of light as she walked among the plants and picked the ingredients she required. She murmured an apology each time before she removed the leaves, caressing the plant before going on to the next one.

Back at the cottage, Agnes stirred up the ashes in the grate so she could start boiling the leaves. Young Matteo's wound was serious, and she needed to prepare the herbs for his poultice. They had brought the boy to her a few days earlier, a deep cut in his leg. She'd cleaned it and stitched him up while he told her how the scythe he'd been using had slipped out of his grip and embedded itself in his flesh, so deeply that he'd thought for a moment they'd have to amputate his leg. She'd laughed and reassured him that as long as she was looking after him, there'd be no need for that.

The leaves simmering gently in a pot, she went down the corridor to the pantry. She lit a candle and held it in front of her, proud of what she had achieved in so little time – the shelves were full of earthenware jars and glass bottles containing chopped, dried herbs, ready-made salves, and every type of lotion she might need for every ailment she could think of.

I'll have to write down the recipes, she suddenly thought. *So I don't forget them, so I can make notes of what works and what doesn't, the right amounts...*

She was rudely awakened from her thoughts by a loud banging at the back door. She grabbed the candle and hurried to the kitchen. One of the servants had already opened the door to their visitor, an old man with a worried look on his weathered face. He jumped as she entered the room, startled.

The knocking woke up everyone else. Riccardo was in his usual place at the kitchen table, while Olivia the scullery maid sat on a wooden stool beside the fireplace, yawning widely as she tossed sticks onto the fire. A couple of other servants stood in the corridor, nudging each other and whispering. Agnes remained standing, waiting for the old man in front of them to speak. She heard her daughter's faint wails coming from upstairs, and hoped he would tell them whatever he had to say before she started bawling.

He cleared his throat, twisting his cap nervously in his hands. She recognised him as one of the gardeners; Giacomo, if she remembered rightly.

'Please, tell us why you've come,' she said gently.

'It's, ahem... well, Matteo.' He stopped.

'Yes?' She tried to keep calm, knowing that any sign of impatience would make him clam up immediately.

'He-he... oh, to hell with it!' The old man looked mortified at his slip of the tongue in front of the lady of the house. 'He died this morning, just half an hour ago, ma'am.'

She clasped her hands to her chest and swayed as her legs threatened to give way. 'No,' she whispered. 'No, it's not possible.'

Riccardo reached her in two strides and took hold of her outstretched hands, clasping them in his. 'These hands can heal, Agnes, but they can't do miracles,' he told her, understanding her turmoil. 'You can't defeat death.'

She squeezed her eyes shut, tears escaping from beneath her lashes. She fell against his chest, sobbing uncontrollably, scenes of death and destruction flashing before her, the sickly stench of rotting carcasses filling her senses. She was vaguely aware of her daughter's cries in the distance, but all she could hear were her husband's words echoing around her head: *You can't defeat death, Agnes, you can't defeat death.*

The tragedy of losing Matteo weighed heavily on her for a long time afterwards. Agnes threw herself into learning as much from Matilda as she could, adding to the old woman's knowledge with her own successes. And failures. Riccardo bought her a leather journal so she could write everything down meticulously. She wrote as neatly as she could, filling every piece of the precious leaves of paper, careful not to waste any. She was determined to teach her daughter, Isadora, the healers' ways, but was also aware of Filippo's threats to herself and her family. Leaving a written record was essential for those who would come after her, and she often sent silent thanks to Lady Elizabeth for having taken the time to teach her to read and write.

After her experience with Filippo in the woods, she and Matilda had made more protective charms. There were charms strewn all over the cottage, hidden under their mattresses, in amongst their clothes in the wooden coffers, on windowsills, everywhere Agnes could think of. Matilda had given her cuttings of herbs from the patch of ground behind her own cottage, which Agnes had dried and then stored in earthenware jars in the pantry. She couldn't wait to add plants from the Grove, once they were flourishing under her care.

'You seem far away in your thoughts this morning.' Matilda interrupted Agnes's dreams of how the Grove would look in a few months. They were in Matilda's tiny cottage, the old woman busy cutting herbs, the knife flying over the chopping board, missing the tips of her fingers by a miracle, while Isadora lay fast asleep in a crib Bob had made for her, gently sucking on her thumb.

'I was thinking about the Grove, and everything I'll be able to do once the plants take hold,' Agnes replied. 'I want you to teach me all the charms, potions, and cures you know, so I can help people in any possible way.'

'It's important to you, isn't it, lass?' Matilda observed.

Agnes paused, the berries half-mashed in the pestle and mortar before her. 'When Matteo died, I felt so helpless, as if I'd let him down. One day we were joking he wouldn't lose his leg, the next he was dead.'

'You won't save them all, get that thought out of your head straight away,' Matilda said. She went over to the table and sat down next to Agnes. 'Sometimes we have to know when it's the right moment to let go. You must understand this, otherwise you will destroy yourself with taking on the cares of the world.' She reached out and grasped Agnes's hand tightly in her own.

Agnes screamed and pulled her hand back, clutching it to her chest.

'Lass?' Matilda looked at her, bewildered.

'It burns,' Agnes sobbed. She turned her hand, shaking, and

gasped when she saw that her fingertips were bright red, as if she'd scorched them on a boiling pot. 'What–?'

Matilda got to her feet and hobbled over to the shelf that held her herbs, unguents and tonics. She returned to Agnes with a pot containing a thick green salve.

'Here, put some of this on your fingers. It'll help the pain.'

Agnes rubbed the salve into her hands, sighing with relief as the burning sensation passed.

'Do you want to tell me what you saw?'

'What do you mean?' Agnes bowed her head, letting her hair fall over her face. She wanted to forget what she'd seen, what she'd sensed, in that brief moment of contact.

'Look at me.'

Agnes slowly raised her head.

'I know you saw something, I can tell from your eyes. And those burns, they didn't come from nowhere.'

'T-the last few weeks, I've been seeing that darkness... that shadow I told you I saw around Filippo,' Agnes said. 'When I pass the villa, it's as if a cloud has passed over the sun and cast a shadow over the house, leaching all the colour away. It was barely noticeable at first, but now...' She hesitated. 'Now it's as if the villa is covered in filth, a grime that can't be washed away. But that's not all. Coming to your cottage today, I saw it again. Above the roof.'

'Here?' The old woman leaned on the back of the wooden chair, her weathered face suddenly pale. 'What else? What did you see when you touched my hand?'

'It was so fast and confused, I'm not sure.' Agnes clenched her fists, images assailing her.

'Lass, I need to know.'

Agnes's voice trembled as she spoke. 'It was hot, boiling hot, smoke and ash filled the air, and I could smell burning. It was a terrible smell, one I'll never forget.' She blinked rapidly and swallowed. 'And I heard laughter. In the middle of all the smoke and confusion, someone was laughing.'

'Who?'

'I didn't see him, but I sensed the evil that poured out of him. It was Filippo.'

'I knew he was getting stronger, but this...' Matilda's eyes blazed with fury. 'He will destroy your family if we don't–' She went again to the pots of herbs on the shelf and grabbed a couple, mumbling to herself. 'Give me your pouch.'

Agnes pulled the leather cord over her head and placed the pouch on the table. Matilda opened it and added a pinch of herbs from each pot, chanting a spell as she did so. Agnes knew better than to speak while she was working, and waited in silence.

'There, that should do it,' Matilda said finally, standing back and putting her hands on her hips. 'I've added some angelica and mugwort for extra protection, and I'll teach you the spell. I want you to do the same with the pouches for your family, and those around the cottage. This is all I've got, until the plants are ready again.' She tipped the herbs onto a piece of muslin cloth, shaking the pots to get the last pieces out.

'What about you and Bob?' Agnes exclaimed, terror in her heart.

'I'm old enough to look after meself, and the young lad is as sly as a fox. He can get himself out of anything. What worries me more is that the count knows your husband isn't the baby's father. He could make trouble for you with his family.'

'They already hate me, he couldn't make it much worse.'

'You married a nobleman and gave birth to another man's child, while pretending to be a lord's daughter. That would be grounds for a stoning in England. I don't know what they'd do here, but I can't imagine they'll be any more lenient.'

Agnes felt as if the bottom had dropped out of her world.

She glanced at Isadora, fast asleep in the cradle, and fear gripped her.

'You need to provide your husband with another child as soon as possible, so there's no doubt as to who the father is of any of your children,' Matilda continued. 'Now that you are married, you must get with child, so no one can cast doubt over you any longer.' She bustled about, collecting more ingredients.

'What are you doing?' Agnes asked.

'Now we're going to make a charm to help you get with child, make things happen a bit quicker, if we can.' She made two piles of herbs on the table. 'Let's see, raspberry leaves, nettle leaves, dandelions, and clover. You leave them to steep in boiling water, and drink a cup every morning and evening.' She swept one pile onto a piece of cloth, and closed it with a twist before handing it to Agnes. 'And with these, we shall make a fertility charm.'

She opened a coffer and took out some items. Agnes watched, fascinated, as she laid everything on the table. She took a pale green stone with a strange symbol painted on it out of a pouch and placed it in a small bowl of water. Next, she lit a candle.

'Put one hand on the bowl, the other on the candle, lass.' Agnes did as she was told. 'Clear your mind of all thoughts, and concentrate on your husband, your love for him, and your desire for a child. Now repeat after me...'

After Matilda had finished reciting the spell, she sat back on her stool and brushed some wisps of hair away from her face. 'Now you tie the charm around your waist, so it hangs below your belly.'

Agnes blushed.

'Come, you're no shy virgin. Recite the spell in your head before and after you lie with your husband, and believe.'

'I just hope we have time.'

'He is stronger, but if I know anything, he must wait for the full moon. All incantations are more powerful then.'

'One month.' Agnes sighed. It would have to do.

'Warn the lad, tell him to be watchful. And don't let the child out of your sight,' Matilda cautioned.

'Don't worry, I won't.'

'I care about you as if you were my own daughter, Agnes.'

Tears pricked at Agnes's eyes when she heard the old woman use her name. She swiped them away before Matilda could see.

'And you have become a mother to me, Matilda,' Agnes replied. The name sounded strange on her tongue, after all this time she'd avoided using it.

The old woman smiled tenderly at her, but Agnes saw the tears in her eyes too.

39

The warmer spring weather arrived, and Agnes dared to hope that none of her premonitions would come to pass. Following Matilda's instructions, she added the extra protection to the charms around the house and to those of Riccardo and Isadora. She bitterly regretted there wasn't enough of the herbs for Bob and Matilda.

'Agnes, I'm a big lad, I can take care of myself,' Bob told her when they spoke about it. It was true. In the nine months since their arrival in Italy, Bob had grown taller and more robust, his daily exercise with the horses giving him a strength he'd never had before. But he was still young, and she feared for him.

He was quieter now, Agnes thought. His bubbly, childish spirit had given way to a more mature approach of dealing with everything around him. The spirited vivacity that had kept them going during the long voyage at sea surfaced every now and then, making them laugh, but not as often as it used to. Agnes knew that the previous year had taken its toll on all of them, perhaps Bob most of all; his family, home and country taken from him, his young eyes seeing things that no child should have to see. She liked this new Bob as much as the other, but every now and then wished she could turn back the clock and save him the heartache.

'Penny for them?' Bob nudged her, an anxious expression on his face. They were standing in the Dragonfly Grove, Agnes proudly showing off the fruits of her labours. The plant she'd brought all the way from England was flourishing, and there were already new shoots pushing out of the ground around it. Dragonflies flitted around the garden, attracted by the small fountain Riccardo had had built in the middle as a gift after Isadora's birth. Her daughter was sleeping in the cottage under the watchful eye of the nursemaid, Vittoria, the morning sun already too hot for her.

'Matilda told me an interesting story about dragonflies,' Agnes replied. 'She said they came from a huge crack in the earth a long, long time ago, when the world was forming. They flew out in an enormous swarm and completely covered the ground. The people came out of their houses, wailing, "What are we going to do now? We can't plant our crops or feed our animals, how will we live?"

'The dragonflies rose in the air and spoke to the people. "Fear not," they said. "We are here to help you, not destroy you. Listen to our wisdom, and you will learn much from the knowledge we have to give you."

'But the people were afraid and grew angry. They threw stones at the dragonflies and tried to drive them away. The dragonflies were sad, but understood why the people reacted that way. "We will help those who ask us for help," they said, before taking to the skies and disappearing.

'Some people followed them, curious to see what the dragonflies could teach them. They journeyed to a gushing spring at the far ends of the earth, this group of people eager to learn. The dragonflies greeted them with joy, delighted that they wanted their knowledge.

'"We will teach you many things, things you can use to spread our wisdom among your people, without causing fear or anger," they told those gathered before them. "You will leave us as different people, with a connection to other worlds that exist without your knowledge. The fairies and sprites, elves and gnomes, all will become your friends and allies, helping you in times of need. You will be able to speak with spirits from the other world, people who are dear to you, others who have a message to pass on. You will learn to adapt to this new world we will introduce you to, it will change your vision and fill you with joy.

'"As you explore these new realms, it will become clear what is an illusion and what is real, in all aspects of your life. Your emotions, your empathy, your sense of *being* will change, and so will you. This knowledge will remain inside you and be passed from generation to generation, never to be lost, an oasis of hope among the rest of humanity."

'The people clapped their hands in delight and were eager to begin their lessons. But the dragonflies had a warning for them. "There will be some among you who will use this knowledge to gain power, to gain control over others. This is inevitable, it is a part of human nature, as we sadly know. You shake your heads, but it will happen. And when it does, we have faith that the others will make sure they do not succeed. And those others shall be called healers."

'The group remained by the spring for many years, following the teachings of the dragonflies, until they could finally rejoin their families. They spoke not a word about their absence, but their knowledge was indeed passed to each generation, right up to today.'

Agnes paused. 'Matilda says that she and I come from that group, and that I have a knowledge inside me I need to reach in order to become a true healer. And that the plant I brought from

England, the plant dear Ted showed me that day in the woods, is the secret to obtaining the knowledge.'

Bob stared at her, his mouth open. 'You mean, you come from those... those *healers*?'

Agnes smiled at his confusion. 'It would appear so. She says the knowledge often lies dormant for many years, and sometimes the healer dies without ever knowing the gift they had. Others are frightened by it and refuse to acknowledge it, preferring ignorance. But the gift carries on regardless, passing to their children, until it can surface once more and be used for good. Or bad.'

'Like Filippo?'

'Yes. Like Filippo.' Agnes sighed. 'We really need to decide how to–' She was interrupted by shouting in the distance.

They both looked up, and gasped. Thick clouds of smoke billowed above the treetops, filling the clear blue sky with swirling grey clouds. Thoughts raced through Agnes's mind as she desperately tried to remember what lay in that direction.

'Matilda!' Bob shouted.

They took off at a run, Agnes holding up the ends of her tunic to avoid tripping as they ran through the woods towards the old woman's cottage. Her breath came in small gasps as she pushed branches out of her way and brambles ripped at her clothes and skin. The air became denser as they drew closer, making it more difficult to breathe. They burst into the clearing, where a terrible sight met them.

The cottage was engulfed in orange flames hungrily devouring the wooden walls, reaching high into the sky with long, flickering fingers. Several people were holding pails of water, looking on helplessly as the fire consumed the cottage.

'Matilda!' Agnes screamed, running towards the inferno. A man caught her by the waist, stopping her abruptly.

'Lady Agnes, you can't go there,' he said sternly.

She writhed in his grip, almost out of her mind with fear. 'Let me go!' she shouted, hitting out at him. 'Matilda... we have to save her.'

'Lady Agnes, I cannot permit you to go in there,' he said, grasping her more firmly. 'No one can save her if she's inside. Look!'

Agnes stopped wriggling, and watched as the fire reached the roof. With an almighty roar, the building collapsed in on itself, sending clouds of smoke and ash into the air.

40

Everyone moved back, coughing as smoke wafted over them. The roar of the fire seemed to become a deep chuckling to Agnes, low at first, then gradually growing louder, until it turned into the rumbling sound of laughter. She looked wildly around her, wondering if the others noticed it, but they were all intent on watching the destructive progress of the flames. The sound echoed around her head, filling her with horror. And then it became once more the rushing, crackling noise of hungry flames devouring everything in their path.

'Matilda.' Agnes collapsed to her knees, sobbing, as the fire continued its work of destruction. Bob knelt beside her, putting his arm around her shoulders, and she leaned against him, weeping with grief. Her distress gradually turned into anger as she realised who was responsible.

'Aye, lass, he's powerful enough now. The moon is full, he will perform the ceremony tonight.'

Agnes sat up at the sound of the old woman's voice. *Matilda? She hadn't been in the cottage after all!* She turned, her arms open wide to embrace her friend, only to be met by an empty nothingness. She searched desperately, confused.

'Lass, I have to go now, my time has come. We will meet again someday, never fear. Remember my teachings, do only good with the gift you have, and pass your knowledge on to your daughter and her daughters. Your family, the Innocenti, will be a great family indeed.'

Matilda's voice faded towards the end to a whisper, and then it was gone. The fire crackled fiercely as it consumed the last of the cottage, the servants having thrown water all around the area so that nothing else would burn.

'Agnes?' Bob tugged at her sleeve.

'She said goodbye,' Agnes whispered, tears rolling down her cheeks. He squeezed her hand, blinking back his own tears.

'Agnes! What in God's name happened here?' Riccardo strode towards her and crushed her in his arms, worry etched on his face.

She opened her mouth to speak, but her face crumpled as she burst into tears once more, the traumatic events suddenly hitting her.

'It's Matilda's cottage, it's burnt down,' Bob said when Agnes didn't speak.

'I can see that,' Riccardo retorted.

'She was still in there.'

'Ah. Oh, Agnes, I'm so sorry.' His tone grew softer. 'How?'

'Your brother,' she spat with sudden venom, so full of hate that Riccardo took a step backwards. '*He* is the cause of this.'

'That's a harsh accusation, Agnes.'

She glared at him. 'It's the truth.'

'I believe you. I will speak with the family about it, I promise. They will know what to do.'

'They won't be able to stop him, he is too strong now. He's determined to destroy you, destroy *us*. Don't you see?'

'Perhaps you're being a little overdramatic,' Riccardo said.

'Overdramatic? Matilda is *dead*, if you hadn't noticed. Who's next? How much do you trust your brother?'

Riccardo stared at her, shocked. 'He wouldn't harm us,' he said firmly, as if trying to convince himself more than her.

'Let's go home, I have something to tell you about your precious brother.' Tiredness crashed over Agnes, making her knees buckle, and she held on to her husband's arm to stop herself from falling. 'Bob, you help the others here. And if you find Matilda... make sure they dig her a grave. We owe her at least that.'

'Don't worry, I'll take care of everything.' He gave her a final hug, then dashed back to the burnt ruins of Matilda's cottage.

'First I have to check on Isadora, then we'll talk.' She held on to Riccardo as they left the clearing.

Satisfied that Isadora was fast asleep in her cradle, Agnes sat down on their bed and told Riccardo about the dragonfly legend, his brother, and what it meant for the future of his family. Unable to sit still, he paced backwards and forwards, his brow furrowed as he listened. When she got to the part about his sister, he stumbled and almost fell, but he remained silent until she had finished.

Agnes watched him as he strode around the room, wishing he would say something, anything. Her heart ached for him, for the thoughts that must be going around his head at this moment. Finally he sat down beside her, the mattress sagging under their combined weight.

'My brother – I will never say his name again, may he rot in hell – how did he come to this?' Riccardo asked Agnes, hurt and pain etched on his face. 'How could he stray so far from us, his family, the church?' His voice trailed off and an enormous groan escaped from his throat.

'The legend talks about good and bad coming from the drag-onflies' teachings,' Agnes said, taking hold of his hand and caressing it. 'I believe that F– your brother – learned from the wise woman, Fiammetta, who lived in Matilda's cottage before we came, and she paid a high price for teaching him. He has gone too far, and will not stop until he has what he wants.'

'You.' Riccardo shook his head in disbelief. 'Why? Is he so envious of me that he must steal my wife?'

'He knows about my gift,' Agnes said softly. She gazed into his amber eyes, lit with golden flecks, pools of molten lava where she drowned in his love every time she looked at him. 'He will use it to become the most powerful man in Italy, more powerful than the Pope, even.'

Riccardo shuddered. 'That must never happen. He clearly is not sane of mind, he will wreak havoc wherever he goes.'

'Tonight there will be a full moon. The time is ripe for him. He has already killed Matilda, I am afraid of what he will do next.'

Riccardo stroked her cheek. 'Then we must stop him. Tonight.'

'How?' she whispered.

Riccardo thought, drumming his fingers on his thighs. 'We cannot tell Mamma and my brothers, they will not believe us. The servants will follow him if they have to choose.' He stood up and began to pace once again. 'We must ask Bob to help us,' he said eventually, avoiding Agnes's eyes.

'No!'

'It's the only way, Agnes. Bob is the only person faithful to us, and the only person I would trust with my life. I will do every-thing I can to protect him.'

'As will I,' Agnes replied. She thought over everything Matilda had taught her, determined to find a charm and a spell that would protect her, Riccardo, and Bob that evening, whatever happened. 'I have much work to do.' She went over to the cradle and looked down upon her sleeping daughter. 'Isadora, at least, will be safe here. We will tell Vittoria to stay with her until morning.'

Riccardo tilted her head towards his. 'No harm will come to either you or Isadora, I promise,' he said, kissing her.

Agnes relaxed against him, taking comfort from his embrace. She noticed he hadn't included Bob in his promise.

41

The afternoon passed slowly. The air was hot and heavy, laden with the threat of a thunderstorm. The servants went about their business half-heartedly, their movements slow and clumsy in the stifling atmosphere. Agnes lay on the bed, watching Isadora, who was playing with her feet and gurgling happily. She was desperately going over everything Matilda had taught her in the last few months, making a mental list of the plants she needed to make the spells that would protect them all. She groaned inwardly at the holes in her knowledge – Matilda had still had so much to teach her when she died.

She prayed to the spirits and the fairies, the sprites and the elves, to help her fight the evil that was threatening her family. Her eyelids grew heavy as a glowing light filled her head. An image of Ted's Dragonfly Grove appeared before her, exactly as she had seen it the last time she'd been there. The stream rushing over its pebbly bed, the carpet of flowers humming with bees, the ancient trees bending their branches towards her, and the mysterious plants that had become a part of her healing lore... the plants, with their silvery leaves and berries, dragonflies swarming above them... the plants... the plants...

Agnes stood, her eyes wide open as she realised what she had to do. Calling Vittoria, she quickly pulled on her tunic over her linen undergarment and gathered her things. She waited impatiently until the girl arrived, her face sweating as she ran into the room.

'Stay with Isadora, don't let her out of your sight,' Agnes ordered. She left without another word, leaving the nursemaid staring at her in bemusement.

Agnes made her way down to the pantry and took her basket off its hook on the wall. She picked up jars of dried herbs and berries, knowing instinctively which ones to take, and placed them in the basket. She took down bunches of freshly cut plants hanging from the edges of the shelves, their fragrance filling the air as she bruised the leaves in her haste.

She closed the pantry door and went into the kitchen. The scullery maid, Olivia, was sitting at the table, gnawing on a crust of bread.

'Lady Agnes!' she squeaked in fright, dropping the bread. She stood up, her head bowed.

Agnes didn't have time to tell her off. She put her basket on the table and took out the jars and plants, lining them up before her. She glanced up at Olivia and smiled.

'I've got something you can help me with.'

'Yes, Lady Agnes, of course. Anything.' The relief on the scullery maid's face was clear to see.

'We'll talk about your behaviour later,' she added. *If there is a later.* She ignored the maid's crestfallen face and told her what to do.

Agnes wearily raised her head when Riccardo entered the cottage a few hours later, and giggled as he looked around him in amazement. She and Olivia were at the table, their faces beaded with sweat, surrounded by pans of every shape and size filled with steaming liquid. A sweet perfume permeated the house, the delicate fragrance of berries, fruits and herbs mixing with the more acrid odour of boiled bark and other mysterious substances.

'You've been busy, Agnes,' he said, gesturing at the pots and pans.

She noticed his hesitance and wondered, briefly, if he believed she were a witch. She pushed the thought firmly from her mind.

'I'll tell you what it's for later,' she replied, glancing at the maid next to her. 'Where have you been?'

'I went to the stables to speak with Bob, but he wasn't there. I left a message to tell him to come here as soon as he can.' Riccardo turned to Olivia. 'Go, and tell everyone to stay inside the cottage until tomorrow morning, no matter what happens.'

'But–'

'Whoever disobeys my order will be sent away, and their family banished with them. Do I make myself clear?'

She curtsied and ran from the room.

'Sometimes you have to be cruel to be kind,' he muttered, rubbing his eyes.

'No doubt she'll be telling the others I'm a witch and you're under my spell,' Agnes said, attempting to laugh but failing. Her shoulders and neck ached, and her body was so tense she wondered if she'd ever be able to relax again.

'You look tired.'

'I am, but after tonight it will all be over,' she replied, making the sign against the devil behind her back.

He buried his face in her hair, breathing in the heady mixture of aromas from the plants she had been working with. 'I hope so.'

They went outside together and sat down on the back

doorstep, the basket full of Agnes's concoctions in front of them. Riccardo leaned over and picked up a large jug. He pulled out the stopper and inhaled. A bitter odour wafted out, making him cough. He hastily put the stopper back in and replaced it in the basket.

'I hope you don't want us to drink that! I know you mean well, but that is...' He wrinkled his nose and grimaced.

'Don't worry, it's not for drinking. We need to sprinkle it around us, in a circle, while I say the incantation.'

'Thank goodness.' Riccardo heaved a sigh of relief. 'Although, perhaps you could throw it over my brother. The smell alone would stop him.'

'If only it could be that simple,' Agnes said.

Thunder rumbled far away in the distance, and the air was more stifling than ever.

'I hope this storm breaks.' She wiped away a bead of sweat from her upper lip.

'It's unusual weather for this time of year.' Riccardo gazed at the grey sky, frowning. 'It will come from over there, when it does break.' He pointed at a mountain, its summit barely visible through the black, low-hanging clouds.

Dusk arrived early. They could hear the servants inside, preparing the evening meal, but neither of them could face eating anything. They remained where they were; nobody came out to bother them, after Riccardo's threat.

'Where are the birds?' Agnes asked all of a sudden.

'What?'

'The birds. The sky is usually full of them at this time, gorging on insects before going home to roost. There aren't any this evening.'

'It's been so hot today, they probably haven't got the energy,' Riccardo replied, but he looked around uneasily. The garden was strangely silent. Even the crickets weren't making their customary concert among the bushes.

Agnes leaned her head on his shoulder. The sky grew steadily darker. Night always fell quickly in the mountains. It never failed to surprise her how it could be light one moment, then dark the next. A breeze ruffled her hair, giving slight relief from the sticky heat of the day.

The moon appeared in the sky, its brightness casting sharp black shadows around them. Agnes gazed upon it, fascinated by its majestic presence. It was so large she felt as if she could almost reach out and touch its cold surface. A wolf howled in the distance, making her shiver.

'Do you think...?' Agnes began.

'My brother may be many things, but he's not a werewolf. A lunatic, yes, but nothing more.'

She turned towards him. His face looked grim in the moon-light. 'I didn't intend...'

'I know.'

She was about to say more when she heard a humming sound coming from the garden. Looking up, she saw a cloud of dragonflies heading towards them, their wings glinting with silver sparks of moonlight, like a fairy trail left in the sky.

'What's that?' Riccardo exclaimed, leaping to his feet. Agnes slowly stood up, her heart beating wildly. The dragonflies reached them, the humming vibration of their wings throbbing in her ears, transmitting the insects' urgency to her. She grabbed her basket.

'The Grove!' she shouted to her husband. She took him by the hand, pulling him with her, and they both ran towards her beloved herb garden, dreading what they would find once inside.

Disorientated, they stopped at the entrance of the Grove, breathing heavily. The cloud of dragonflies dispersed, leaving behind a deathly silence. Agnes searched frantically for whatever had caused the disturbance. The fruit trees cast heavy black shadows across the ground, perfect for hiding someone.

Riccardo tugged on her elbow. 'There,' he said, his voice low.

Filippo was standing beside the fountain, his arm around Bob's neck. Agnes saw the unmoving bodies of dragonflies spread over the white marble, others floating on the surface of the water. Now she understood what had disturbed the insects, and why they had come to warn her.

As Agnes and Riccardo walked towards them, she noticed the dark shadow of a bruise on the side of Bob's face, and saw his eyes were half-rolled up in his head. There were scuff marks on the ground, as though he had struggled before being overcome.

'Riccardo, brother. I'm glad you came.' Filippo shifted his feet, compensating for Bob's weight leaning against him, and Agnes gasped as she saw the metal blade of a dagger against the boy's throat.

'You're no brother of mine.' Riccardo stood still, arms folded across his chest, his face stern.

'I see your lovely wife has been talking about me,' Filippo said with a laugh.

'Let the boy go,' Riccardo ordered.

'Who, Bob? But he and I have been getting on so well, we're good friends now.' Filippo shook Bob's shoulders, making the boy groan. 'Besides, I'll be needing him soon. The time is almost ripe.'

'What do you want?'

Agnes blinked, surprised at how steady Riccardo's voice was; she was trembling all over, her legs suddenly weak. She put down her basket, unable to hold it any longer.

'I think you know. I see you've brought your potions, Agnes, but you may as well leave them there on the ground. They won't be of any use to you. Not tonight.'

Riccardo stepped in front of Agnes, shielding her from his brother's sight. 'What's so special about tonight? Are you so deluded that you think you have magical powers, just because there's a full moon?'

Agnes quickly bent over her basket and slipped some pouches of herbs up the sleeves of her tunic while they talked.

'You may sneer, brother, but the witch taught me many things before she died.'

'Before you sent her to her death, you mean,' Riccardo interrupted.

'Our family was heading towards ruin before I took over,' Filippo said, ignoring him. 'Our father wasn't very good at running things, throwing away money by sending you all over Europe to buy those damn horses while here the crops were rotting in the fields. All he cared about was the horses. It's ironic, if you think about it; falling from his horse and breaking his neck when it got spooked like that. But luckily I was around to take over and save the family from further embarrassment.'

'You?' Riccardo took a step forward, his fists clenched.

'It was for the good of the family, brother. Like sending Rossella to the village saved us from the plague. No one here got sick, did they? Our family is wealthy, and more powerful than it has ever been, isn't it? So, dear brother, I don't *think* I've got magical powers, I *know* I've got magical powers. And if you opened your eyes, you'd see that your English wife has them too.'

'Agnes is special, yes, but she is nothing like you,' Riccardo snapped.

'Insult me all you like. You and your children will be cursed from now to eternity, to live in poverty and hatred, while I, Filippo Innocenti, Conte di Gallicano, will spit upon the ground you walk on. That's why the curse had to be cast here, in this paradise Agnes has created. Poetic justice. Very appropriate, don't you think?'

'You hate me so much?'

'Hate you? No, this isn't personal, brother. The witch showed me my future, what I will become. Fate, destiny, God's will, call it what you want, this must happen.'

Agnes stood behind her husband, quietly reciting the incantations Matilda had taught her, calling upon every being she could think of to help them. Vague shadows fluttered at the edges of her vision, but when she turned her head they dissolved into nothingness, only to reappear as she looked away.

'Don't you see how crazy this is?' Riccardo said, spreading his arms wide. 'Magic spells, curses, the full moon. How can all this be real?'

Filippo raised his eyes to the moon as he held Bob, the boy's body slumped against him. 'Enough. It is time.'

gnes grasped Riccardo's arm, alarmed. He motioned to
her to remain behind him. Filippo thrust Bob upright,
and with a deft movement drew the dagger across the boy's
throat. A thin, red line appeared, then blood gushed from the
wound. He threw Bob to the ground, where the boy lay, gasping
feebly as his life's blood drained from him.

Agnes screamed, fighting to escape from her husband's grip
as Filippo crouched beside Bob. He held up the dagger in the
moonlight, the blade glinting wickedly, then ran it across his
palm. The wound bled immediately, huge red drops falling to
the ground and mixing with Bob's blood, soaking down into the
earth.

Filippo spoke, his voice low at first, then rising to a
crescendo as he recited the curse.

'*My blood for revenge, a plague on my brother's family, misfortune, disaster and death...*'

Agnes could see the madness in his eyes as he uttered the
words, and shuddered. 'You must do something, Riccardo,' she
whispered.

Her husband turned to her, tears glistening on his cheeks.

'That it must come to this,' he said, his voice breaking. He strode towards his brother, still crouched beside Bob's lifeless body, and Agnes saw a short sword tucked in his belt, behind his back. Filippo looked up at him and smiled.

'It is too late. The curse is set in motion, there is nothing you can do now.'

Agnes grabbed the jug with the bitter concoction, removed the stopper with her teeth, and followed her husband.

'I can kill you.' Riccardo looked down at his brother, hatred on his face.

Filippo's expression changed. His eyes grew narrower and his mouth contracted in a roar that revealed sharp, pointed teeth. Thunder rumbled above them, closer now, and the first draughts of air began to rush through the trees all around them. Riccardo took a step back as his brother stood, brandishing the dagger he'd cut Bob's throat with, dark liquid glistening on its blade.

Agnes poured the concoction on the ground, creating a wide circle around them, and called on the moon, the sprites, and the spirits to help them.

Filippo leapt at Riccardo, his lips raised in a snarl, aiming for his brother's throat. He crashed into him, sending him flying back towards the edge of the circle. As Riccardo lay stunned, Filippo lifted his hand, the dagger held point down, and lunged at him.

With a grunt, Riccardo rolled to one side and the dagger plunged harmlessly into the ground, right up to the handle. As Filippo tugged to free it, Riccardo bowled into his side, knocking him down. He threw himself on top of Filippo and the brothers rolled over and over, a confused tangle of limbs, one grunting, the other snarling.

Agnes screamed, and doubled her efforts in reciting the incantation, the dull thud of fists hitting flesh striking terror into her heart. The dagger remained buried in the earth, forgotten, as the two men hit each other. She caught a glimpse of Riccardo's bloodied head as he scrambled to get away. Filippo reached out with a clawed hand and grabbed at his brother's leg, trying to pull him back. Riccardo lashed out with his foot, striking Filippo in the stomach, and crawled away on his hands and knees, sweat and blood pouring from his face. He scrabbled desperately for the sword in his belt, shouting in triumph as he drew it out. He turned, panting, and held the sword in front of him.

As he faced his brother, shadowy figures suddenly appeared within the circle. They swept over Riccardo, ignoring him, and hurtled towards Filippo. He stopped, a confused expression on his face, as the figures surrounded him, hiding him from view.

'Get out of the circle!' Agnes shouted, running towards her husband. Riccardo turned and looked at her, desperation on his face, as high-pitched screams came from the swirling wall of shadows behind him.

Agnes stopped. 'Help him,' she whispered, tears streaming down her face.

A glittery stream of lights flashed past her, entering the circle she'd created. They swarmed around Riccardo, enveloping him in a whirling twist of dazzling light, and guided him out of the circle. He fell to the ground with a heavy thump, and Agnes ran to him.

They sat together, arms around each other, as the lights went back into the circle and joined the shadowy mass. Filippo's screams had diminished to soft sobs, muffled by the crushing force of shade and light.

Agnes raised her face to the moon, basking in its cold glow, feeling its force and energy flowing into her body. She could see as clearly as if it were daylight, perhaps more, and the pulse of the world around her beat in time with her own heart. She was connected with the ground, the trees, the plants, the insects and animals. Every movement, every blade of grass fluttering in the breeze, every whisper carried on the wind, poured into her and touched her soul. She shuddered as she felt Filippo's life leave his body, his final breath drifting away in the night air.

She turned to the circle. The shadows were gone, and Filippo was lying immobile on the ground. The expression on his face would haunt her dreams for many years to come, his muscles rigid with terror, as though he wore a grotesque death mask.

The lights hovered in the air above him, calling her. 'The curse. I have to remove the curse,' Agnes said to Riccardo. She pulled herself from his grip, as reluctant to let him go as he was her, and stepped within the circle.

She pulled the pouches from her tunic sleeves and emptied their contents over the ground, and over Bob's and Filippo's bodies. Stretching her arms up into the air, her sleeves falling back so that her arms were bare, she turned to the moon and began to chant.

Low at first, her voice steadily grew louder, the words forming lilting notes as she sang. A dragonfly flitted above her, its wings glittering in the silver light as it circled her head. Others arrived, and more again, until her head, shoulders and arms were hidden beneath their jewelled bodies. Still more flew to her, fluttering in the air, the vibrating hum of their wings in tune with her song, until the whole Grove reverberated with their harmony. White shadows drifted across the ground, wispy shapes that changed form as they moved, like clouds in a stormy sky. They created a wall of mist around Agnes, billowing in and out with the cool breeze that was steadily getting stronger, a precursor of the storm on its way.

The little dots of light flashed around her, leaving sparkling trails behind them. Agnes raised her voice, feeling energy flow into her from the moon, the dragonflies, the spirits and the fairies. Her chant changed, and she recited an ancient language she had never heard before, her mouth forming the words as though she had spoken them all her life. She stretched her arms as far as possible, reaching to touch the moon with her fingertips, while chanting the final words. The light from the moon glowed brightly, illuminating the ground all around as she spoke. Then her voice faded away and she stood with her head bowed, her energy spent. She lowered her hands and the dragonflies flew into the air. She stood motionless as the shadows dispersed, until she and Riccardo were alone in the Grove once more.

She turned to Riccardo, afraid of his reaction. He was on his feet, staring at her wide-eyed, his face pale in the moonlight.

'I...' she said, then stumbled, her legs buckling beneath her.

In a few strides he was there, holding her close to him, kissing her hair, her cheeks, her mouth, his tears mingling with hers. She clung to him, her body shaking after the tremendous effort.

'It was incredible,' he murmured in her ear. 'In all my life, I would never have imagined to see something like that. Matilda was right – you have a gift.'

'It wasn't enough.' Agnes sobbed against his chest.

'What?'

'The curse was too strong.' She lifted her head and took several deep breaths. 'I couldn't remove it.'

'Come and sit down,' Riccardo said gently, leading her over to the fountain. They sat on its edge, the smooth marble cool against their skin. He pulled Agnes to face him, so that she couldn't see the two corpses a short distance away.

Agnes trailed her hand in the water, silver drops cascading from her fingertips. 'I don't know why, but I had a feeling he might come here this evening. If I'd known what he had in mind, I'd have–' She put her head in her hands, reliving the nightmare.

'You couldn't have foreseen all this, Agnes,' Riccardo said, smoothing her hair.

'Bob...' She couldn't go on, her heart breaking at the thought of his sacrifice.

'He will have an honourable burial,' Riccardo replied. 'I know it will never repay what happened to him, but he will never be forgotten. His death wasn't in vain, Agnes.'

'How can you say that?' she shouted, anger surging through her body. 'Matilda, Bob, your father, your *sister*... so many lives lost, and for what? So that your brother could become more powerful? So that your family could rule over this area, and eventually the whole of Italy? How can that justify their deaths?' She stopped, her chest heaving, waiting for her husband to reply.

His shoulders slumped. 'I don't know the answers,' he said sadly. 'But you and I met for a reason, on board the ship, and you came here to... what, help me? Was it preordained in the stars? Was it our destiny? My brother was already lost, and without you our family would have been destroyed by him. How many more would have died if you had not been here tonight?'

Agnes sniffed and wiped her nose with the back of her hand. 'But the curse–'

'We will live with the curse, if needs be,' Riccardo said. 'Whatever happens after this, we will get through it.'

'I tried so hard, we *all* tried, but it was too strong. The blood sacrifice; he knew what he was doing. A friend, a good person, he needed that blood to strengthen the curse. Damn him!'

'Agnes.' Riccardo reached out for her hands. 'You did your best.'

'I managed to weaken the curse. I–' She recalled the dragon-flies and shadows that had surrounded her and corrected herself. 'We called upon the moon to help us. He thought the full moon was necessary for his dark magic, but it is not so. Matilda taught me that the full moon is used in many healing spells. Its energy heals, it doesn't destroy.'

'That song?'

'It was an incantation, to help heal the land. A b-blood sacrifice is strong, but we used the moisture in the ground to wash away the blood, and the curse.'

'Go on.'

'Something has remained. Some evil that got into the ground from your brother's blood. We couldn't penetrate the ground around it. He must have put a protective charm on it.'

'What does that mean for us? For our family?'

Agnes rested her head on Riccardo's shoulder, exhausted. 'It means that anyone could succumb to its influence, if they are weak or are already so inclined. It will enter their bodies, their minds, and gradually take over, until either they are driven mad or fall under its spell. We must be vigilant, Riccardo, and take care not to let this happen.

'I will teach Isadora the ways of the healers, and she will teach her children, and so forth, for every generation that is to come. We will do good here, and not let the evil out of the ground. We will become healers. That is how I intend to honour Matilda, Bob, and all the others who have died. This I swear to you, to the plants here in the Grove, to the dragonflies, and to *her*.' She raised her eyes to the moon above them. 'And to our unborn child,' she added, almost in a whisper. She felt Riccardo's body jerk beneath her head, but he didn't say anything. He put his arm around her and they remained there in silence, under the watchful eye of the moon.

43

1360

The young girl crouched down next to the plant, studying it carefully before choosing which leaves to pick. As her fingers pinched each leaf from the stem, she said a brief prayer of thanks before putting it in her basket. She repeated the action time and again, until her basket was filled with sweet-smelling herbs.

'Is this enough, Mamma?' she asked, turning to the woman watching her.

'It's perfect, Isadora,' Agnes replied. 'Now, what else do we need to add?'

Her daughter rattled off the list of ingredients they needed for their cordials and ointments. Agnes had perfected the recipes over the years, writing each one down in the leather-bound book Riccardo had given to her all those years before. She had insisted that her children were taught to read and write from an early age, terrified that she would die before she could pass on her knowledge. The twins, Alfredo and Guglielmo, weren't interested, but Isadora had followed in her mother's footsteps as soon as she could walk. They had spent many hours together in the Dragonfly Grove, Isadora listening, enthralled, as Agnes explained each plant to her and how to use it.

Now eleven years of age, she could easily find any plant Agnes asked for, and knew how to look after each one. She loved to read through her mother's recipe book, and had added some drawings of the plants on each page. Agnes had taught her daughter, just as Matilda had taught her. Isadora had been an eager student, quickly learning the ways of the healers.

Agnes was glad. Her bones ached most of the time, the cordial she drank no longer effective against the pains that racked her all day long. The night she had tried to remove the curse had taken its toll on her body, leaving her feeling as old as Matilda. She found it difficult to bend down and pick the ingredients she needed, and relied more and more often on her daughter's help.

She glanced over at Isadora, smiling at the sun glinting off her braided blonde hair. Ted's hair. She had never said anything to Riccardo, but her daughter took after her father, from her snub nose to her quick-witted humour. She knew that he must see it, but he had never said anything to her. In his eyes, Isadora was his daughter, nothing more, nothing less. Agnes loved him even more for it, and knew how lucky she had been to find him. *Was it luck or destiny?* she mused.

'Mamma?' Isadora's voice broke into her thoughts, making her jump. 'I have everything, we can go now.'

'All right, let's go and get ready.' Agnes took hold of her daughter's arm, leaning on it as they went back to the house.

Riccardo stood with his head bowed as the priest recited his liturgy. The boys shuffled their feet next to him, itching to go back to running through the woods. Agnes glared at them and they stood still, grinning and nudging each other. Isadora had placed the bouquet on top of the grave, the mixture of sweet perfumes filling the air. Lavender, sage, and rosemary were some of the flowers in the bouquet they placed on Bob's grave near the river, while the priest said his prayers. Riccardo had said that they would honour Bob's death, and they did so, without fail, every year. Agnes visited his grave regularly, keeping it free of weeds, cleaning the marble headstone, and talking to him whenever she felt the need. Over the years, he had helped her solve many problems, listening while she spoke, guiding her thoughts to the correct solution.

Her mind wandered back to those terrible times as the priest droned on, his voice lulling her to sleep. She and Riccardo had sat in the Dragonfly Grove until dawn, when they had risen stiffly and gone indoors to tell the servants to take care of the two bodies. Then they had gone up to the villa, where Riccardo had broken the news of his brother's death to his mother. She had fainted from shock and never fully recovered. Six weeks after Filippo's funeral, the contessa had joined him in the family mausoleum, her heart having given out from grief.

Bob's funeral had been a quiet occasion, with only Agnes, Riccardo and a sleeping Isadora present. The priest had protested against burying him in unconsecrated ground, until Agnes had taken him aside and spoken quietly, but firmly, to him. Since then, he had been wary of her, but carried out her wishes in a dignified manner.

While Riccardo's younger brother Umberto had taken over the running of the family estate, Riccardo and Agnes remained in the cottage. She had become renowned as a healer, and people from all over the valley and mountains journeyed to the cottage for her remedies and cures.

Riccardo worked the land, enjoying the manual labour and working with the locals. While the rest of his family remained aloof, he befriended many of the labourers and would often invite them to the cottage for some of his wife's home-made ale. Agnes was proud of her husband, glad he accepted her less than noble origins, and that he embraced her way of life.

The twins had been born eight months after that terrible night. They had been two bundles of energy right from the start, hardly sleeping for the first year. Agnes had felt permanently exhausted, with a toddler to run around after and two screaming newborns. But they had all survived, somehow. She grimaced as she watched them, making faces at each other while the priest slowly arrived at the ceremony's conclusion. She loved her children dearly, but sometimes her sons worried her. No, not worried. They *scared* her. Her heart jolted as she finally admitted something she'd been holding inside for a long time. She gasped as her heart suddenly pounded in her chest, her muscles contracting in pain, until the sensation passed as suddenly as it had come. She raised her head and found Alfredo staring at her. He smirked, then turned to his brother and whispered something, nudging him. Agnes clenched her fists tightly. She may be weaker, but she still had some fight in her. She was determined her sons would not succumb to the evil Filippo had left behind, however long it took.

44

1365–1370

'What are you working on now, Mamma?' Isadora peered curiously over her mother's shoulder at the tapestry on the small loom standing on the low table in front of her. Agnes looked up from her work, frowning at the disturbance, then relaxed when she saw her daughter's inquisitive face. It seemed only yesterday she'd taught her how to tend the plants in the Grove, and now she was a woman of sixteen, about to marry Niccolò.

'This is the village where I used to live in England,' Agnes said, showing Isadora the intricately woven picture she had started working on. She sat back and flexed her fingers, bent from the rheumatism that afflicted her.

Isadora pulled up a chair and sat next to Agnes. 'It looks beautiful. Where's your house?'

'Here.' Agnes pointed at the manor house in the background, surrounded by forest. 'I was maid to Lady Elizabeth Funteyn. She was the same age as me, and we had lots of fun together. She was the one who taught me to read and write.'

'And this?' Isadora pointed at a tall tree trunk, gaily decorated with bright ribbons and with children dancing around it.

'That's what we did on May Day. Lady Elizabeth gave us the ribbons, we tied them to the trunk, and then we danced around it, weaving in and out of one another until it was completely covered. Then we chose the May king and queen.' She pointed at two tiny thrones nearby. 'They were crowned with a wreath and led the festivities.'

'The thrones are empty, though, Mamma.'

'That's because the dance has to finish first.'

'Were you ever a May queen?' Isadora asked.

Agnes felt tears prick at her eyes. 'Once, only the once.'

'And who was the king?'

Agnes shook her head. 'That's enough, Isadora. Not now. I need to concentrate on my work.'

'Sorry, Mamma. I didn't mean to upset you.' Her daughter stood up. 'I'll let you get back to it.'

Agnes held up her hand. 'It's all right. I want to get it finished before...' Her voice trailed away. 'Would you pass me those threads over on the table? My knees hurt so much today.'

'Of course, Mamma.' Isadora handed her the tray. 'Weren't those the ones you left soaking in some concoction the other day?'

Agnes took the tray and picked up a bright yellow thread. 'Hmm?' she asked, her thoughts elsewhere.

'Never mind. I'll leave you to work now,' Isadora replied, and left the room.

Agnes leaned back with a sigh. The idea had come to her a few weeks earlier, during a visit to Bob's grave. She needed to leave something behind, something to tell her story, something that could break the rest of the curse. Something that would survive the passing of time, impregnated with the juice of the plant from the Dragonfly Grove, its magic transmitting her message to a future healer.

That was when she'd thought of a tapestry. She could soak

the threads in a brew made from the silver leaf plant and use them to weave the magic into her story, impressing each image with her memories and feelings. She'd taken the dry threads in her right hand and images had flashed through her mind – May Day, sitting on her throne beside Ted, proudly wearing her wreath, giggling as the others stepped forward to pay homage to them, even Lady Elizabeth curtseying before her; the Dragonfly Grove in the forest, with the limpid waters of the gurgling stream rushing through the clearing over its stony bed, dragonflies flitting above their heads as she and Ted made love; finding Bob in the stable when she thought she was all alone, everyone else dead from the plague, and her relief when he got better; Constance, dear, sweet Constance, who took them in and gave them her love when no one else would...

Tears streamed down her cheeks as the memories tumbled through her mind, jostling each other in their rush to be included in the tapestry. She held them back, berating them for their impatience, telling them that each one would be woven into the fabric in due time. Her pains forgotten, she bent over the loom, lost in a faraway world that only she could see.

It took her the best part of five years, working on it in every spare moment, but Agnes finally finished the tapestry. She straightened her back, wincing as her muscles protested painfully, and gazed upon her creation, glad it was over at long last. The tapestry depicted the two parts of her life – on the right, Forest Brook in England, with tiny figures of the people she had loved there; on the left, the villa, nestled in the mountains above Gallicano, with the cottage, the Dragonfly Grove, and the woods around them. But, even though she'd used the same brightly coloured threads, the left side seemed darker somehow, and she was afraid to touch it.

'Good morning, Mamma. How is Papà today?' Isadora stepped through the door, groaning as she sat down at the kitchen table.

Agnes looked at her daughter's swollen stomach, and prayed it would be a girl this time. 'Oh, you know. Same as yesterday, and the day before. The pain's getting worse lately.' Riccardo had been in bed for the last two weeks, the tumour consuming him on the inside, causing atrocious pains that made him cry out. 'And you? It's not long to go now, is it? I can see little one is eager to enter the world.'

Isadora grimaced. She stroked her belly as she shuffled on the chair, trying to get comfortable. 'I'm sure the boys weren't as lively as this one. It's been kicking all night, I'm exhausted. I hope it comes early, I'm getting a bit tired of its somersaults in there!' She glanced over at the loom. 'Oh, is it finished?'

'Yes, just before you arrived, in fact.'

Isadora laboured to her feet and walked over to have a closer look. 'It's beautiful, Mamma. Such detail. You can see every blade of grass, every flower, every leaf on the trees. How did you do that?' She reached out and touched the tapestry with her fingertips, awestruck.

'Isadora!' Agnes's reprimand came out harsher than she intended, but she didn't want her daughter touching the tapestry.

Isadora withdrew her hand as if she had been burnt. 'Mamma?' she cried in wonder. 'They moved.'

'What?' Agnes went over to her daughter and took hold of her hand. 'Come, sit down. It is hot today, you must rest–'

'No, look, Mamma. The children around the maypole, they're dancing and singing. Can't you see them? Can't you *hear* them?'

Agnes heard faint notes of childish singing and giggling, far off in the distance, silly nursery rhymes she had sung to her brothers and sisters.

'Nonsense,' she said brightly, and pulled Isadora's arm. The singing suddenly stopped, and the images were still once more. 'Come, I need to talk to you.'

Isadora glanced at the tapestry, then followed her mother back to the table.

'Here, drink this.' Agnes ladled some steaming, sweet-smelling tea from a pot over the fire into a cup and passed it to her. 'It will calm the baby and help you rest before the birth.'

'Thank you.' Isadora sipped the tea. 'I hope this works, I'd like to get some sleep tonight.'

'The recipe's in the book, you can make it any time.'

'You said you needed to talk. Is it about Papà?'

Agnes flinched. Nothing escaped her daughter's notice, she realised. 'His condition is getting worse, he can hardly sleep for the pain.'

'Is there nothing you can do?'

'My cordials helped keep it at bay for a time, but they no longer help,' Agnes whispered, her heart breaking. 'It's like a darkness, eating him on the inside, burning its way through him. There is nothing more I can do. Believe me, I've tried.'

'How long does he have?'

Agnes saw the pain in her daughter's face. Even for a healer, perhaps especially so, death was never easy. 'I don't know. It could be days, or months.'

'But he's suffering.'

'Yes. Very much so.'

Isadora was silent for a moment. 'There is one thing you can do to help him.'

'Such as?' Agnes held her breath, wondering if her daughter was thinking the same as her.

'There is only one way to relieve a person's suffering when our cures won't work. You taught me that, Mamma. Whatever you choose to do, I will understand your decision. As will Alfredo and Guglielmo. You know how much they respect and love you.' She reached out and took Agnes's hand, squeezing it gently.

They were silent for a moment, both remembering the other people Agnes had helped during the years, as they begged her to give them relief from their pain.

'W-when it happens, your father must go in the family mausoleum,' Agnes said.

'Mamma–'

Agnes held up her hand. 'Let me finish. This isn't easy for me.'

Isadora nodded.

'We must follow his family's wishes, and he will be placed in the mausoleum at San Jacopo.' Agnes got up and went over to a cupboard, then returned with two silk bags, one red and one white. 'You must make sure that this charm is placed inside his coffin.' She held up the red one.

'What is it?' Isadora asked, taking it in her hand. It released a faint perfume.

'It is a charm to protect against evil, but I have also infused it with my love for him, with a part of my soul, so that we can remain together for all eternity.' A few months earlier, Agnes had told her daughter about that long-ago evening when Filippo had cursed their family.

'You can do that, when it is time.'

'Of course. But if I'm no longer here, you must do it. Promise me,' Agnes implored. 'The other is for me. It contains a part of your father's soul. It wasn't easy, but I showed him what to do and he did it. For me. You must put it with me, in my grave.'

'I will, Mamma, I promise,' Isadora said solemnly.

'I won't be buried in the mausoleum. The Innocenti will not

allow it, nor do I want it. Your father has arranged for me to be buried in the graveyard at San Jacopo. There will be no head-stone, but a statue of an angel to guard over me. These are my wishes.'

'I will see that it is done,' Isadora said, tears in her eyes.

'I hate to speak of such things, but it must be said.' Agnes sniffed, her own eyes watering. 'The book will be yours, to hand down to your daughter, and her daughter, and so forth, for generations to come. The cottage too will become yours, and must pass from healer to healer. The Dragonfly Grove is the source of our magic, and the source of the curse. It must be tended carefully and guarded over, we must heal and protect those around us. The cycle must never be broken, and the Inno-centi name must go on for eternity.'

'I understand.'

Agnes glanced over at the tapestry. 'One day there will be a healer who is stronger than all of us, even me, and she will rid our family of this curse so that we can live in peace. Until that day, we must continue to heal others, and keep the wolves from our door.'

'I will do my best,' Isadora promised.

'I know you will. That is all any of us can do.' Agnes got to her feet with a groan. 'I must tidy away my things and go to your father.'

'I'll come again this afternoon, Mamma. Perhaps Niccolò will come with me, I'll tell him to help you in the Grove.'

'Thank you, that would be lovely.' Agnes hugged her daugh-ter, then placed a hand on Isadora's stomach. She smiled. 'This time you're carrying a girl,' she whispered in her ear. 'Teach her well.'

.   .   .

After Isadora left, Agnes went over to the tapestry and removed it from the loom. Holding it tight between her hands, she closed her eyes and infused it with her thoughts and wishes, and her memories. Then she placed it into an oiled silk bag, pulled the drawstrings tight, and recited an incantation as the energy flowed from her to the bag.

She knew that she had to hide the tapestry, it would never do if the wrong person found it, and the wooden chest that Ted had made her was perfect. Many years earlier, Bob had made a false bottom for it, leaving a small space where she would hide their money while they were travelling. Now it would hide the tapestry from prying eyes, to be passed unknowingly from generation to generation, until it made its way to the right person.

She placed the bag on a tray, next to two cups. She hobbled along the hall to the pantry and went back to the kitchen with a bowl of black berries soaking in water. She removed the berries and poured the infusion into the two cups, adding some of the sweet-smelling tea she'd given Isadora earlier.

While she waited for the concoction to cool, she took out the recipe book and sat down to write.

Used in higher doses, the berries of the banewort plant will cause a quick, painless death...

She closed the book and left it on the table, picked up the tray with the cups and tapestry, and made her way upstairs to where her husband lay in bed.

JENNIFER

45

I floated in an inky blackness, not knowing if I was upside down or right side up. My head spun as I fought to understand where I had to go, the murky darkness closing in on me, confusing me. I opened my mouth to scream and choked on the foul air, its cloying, suffocating denseness filling my lungs. Then I saw a pinprick of light in the distance, a single spark before it disappeared, but I kicked my legs with all my might, heading towards it, towards what I hoped was salvation. It appeared again, brighter this time, shining steadily like a beacon as I struggled to reach it.

My body broke through the dark surface and I was surrounded by a brilliant white light that brought warmth to me after the panic just moments – or was it hours? – before. A figure stepped towards me, its arms outstretched, and my body was flooded with a calm, peaceful feeling. The woman, somehow I knew it was a woman before I heard her voice, spoke to me, the words filtering through to my mind. I wanted to reach out, to go with her, but something was stopping me, something was pulling me back. The light faded as the figure receded, and I screamed...

'Jen!' Francesco cradled me in his arms, rocking me back and forth as I screamed once again, the sound harsh in my ears. 'Jen, it's me. Come back, Jen.'

I opened my eyes to find Francesco and Agnese hovering over me, worried expressions on their faces. Bella licked my hand and whined. I tried to sit up, but fell back, exhausted.

'Lie still,' Francesco said. 'I've got you.' I lay in his arms as I slowly regained my strength. Agnese brought me over a coffee, holding it to my lips as I sipped.

'I've put lots of sugar in it, you'll be feeling better soon,' she said.

'Thanks.' I gulped greedily; it felt like I hadn't eaten or drunk anything for days. 'How long was I out?'

Agnese and Francesco glanced at each other.

'We started this morning, about ten,' Agnese said.

'What time is it now?' I looked around the room. The shutters were still open, and the sky outside was dark.

'It's ten at night,' Francesco said.

I was stunned. 'Twelve hours? I was out for twelve hours?' The first time it had happened, I'd only been out for a couple of hours at most.

'We were starting to panic,' Francesco admitted. I saw how pale he was, with dark shadows under his eyes.

'We called you a few times, but you didn't even move,' Agnese added. 'Then you started thrashing about, like you were drowning, and you screamed.' She shuddered. 'It was awful. We were calling you, Bella was barking, but it was as if you were too far away.'

'Well, I'm back now.' I shivered, and pulled the blanket tighter around me. I knew that if it hadn't been for them, I would have followed the woman and never come back.

'Before you tell us anything, you're going to eat,' Francesco said firmly.

'Yes, sir.' I tried to salute, but my hand felt as heavy as lead.

'Stay here, don't move, don't talk, and wait,' he ordered, going to the kitchen. I heard the rattling of pots and pans as he made himself busy.

'Can I at least go to the bathroom?' I called.

'If you must,' he replied with a sigh.

Twenty minutes later we sat at the table, devouring enormous plates of spaghetti. I hadn't realised I was so hungry. Judging from the speed at which they emptied their plates, Francesco and Agnese were starving too.

'Didn't you eat today?' I asked, leaning back in my chair, my belly full.

'We were too busy looking after you,' Agnese said, wiping her plate clean with a piece of bread.

'Seriously? You stayed with me all that time?'

'We said we would, didn't we?' Francesco stood up and collected the plates.

'Yes, but I wasn't expecting it to last twelve hours! Poor Bella.'

'Oh, she slept most of the time, except when she asked to be let out in the garden.' Francesco scratched her head as he passed by her, a wag of her tail the only acknowledgement.

'I know you must be exhausted, but I can't go to bed without hearing all about it,' Agnese said.

'I'm not that tired, actually,' I replied. It was true; my mind was buzzing with everything I'd seen, and I was sure I wouldn't be getting much sleep that night.

'I'll make us another coffee, then you can tell us everything,' Francesco said. He glanced at the pile of plates and pans on the side.

'Leave them, I'll do them tomorrow,' I said. He grunted, and got on with making the coffee.

Cradling my steaming cup, I began to tell Agnes's story. The images were clear in my head, almost as though they were my own memories; which I supposed, in a way, they were, having seen Agnes's life through her eyes. I told them about the manor house, the May Day celebrations, Ted, and the Dragonfly Grove.

'Really? She called it the Dragonfly Grove?' Agnese exclaimed.

I nodded. 'It was beautiful, too, like something out of a film. It had a stream running through it, a grassy clearing dotted with flowers, and trees casting their shadows over everything, and hundreds and hundreds of dragonflies.'

'Incredible. But what's the connection with the Grove here?' she asked, impatient.

'All in good time,' I replied with a wink.

'Oh!' Agnese crossed her arms and huffed.

'Go on.' Francesco leaned forward, interested.

Talking about the deaths Agnes had witnessed from the plague was hard, and tears were streaming down my face by the time I finished. Mrs Smythe, Lady Elizabeth, even Lord Funteyn, had become as dear to me as they had been to Agnes, perhaps even more so. Their faces were as familiar to me as those of Francesco and Agnese; I had come to know and love these people. The timelines blurred, and I began speaking in the present tense as I continued to recount my story.

Agnese and Francesco listened intently, not interrupting me anymore as I spoke about Bob, the long voyage at sea, Agnes falling in love with Riccardo, and Matilda teaching her the ways of the healers, the strength of Agnes's gift. I told them about the legend of the dragonflies, remembering it word for word, seeing their reaction as it suddenly dawned upon them.

'You mean, you come from those people?' Agnese gasped.

'It would appear so,' I replied. 'If you think about it, it makes sense. They said the gift would be passed from generation to generation – some would use it, others would be afraid of it and try to hide it, and others would maybe die before realising they have it. Luisa wasn't the last of the healers, after all. Bruna should have taken over from her, but refused and left for England instead. My mum could have been the next healer, if she'd known about it.

'I've always thought there was something special about Mum – she always seemed to know when there was trouble and turn up to help sort it out. If I let her.' I grimaced, thinking back to my drunken days when I would yell at her to go away and leave me alone. 'You remember how she turned up that evening Mark was attacking us? At the time, I didn't really think about it, but how much of a coincidence was that? You and I are fighting a madman, and she rings the doorbell, standing there like Mary bloody Poppins, and starts hitting him over the head with her umbrella! She knew; deep down inside her, in her subconscious, she knew.' I took a deep breath, suddenly overwhelmed by it all.

'You're right,' Agnese said, shaking her head. 'I've never thought about it, but it was incredible how she turned up at exactly the right moment.'

'And then there's me.' They both looked at me, waiting for the next revelation. 'I came here to get away from my life in England, and ended up being the next healer. All because I drank Luisa's special juice and touched the letter she'd written. Oh, and of course there's the curse.'

'Curse? What curse?' Agnese said.

Francesco ran his hand through his hair, a bemused look on his face. 'This is getting a bit weird, like a fairy story.'

'Tell me about it,' I replied. 'Okay, so here comes the interesting part.'

'Because everything else was boring?' Francesco said, raising his eyebrows. 'I can't wait to hear this!'

The expressions on their faces were priceless as I told them about Agnes learning to make charms to protect her family from Filippo, chanting incantations and drawing on the energy from the world around her to help strengthen her spells. I almost mentioned the charm Matilda had given her to help her have another child with Riccardo, but something stopped me. That I would keep to myself for the time being. When I arrived at the part where Filippo cast his curse after cutting Bob's throat, Francesco leapt up, shoving his chair back noisily. I looked at him, baffled.

'What's wrong?'

'This. Curses, spells, and charms. Do you really believe in all that stuff?' He paced back and forth, unable to sit still.

'After everything I've seen and been through this last year, yes, I do believe in "all that stuff",' I replied coldly.

He stopped abruptly, his shoulders slumping. 'I'm sorry. It's just... it's so much to take in. Things from hundreds of years ago, affecting our lives today.'

'You saw me go into those trances, you encouraged me to do this to find out what's going on,' I snapped. 'And now it's a load of hocus-pocus to you?'

He strode over to me and put his hand on my shoulder. I sat stiffly, unwilling to give in.

'I'm sorry.'

'You've already said that.' I wasn't going to make it easy for him.

'I know. You must admit, though, it's a lot to take in. To find out that the woman you love is actually a...' He paused.

'Say it,' I said through gritted teeth.

'A witch.' He stepped back, hands in the air in resignation. 'You told me to say it!'

I burst out laughing. 'Your face. You know, I feel exactly the same as you about it. I've been in a trance for the last twelve hours, watching Agnes's life unfold, living it with her, and I still can't believe everything I've seen. I can only imagine how difficult it is for both of you. And I haven't even got to the best part yet.'

Francesco sat back down and wiped the beads of sweat from his brow. 'I honestly thought you were upset with me,' he grumbled. 'I thought I'd have to grovel to get back in your good books.'

'I couldn't resist. It's my British sense of humour.' I leaned over and ruffled his hair. 'Forgive me?'

'Yes,' he said, trying not to laugh and failing.

'Okay, now that your lovers' tiff is over, maybe we can get back to the story,' Agnese interrupted. 'What's the best part?'

'Towards the end, Agnes spoke about a healer in the future, one with even more power than she had, who would break the curse on the family and set things to rights. She put the tapestry in the hidden compartment in the wooden chest, where it would stay until the right person found it.'

'You found the tapestry,' Agnese whispered, her eyes wide open in awe. '*You're* the person she was talking about?'

'Apparently so.' I shrugged. 'I don't know what I'm supposed to do, though. She didn't say any more, and that's when I woke up.'

'It ended like that?' Agnese thumped her hand on the table. 'That's so unfair, we'll never know what happened to her.'

'Actually, we do,' I said. 'Riccardo was extremely ill, from her description I imagine he had cancer and was in a lot of pain. She made two cups of tea and added some belladonna.'

Agnese gasped, her hand over her mouth.

'Sounds familiar, right? She wrote the recipe in the book. The same recipe both Luisa and Tommaso used.'

'Wow,' was all Agnese said.

'Then she went upstairs, up those very stairs over there,' I pointed, 'with the cups and rolled-up tapestry on a tray. That's when I woke up.'

'She killed Riccardo and herself?' Francesco asked.

'Yes. She was only thirty-seven. She probably had many years ahead of her still, but I imagine she couldn't bear to live without him. She told Isadora she wanted to be buried in an unmarked grave at San Jacopo in Gallicano, with a statue of an angel watching over her. I think I saw it that day M– *he* took me up there. I kept turning around to look at it. I remember feeling as if it was calling to me.'

'We'll go back and check it out. I know the priest, he'll let us in,' Francesco promised.

'Thank you.' I felt tears prick at my eyes, tiredness and emotions suddenly hitting me. 'There's nothing else to tell, really.' I hoped they wouldn't ask about my return to the real world, I didn't want to remember the dark emptiness I'd been trapped in. A thought niggled at my mind, but I ignored it, too tired to focus on anything else.

'I'd say we've got enough to think over,' Francesco said. 'It's late. We'll talk about the curse and how you can break it tomorrow.' He glanced at Bella. 'You two go to bed, I'll take her outside before I come up.'

Agnese and I said goodnight to Bella and made our way upstairs.

''Night, Agnese,' I said. 'Sweet dreams.'

'What's the betting that the one night Malva's at Mamma's, I can't get to sleep?' Agnese said with a rueful smile. 'Your story is going to keep me awake for ages.'

I kissed her on the cheek and went into the bedroom, the soft bed calling out to me. I hoped for a long, dreamless sleep.

46

We were woken the next morning by a loud knocking at the back door. Rubbing my eyes and yawning, I made my way downstairs. Bella barked when she saw me, running from the door to me and back again. I groaned as my head thumped with the noise. It felt worse than any hangover I'd ever had.

'Ciao, Jennifer,' Beatrice shouted as she barged into the house and wrapped her arms around my waist, almost knocking me over. 'Ciao, Bella! Shall we go outside and play?' Dog and child ran out into the garden, scaring a flock of sparrows pecking at the ground. They flew away, twittering angrily at being so rudely interrupted.

'Good morning,' I said, fixing what I hoped was a welcoming grin on my face. Aunt Liliana bustled into the room with Malva in her arms, followed by Giulia with Antonio in hers.

'We've left the prams outside, the wheels got a bit muddy after last night's rain,' Aunt Liliana said. 'Did we wake you?' She peered at me. 'Never mind, it's gone nine. It's about time you were up anyway.'

Giulia glanced at me apologetically. I smiled, and tried to

make my brain focus. 'Why don't you get some coffee on, Aunt, while I go and get the others up.'

'Late night, was it? I'll make it nice and strong, that'll help. The men are back at the house, taking care of some pots I've left on the stove. We shouldn't be too long, though – goodness knows what they'll get up to! I thought I'd make lunch for everyone today, and it seems like it's a good idea, judging from the state of you!'

I groaned inwardly as I went back upstairs to tell Agnese and Francesco the good news. Our plans to work out how to break the curse would have to wait.

As always, the family lunch was full of laughter and heartfelt discussions. Uncle Dante was his usual taciturn self, his silence made up for by Aunt Liliana's non-stop chatter. Piero and Lorenzo kept up their customary banter, making jokes at Francesco's expense, but I sensed an undercurrent of tension between them.

Lunch over, we divided into separate groups as usual: Aunt Liliana in the kitchen, refusing anyone's offer of help, saying she'd be quicker doing it herself; Giulia, Agnese and I in the living room with the children; and the men outside in the tiny back garden, talking while they smoked.

'They look serious,' I remarked, nodding at the four men outside.

Giulia glanced at Beatrice, who was absorbed in a cartoon on TV. 'Piero said he needed to speak to Francesco, but wouldn't tell me what it was about,' she said quietly. 'But he and Lorenzo went down to the valley the other day, and they've been strange ever since.'

'I noticed they were a bit tense,' I said.

'Do you think it's anything to do with *him*?' Agnese looked pale, and she held Malva tightly to her chest. The baby made small noises of protest and pushed against her mother with closed fists.

'I'm sure Francesco will tell us,' I said. 'Here, give her to me.' I held Malva in my arms, breathing in her gorgeous scent. A memory flashed into my mind of Matilda and Agnes, making their special charm so that Agnes would fall pregnant with Riccardo's child. My breath caught in my throat as I realised that, even though it wasn't in the recipe book – or the spell book, as I'd taken to calling it – I now knew how to make one for myself.

'Are you all right, Jennifer?' Giulia asked, looking concerned.

'What? Oh, yes. We had a late night, we're all a bit out of it today.' I felt my face flushing, and changed the subject. 'So, is little Antonio sleeping better now?' Giulia had complained regularly that she hadn't had a full night's sleep since he was born, and had finally resorted to asking us for help. We'd come up with an ointment she could put on a cushion near his cot, the mixture of herbs releasing a gentle perfume in his room that would help him fall asleep.

Her face brightened. 'I don't know how you did it, but it worked! He's slept all night for the last week. I've started recommending it to my friends, so expect them to come knocking on your door any day soon. What on earth did you put in it?'

I let Agnese explain, while I settled back on the sofa, a sleeping Malva in my arms. Their murmuring voices, together with the lack of sleep from the night before, lulled me into a relaxed state and I started to drift off. A white light filled my head, reminding me of the moment when I'd broken through the dark blackness when returning from Agnes's memories. Confused, I tried to open my eyes, but my body wouldn't respond. I watched as the white figure came towards me, her arms outstretched as before, her mouth opening and closing, telling me something, something important, but I couldn't make it out, I couldn't hear what she was saying, she needed to get closer, she was whispering in my ear, saying–

'Jen?' Francesco was on the sofa next to me, gently shaking my arm. 'Hey, Jen, wake up. It's four o'clock, it's better we get back home. Bella will be going crazy wondering where we are!'

I blinked, muddled thoughts rushing through my mind as I slowly came to. 'I've been asleep?' I mumbled.

'For about an hour,' Giulia said. 'We didn't want to disturb you, you both looked so comfortable there.'

Malva was still asleep in my arms, snorting as she moved restlessly. 'Here, I think she's starting to wake up as well,' I said, handing her to Agnese.

'Good. That way we can get back to the cottage before it's time to feed her.' Agnese gathered up her bits and pieces, expertly holding Malva against one shoulder while putting everything in her bag with one hand.

'You all right?' Francesco asked.

'Yes,' I snapped. I took a deep breath and tried again. 'I'm sorry. You know what it's like when someone wakes you from an afternoon nap. I feel a bit groggy, that's all.'

'A walk back to the cottage will make you feel better,' he said with a grin. 'Ready?'

We said our goodbyes to everyone and left about half an hour later. Aunt Liliana, with Beatrice jumping around next to her, called out to us to come back soon as we walked down the narrow street.

'I do miss them,' Agnese sighed, 'but it's lovely to get back to the peace and quiet of the cottage after a while.'

I laughed. 'It's like turning off the TV after it's been on all day at full volume.'

'With episodes of your worst programme on a loop,' Agnese added.

'Or walking out of a Metallica concert with your ears whistling,' Francesco remarked.

We both stared at him.

'In my younger days, many moons ago!'

'You were quite the rebel, weren't you?' I was glad his taste in music was a bit tamer these days.

'You have no idea,' he replied, raising his eyebrows and smirking. I slapped his arm.

'You're never going to convince me you were a wild child, I know you too well, Signor Conti. You're far too respectable.'

'Okay, okay, you've found me out!' He raised his arms in mock surrender. 'Just don't tell everyone else, I've got to keep my so-called reputation intact.'

'Oh, your secret's safe with us,' Agnese said, giggling. She made a zipping motion across her mouth. 'The ultimate rock rebel, talking about his Metallica concerts, AC/DC, Guns N' Roses; but we've seen your Madonna CD in the van!' We burst out laughing, causing people to look at us as they passed by.

'So, what were you men talking about at Aunt Liliana's?' I asked a little later, after we'd calmed down.

'I can't keep anything from you, can I?' Francesco replied. 'Do you read minds as well, now?'

'It doesn't take a mind reader to sense the tension between you lot,' I retorted. 'And Giulia said she thought Piero and Lorenzo had something to tell you, but didn't know what.'

Francesco stopped and looked at us, his face serious. 'Okay, I'll tell you but don't freak out. They went down to the valley a few days ago. They needed some electrical equipment they couldn't find locally–'

'All right, you can skip this part,' I said impatiently, stamping my foot. 'They saw Mark, didn't they?' I shivered as I said his name, and thought that Matilda was right; names did have a certain power and it would definitely be better not to evoke it.

'They're not sure. They don't really know him, so it could have been anyone. But,' he added hurriedly as I opened my mouth to speak, 'they think it was him. There was a man trailing them around the town. Everywhere they went, they saw this guy hanging around. It was like he wanted to approach them, but couldn't. As if something was holding him back.' He looked pointedly at me.

'They were carrying the charms I made?'

He nodded.

I punched the air in joy. 'I knew it! I knew they'd work, even if no one else believed in them!'

'You haven't heard the rest. They went over to him, to ask him what he wanted. He had his back to them, and was pretending to read a menu. Piero touched his arm, to get his attention, and he jumped out of his skin, as if Piero had punched him. Mark ran off, clutching his arm, but they lost him down one of the side streets.'

I was stunned. 'I would never have thought in a million years...' I was unable to continue, my emotions overwhelming me as I realised the gift I'd inherited. Francesco wrapped his arms around me.

'Er, guys. I hate to break this up, but it's starting to rain,' Agnese said. She was right; huge drops of rain fell out of the overcast sky. We broke into a run, determined to get back to the cottage before the storm broke.

47

The next day was glorious, as if the storm had washed away all the dust and dirt. The leaves on the trees sparkled, the sky was a brilliant azure, the clouds white and fluffy. I watched as Francesco drove off to work in his van, whistling loudly.

Agnese and I took advantage of the beautiful weather by working in the Grove. Malva lay on a blanket under the shade of the apple trees, cooing happily as she played with the toys we'd placed around her. Bella lay a few feet away with her nose on her paws, one eye always on the baby.

We tended the plants, clearing away the new-grown weeds that always seemed to spring up as soon as our backs were turned. Dragonflies whizzed around our heads as we disturbed them, and the Grove was alive with splashes of vivid colours and the humming drone of busy insects.

Bella suddenly sat up, her ears pricked and her body alert.

I put my trowel down, curious. 'What's up, Bell?'

She ran to the gate, her ears flat against her head, growling furiously, then ran back to me. I heard footsteps coming down the path, a faint whistling as whoever it was approached.

'Jen, the dragonflies,' Agnese whispered.

Startled, I looked around. There wasn't a single dragonfly to be seen, or any other insect for that matter. The Grove was ominously quiet. I gripped Bella's collar, my mouth suddenly dry, and fixed my eyes on the gate, waiting. The charm I'd attached to the latch swung gently in the breeze. I hoped it would be enough. Clenching my fists, I turned to Agnese.

'Go to Malva.' I didn't need to tell her twice. Her face pinched with fear, she ran over to her daughter and sat down on the blanket, her arm spread protectively over Malva's body.

'Hello, Jennifer.' Handsome as ever, still sporting the sexy stubble look, Mark stood on the other side of the gate, smiling at us.

I glared back. Bella growled softly beside me. 'How did you get in?'

'The front gate was open. Bit silly of you, I'd have thought you'd always make sure it was locked. You know, ever since you saw me in Lucca.'

I gasped. 'You know I saw you?'

'Oh yes. I'd seen you in town a few times before that, and thought it would be fun to let you catch a glimpse of me. How did it make you feel?' He winked, leering at me.

'You're an arsehole,' I replied. 'We called the *carabinieri*, you know.'

'I imagined you would. I left Lucca that same day, and I've been moving around since then.'

'Why are you here? You could have gone back to England, no one would have been any the wiser and nobody would be looking for you now.' I wouldn't let his words get to me, or give him the satisfaction of hearing the fear in my voice.

'That wouldn't have been much fun, would it? And besides, I have a child now. I wanted to see it, that's why I'm here. Ciao, Agnese! Missed me?' He looked over my shoulder at Agnese and Malva.

'Piss off.'

I smiled at Agnese's words, ringing strong and clear around the Grove. I surreptitiously felt in my pocket for my phone, taking advantage of Mark being distracted. Francesco had made us practice over and over again until we could find the speed dial button on our phones in any situation. It had seemed easy then, when there wasn't the added stress of Mark standing right in front of us. My fingertips had lost all sense of touch, I couldn't tell which way round the phone was... I took a deep breath and cleared my thoughts, concentrating on what I was doing. *There*! I pressed the button, mentally crossing my fingers that it was the right one, and turned back to the conversation between Agnese and Mark.

He laughed, an ugly sneer contorting his face. *What did we ever see in him*? I wondered.

'Come on, show me my son. Or is it a daughter? Whatever, I'd like to see it. I have rights, I'm the father!' He raised his voice, his hand reaching for the latch on the gate.

'I'll let Bella go,' I threatened. 'She tore your arm up last time, I hope she goes for your throat now. I won't pull her off, I'll be happy to watch her.'

'I thought you might say that, so I brought this with me.' He reached behind his back and produced a knife with a long, serrated blade that glinted in the sunlight. 'I'd advise you to keep a hold of that brute of an animal.'

I glanced round at Agnese. She was holding Malva tightly in her arms, her face white with fear. I touched my pocket, hoping she'd notice and understand that I'd called Francesco. A shadow of a smile passed over her lips, letting me know that she had. I turned back to Mark.

'I'm calling the police,' I said, taking the phone out of my pocket.

'Don't,' he snarled, reaching for the latch again. Everything seemed to happen at once. There was a blurred chaos of bright colours as a cloud of dragonflies rose up from nowhere and surrounded him. Bella struggled free from my grasp and launched herself at the gate, her deep barks filling the air. I heard Agnese shout behind me, calling her back, but it was too late. Bella barely stopped, then cleared the gate with space to spare. Mark raised his arm, and swept the knife towards her, aiming at her unprotected stomach.

I ran forward, yelling at Bella, at Mark, sobbing as I fought with the latch, my fingers fumbling. Finally I lifted it free and pulled the gate open with a crash. I took two steps, then stopped, stunned. The cloud of dragonflies swarmed around Mark, the vibration from their wings filling the air with a thrumming that I could feel deep within me. He swiped at them ineffectively with the knife, then cried out as Bella's jaws closed around his arm and she dragged him to the ground. He dropped the knife. I darted forward to grab it, relieved to see there was no blood on the blade, then threw it under a bush, out of harm's way.

The dragonflies scattered, and disappeared into the Grove. Bella's growls and snarls became louder as she mauled Mark's arm, his screams echoing around us.

'Call your damn dog off, you bitch!' he shrieked. 'I'll call the police, I'll have it put down as a dangerous animal–' He cried out again as Bella's teeth sank in deeper.

I put my hand on her collar, and she released his arm. She stood beside me, hackles raised. 'You're trespassing on private property,' I said calmly, raising my voice to be heard over Bella's snarls. 'I've already called the police. You should leave before they get here. Before I let Bella go for your throat.'

He looked around, bewildered. 'Where did the dragonflies go?'

'Dragonflies?' I assumed an innocent air. 'I didn't see any dragonflies.'

He scooted back away from me, cradling his injured arm. 'Witches. You're witches, the pair of you. I-I–'

'You'd better get out of here before we put a curse on you, then,' Agnese said from beside me. She chuckled, a deep, throaty sound full of self-assurance.

He glared at us, hatred pouring out of him. 'Your family, you're cursed. You know that, don't you? Go look in the library, do some research on your damn family. The so-called Innocenti. Innocents, my arse!'

'I know all about our family history,' I replied coldly. 'The only curse we have is that we keep meeting arseholes like you, in every bloody generation, and we have to keep getting rid of them. By any means possible.' I glared at him. 'Any.' I kept my hand on Bella's collar but let her take a couple of steps forward.

He got to his feet and turned to go, then hesitated. Bella barked madly, straining against me, desperate to leap at him again. That seemed to make his mind up. We watched as he ran back through the garden, and made sure he didn't go into the cottage. The dragonflies came back to hover over the entrance to the Grove, brightly coloured guardians determined to protect us. I grinned as he fled down the driveway, then I let go of Bella's collar. She stayed beside me, her tongue lolling out of her mouth as if she were pleased with her day's work.

'He's gone,' I said to Agnese, my body shaking as the tension drained away. We held on to each other, laughing and crying at the same time. 'We did it.'

'With a little help.' Agnese gestured at the dragonflies, still swarming above the gate. Malva stretched in Agnese's arms, struggling against her mother's grip, her pudgy hands reaching out towards the glittering insects. One flew over and landed on her outstretched fist, its wings brushing gently against her skin. She blew a raspberry, giggling at the feathery touch.

'And Bella.' I bent over and stroked the dog's head. A thought occurred to me. 'I'd better make sure he's not hiding somewhere. You wait here with Malva.'

'Wait. Take this.' Agnese handed me the knife, the handle wrapped in a cotton handkerchief. I stepped out of the gate and ran down the garden, Bella close at my heels. I was glad of her presence. We headed down the driveway, past the clump of trees that hid the cottage, and round the curve. I stopped when I saw the double gates ajar and Francesco's van parked in the middle of the road, the driver's door wide open. I looked frantically around, dreading the worst.

Bella gave a bark and ran over towards some bushes by the gates. I almost cried out in relief when I saw Francesco stand up and wave to me.

'Thank goodness you're okay,' he said as I approached. 'I came as soon as I got your call, I could hear shouting in the background, but it was all muffled. I guessed this piece of shit had come back.' He gestured with his foot, and I saw that Mark was laid out on the ground before him. 'Bella, keep away from him, you might catch something.' She moved a little distance away and sat down, growling.

'What did you...?' I hardly dared to ask.

'I gave him a good punch in the stomach, that put him out of action.' He grinned. 'I almost felt sorry for the arsehole. Almost. What happened to his arm?'

'Bella.'

'She did that? Agnese, Malva, are they all right?'

I heard the sounds of sirens in the distance, steadily getting closer. 'They're fine, they're in the Grove. Did you call the *carabinieri*?'

'Yes, on the way here. I was worried I wouldn't arrive in time. Did he do anything to you, hurt you?'

'No, he didn't get anywhere near us. The charm I put here, though, I don't think it worked.' I looked at the large metal gates, disconsolate. 'He got in. Thank goodness for Bella, or he would have got in the Grove too.'

Francesco took something out of his pocket, looking guilty. 'That might have been my fault. I removed it.'

'What?'

'It was damaged by the storm last night, it was a pulpy mess on the ground. I didn't have time to tell you, so I took it away with me this morning. I meant to phone you, but I forgot.'

'Typical,' I said, but I wasn't upset. Agnese and I had faced our worst nightmare and we'd come out stronger than ever.

'So maybe the one in the Grove would've worked.'

'Maybe. It doesn't really matter now, does it?' My voice faded away as my legs suddenly started shaking and my vision blurred.

'Woah,' Francesco said as I swayed, my head spinning. He held me in his arms until I stopped shaking.

The sirens became unbearably loud, and a police car came to a screeching halt next to Francesco's van. We watched as they talked to Mark, trying to ascertain if he was conscious; satisfied he was in no danger of further injury, they helped him to his feet and led him over to the car.

'We'll need a statement later,' one of the *carabinieri* told us.

I handed him the knife I was still holding. 'You'll probably want this. He threatened us with it.'

The *carabiniere* took out a plastic bag and slipped the knife inside, then gave a curt nod and returned to his colleague.

'Is it over?' Agnese asked from behind us.

I turned and gave her a weak smile. 'Yes, it's finally over.'

We stood and watched as the police car tore down the road, the sound of the sirens echoing around the mountains, until finally there was peace and quiet.

48

It took a few days for the excitement to die down. News quickly spread, and locals dropped in at all times on the off chance we had some cordial or other, and for a long natter about what had happened. Aunt Liliana was in her element. She arrived at the cottage early every morning, and spent the day making coffee and offering cake and biscuits to whoever turned up. They would sit outside in the back garden, and I could hear their oohs and ahhs from the laboratory, where I'd holed myself up with the excuse that I had to make new batches of products. Agnese escaped to the Grove with Malva and Bella, the area off limits to the uninitiated.

With pots and pans bubbling on the stove, and various herbs steeping in bowls on the side, I passed hours looking through the spell book, desperately searching for the charm Matilda had given Agnes. I guessed it had to be somewhere near the beginning, if Agnes had even written it down. Perhaps she hadn't wanted to leave a written record. I finally found it, half-obscured by a drawing of a sage plant. Isadora's drawing. I lightly ran my finger over it, marvelling at the details in the sketch. It reminded me of the dragonfly sketches I'd found in Tommaso's study after his death, now hanging in frames on the walls of the living room. The Innocenti were evidently artists as well as healers.

I set to copying the recipe the best I could, guessing at some of the words covered by the ink drawing, using my memories to fill in the blanks. Once I'd finished, I sat back in my chair and closed my eyes, evoking images of that time, long ago in the past, when Matilda had made the charm for Agnes. The recipe complete, I set to making the charm. It was to be my secret for the time being. I couldn't face telling Francesco or Agnese and witness their pity if it didn't work.

Agnes had worn the charm in a pouch around her waist. That was impractical for me, and would be difficult to hide. I thought hard about an alternative solution, and Matilda's lessons on passing energy to a personal item came to mind. I found a silver locket Mum had given me years before, on my eighth or ninth birthday. It was a big, chunky old thing, and I'd hardly ever worn it. I gave it a polish and started wearing it around my neck day and night, to get used to it.

By the end of the week, the ingredients for the charm were ready. The cottage was finally silent, the visitors more sporadic now that we were old news. Aunt Liliana hadn't turned up, a good sign there was no more gossip to be made, and we could breathe again at long last.

'Do you need some help in the laboratory?' Agnese asked. 'I feel guilty, being out in the Grove in this beautiful weather while you're stuck in there.'

'The laboratory is no place for Malva, she needs fresh air and she loves staying out there with you and Bella,' I said nonchalantly, my stomach clenching. I didn't want her finding evidence of what I'd been up to, even though I'd been careful to return everything to its place at the end of every day.

'Are you sure? You're looking a bit pale, you could do with some sun,' she said. 'It's not good to shut yourself away like that.'

'Orders to fill, money to make,' I said, laughing. 'White's my natural colour, I'm British, remember? I'll finish today, then you can take over on Monday. What about we take the weekend off and go for a day trip somewhere? How does that sound?'

'Sounds perfect. I know just the spot for a picnic, up in the mountains near a river. You'll love it. And you might even get a tan, take an edge off that brilliant white glow you emit,' she added.

I threw a cushion at her. 'I'll have you know I like my pale skin. It makes me stand out.'

'Oh, yes, it definitely does... like a beacon!' Agnese shrieked and dodged another cushion. Bella jumped up and barked, puzzled at all the noise.

'Don't you start as well,' I said, heading outside. 'You can bring me a coffee later,' I called over my shoulder to Agnese.

'As long as you don't throw it at me,' she shouted back. I heard her giggling as I went into the garden.

The morning passed quickly as I worked, absorbed in my task. The herbs were ready, but I had to prepare everything for the incantation – set the candles, clear my mind so that I could focus, perform the spell that would bring me my heart's desire. The door was locked, my mobile phone was back at the cottage, Francesco was at work. There would be no danger of interruptions. I rolled up my sleeves, wiped the sweat from my brow, and started.

As I tidied up the laboratory that afternoon, I could feel the locket against my chest, the silver warm against my skin. It was heavier, filled with the potent charm I'd made, and with the energy I'd transmitted to it. Deep inside my head, a little voice of reason tried to tell me not to be so silly as to put my faith in this hocus-pocus, but I pushed it aside.

'I believe,' I whispered, holding the locket tightly in my fist. I brought it to my lips and kissed it.

'I believe,' I said more firmly, glancing at a dragonfly passing outside the window.

'I believe!' I shouted as I poured all my emotions into the charm in my hand, tears streaming down my cheeks.

I stayed in the laboratory a while longer, proudly surveying its gleaming surfaces and well-stocked jars of herbs. My tears subsided as I thought of everything I'd achieved over the last year, how much my life had changed. A healer. I'd become a healer – what some might call a white witch, but I knew it was more than that. The dragonfly legend came to mind, how that one small group of people had changed the course of my life. The dragonflies had been a part of it all, ever since my arrival, I mused, and long before that, when they'd told Luisa how to make the juice that had awakened my powers. The cottage, the Grove, the dragonflies, all were linked. And the curse, the bane of my family, had been woven into the fabric of our lives that long-ago night. The curse, cast at midnight under the full silver moon... darkness and light... good against evil... Agnes, her bare arms thrust towards the glowing orb of the moon, a stark figure against the night sky... a figure, bathed in white, coming towards me as I emerged from the murky darkness... the figure, whispering in my ear, urging me to...

'Call for the dragonflies,' I whispered. Now I remembered everything, and I knew what I had to do.

I had to wait a week for the moon to be in the right phase. In the meantime, I studied the book, gleaning any information I could from it, and googled the magical properties of the plants in the Grove to find out which ones I could use for breaking a curse. My dreams were full of bizarre symbols that I drew as soon as I woke up, the images impressed clearly in my mind like a photograph. The coffee table was strewn with my sketches and pieces of paper covered in notes I feverishly wrote as ideas came into my head.

To Agnese's delight, I took to sitting in the Grove for long hours, freeing my mind and travelling to distant places, looking for answers. She would often find me beneath one of the fruit trees, its shady branches shielding me from the sun, dragonflies hovering around my head as I gazed into the sky. *The* dragonfly, the one who had called to me from the beginning, became my constant companion as I sat there, meditating.

By the end of the week, the moon was full and I was ready.

'Agnese, you'll stay in the house with Malva and Bella. No buts,' I added as she opened her mouth to protest. 'It's probably not dangerous, but I mustn't have any interruptions while I'm performing the incantation.' I preferred to call them incantations instead of spells, it seemed less witchlike and more healer-like, in my opinion.

'All right,' she said, pouting. 'But I'll be watching from the upstairs window. I don't want to miss this.'

'That's fine,' I replied, smiling. 'And thanks.'

She hugged me. 'I can help you set things up, though, can't I?'

'Of course. Everything's ready in the laboratory, we only need to take it down to the Grove.' I'd etched the symbols from my dreams into the candles I'd made, infusing them with some of the herbs from the garden. The silver-leafed plant was an essential part of all my preparations, from the candles to a special infusion I would drink just before performing the ceremony.

'What do I need to do?' Francesco asked. Both he and Agnese wholeheartedly supported me in everything I did, and I loved them both for it.

'Bring a spade and follow me to the Grove. You can come too, Agnese,' I added. I picked up a silver bowl I'd prepared the day before by cleansing it with pure mountain water from a nearby river, then transferring my energy to it.

I went over to the grave in the centre of the Grove, where Bruna's daughter, Malva, was buried. I crouched down, running my left hand over the ground, my eyes closed as I followed the energy patterns beneath me. I heard the whispering movement of ants' feet as they worked below the earth in their nest, busy with their duties; I felt the vibrations of a worm burrowing through the soil, blindly heading towards who knew where; I sensed the sucking motion of the plants as they drew the water and nutriments they needed into them, while dead leaves rotted into the ground, replacing what they were taking. *There!* There was a break in the earth, a place where no insects trod and no plants thrust their roots, a dark, barren channel that pulled at my soul, hungry for my energy. I stood and took one step to the right.

'Okay. If you can dig a hole here, one that's large enough for this bowl so that its rim is just beneath ground level,' I told Francesco.

Once he'd dug the hole, I placed the bowl inside, filling the gaps at the edges, then I placed the candles in a circle about two metres wide around the bowl. I brushed the soil from my hands, satisfied.

'Everything's ready.'

'Will you at least tell me what the bowl's for?' Agnese asked, holding Bella back. 'I don't think it's for you, Bell!'

'It's for the curse,' I told her. 'You've heard of dreamcatchers, right? Well, this is a cursecatcher.'

Francesco shook his head. 'I can see that tonight's going to be, um, interesting.'

49

It was eleven thirty. Francesco and I left as quietly as possible so as not to disturb Malva and Bella, and made our way down to the Grove. I glanced back and saw Agnese at the upstairs window, her nose pressed against the glass. I raised my hand, then turned my mind back to the upcoming ceremony. Francesco followed me, silent as a ghost, understanding my need for calm so I could gather myself for what I had to do.

The Grove was deathly still as we entered. The glow of the full moon created distorted shadows among the trees and plants. The bowl was barely visible, except for a sliver of light glinting off the bottom as we neared.

'Stay here,' I said to Francesco as we reached the circle of candles. I quickly lit each one, their flames casting flickering shadows. He stopped outside the ring, waiting until I'd finished.

'Call if you need me,' he said.

'Don't worry, I will,' I replied with a nervous smile. I turned and kissed him on the mouth, a long kiss where his love filled me with hope and belief in myself.

'Thank you,' I whispered, and stepped through the circle.

It hit me instantly; a dark, bleak desperation, identical to the channel I'd found earlier. It filled my lungs as I breathed it in, spreading through my veins, throughout my body, racing towards my heart to tear my emotions and my feelings from me. I panicked at first, then slowed my breathing, concentrating on the pulse of my heart, pushing back against the darkness inside. I raised my head to the sky, my eyes fixed on the pale moon far away, and called for the dragonflies.

Nothing happened. I called again. Not a blade of grass stirred. Fighting the panic rising in me, I stood, straight and tall, closed my eyes, and raised my arms to the sky, as Agnes had done centuries before. There was a whirring sound and a sudden breeze ruffled my hair. I opened my eyes. The circle was full of them. There were dragonflies everywhere, their jewelled bodies sparkling blue, red, green, and yellow in the candlelight. Hundreds of them, maybe thousands, settled onto my arms, head and shoulders, tickling my skin. I felt the darkness inside me recede, surging with anger as it realised it couldn't reach my heart. I opened my mind to the dragonflies, letting their light fill my body, and pushed away the darkness. I followed it as it flowed back through my veins, out of my mouth, out into the air once more, sinking back down into the earth.

I fell to my knees, the weight of the dragonflies suddenly too much for me to bear. They guided my hands downwards, until they rested, palm down, on the ground. I felt the energy flow through my body, down my arms, to my palms, then down into the earth, forcing its way to the dark channel, drawing moisture from the soil as it went.

As if in a trance, I began to recite.

> 'Water, pure and clear, hear my plea,
> Cleanse this curse and set us free.
> Banish the dark and welcome the light,
> Help us in this time of plight.'

The ground vibrated beneath my hands, and deep below I felt the stirrings of something awakening after years of slumber. The water coursed down towards it, carving its way through the ancient soil, untouched for so long. The dragonflies remained perched on my body, their wings adding to the vibrations all around me, giving me the strength I needed.

A violent shock passed through the ground as the water arrived at its destination. My whole body shook with the impact, but the dragonflies kept me in place. I spoke the incantation over and over again, faltering when I sensed the water change direction and return up to the surface, bringing whatever lay beneath with it. I kept my eyes and my mind focused on my hands, my mouth speaking the words automatically.

Out of the corner of my eye, I noticed a wind stirring inside the circle, making the candles flicker. A few leaves floated up in the air, twisting and turning in the current. The wind became stronger, picking up more debris from the ground. The closer the water came to the surface, the stronger the wind became, until it was a violently swirling vortex all around me. The dragonflies and I remained motionless, as though in the eye of a tornado, my voice strong and sure as I drew the curse from the earth. I could no longer see Francesco or the Grove outside the circle, and prayed that he would remember my warning not to disturb me, whatever happened.

Between my hands, a trickle of water appeared. It flowed along the ground, towards the silver bowl, slow and viscous. I gasped as it dripped into the bowl, dark red drops splashing in the bottom. I turned back to the small fountain breaking out of the earth, gushing more strongly, and realised it was blood. My head started to spin as images of Bob, blood spurting from his cut throat, filled my mind. The curse had been cast in blood, that of Filippo and Bob, and now the water was drawing the blood from the ground, to rid the land of the curse. I wanted to pull my hands away, disgusted as yet more of the dark liquid emerged between them, rolling slowly towards the bowl.

The dragonfly, *my* dragonfly, flitted in front of me and hovered there. I stared into its bulbous, mystical eyes, finding the courage I so desperately needed to finish the incantation. It held my gaze for minutes, hours, eons... until it broke the connection and flew away. I noticed that the wind had died down. Glancing at the ground, I wondered how much more blood there was to come, and was surprised to find clear spring water gurgling from the hole.

The bowl was half full with a thick sludge of a gelatinous mass that rocked back and forth. It gradually slowed as I watched, until it finally stopped moving. The clear water rushed past me, dividing into two streams when it arrived at the edge of the bowl, only to reunite at the other side and disappear back down into the earth.

The dragonflies took off into the air in one enormous swarm, their work done. My dragonfly reappeared before me, flitting from side to side, until it darted off to some corner of the Grove. I stood up and stretched, my back aching from crouching for so long. I felt as though I'd just awoken from a long sleep, so disorientated I didn't even know what time or day it was. I noticed then that the candles had gone out; the only light came from the moon in the clear night sky.

I turned to Francesco and smiled.

'Is it over?' he whispered.

'Almost,' I replied. 'There's one more thing to do.'

I carried the silver bowl through the garden and into the woods, down to the river where I'd cleansed it the day before, Francesco close behind. The path beneath the trees was barely visible, but I had no need of light. I knew my way as if I'd travelled it hundreds of times already. Just as I knew that Bob's grave was nearby, hidden from prying eyes in the undergrowth, forgotten as the centuries had passed.

The river reflected the starlight, twinkling dots flashing off its surface as it rushed past us on its way to wherever it had to go.

'This is where we get rid of the curse,' I said to Francesco.

'Will it be like before?' Even though his face was in shadow, I could sense his fear.

'The worst is over. This part is easy.'

I knelt on a tussock of mossy grass beside the river, the bowl still in my hands. The viscous substance lapped against the side, as if it sensed what was going to happen to it.

'Is that what I think it is?'

'Blood? Yes, it is. Centuries-old blood.' I turned to him, smiling at the disgusted look on his face.

'I didn't want to ask before. You were so serious, back there, so incredible.' He threw his arms in the air. 'I never thought...' He stopped. 'I'll never doubt you again, Jennifer. What happened was unbelievable, and yet I saw it with my own eyes.'

I blushed. 'I didn't really know what I was doing. It was the dragonflies, they helped me.'

'And now? Do you know what you have to do?'

'Oh, yes.'

I leaned over the surface of the water, my arms holding the bowl out as far as I could reach. I felt Francesco's arms wrap around my waist, keeping me anchored to the ground.

> 'Water, pure and clear, hear my plea,
> Cleanse this curse and set us free.
> Wash away the blood from this bowl,
> Return the goodness to its soul.'

I placed the bowl in the river, the water quickly filling it and washing away all traces of blood. My muscles strained against the current, and I tightened my grip on the bowl, afraid it would be ripped from my hands. I repeated the incantation three times, then sat back on my heels, the dripping bowl in my lap. Francesco sat beside me, holding me, until I felt strong enough to go back to the cottage.

Once more in the Grove, we stood in the middle of the circle of candles. The clear stream of water was still flowing from the ground, gurgling merrily. I placed the cleansed silver bowl back into its hole, and we both gasped as the two streams of water united into one and splashed over its edge. It quickly filled, and the overspill went back down into the earth, to rejoin the stream underground, I supposed. I whispered a silent prayer of thanks, filled with wonder and joy.

'It looks like we've got a new fountain,' Francesco said. 'The dragonflies will be happy.'

'As long as Bella doesn't use it as a drinking bowl,' I remarked dryly, and he burst out laughing.

'Well done, my beautiful healer,' he said, bending down and kissing my ear. 'Now let's go to Agnese, she's going to want to know everything.'

As I closed the gate behind me, I looked back at the Grove, serene in the moonlight. There was a new sense of calm and tranquillity that hadn't been there before. I touched the locket around my neck, and made a wish.

50

The cottage was a hive of activity as people ran around shouting if anyone had seen their hairbrush, or hat, or earring. I escaped upstairs into my room and closed the door against the commotion outside. I sat down on the edge of my bed and stared at my reflection in the mirrored wardrobe door.

'Don't touch your face,' Giulia called from the hallway. I snatched my hands away guiltily. 'Or your hair. You've got ten minutes, then I'm coming back to finish you off. Oh, Bea, what are you up to now?' Her voice drifted away as she ran after her daughter.

I looked at my heavily made-up face and grimaced. The urge to rub my eyes or cheek was strong, so I sat on my hands. My hair was done up in an immaculate chignon, with some stray curls at the sides to soften the look. Giulia had spent hours perfecting the style, until we were both happy with the result. I glanced at the ivory-coloured dress hanging from the edge of the wardrobe. Simple but elegant was how Mum had described it when she'd seen it, tears brimming in her eyes at the thought of me wearing it on my wedding day.

My wedding day. Today. We'd wanted a quiet ceremony with

little fuss, but Aunt Liliana had had other ideas. Hence the house full of female relatives all in a tizzy. My only consolation was that Mum had arrived two days earlier. Her presence had helped calm me down immediately, squashing the butterflies I seemed to have had permanently ever since we'd set the date.

There was a gentle knock at the door. 'Can I come in?'

'Of course, Mum,' I called back.

She opened the door and slipped into the room, closing it behind her. She was already in her wedding outfit, a gorgeous pale-blue dress that brought out the colour of her eyes. I patted the bed next to me.

'Come and sit down here.'

'You look beautiful,' she said, gazing at me in admiration. 'When are you going to put your dress on? I want to take some photos.'

'Giulia wants to do some finishing touches before I get dressed,' I replied. My mind was transported to another wedding, decades earlier, the bride-to-be in this very room having a heart-to-heart talk with her mother. All were dead now. They were only memories, ones I would carry with me forever.

'It's chaos downstairs,' Mum said, sighing. 'I think the men had the right idea – a glass of whisky at Liliana's while they get changed, then hang around until it's time to go to the venue. What with hyperactive kids and Liliana running around like a headless chicken, it's bedlam!'

'How's Kevin getting on?' Mum's boyfriend had insisted on accompanying her, even though she'd been worried about introducing him to everyone. He'd spent the last two days in shock, surrounded by my overwhelming family who had showered him with affection. Francesco, Piero and Lorenzo spoke English, which made things easier, but I couldn't help smiling at the bewildered expression he had on his face most of the time.

'He's fine. I thought he'd take the first plane back to England, but he says he's enjoying himself. I've just spoken with him – he says Francesco is jittery but coping well. Apparently, there's a cousin there who's keeping him calm.'

'That'll be Luca, he's Francesco's best man. They don't see each other often, but they were best mates when they were little.'

'And what about you? How do you feel today? Are you ready to become *la Signora Conti*?'

I took a deep breath. 'I'm all right. I can't quite believe it's happening, it's like a dream, or like it's happening to someone else. But no matter what it says on my marriage certificate, I'll always be an Innocenti. It's in my blood now.'

'Our family tends to have that effect on you,' she joked. Then she became serious once more. 'And you're sure? It's not too late, you know.'

'I'm positive. He's my soulmate, Mum.'

'Glad to hear it.'

'A couple of months ago, after breaking the curse...' I stared at her, daring her to say something, but she merely nodded, so I went on. 'We went to the graveyard at San Jacopo. The priest met us outside and gave us the key, and told us to give it back to him when we'd finished. We went to Agnes's grave. It's the only one with an angel statue over it. When I touched the statue, I could sense her there, watching over us, her soul at peace, as if she could finally rest after all this time.'

Mum knew about the evening I'd broken the curse. I'd Skyped her the next day to tell her about it. She hadn't said much, and I wasn't sure if she'd believed me or not. I carried on, regardless. 'Then we went to the family mausoleum. We found them – Riccardo, his mother and father, his brothers and sisters. Filippo was there too, but when I touched his tomb, I felt nothing. There was no presence of any soul, neither good nor bad, only a grey emptiness. I hope this means that the Innocenti can rest in peace now. Anyway, I'm glad we went.'

'I'm pretty sure you helped them finally rest in peace,' Mum said, fiddling with an earring.

I raised an eyebrow, sceptical.

'I'm not joking. I know I haven't said much since you told me about that evening, but to tell you the truth, I was too shocked to react. To think my daughter has this wonderful gift. I'm so proud of you, sweetie.'

I gulped. 'Don't make me cry, Mum, Giulia will have a fit!' I touched the necklace around my neck, a habit I'd got into whenever I felt emotional.

'You're wearing Bruna's necklace,' Mum exclaimed.

'What? Didn't you give it to me when I was little?' I asked, confused.

'Yes, but my mum gave it to me on my wedding day. I didn't like it much, it wasn't really my style. I put it away and forgot about it until you went through my jewellery box and found it. You loved how shiny and sparkly it was after we polished it, so I gave it to you.'

'I found it among the things I brought from England, I've no idea how it got in there.' I almost told her about the charm but again, something stopped me. I tucked it back inside my top, away from prying eyes. It was my secret, for now.

The door suddenly opened and Giulia burst into the room, followed by Agnese carrying a glass.

'Right, it's time,' Giulia said. 'Rita, could you go and help look after the kids? Liliana really needs you.'

Mum nodded. 'Call me when you're finished, though, I want to be the first to see her.' She blew me a kiss as she left the room.

'Okay. Let's touch up your make-up, then you can put your dress on,' Giulia said.

'Here, I've brought you a glass of Luisa's juice.' Agnese winked at me. 'I thought it might help you get through the day.'

I took a large mouthful, gasping as a sudden warmth spread throughout my body. 'What would I do without you?' I said, grinning at her.

The eighteenth-century farmhouse in the hills overlooking Gallicano was the ideal setting for our wedding. The pretty white gazebo in the courtyard was decorated with ivy and roses, while the grey slate flagstones were strewn with rose petals. Everyone turned in their seats as I entered beneath the archway, a collective *ahhh* filling the air. Clutching Dante's arm, I made my way along the white carpet between the chairs, my eyes fixed on Francesco waiting for me at the front. I clutched my bouquet, nervous under the gaze of friends and family, terrified I would stumble at any moment. I reached the top safely, vaguely aware of Mum in the front row, her hand over her mouth as she proudly watched.

Dante removed my hand from his arm and patted it awkwardly. 'Go and get married,' he said gruffly, rubbing at his face as he turned to find his place next to Liliana.

I only had eyes for Francesco. Seeing him standing there, a look of wonder on his face as he saw me for the first time that day, my heart overflowed with love for him. I was ready to become Signora Conti.

The afternoon passed in raucous celebrations, getting steadily noisier as the wine flowed. Music pumped from the sound system, and everyone was having fun. Francesco and I paused for a breather, the music still vibrating through our bodies.

'Have I told you how beautiful you look today?' he asked, gazing at me.

'Only about a hundred times,' I replied.

'Must be true, then,' he said, leaning over and kissing me. Several people nearby cheered, raising their glasses to us.

'Mmm,' I said as I kissed him deeper. Then I pulled back, my eyes wide open in surprise. 'Well, look at that,' I whispered, nudging him. Over in a corner, beneath the drooping branches of a weeping willow, Agnese was standing close to Luca. He brushed some hair away from her face as they talked.

'Do you think romance is in the air?'

'Could be. He's a great guy,' Francesco said. 'But that's enough speculation, let's get back to us.'

We kissed again, amidst more loud cheers and whistles, as the guests gathered around us. As my eyes closed, I felt their presence: the healers, Agnes, Matilda, Luisa, and their men, Riccardo, Bob, Tommaso; they were all here with me, celebrating these new beginnings for the Innocenti. I'd released the family from the curse and I knew that whatever happened, wherever my life took me, my family would be here with me forever.

A faint humming vibrated near my ear, and I opened my eyes to see a brightly coloured dragonfly hovering before my face. It circled my head three times, its transparent wings brushing against my forehead as if blessing me, then settled on my shoulder. It was my dragonfly, my saviour, the one who had started me on this incredible journey when, on that long-ago evening, it led me to the Dragonfly Grove.

51

EPILOGUE
JUNE

It was the middle of the night and I was comfortable under the covers, but I really needed to pee. I swung my legs over the edge of the bed and carefully got to my feet. I made my way across the room but had only reached the end of the bed when I started to sway, my head pounding. I gasped and placed my hand protectively over the extended roundness of my belly.

'Jen?' Francesco's voice was groggy with sleep. I heard him rummaging about, then the room suddenly lit up as he turned the light on. He wriggled to a sitting position, rubbing his eyes, his hair sticking out in all directions. 'Is something wrong?'

'No, nothing,' I tried to reassure him. 'I need the loo. Go back to sl–' I froze as water gushed between my legs, splashing my feet as it hit the floor. 'Oh,' I said, then gasped once more as the first pains hit me.

'Okay, it's D-Day.' Francesco leapt out of bed and grabbed his clothes. Hopping on one leg, and then the other, he pulled his jeans on. Pausing briefly to kiss me, he shoved his head through his T-shirt. 'Where are your clothes?' he asked, glancing wildly around the room.

'Over on the chair, where they usually are.' I winced again at the contraction running through my body. 'But I'm not sure I can get dressed...' The water had stopped, but I was scared to move.

'Hey, it's the middle of the night, what on earth is all this noise?' Agnese appeared at the bedroom door, blinking and yawning. She took one look at the scene in front of her and understood immediately what was happening.

'Francesco, ring the hospital and let them know you're on your way,' she said, taking command. He picked up his phone and headed downstairs. 'And start the car,' she called after him.

She put her arm around me as I grimaced again. 'This is the worst part, Jen. You've just got to grit your teeth and get on with it.'

'Thanks,' I groaned.

'Oh, come on. If I can do it, anyone can.' She grinned at me and I tried to smile back. I failed miserably.

'I'm scared, Agnese. What if...?' My unspoken thought hung between us. It had been at the back of my mind since the day I'd found out I was pregnant. All those months of worrying, wondering if each day would be the last, until finally the danger moment was past and I could relax, knowing that my baby could survive this time. Until now. Now, anything could happen, and I was powerless to stop it.

'Everything will be fine, you'll see.' Agnese placed my dressing gown over my shoulders and helped me put my arms into the sleeves. 'Oh, Jen, you're going to be a mum!' she exclaimed, hugging me tightly. 'I wish I could be there.'

'I'll get Francesco to call you as soon as, you know. Give Malva a big kiss for me in the morning.'

She helped me down the stairs and into the car. As she strapped the seat belt around me, she squeezed my hand. 'Good luck,' she whispered.

. . .

I lay back, resting my head on the pillow, the crisp cotton cooling my skin. The last few hours had passed in a blur. I vaguely remembered us arriving at the hospital and Francesco calling for help as my body was racked by painful contractions. Nurses had come running down the hall and sat me in a wheelchair, their calm professionalism washing over us and settling the rising panic. We'd rushed through the brightly lit lobby, lights flickering at the corner of my eyes as we entered the labyrinth of corridors. They'd helped me onto a bed, and then everything else was a jumbled chaos of images, pain, voices, and more pain.

'Jen?' Francesco wiped my skin with a towel soaked in cold water, soothing the heat raging through my body. The pillow was already drenched with sweat.

'I'm sorry,' I said through clenched teeth, my eyes still closed. 'I did everything I could but...' The words from the other Malva's grave appeared in my mind: *but I wasn't good enough.* Tears poured down my cheeks.

'Hush now, don't be silly.' Francesco wiped them away and stroked my brow. 'You're not the first woman to have a caesarean, and you won't be the last. The important thing is that both you and the baby are all right.' He cocked his head as a strident wail filled the air. 'And it sounds like junior is fighting fit. Listen, Jen. That's our son.' He waited, watching me as more cries rang around the room.

I burst into tears again. 'A boy? He's a boy?'

'A little blond-haired boy who's going to grow up big and strong like his daddy and take over the family business one day,' Francesco said with a grin.

I smiled dreamily. 'Ted.'

'Tommaso,' Francesco said at exactly the same moment.

I laughed. We'd been fighting over names ever since the seventh month, when we'd dared to hope that our baby might survive. We'd both immediately agreed on Luisa for a girl, but couldn't decide which name we wanted for a boy.

'I've been thinking,' I said.

'Wondered what the noise was,' Francesco joked.

I ignored him. Sometimes I wished I hadn't taught him my British sense of humour. 'I was thinking...' I glared, daring him to make another wisecrack. Sensibly, he kept quiet. 'What about Edoardo Tommaso Conti? Ted is short for Edward, and I quite like it.'

'I love it,' he said, and bent over to kiss me. 'Thank you.'

'For what?' I whispered.

'For everything.'

'I love you.' My voice cracked on the last word.

'Excuse me, *signora*.' A nurse approached us, holding a bundle in her arms. 'We've checked him over, everything's fine. You can hold him now.'

She held the bundle out to me and placed it in my arms. I looked down and saw my son's face for the first time. I thought my heart would burst with the love I felt as I gazed upon him, memorising his miniscule features, imprinting them on my mind so that I would remember this moment for the rest of my life.

Francesco sat on the bed beside me and rested his hand on the blanket. I turned to him and saw the wonder and love I felt reflected in his face.

'You did it, Jen.' He kissed away my tears as his own poured down his cheeks. 'I have no idea how, but you did it.'

I touched the necklace I always wore, with the secret talisman hidden inside the locket, and sent a silent prayer of thanks to the healers. And to Agnes, the one who had shown me her life and revealed so much more. The immensity of the gift she had given me suddenly hit me, as I realised that from now on, my life would never be the same again.

THE END

ACKNOWLEDGEMENTS

Thank you for reading *The Healer's Secret* and *The Healer's Curse*, I hope you have enjoyed Jennifer's magical story as much as I loved writing it! The next books in the series will feature healers from the past, starting with Sara Innocenti in *The Healer's Awakening*.

I've always been fascinated by medieval times, so when I decided to set the origins of these books in that era, I enjoyed all the research I had to do. While I have tried to keep everything as historically factual as possible, some details have been changed to fit the story, and any errors are my own.

I'd like to thank Morgen Bailey for editing the manuscript, and everyone at Bloodhound Books for all their hard work.

A huge thank you to my street team, their support has been invaluable, and I appreciate everything they do. Thank you also to everyone who interacts on my Facebook page and social media, it's lovely getting to know the people who read my books.

The Facebook group Skye's Mum and Books deserves a special mention, it's such a friendly, welcoming group where we talk about anything and everything!

Special hugs go to Kayleigh and Sarah for being there for me during such an awful year. I treasure their friendship every day.

As usual, the last thank you goes to my husband, Ivan. Your support and love mean everything to me, and always will. *Ti amerò per sempre, amore mio.*

You can sign up for my newsletter at: https://sendfox. com/lp/1knl41
for up-to-date information on my books, behind the scenes details, chat about life in Italy, and freebies/promos of other authors' books I think you may like.
I only send my newsletter out once a month or so, unless I have any exciting news to share with you!

You can also follow me on:
Facebook
Twitter
Instagram

Printed in Great Britain
by Amazon

48957045R00190